I0451429

The Broken Prophecy

by Thomas Knapp

Copyright 2013, all rights reserved

Cover art by Fred Gallagher and Jorge Rivas

Edited by Patrick Coyle

Prologue

When I was a young girl, I scoffed at the prophecies and the myths that came from ages past. They were nothing but fanciful stories to me, full of confusing images and unclear meanings, something that no longer held any significance in this sophisticated era.

But then, in a stretch of a half staryear, I finally came to understand. The stories were anything but fiction, and I realized why the prophets had used such vague language to describe what they had seen in their visions...

...Because no words could ever do the truth justice.

Rumil put down her stylus and carefully looked over the words she had written onto the thick pad of paper before her. Finally satisfied, she peered down forlornly at the large pile of failed introductions she had rejected. The mess was almost enough for her to reconsider typing everything on a terminal, but she rejected that thought quickly, having promised herself that she'd at least write it down first.

There was a peculiar majesty to writing something on a page, letting her hand guide her words, something that a console display just didn't convey. While she had no doubt that this book would eventually be transferred to the GalNet and other electronic media, the idea that you would still be able to find it in a physical form, bound with a plastic fiber cover, was surprisingly comforting.

She ruefully thought to herself that her opinion might change after she wasted a few more reams of paper... but for the moment, she was firm in her decision.

She took a deep breath, and set aside the page she had just written. As she prepared to press her stylus against the paper once more, her head buzzed with a familiar mental presence, a psionic signature that she almost couldn't believe was there. She jumped up, knocking her chair and her wastebasket over in the process, and dashed out to the balcony.

The gentle snowfall and the nighttime cold barely registered in her mind as she stepped out onto the snow-covered deck in nothing but slippers and a thick nightgown. As she narrowed her focus on the source of the presence, her eyes followed until she found what she was looking for.

He was covered in what appeared to be a light gray cloak, the hood drawn over his head and shimmering with a reflective coating. He didn't look up at her, but paused at the entrance of the memorial less than half a TackMet from the front door of her home. It was clear he wanted her to follow.

She didn't bother dressing, and dashed down the stairway at full speed, not caring who she awoke in the process. She practically jumped into a pair of thick boots to keep her feet warm, and grabbed the first coat she found in the closet; a pale blue jacket meant for springtime wear, but hardly of concern to her at the moment.

She was out the door just as quickly, sprinting across the snow as fast as her feet could take her. Nonetheless, it took her almost five ticks to cover the distance between her home and the memorial through the snow piling on the walkway, despite frequent plowing.

The memorial was nothing more than a pearl-colored stone circle about thirty tacks in diameter with names carved along the inside of the ring, and a small gap that allowed for entry inside. In the center of the ring stood a towering four-sided obelisk, ten tacks high and cut from the same stone, with more carved words on the side facing the opening.

She could guess why he wanted to come here. He hadn't been present when the memorial had been dedicated. As a matter of fact... she was rather curious where he had been.

"I knew that you survived somehow," she said to the figure, who was reading the text on the obelisk.

He didn't look at her when he said, "Did you see it in a vision?"

"Something like that," she replied, then testily said, "Look at me."

Finally, the man turned to her, but to her dismay she couldn't see his face... couldn't tell if it was what she hoped... or what she feared.

She felt ready to ask the question that she dreaded asking, but once again, her courage failed her. "Jonathan and Julianne are with me now, in case you didn't know. They think you're dead."

"That's probably for the best, at least for the moment," he stated. "I'm not sure I'd be able to face them right now. How are they doing?"

"Well, they're obviously still not quite over everything that's happened... but they're moving on. Jonathan's talents are becoming more pronounced with every day. Eventually we're going to need to convince his master to leave Kiros and train him like he was supposed to."

"That won't be necessary," he replied, almost angrily. "I'll do it myself in time. I should at least do that much."

She felt slightly relieved that he remembered the pair. She wasn't sure why he wouldn't... but then again, she would never have dreamed the change he had undergone was possible.

"There's something you want to ask me," he correctly observed.

"I'm not sure how to ask it," Rumil said, waffling between just getting it over with, and wondering if it was better to not know at all. "Do you remember how this all started?"

"Why do I get the feeling that's not the question really on your mind?"

"I'm leading to it..." she said, with a hint of exasperation. At least he could still be as aggravating as she remembered. "It's rather amazing thinking back where it all started, and seeing where we are now. I just want to know if *you* remember..."

Chapter One

Rumil's eyes scanned across her surroundings once again. A wall of grid panels stood vertically on each side of her, extending about three Tacks above her head, and like the identical floor beneath her, their lines slowly came together against a horizon that seemed to go off into nowhere. The lines dignifying the grid frame shone with a pale yellow light against the uniform purple of the panels. Digital characters on each vertical panel around her bore the name "Archives: 3300-3310."

Rumil frowned disdainfully. "Wrong century," she muttered, and reached down into her waist pack. She pulled out a small device about the size of her fist and held it in front of her face. The device barely fit into her palm, and it was mostly of a black analog display with small white crosshairs marked in the center, signifying her location. The screen was then rimmed with a light gray plastic border, the top left corner being where the model code *would* have been… had it not been rubbed off with a file. The internal programming of the device had also been wiped, to prevent anyone from locating its source of manufacture or buyer.

So far, the screen remained completely black, meaning that the security programs had not detected her yet. "Well, that will probably change rather quickly," Rumil noted, and then turned towards another grid corridor that led to earlier dates in the archive.

Once she found the decade she desired, she encountered a heavy security lock that resembled a large green metal door with a keypad on the left side. Dutifully tapping in the pass code she had acquired, she awaited clearance or rejection. From an immaterial speaker system, she heard a computer-generated female voice declare, "The data contained in this module is restricted to Level Ten clearance. Your current clearance is Eight. Access to this module is denied."

"So… my little friend wasn't as high up the chain of command as he claimed." Rumil sighed softly to herself. She had guessed that any man who so willingly gave up his clearance codes after a few drinks wasn't terribly high up the ranks, but she had taken the chance anyway.

Rumil frowned angrily in spite of her own reasoning and began to think about ways to work around the firewall, when her waist pack suddenly vibrated. She didn't need to examine the detector to know what was happening; she already knew, but she pulled the analog screen out of the pack just to confirm her fears.

Four white lights were beeping on the edge of the display, but she knew that the security sentries would close the distance rapidly. With a dejected sigh, Rumil reached up to her right ear, and tapped on the space above it with her index finger twice.

The lighted grid frame disappeared abruptly, and was quickly replaced with a more detailed scene, although in some ways it was just as barren. The small tavern had likely been abandoned for years, for now only cobwebs and dust were its regular patrons. Sliding the red-tinted visor of her virtual display helmet into the slot on the temple, she examined her surroundings a little more closely.

The small bar counter ran from the middle of the west wall about two Tacks and a half to the north, then ran to the east, stopping just shy of the far wall to allow a vertical flap that opened for entry behind the bar. Even through the dust, the counter was a shade of red that would have looked absolutely gorgeous if given a tenth-cycle's cleaning and polishing. Behind her, a large shelving unit, stripped bare of any contents, filled almost the entire space behind the counter.

The rest of the room was occupied with twelve equally elaborate oak tables, spaced evenly throughout, carved and polished in the same beautiful red hue. On each table were four wooden chairs placed upside down on the tabletops, their backs hanging down over the edge. Five of the chairs had fallen from their perches: two from the northwest corner table, one from the southeast, and two from the center table that had been smashed in the fall.

The walls were made of a normally drab fiberwall that was being used in all buildings for the last century, but in this establishment, it had been molded and decorated to resemble white granite, and Rumil had to admit it did the job impressively. The door, made of a harder fiberwall composite, had been formed and painted to mimic a thick wooden door, but without the weight and bulk. The door had separated from its lower hinges, but still was able to close, allowing Rumil some desperately needed solitude. Hacking was a delicate and largely illegal business, best not done in a public place with many eyes about.

All in all, the bar looked like it should have been in an antique store, rather then wasting away, abandoned to be claimed by inactivity. Such robust pieces of woodwork and skill didn't deserve such a lackluster fate.

Nonetheless, said fate was precisely the reason she chose it for her hiding place. The only people who came around here were historical renovators, or something of the sort, and they had absolutely no reason to come around in the depth of night.

Rumil tugged the light helmet off her sandy blonde hair, quickly swishing her short shoulder-length mane a few times to free the follicles from where they had plastered to her cranium. After plucking her interface gloves off, finger by finger, she disassembled the four interconnecting plates of the helmet, and put all the items into the satchel hanging off her right shoulder. Once more, she appraised the abandoned bar, and a slight smile worked on her face.

"Maybe after I get my last little paycheck… I might just buy a place just like this. Settle down, run a quaint little bar, hire some nice dancers…" Rumil mused, then chuckled in spite of herself. The concept of staying in one place wasn't one that Rumil felt she could ever enjoy. Even after the conclusion of her hacking career, she'd have to stay quiet for twenty staryears or so, while the statute of limitations on her crimes had expired.

She slid off the small, red leather barstool she had been sitting on, and extended her two-Tack frame to her toes, working the kinks out of her spine, and rolled her head from one side to the other three times. She always got unusually tense when she was hacking, and she doubted it was any good for her posture. Striding to the door on her thin frame, she grabbed the handle, and started to pull the wounded doorway open. Stopping, she fondly regarded the lonely bar one last time, then slipped out the entry silently and gently closed the door.

Looking up at the blackened alleyway she now found herself in, it was like stepping through a portal three hundred staryears into the future, in which she came from the full, colorful tavern of yesteryear into the monotonous deep gray present. The buildings across the alley loomed upward several stories, tall banal blocks shrouded in the darkness of the alley, the occasional speck of lighted windows breaking their cold exteriors.

Despite the futuristic design, the only light being provided was from the moon of Talos, hanging in orbit, and even that light was a dim one indeed thanks to heavy cloud cover. As it was, Rumil couldn't see the tops of the drab buildings flanking the alley, and didn't even realize that she was not alone in the alley until she turned right into him.

The stranger seemed to be clad in something hard, but he was not heavy, as she could feel him stagger backward with the collision. He didn't fall on his bottom like she did, however. She landed hard next to a trash canister that – judging from the smell – had not been left alone quite as long as the bar next to it. The sudden movement set off the motion lights across the alleyway, and it cast the narrow passage in a soft white luminescence, giving Rumil a better view of her new companion in the alley.

The first thing she noticed was that he wouldn't be much taller than herself, if even that, and his frame had the appearance of a young boy.

Her eyes came to rest on the hard carbide breastplate, molded to fit the exact shape of its wielder, and colored a deep brown. Abdomen and chest muscles were clearly defined in the alloyed material thanks to the newfound light. The shoulder plates were hinged to the breastplate, allowing free movement of the man's shoulders. Cylindrical carbide wrapped around his toned upper arms. Below the elbows, his forearms were covered by gauntlets noticeably bulkier than the rest of his armor, with gloves of metallic mesh over his hands and a flattened plate attached to his right gauntlet as a small shield.

His legs were like the rest of his body – thin but well toned, covered in shells of carbide, down to the mesh boots that gave way to black soles at the bottom of his feet. Where she could see underneath the brown alloy plating, a lighter brown tight-fitting bodysuit clung to the man's frame.

Hoping to get a look at the stranger's face, she was foiled by the tinted visor that extended from the temple of his brown helmet to his chin piece. However, she didn't need a face to identify him. Blazoned in small gold letters upon a black bar on left side of his breastplate were the words, "Honore, Timothy." Seeing that name, she glanced back down to the belt around his waist, and confirmed her worst fears when she took note of the startling lack of equipment. Where a common soldier would normally hang a bevy of weapons and field equipment, only a small plasma pistol and sword took residence among some small belt pouches, and she was pretty certain why.

Only the ignorant didn't know the Honore family and the history it had. The man in front of her was an Erani. More importantly, he was a member of the Solarian army. And *most* importantly, he was a Solarian Knight.

Despite their smallish stature, the Erani were not a people to take lightly. They were swift of foot and light in their movements, and the military training their soldiers took honed those natural gifts to a keen skill. It was very likely that the Knight in question had been following her since she left her hotel room, and she had never noticed, despite his armor.

Of their kind, of whom none were to be trifled with, the Solarian Knights were indeed the utmost of the lot. They were the ones in which the blood of the Se-Lan race ran the strongest, and it manifested itself in the ability to manipulate the universe around them with but a thought. A Solarian Knight could ignite a bonfire with no kindling or devices, heal in mere seconds wounds that would have bled for hours, and even warp the boundaries of space and time, moving the span of TackMets in the blink of an eye.

Rumil did not consider this good news. She must have *considerably* upset someone on the Solarian capital of Centris with her hacking, and that the Solarians were now starting to get serious. Judging from the aggressive posture of the Knight standing in front of her, it appeared that his orders did *not* necessarily include taking her alive…

In her panic, she almost didn't hear the Knight speak. His voice was soft, but firm, and betrayed no emotion. "Rumil Bonamede, I suggest you come with me. Let's not make this any more irritating than it's already been."

"How…" she began, unable to finish her thought.

Timothy finished it for her. "Did I find you? We've been watching your transactions since you logged into our database. Do you *honestly* think that someone would divulge their security clearance after a couple giacanos?"

Rumil was somewhat disappointed that she hadn't anticipated the ploy her adversary had used. She had been under the impression that she had ordered something stronger. Gathering her wits, she realized the sort of planning such a deception would take. They must have been following her since her last hacking raid… plotted out where she'd go next, set up the scene in the bar she went to, paid off the bartender… and she eventually reached one conclusion. "Sounds like you've been planning this sting for some time."

"Since I was assigned to lead the case," Timothy admitted.

"How long has *that* been I wonder…?" she said, letting her voice drop off, trying to buy some time to think up a plan.

It appeared that the Knight saw the ruse for just what it was. "I do not need to answer *any* question of yours." Reaching down, he grabbed her shoulder, and pulled her to her feet. His grasp was firm, but not painful, until he took her by the wrist. Even then, Rumil admitted that her pain had nothing to do with the Knight. She bit down a yelp, then had to sink her teeth into her lower lip when her arms were pulled behind her back and cold restraints clapped over her wrists.

He leaned in next to her ear, and whispered softly, "I don't *want* to get rough with you, but if you give me a hard time, I *will* make your life *very* uncomfortable. Now move."

She dragged her feet initially, but the uninviting feel of a hypersteel blade against her back convinced her to pick up her pace. Even now her eyes scanned about, looking for any possible avenue to escape her current predicament.

To her immense luck, it appeared that such an avenue came to *her*. As they were about to enter the main road, another voice from the alley playfully called to them, "Pardon me, dear sir, but just where do you think you are going with yon hacker?"

Timothy whirled about, and Rumil had no choice but to follow. Her eyes then caught sight of the speaker as he emerged into the lighted part of the alley, and then she couldn't help but smile.

The second man was clad in a similar fashion as her current holder, but his armoring was colored a royal blue. His attire and lack of equipment suggested that he too was a Knight of his respective faction. Gold letters similar to the ones on Timothy's breastplate read, "Feroz, Justin." While she couldn't see Timothy's face through his visor, she didn't doubt for one second that he was absolutely glaring.

If he was, his voice didn't show it, as he spoke as plainly as before. "Where I am going should be obvious even to your ignorant kind," Timothy retorted. "Now I suggest that you return to wherever you came from. This is no concern of the Kiros."

"I beg to differ," the blue-armored warrior said somewhat threateningly, and he stepped even closer, his right hand crossing his body, starting to linger over his sword hilt. "The Kiros have quite a stake in delivering this hacker to justice, and I was ordered to bring her in at all costs."

"Your orders are of little concern to me, Kiros," Timothy shot back coldly. "Now I suggest you crawl back into whatever hole you slithered from, unless you wish to be severely hurt."

"I think I'll take my chances. I've wanted to test my skill on someone deserving of it," Justin replied. As with Timothy, Rumil couldn't see through the blue-clad warrior's tinted visor to see if his face revealed confident swagger, or insecure posturing.

With a shrug, Timothy pushed Rumil back against the trash container that she had fallen into when they had first run into each other. "Stay right where you are while I deal with our new friend. Do *not* move as much as an eyelash, because I'll be watching you."

Timothy then once again turned to face his foe, and Rumil thought that now was a good chance to possibly slink away. However, the moment she moved her left foot, a plasma round ripped through the air with a burning crackle, and sizzled through the fiberwall inches ahead of her nose. Turning back to the fight scene, she saw Timothy's pistol trained on her. Guessing from the angle of the weapon, she decided he wasn't going to fire a second warning shot.

"What did I just say?" Timothy reminded sternly.

Rumil grinned in reply, and said coyly, "I don't think you should be wasting so much attention on me."

In response to that statement, Timothy whirled back to face his opponent, sword swinging upward to deflect the blow from Justin, who slid with the strike, and nimbly rolled back to his feet, his sword again at the ready.

"Attacking a man from behind. That was quite dishonorable of you," Timothy chided. "Not surprising considering the source of the attack though."

Justin huffed, and answered casually, "I knew you would react in time to stop me. If you hadn't, then you wouldn't have been worth the energy I'm about to spend." Then with a slower drawl, he added, "Besides, *someone* had to start us off."

"Right…" Timothy retorted, clearly unconvinced, before closing the gap with a strike of his own. Justin turned aside the blow with a quick swipe, and countered with a low sweep, hoping to get Timothy to jump over the blade. Instead, Timothy stopped the blow with his own weapon, forcing Justin's sword downward, and swung his right arm in a vicious uppercut that probably would have dealt some serious harm to his Kiros counterpart, had Justin not leaned back away from the blow. The Kiros Knight, rolling backward and to his feet, lunged forward as soon as he had regained his balance.

Timothy responded by spinning to his left, and the ensuing thrust caught empty air as Justin flew completely by. Timothy then brought his sword around with a low sweep of his own, and Justin responded by pushing his entire body into the air off his left hand, flipping in a graceful somersault, and landing a Tack away squarely on his feet. The two combatants once again faced each other, taking a couple sidesteps, swords at the ready for the next exchange.

Rumil almost forgot she was trying to get away; the fluidity of the two Erani's combat had nearly lulled her into an awed trance. Shaking herself out of her astonished stupor, she once again started looking about, waiting for her opportunity to make a break.

"I said do not move," Timothy reminded her again, although it did not appear he had taken his eyes off his opponent. "How many times must I remind you?" Finally, he appeared to address Justin, adding, "You *could* keep an eye on her too, since you seem to be so intent on bringing her in yourself."

Justin jerked slightly as if slapped, then shot back casually, "Who says I'm not?" Then, as if to take the attention off the topic, he attacked again. This time his attack was in the mold of a standard fencing strike, thrusting the point directly forward in an attempt to pierce the carbide of his opponent. When Timothy deflected the blow aside, Justin's right hand followed, his palm filling with a glowing orange ball of energy moving towards his opponent's face.

But Timothy had a response even to that, and when Justin released the small ball of psionic flame, it bounced off an invisible barrier that had suddenly popped up between them. The sphere of energy ricocheted upward into the black sky, lighting up the darkness above them as it traveled, and no doubt drawing the attention of the people inside the small lighted windows of the buildings around them.

"Impressive," Justin said, his voice tinted with a begrudging appreciation. "Not many can construct a psychic mirror that quickly."

Timothy grunted in response. The unwritten rule between warriors that had kept this solely a martial affair had been violated with Justin's fireball. Now Timothy figured that every tool in his repertoire was at his disposal. Focusing his energies for less than a demitick, the Solarian then used a quick burst of power to leap several Tacks above Justin, and while airborne, sent a cascade of small blue-white electric bursts down into the narrow alley. However, Justin was not without a defense either, as the bolts struck a similar barrier as the one Timothy constructed, sending the shards of energy screaming in various directions.

Rumil yelped in surprise as one of the whistling white-hot bolts struck the ground a mere Tackem from her left foot, the residual electricity shooting painfully through her foot and ankle. A sudden crack from above her drew her attention, and it became apparent that one of the bolts had struck the heavy fiberwall above her, sending large chunks on top of her seated form.

After an agonizing pause, Rumil realized that the falling debris hadn't killed her. Dropping her hands from her head, she allowed her eyes to adjust to the sudden darkness and appraise her position.

A large slab of the fiberwall rested above her head, one end leaning on the edge of the trash container next to her, the other slanted down to the alley road, and effectively supporting the rest of the collapsed wall from crushing her.

Breathing a sigh of relief, her attention was then drawn to her right, where she saw the lower half of the doorway to the bar. In the sudden collapse of the wall above it, the door had fallen inward, leaving a small crawlspace back into the bar.

Rumil smirked at the sudden change of her fortune. There was a stairway behind the bar counter that led to the next higher floor, and quite likely, another exit. Sliding on her stomach – her arms still bound behind her – she slipped back into the bar. Crawling to her feet as quickly as she could, she crouched underneath the flap leading behind the counter, and rushed for the stairs.

Meanwhile, two Erani Knights dug through the rubble, one quite vocal in his displeasure.

"You are an idiot!" Justin shouted as he frantically pushed chunks of fiberwall and fragmented hypersteel supports aside. "If you've killed that hacker…"

"We'd both be off the hook," Timothy replied flatly, although he was just as frenzied in removing the rubble.

Justin paused to ponder this for a moment, and was jolted when Timothy said with a hint of disgust, "Do you think you could help me move this anytime this staryear?"

A large slab of fiberwall was resting against the trash canister that Rumil had been sitting next to. Justin knelt down, and dug his fingers in between the slab and the ground, but then Timothy paused. He put his left hand under his chin, and said, "Don't mind that. There's no point after all… she's escaped."

"Just because you can't feel her life aura, doesn't mean her body isn't under here, buffoon," Justin snorted. In response, Timothy just pointed above Justin's head, and let the Kiros's eyes take him to what he was referring to. Above the slab, the top of the doorway behind it was visible. The door obviously had fallen inward in the mayhem, giving a wide-open passage for anyone under the rubble to slide back into the building.

"You have *got* to be kidding me…" Justin sighed. "Well, way to go. You've just let our target get away." He stood up, got face to face with his counterpart, and replied with a menacing hiss, "I'm of half a mind to send you back to Solaria in a casket…"

Justin's rant was interrupted by the sound of approaching sirens, no doubt the peacekeeping force of the city arriving at reports of the mysterious destruction. Justin looked around the alley into the main street, and groaned, "Are you in any particular mood to explain this to the Talos Peacekeepers?" When Timothy didn't reply, Justin turned back to where the Solarian had been standing... to find nothing.

"Sly Solarian bastard..." Justin mused with a sour chuckle. Then gathering his sword, Justin quickly teleported away from the scene, leaving the alleyway empty once again.

Chapter Two

His eyes flashed open, and his left hand instinctively shot over to the alarm at the side of his bed, mere demiticks before it began blaring. Sitting up swiftly, Timothy Honore folded back the covers neatly, and turned out of the bed as if he hadn't been in deep REM sleep just moments ago. Pausing for a moment on the bed's edge, he moved his hand rapidly in front of the motion sensor just beside the headboard. The fluorescent lighting module on the center of the ceiling flickered slightly, as if it was somewhat unwilling to rise at the hour Timothy had designated, then fully activated to cast the small suite into light.

The white rough-textured ceiling gave way to fiberwall supports, molded and painted to resemble plywood planks. The carpet was of a cheap sort, woven in a rather gaudy red and gray fiber pattern. Judging from the feel under Timothy's feet, the proprietors of the hotel had not even spared the expense to place a padded layer underneath.

Timothy didn't give much further attention to his surroundings, instead bending over a large luggage pack that was almost a Tack square, and a half-Tack deep. His fingers nimbly plucked the clasps, and the top of the pack jumped open with such force that it nearly sent the whole pack tumbling backward, despite the weight inside. Timothy righted the case quickly, averting said disaster, and began looking for his day's attire.

He first pulled another form-fitting brown body suit from the interior, and slid it over his lean frame. From there, he pulled out three different shades of white shirts, the first long-sleeved and the next two short, before settling on a sleeveless russet leather vest. The Solarian slipped his arms through the armholes, and tugged the fabric over each shoulder, leaving the clasps unhooked, the opening flapping loosely across his taut abdomen. Reaching into the pack again, his eyes appraised four different pant options, finally deciding on long-legged, light brown casual pants. He regarded his mesh armor boots for a brief second then passed them over for black slip-on low heels.

Methodically, he folded each item he passed over and placed them, heaviest items first, into the pack, save for his mesh boots which he slid to the far right corner of the bed. Satisfied that everything was back in its proper place, he moved the three Tacks to the small desk of his one-room inn suite, where his personalized computing unit awaited use. Other suites, much more spacious, had been available, but for costs that Timothy was not comfortable with renting. Besides, he rationalized that this was all he really needed, and that to get anything larger would have been a waste of his funds.

And yet, he reluctantly admitted that he would have liked just a little more room to operate in. As it was, he could barely fit a chair in between the bed and his desk, and as he pulled the folding chair out, he felt the thud of its small aluminum back against the frame of the bed. Sighing, he sat down, leaning his back against the padding, and scooted forward until he was in a proper operating position. He passed his thumb over the lip of his book-sized PCU, flipping the catch that released its three sections and unfolding them to form a single touch-sensitive keypad, with an opaque holographic display appearing just above and behind it.

With a pained groan, the first thing he saw was a daily news headline and a picture of the alley that he and that Kiros, Justin Feroz, had scuffled in the night before. There was no report of any bodies being found, confirming his hypothesis that the hacker Rumil had escaped. His eyes continued to peruse the article before stopping to read one section more closely:

> It is still to be determined what caused the abandoned bar house to partially collapse, but witnesses to the scene reported several flashes of light from the alleyway adjacent to the prospective landmark, as well as sounds of fighting. Peacekeepers have no leads to connect the events prior to the collapse to any person or group, and none have claimed responsibility.

> Hoef's Grand Tavern had been out of operation for 4 staryears, but the Talos Historical Committee had been in the process of purchasing the lot, and restoring it as a planetary landmark. The Historical Committee has not given any indication that they will proceed with plans to purchase the building.

Timothy shook his head. The last thing he needed was for the fault of damaging a potential historical landmark to be placed on him. All thanks to that obnoxious Kiros, he had lost his target, and would likely get hit with a nice, big damage assessment. All Timothy could hope for was to find Rumil quickly, and get off the planet without further incident.

Thoughts of the hacker triggered something in the Solarian's memory. In that brief moment that he had been touching her, he had felt a tingle in the back of his head, similar to a slight psionic shock. It baffled him, and allured him at the same time. When he'd been given the case to pursue, he had not thought much of the shapely blonde who looked like she probably would have fit in better at a gentlemen's club than the seedy underworld...

All of a sudden, it struck him. He knew where he had seen the hacker before.

*   *   *   *   *

Through the dimly lit surroundings, Timothy looked down at the small mono-mobile PCU in his hand, but it only confirmed that of which he was already certain. From his position, near the rear of the Sultry Siren Gentlemen's Club, he saw Regis Gallan, with some cosmetic alterations, living the "good life" at the front row of the catwalk. Gallan was cheering heartily at the erotic dancer taking swaying strides off the raised stage, which the Demodian pirate leader turned to jeers as the woman was about to disappear. Recognizing this, she turned around and gave him a suggestive wink, pointing to the back rooms.

Gallan stood with a smug grin and began to work his way to the exit leading to the dancers' private quarters, while the two hulking Ubeks guarding the passage stepped aside in anticipation of Gallan's passing. Timothy started to stand, preparing to follow the pirate leader, when motion on the stage broke his attention.

The club owner, a bulbous, short, balding excuse for an Arcadian, hastily shuffled his portly body as fast as he could, slipping his broadcast comm into his mouth as he did so. By the time Timothy had turned his attention back to the pirate, he had already disappeared through the exit, the bouncers again flanking the exit. Nearly cursing, he sat back down, hoping to get another chance at the pirate when the man had concluded his... business.

The club owner giggled obnoxiously, then said, "Don't worry, gentlemen, Sasha's ridden harder and longer men than *that* sir, and she'll be back at the top of the hour as scheduled. Let's hear it for Sasha once again!"

A round of raucous applause followed, complete with whistles and yells, and the horizontally gifted, vertically challenged Arcadian soaked it up. Timothy grudgingly joined in with his own nonchalant clapping, trying to blend in with the crowd as much as possible, but he was simply unable to immerse himself in the moment like everyone else.

When the din died down sufficiently, the club owner giggled again, and said, "Well, dear sirs, do I have a special treat for you. No one knows her name, and she will only give it to the one man who captures her heart." He paused in an attempt at suspense, before adding, "Perhaps it will be one of you fine gentlemen out there?"

Timothy scoffed. The upcoming dancer likely had given more than just her name to a great number of patrons of this particular bar, and possibly several others. Predictably, there were some confident affirmatives from the audience, and ignoring them, the owner announced with a hushed voice that rose into a declarative yell, "Here she is… the beautiful… the mysterious… the Beauty of Baramak!"

The long-legged blonde that emerged, clad in navy lingerie and a transparent slip of matching hue, quickly caught Timothy's eye, but for more than the obvious reasons. He admitted that he was drawn to her ample chest, flaring hips, and smooth curves, but there was something else… something that tingled in the back of his head, a sensation that he should not have felt upon the woman's entry, due to her obviously Arcadian descent.

The woman's green eyes scanned the crowd with a playful gleam, and she moved with such perfect balance out on the catwalk that it seemed like she floated out to the front. She slid down smoothly until she was sitting across the edge, and lifted her right leg towards a man in the front row. She said something that Timothy couldn't hear clearly, even with his naturally superior hearing, and the man leaned forward to remove her high-heeled shoe. She quickly shook her head, and made a quick, sensual biting motion with her teeth.

Catching onto the hint, the club patron leaned forward, took the pointed tip between his front teeth, and slowly slid the heeled shoe off the dancer's foot. Once removed, she pulled her leg away then lifted her left foot to yet another front row patron. After her left shoe was removed in the same manner, she stood up again, swaying her hips as she approached a thin pole that extended from the middle of the catwalk to the ceiling.

She planted her right foot between the floor and the pole, then spun twice around it, her long gathered tail of hair following in long arcs. She strode to the edge of the catwalk again, knelt down, then began to flirt with a trio of men in the front. As she did so, Timothy's eyes narrowed, still trying to work out the perplexing sensations he was experiencing.

Somehow, the alluring dancer sensed his eyes on her, for she lifted her head and looked up, her eyes focusing on the determined glare he was casting her way. She smiled toward him seductively, mistaking his gaze for something else, and her eyebrows rose in a playful manner.

The three closest to her obviously objected to her suddenly turning her attention away from them. One, a red-haired humanoid that Timothy recognized as Demodian from his four-fingered hand, suddenly shouted over the crowd, "You were talking to us, you filthy whore!"

Timothy was jolted out of his scrutiny as two of the men flanking the Demodian jumped up onto the catwalk, grabbed the stunned dancer by her elbows, and pushed her down so that she was leaning over her knees. The Demodian then jumped up beside her to the cheers of his fellow patrons. With a sneer, the red-haired humanoid ripped the navy slip clean off the dancer's body, and shouted, "Did you forget that you were here to entertain *us*? I think you owe us an apology."

She muttered a quick, timid, apology, but that proved not to be enough for the Demodian. He turned to the patrons on the floor proper, and said, "Maybe this little slut should kiss my feet? Better yet... she should *lick* my boots clean. Any of you out there favor that idea?"

The cheer was enthusiastically in the affirmative, and Timothy's eyes narrowed again, this time in concern. The situation was increasingly turning into one that crossed tolerable bounds even for this manner of establishment, and with a quick glance to stage left, he noted the club owner once again giggling uncontrollably, suggesting that the dancer would find no aid there.

On the other hand, making a move to stop the assault would certainly require him to reveal more than he had wanted until *after* he had Gallan in custody, and to do so now would likely tip off the pirate leader and allow him to escape.

Onstage, the humiliating display began, the dancer's small pink tongue touching the leather boot, running along the surely filthy sole. Two tears escaped the young woman's lashes, falling unheeded – save by one person – to the catwalk below.

Despite every thread of his common sense almost screaming not to interfere, it was as if another part of him would have none of it. Something had been compelling him to come to her aid, and the sight of her tears set him into motion. Slipping through the mob that was quickly massing as close as they could to the catwalk, he used his smaller stature to wedge his way to the front of the crowd. He effortlessly leaped to the catwalk, and tapped the Demodian on the shoulder.

"Don't rush me... you'll get your turn," the red-haired humanoid said, not even looking back.

Timothy snorted, and replied, "I'm not here for my *turn*. I'm here to tell you to stop… right *now*."

The Demodian turned around slowly, and Timothy found that he had to tilt his head up to look the man in the eye. The four-fingered humanoid hissed, "Could you care to repeat that, little man?"

Normally, being stared down upon led to a small degree of intimidation, but Timothy, like most Erani, had become used to the fact that they simply did not possess the same physical stature as other sentient races. Unperturbed, the Solarian Knight said, "Let me put it into words your drunken, narcotic-addled brain can comprehend. Cease and desist, before I rip that foot of yours *off*, and give you the opportunity to lick it clean on your own."

In response to that unsociable threat, the Demodian reached out with his right hand to shove Timothy aside. Timothy grabbed the intruding limb and dug his fingers into the thug's knuckles, pinching the nerve endings in a way that he knew would be excruciatingly painful from his study of Demodian anatomy.

The red-haired man squealed as pain shot up the entire length of his arm, and he dropped to his knee. His companions regarded the development cautiously, unsure what to make of this stranger. Slowly, they stood, observing the scene warily, dragging the dancer up with them.

The Demodian finally wailed, "All right! All right! I'll stop!" prompting Timothy to release his victim. The red-haired man stood once again and staggering back to his two friends, whose gaze kept switching between their leader and the waif-like stranger glaring at them. "What are you dolts waiting for?" the Demorian said to his companions, "Take care of that punk."

After a moment's hesitation, the two complied, but fared even worse than their leader. One found himself the recipient of a vicious kick to the gut, and the second charged at Timothy, only to be cut at the legs when the Solarian crouched, sending the thug into the crowd. Timothy turned his attention back to the first assailant and threw another kick, connecting against his jaw. The thug crumpled, and tumbled off the catwalk. In his attempt to climb back on, he treated one of his fellow patrons a little too roughly, and the patron pushed back. From there, the violence spread like a ripple of water in a pond, until the entire club had burst into fighting.

Dashing past the gang's leader, who was still nursing his hand, and ducking an airborne barstool, Timothy quickly circled his arm around the dancer's waist. She yelped in surprise as he then lifted her off her feet, and with one graceful leap, jumped off the catwalk to land behind the bar several Tacks away.

He set the startled dancer down gently, and said, "Stay behind here, and *don't* move until I tell you it's clear." Without waiting for her confirmation, he then addressed the barkeeper, who was crouched behind the bar in cover. "You keep an eye on her for me, okay?"

After receiving the barkeeper's hurried nod, Timothy then jumped on top of the bar, pulling out his pistol in one smooth motion with his left hand, his right going to his creditfold where he kept his identification. He raised his pistol to the ceiling, and fired three rounds upward. The crackle of plasma fire quickly settled the small riot, while inciting a bevy of screams from in back of the club. Once Timothy had the patrons' attention, he let the bottom third of his fold slip out, revealing his Rank Shield.

"I am a Solarian Knight, and while I do not have jurisdiction here, I am not averse to applying due force to get what I want," Timothy stated calmly. His lowered the aim of his pistol, hovering it around the patrons beneath him. "If any of you do not wish to make an overnight visit to confinement or the recovery ward, I would suggest that you all leave immediately."

It became apparent that the vast majority of the patrons did not wish to do either, and slowly began to filter to the nearest exit. Even the trio of troublemakers had fled, leaving the club as empty as if it had just closed.

The club owner, seeing a good nighttime's revenue slipping out the doors, rushed to Timothy, and angrily ordered, "You have *no* right to bust in here and run out my business! I want your Rank Shield Identification and the contact protocol for your highest superior. I will *not* tolerate your…"

The stout Arcadian's monologue died off when Timothy trained the pistol on him. The Solarian said simply, "You are free to have it, but would you like me to inform the enforcement office here as to exactly what goes on behind that guarded doorway?" he said, motioning with his free hand to the doorway leading to the back rooms, where even the Ubek bouncers had fled the scene.

Licking his lips nervously, the club owner finally stated, "Okay… but don't expect me to be so kind *next* time. Now if you pardon me, you've given my girls an awful fright. I should calm them down now." Bolting away, the owner disappeared into the back.

Timothy still could not hear any enforcement agents approaching, and he did not feel particularly inclined to wait for them. He looked back down behind the bar, and said, "It's clear. You can come out."

Two heads emerged, but the only one that held any interest to him belonged to the dancer, whom he assisted in climbing over the bar. Realizing that he was about the same height as her, he pulled off the light jacket he wore, and put it over her shoulders. She gratefully accepted it with a voiceless "thank you", and pulled it around her scantily clad body.

Timothy then remembered why he was in the club in the first place. For a second, he thought about investigating in back, but decided that Gallan had most definitely fled the scene when all the commotion had began. Deciding that he would have another chance to bring down the pirate leader, he waited in silence with the dancing girl until he heard the approaching sirens that indicated that enforcement officers were approaching.

As he made to leave, he offered the dancer a small piece of advice. "I would strongly suggest, madam, that you *quickly* find a new line of work." With that, he rushed out the north exit, farthest from the approaching sirens, and turned left onto the street.

*   *   *   *   *

With a sigh, Timothy folded his PCU closed again and slid out of the chair. Once he was standing, he folded the chair up, and leaned it against the wall between the bed and the desk. Checking to make sure that he had everything he needed, he prepared to leave the room.

Just as he was about to grab the door handle, three swift knocks sounded from the other side. He didn't need any psionic ability to have a pretty good guess as to who had come calling. There was only one person who had any business rapping on Timothy's suite.

Timothy immediately opened the door, to reveal the tall Arcadian hotel manager. The gaze that fell on Timothy was one of barely tolerated disdain, but the Solarian acted as if nothing was the least bit amiss.

"Hoef's Grand Tavern was nearly demolished last night. Witnesses say there were odd lights and fireballs, and the sounds of fighting," the manager said, in a failed attempt to talk casually. "I wonder if you had anything to do with it, hmm?"

"If any damage was done to any part of this planet, it was not by my hand," Timothy replied coldly, which he honestly felt was the truth. He had very carefully deflected Justin's fireball so that it could do no harm. However, the Kiros's haphazard shielding was not nearly so precise. *That* was what had caused any undue destruction of person or property.

"Well… even if you *are* telling the truth, which I highly doubt, it always seems that where you religious fanatics go, a nice little swath of destruction follows, usually of things *normal* people hold dear." The manager stressed the word "normal," an obvious jab at Timothy's Erani lineage.

However, Timothy found it to be pretty pathetic attempt at an insult. "If Hoef's Tavern was held so dear, why did it have so little business that it had to shut down?"

Timothy took the half-tick the manager took to react to the question to slip aside, and strode purposefully down the hall. From behind him, the manager called out, "If you want to rent this suite for another three days, payment must be made before 5 LT!"

"Hopefully, I won't have to book a further stay," Timothy called back as he stepped into the lift at the end of the hall. "I would say it's been a pleasure, but then I *would* be lying." The lift doors closed, and he rode the mechanism to the ground floor.

Once out onto the ground floor, he stepped into the main lobby. Five expensive-looking gold and crystal chandeliers hung in a neat line leading from the lift to the main exit. Carved columns were spaced about the lobby, two of them forming the corners of the main desk. Passing by the desk, he gave a passive wave to the early shift receptionist, but didn't bother to note her response. Timothy purposefully strode through the glass double doors, and outside, where the system's primary was beginning to creep over the slope of the planet.

He paused underneath the covered walkway leading to the sidewalk, his eyes darting back and forth. His mental sense caught a slight tingle of another gifted psionic nearby, vainly trying to keep his aura hidden. Timothy correctly reached the most logical conclusion, but refused to let it bother him. If that inept Kiros wished to tag along on the hunt, then so be it.

Meanwhile, Justin Feroz exhaled in relief as Timothy finally left the walkway, and began to take a leisurely pace down the side of the relatively vacant street. For a brief second, Justin had thought that his Solarian counterpart had detected him, but that didn't appear to be the case.

Keeping a safe distance away, Justin slinked after his target. The Kiros Knight had no idea where Rumil might be hiding, but was taking a gamble that Timothy Honore did. If the Solarian did have a lead, Justin wanted to be present when it panned out.

Timothy abruptly turned right at the next intersection, and the Solarian's psionic aura disappeared soon after. Thinking that Timothy had teleported away to escape pursuit, Justin rushed around the corner, hoping to pick up a hint of the warp trail. Instead, he walked right into a lightning-fast jab to the throat.

Justin collapsed to the ground, and Timothy stood over him while the Kiros Knight fought a losing battle to remain conscious. As blackness filled Justin's vision, Timothy muttered, "*That* is how you dampen a psionic aura. Consider it my first and last lesson to you."

Chapter Three

Rumil didn't notice the rapidly approaching dawn. Instead, she twiddled her thumbs restlessly as she sat in a small plastic chair in a dark corner on the downstairs level of the locksmith's shop. The basement was but a single room about seven Tacks square with a small exposed light hanging from a chain in the center. The walls were fashioned out of brick, not the modern fiberwall found in most recently built establishments. The bricks themselves were a deep gray, and thus didn't reflect much illumination onto the rest of the surroundings, which were probably pretty dismal anyway.

Fifteen other guests were in with her, quietly discussing business of the less than legal sort. Four Arcadians and an Ubek were in the corner furthest from her, too far for Rumil to overhear, but judging from the tight circle and open sterilization bags they were likely dealing in narcotics. Two Demodians were in the center of the basement, probably interstellar pirates, trying to sell some of their wares to the six Arcadians around them. Finally, two Arcadians were the closest to her, just two Tacks away, and were discussing another narcotics deal. Seven Ruma, reptilian descendants with bony plates that extended from the top of their heads, roamed between them, serving as runners for the owner upstairs, delivering drinks or messages.

The locksmith business that she currently sat in, like many other businesses all around the galaxy, had two parts. One was the legitimate business that took place above ground, and then there was the underside, where businessmen took in their *real* profits. However, that business often took a backseat to the legit one, and thus Rumil had been waiting for several tenth-cycles for assistance.

Finally, a Ruma came close enough for Rumil to reach out with her foot, and trip the small reptilian being. It stood quickly and glared at her, its eyes shrinking to pin-width slits and the eyelids narrowing threateningly. For a moment, Rumil looked uneasily at the bony plate that extended vertically from its scaled cranium, as it appeared that it had been sharpened. Such a natural weapon promised pain to those that crossed its owner.

Instead, the Ruma attached to the plate said with false sweetness, "May I be of assistance to you, somehow?"

"Yes," Rumil said, "Can you please inform your employer that I am growing extremely impatient?"

The features of the Ruma went flat, and it said dryly, "There's considerable business in lock-smithing… she will be with you as soon as she is able. Had you made an *appointment…*?" It let its voice drop off, mocking her.

"Sorry, I couldn't anticipate being nearly arrested," Rumil interrupted acidly. "Next time, I'll be sure to let you know when I intend to be apprehended again."

Either the Ruma didn't get the sarcasm, or it chose not to care, since its reply was, "Yes, that may be beneficial for prompt service." Then it walked away.

Had Rumil's arms been free, she probably would have thrown the chair she was sitting in at the retreating reptilian. Instead, the frustrated woman settled for a completely ineffectual kick in the Ruma's general direction. Slumping dejectedly back into her seat, she exhaled depressingly.

The two Arcadians closest to her found interest in the young beauty in the chair. Ceasing their business arrangements, they approached Rumil, who recognized the gleam in their eyes. She had seen it in many a man… although she had been at least partially in control of the circumstances before.

The one who stood right before her had brown hair and eyes, with a small scar on his left cheek. "Well, well, pretty little thing…" he began. "What brings you here?"

"Oh you know… I like tormenting ragged excuses for men like you, letting you know that you'll *never* land a girl like me," Rumil replied darkly. She was not particularly in the mood to deal with hormone-driven addicts.

"Is that so?" the Arcadian hissed, "Looks to me like you don't have much say in the matter, seeing how you're kinda… tied up… at the moment." The man laughed at his own joke, obviously finding humor that Rumil didn't share.

She sighed, then replied with a voice coated in honey, "Yes… perhaps you're right. Why don't you come a little closer, and I'll show you just how sorry I am for teasing you…"

With a triumphant smile, the scarred Arcadian said, "That more what I'm talking about." He took two steps forward, and then Rumil sneered maliciously, sending her left leg up, striking with considerable force between her target's thighs.

The dealer's eyes rolled into his head, his jaw dropping open, and he staggered back a Tack before dropping to his knees, then falling to his left onto the cold concrete floor, clutching his wounded genitalia and moaning in pain occasionally. The other denizens of the basement stopped their transactions for a brief second to analyze the situation, but quickly returned to their business. One good thing about black market operators: they weren't particularly nosy.

The Arcadian dealer's partner, a black-haired, well-built specimen, at first gaped in disbelief, then turned towards Rumil angrily. Lashing out with his left hand, he slapped her across the face. The force of the blow knocked her completely out of her chair as she accidentally bit down into her lip. With her arms bound found she had to struggle to return to a reasonably upright position, while blood from her bite began dribbling down toward her chin. She could have easily sucked on her lip to keep it under control, but she felt it that letting it run freely was more appropriately defiant.

The Arcadian probably would have struck again, had he not been tackled from behind by a pair of Ruma messengers, who succeeded in dropping him to the ground, and pinning him firmly to the floor. Another Ruma appeared from the stairs, its brown scales lifting off its skin angrily. "While this basement may not be one of the most savory places on this planet, I will *not* tolerate violence here." The Ruma locksmith then turned in Rumil's direction, and sighed. "I was told that I might have to aid you, Miss Bonamede. Come upstairs, and I'll escort you to a private room we can assess your situation in."

The two Ruma restraining the violent Arcadian promptly released him, and motioned for Rumil to follow them. They climbed up the long set of steps, and led her around a back hall behind the main business floor. Rumil mused that if the legit customers knew there was only a thin fiberwall partition separating them from thieves who were in the process of learning how to crack the very locks they were purchasing, they'd never have any faith in security ever again.

The two Ruma led her to a very small room that probably would have better served as a closet, and likely had been its initial purpose. She sat on a long wooden unpolished stool, and looked gloomily on the gray brick framing a bare concrete floor that only gave about three square Tacks of space. Half a tick later, the brown-scaled owner of the establishment entered and smiled. "I apologize for your wait, Miss Bonamede." Without waiting for a reply, the Ruma placed its orange hypersteel workbox on the floor, and spun around to Rumil's back, analyzing the hacker's bonds.

The Ruma made a trilling hiss in what Rumil assumed to be the reptilian equivalent of an impressed whistle, which to her ears sounded more like a canine pup being dragged along a cheese grater.

"Hmm… Your last boyfriend get a little kinky, dear girl?"

Rumil snorted at the idea, then had to bite down a scream as the Ruma grabbed the hacker's wrists roughly to examine the restraints more closely. It opened the scabbing wound on her lip again, and this time she sucked her lower lip into her mouth to keep it from bleeding once more.

"This is quite the specimen indeed, young lady…" the Ruma nodded appreciatively. "This is Solarian made, and quite an impressive restraint indeed."

"I rather gathered," Rumil acknowledged ruefully, her tongue involuntarily licking her broken lip right afterwards. "Can you get it off?"

"I can… but it depends on if your credits are good or not…" the Ruma replied with a wary eye.

Rumil sighed. "If you know who I am, then you know who my employer is. Trust me, my credits are good."

The locksmith twitched, as Ruma often did when in thought. "I suppose they would be… but credits in the underworld can disappear in the blink of an eye. Those on top can quickly find themselves on the bottom."

"Well, I can assure you my employer isn't going to be falling off his perch anytime soon."

The Ruma didn't seem terribly convinced as it said, "Perhaps not…" Nonetheless, the reptilian locksmith reached into its workbox, and pulled out a remarkable collection of picks and rods, setting to work on Rumil's restraints soon after…

*   *   *   *   *

Three tenth-cycles later, a varied assortment of metal rods was sticking out in random angles from the keyhole of the restraints. The locksmith said with a wipe of her eye ridges, "Fortunately for you, this is not the first time I've seen a crysalline restraint." With one more turn of a pick that the Ruma had slipped in among the already numerous mass, the restraint fell open.

Rumil examined her sore wrists as the Ruma picked up the restraint to examine it appreciatively. As the reptilian did so, a small, clear, spherical object dropped to the floor. The Ruma curiously picked it up, and then its eyes nearly bulged out of its skull.

It quickly pushed Rumil to her feet, and said, "Get out of my building *now.*"

"Why?" Rumil asked, then saw the item in the Ruma's hand. *Well... this Solarian is a devious little sort...* she thought, ironically impressed by his ingenuity.

"Trust me... it's not for your sake, but for *mine*. The last thing I need is a Solarian ripping up my place looking for you. Now *go!*"

Rumil rushed out of the room as the Ruma quickly smashed the minute device with a hammer in its workbox. "Out the *back!*" it shouted as Rumil turned to her right, to leave from the main entrance.

The hacker quickly did an about-face, and ran down the left hall, barging out a small wire-covered emergency exit, then jumping down the small flight of metal steps that led to the back lot where the trash was collected. Rumil squinted as the light of the rising sun blinded her, then as soon as her eyes adjusted to the dawn she bolted through the back alleys, hiding in the darkest shadows she could find.

She didn't dare return to her old hotel room... it was likely that the Solarian Knight following her was keeping watch on it. Added to the fact that there was a Kiros Knight lurking around somewhere that no doubt wanted just as badly to bring her to justice, she knew she had to get off-planet quickly.

Morning was in full bloom by the time Rumil felt desperate enough to come out onto the main streets. Finding her way to a small ducha house, Rumil sighed in relief when she saw that several computing consoles were lined around the walls inside. Slipping inside quickly, and trying to keep casual without rousing any undue attention, she sat down on a stool in front of the third console on the wall adjacent to the window. She leaned forward into the divider separating the terminals, trying to make sure that no one could see her face from outside.

There was a tap on her shoulder, and it was everything Rumil could do to keep from jumping straight into the air. Turning her head cautiously, she saw a thin teenage Arcadian girl wearing a dress shirt of red and white vertical stripes and a name plaque reading "Kaylee," with "Welcome to Ducha Delight" in very fine print above it, and "I am Here to Help" at the bottom. Her adolescent face was creased with uncertainty, and her chocolate brown eyes looked like those of a young girl afraid to be bitten.

"Umm... miss?" Kaylee said nervously. "Only paying customers can use the consoles."

"Oh," Rumil said, trying to veil the relief she was feeling. "Of course. Where do I place an order?"

Kaylee straightened, then pointed to a counter top on the other side of the café, her full-bodied brown ponytail bobbing. "Over there at the counter. It'll only take a tick, and you'll be able to browse GalNet with no trouble."

"Thank you," Rumil said kindly, and did as instructed. As she approached, a Ferian with yellow fur dappled by orange spots suddenly popped up from some task beneath the counter, and Rumil gazed in dire wonder at the knife-like teeth in its mouth as it spoke. She was so enthralled that the Ferian had to repeat itself; "What can I get you today, madam?"

"Oh… can I just get a mixed-fruit mineral water?" Rumil said, shaking her head clear. "Two of them?"

"Certainly," the Ferian replied, tapping the order onto the console in front of it. "It will be 246 credits."

Rumil swiped her currency card through the digital reader, and the Ferian nodded appreciatively as the card cleared the transaction. The cat-like being pointed her to the console she had been sitting at, and said, "Just have a seat again, and I'll bring your order right out to you."

Rumil returned to the stool, and accessed her electronic messaging account. She didn't expect any mail to be there, since it was only used for business and not personal affairs… even if she *had* any personal affairs to speak of. She only accessed it out of habit most of the time, as she could never be certain when plans might change.

However, there was not just one, but *two* messages in her record. She examined the sender protocol addresses, and neither one was on the list of typical protocols she had memorized. Opening the first message, she discovered it to be from the locksmith owner she had went to earlier:

Don't ask how I was able to locate your message protocol, let's just say I know a few of the same people you do. I convinced them that I had news that you needed to learn quickly.

Your Solarian "friend" showed up at my shop as I expected, just half a tenth-cycle after you left. At first I thought he was just a skinny Arcadian, since he was a little taller than I've known most Solarians to be, but when

I was able to see through the hair that he kept real scruffy, probably to hide his Erani ears, I figured it out pretty quick.

Rumil nodded to herself. Solarians and Kiros shared many physical traits, one of them being slight points at the top of their ears. They were unique to the humanoid races, likely a genetic tie back to their Se-Lan ancestors.

Anyway, he initially said that he was your boyfriend, and that you had disappeared last night. Once he realized that I was on to him, he became very stern and cold. He told me that if he found out I was hiding you, "things would happen to my business".

*As if to prove it, every single flammable thing on my counter burst into flame. I could see that gleam in his eye... he was giving me a sample of what he could do. I would have attached his picture to this message, but I discovered just now that all my security recorders had been totally fried as well. Gods above, girl, you didn't tell me a Solarian **Knight** was after you. Those are some of the most dangerous people to get on the wrong side of, and I know some **dangerous** people to be on the wrong side of.*

Rumil sighed. She already knew from experience what her pursuers could do.

*You have got to get off this planet quick, and hope to whatever god or gods you worship that you never hack a single thing again. Even then, he **still** might find you.*

"That's what I'm planning to do," Rumil softly muttered to herself as she closed the message.

Then she opened the second, and nearly fainted right out of her seat when she saw its first line. It didn't say whom it was from... but she knew.

You can't run, Miss Bonamede. Don't make this any harder than it needs to be. I don't want to have to really use force.

For the first time in a long while, Rumil was starting to get scared. The Solarian after her now was not like the incompetent investigators she had eluded at the start, when she had first been given her task. The Knight she was up against knew what he was doing, and didn't appear to be against bending some rules to get what he wanted.

Her fingers trembling, she slowly tapped in the site protocol for the nearest starport, and began procedures to book transport off Talos. Eventually, she was prompted to scan her currency card, but when she did so, she was unexpectedly rejected.

She tried again, her eyes widening in disbelief. Once again, her payment was rejected.

She attempted a third time, and with her third rejection, an explanation appeared on the display:

This card account has been seized for investigation of currency fraud.

Please contact your credit institution if you feel this is an error.

Finally, at the bottom of the display, it said in small type…

This console address has been recorded to prevent illegal usage.

Rumil jumped from her stool in an almost blind panic, surprising the portly Arcadian businessman next to her into spilling his ducha into his lap. Rumil didn't even recognize this, however, as she had bolted out of the café in terror.

Meanwhile Kaylee had come out of the back room with two bottles of mixed-fruit mineral water, just in time to see her customer rifle out the door like a plasma round, nearly knocked the sliding door off its railings in her impatience.

"Hmm," the girl mused with a chuckle. "Seems like she didn't need any ducha anyway…"

Chapter Four

Rumil found herself hiding in a cardboard box tipped on its side, and she couldn't help but recognize the irony.

"Fifteen staryears later, and I'm cowering under boxes again," Rumil muttered to herself.

She started to think about that time, but she quickly suppressed the memory. She needed sleep desperately, and she wasn't going to get it thinking back on her past.

Even then, sleep did not come easily to her. She was certain that Timothy Honore was lurking just around the corner, waiting for her to fall asleep. Even if she somehow escaped him, no doubt it would be right into the clutches of Justin Feroz, who was surely also waiting for her to make a mistake.

When she finally did manage to sleep, she was plagued with the same nightmares that have haunted her since she was a child. She dreamed of being surrounded by complete pervasive darkness, save for a large clawed hand that was rising out of the void, as if trying to snare her very soul. No matter how she tried to avoid it, the red-scaled hand flecked with flaming red hairs kept getting closer, until the ichor-stained claws disappeared from her vision. From between the gaps of the menacing fingers, she could see the outline of horns, and of teeth that would make a Ferian seethe in jealousy…

Jerking awake, and nearly ripping the box with her flailing, she fought back the initial impulse to scream. She instead panted heavily, wiping away sweat that threatened to slip through her saturated eyebrows. Peeking up outside the box, she noticed that the sun had set, and that darkness once again reigned over that hemisphere of Talos.

She knew what she had to do now, even though she didn't like it, and no doubt her employer would not, either. But she had no other choice. Stepping out of the box, her eyes scanned the darkness for the network terminal that usually rested outside every building with a GalNet connection. Fortunately, she spotted one right across the alley, running across the fire escape steps.

She liked that idea because it meant she didn't have to go out in the open street. She wasn't even sure if she was safe in this alley, much less out in the open, nighttime or not.

She managed to hook the nails of her thin fingers underneath the terminal cover. With a grunt of exertion, the cover came off, flying out of her hands and landing with a loud clang on the alley floor below. Rumil froze, her eyes and ears probing her surroundings for any signs that anybody was approaching to investigate.

Five ticks passed before Rumil dared turn her attention back to the GalNet terminal. She examined the haphazard mess of wires; a tangle of red, yellow, brown, and blue. Judging from the fused portion of the red transfer cable that led to the network splitter, it appeared that she was not the first person to do what she planned to do to this box.

"Good thing, too… I don't have the proper cutters with me," Rumil muttered, and proceeded to work the fused section apart. Taking the smaller copper-colored wires inside the plastic cover, she unwove them and reconnected the plugs. Removing her PCU from her satchel, she confirmed her initial concern: the GalNet box was a significantly older model, and the plugs inside were incompatible with the slots on her unit. With a resigned sigh, she reached back inside her satchel.

After some rummaging, she took out a remote networking adapter, resembling nothing more than a small black cube a little less than a Tackem to a side. She connected the network box's plug to one slot on the adapter, connected the adapter to her unit, then opened and turned on the unit as she sat down and placed it across her legs. The size of her dual-mobile model was inconvenient at times, but mono-mobiles didn't have the power or capacity she sometimes needed, and carrying two PCUs for hacking meant there was twice the liability if one was confiscated or stolen.

Her login screen appeared on the display and she entered her password, then accessed her network features. To her expectations, the GalNet flared to life before her, and she quickly typed in the address to the general access chat sites. Working entirely from memory through the network quagmire, she typed in requests for a very specific user to join her.

Normally, such requests were not answered promptly for any number of reasons, but she knew that the user on the other end would reply quickly, and true to form, he did.

>>*This had better be good, Bonamede.*

Rumil didn't have much patience for her contact's attitude.

>>**Stuff it. I'm in a real bind here. I've got a Solarian and a Kiros Knight on my tail, and I can't get off planet.**

>>*I see. The Solarian Military has seized your currency card... You've put us all in danger just contacting me.*

>>**How else was I supposed to get out of here?**

>>*You won't. I'm leaving now.*

For a brief moment, Rumil was about to panic, then regained her cool long enough to type:

>>**You know all too well that I'm the only one that has any hope of getting into the Kiros and Solarian servers. No one else in the organization has my skill.**

There was another pause from the other end, and Rumil was beginning to worry that her contact had indeed left. Finally, the reply came:

>>*All right... you win. I'll arrange passage for you to get off planet. You'll find the instructions on your fifth messaging protocol. Do not contact this protocol, through message, or chat, ever again, as it is probably already been compromised.*

>>**Understood.**

>>*You better come through for me, Bonamede. The boss is not going to look kindly on this action.*

>>**I won't fail. I can't fail.**

>>*You're right, you can't.*

With that, the connection terminated, leaving Rumil alone again. She discovered she was trembling, but not due to any chill. It didn't matter where she ran to... she was terrified of every side.

* * * * *

As Rumil's contact feared, the chat room had been compromised. From the PCU resting on his lap, Timothy Honore monitored the conversation. He frowned at the contact's parting orders. Timothy had only managed to detail out *four* of Rumil's messaging protocols, and those had been tough to divine to begin with.

Rumil used public-domain protocols, and no doubt her contacts did as well. These protocols could be totally anonymous, meaning they didn't require any personal information whatsoever to start one. People wanting to use such protocols could leave every information field blank, if they so desired. It made it very hard to track down potential criminals.

Fortunately, he did get something out of the discussion. Like Timothy had suspected, there was a higher influence running the show, and Rumil was not their only hacker... but from the tone, she was one of their best.

He had to admit that she was quite wily. She had discovered his carefully placed tracking module, as well as eluded capture when he had closed his sting. The young blonde had managed to keep one step ahead of him so far, but he was determined that it not remain the case for long.

Her parting words to her contact continued to ring through his head. She had said she "couldn't fail." Why? What was her employer holding over her head that she felt she *had* to succeed?

Timothy was not comfortable with so many questions, as it made his job considerably tougher. If Rumil was being coerced somehow into hacking for whoever was employing her, he didn't want to get too rough, not if he wanted to keep a clean conscience.

He finally lifted his head from his display, and analyzed the starport around him. It was dismally empty, which was somewhat surprising for a metropolis of this size. Artificial lighting was lined up in rows across the white textured ceiling, and it cast light down onto sixteen rows of red cloth chairs, ten to each row, with a long aisle dividing them down the middle. He sat in the farthest northwest corner seat, with a clear view of the main entrance so he could analyze all the comings and goings into the area. Only three people were in the waiting area with him, but from his position, he couldn't tell much beyond the fact that they were male, judging from their hairstyles and manner of dress.

He had anticipated that Rumil would attempt to leave tonight, but judging from the implied meanings in the chat, that wasn't going to be the case. That meant she could feasibly wind up heading to any of the three starport regions in the city, and at any time.

He had to start his search almost from scratch. He considered questioning the staff from the Ducha Delight, Rumil's last confirmed location, but decided that they probably wouldn't have much information to give him. Besides, gathering the staff for such questioning would probably take time he couldn't afford.

As that thought passed, his comm unit beeped three times, and he quickly snapped it up and flipped open the small black device. Timothy had never counted on luck in any of his investigations, but he never complained when he got any, as he did right now.

A thin, red-haired Arcadian face with bloodshot green eyes popped up on the minute screen, and said, "Knight Honore, we have found something you might find useful. A GalNet transfer box was broken into on an alley between 110 and 112 East Severn Causeway. It might be your hacker... but I doubt it. A lot of hackers use that trick to get into the GalNet, and remain out of public eye."

Timothy nodded. "Right now, I'll take anything I can find. Thank you. You've been a great help, Captain."

The enforcement officer huffed, and replied, "Well, anything that gets you and that hacker off my planet, I'm completely game for."

Timothy didn't respond to the comment. There had always been tension between Arcadians and Solarians. Fortunately, that didn't stop them from assisting each other as much as feasibly possible. Finally, Timothy said, "Regardless, I admire your assistance, despite your concerns."

"Yeah well... perhaps you aren't such a bad character yourself, Honore. I'd advise you not to stick around too much longer before I change my mind."

"Have you heard any reports about a Kiros Knight in the area?"

"Not as of yet. All I know is that one arrived about a day after you did. He hasn't contacted us at all."

"He seems pretty content on having me do the work, and then swoop in like a vulture... typical Kiros, I suppose."

"And typical Solarian too," the officer stated dryly. "I'll be honest, you've been the first Erani investigator I've seen who's actually been willing to do any dirty work at all. They've always had us handle the job, then take the credit for it, Kiros and Solarian alike."

Timothy cringed at the thought, and didn't like the idea of his fellow Knights and Army comrades being labeled in that fashion, even if he ruefully admitted to himself that it was somewhat accurate. Finally, he laughed softly, and said, "Perhaps I'll end this transmission while we still are on talking terms. Good night, Captain. Get some sleep. You look like you need it."

"I'd wish the same for you… but I doubt that you will get much tonight," the officer said tiredly, rubbing his eyes with his right hand. "Good night, Honore."

Timothy closed the comm unit with a smirk and folded up his PCU, sliding it into his luggage pack and closing up the hard-covered container that was nearly as large as he. Nonetheless, he effortlessly lifted the pack in his left arm and, while holding his right arm out for balance, carried it off to the security modules along the back of the waiting area. Timothy examined the module numbers for the one he had reserved earlier, and tapped his combination onto the keypad. Opening the heavy hypersteel door, he slid his luggage pack into the large interior and closed the module again. The door snapped shut with a reassuring clang of hard, unyielding metal, and Timothy strode away, leaving the waiting area, and out the main entrance to the starport.

Meanwhile, as Timothy left, the person farthest in the front of the waiting area regarded him cautiously. Justin Feroz wished he had brought sound enhancement equipment with him; then he could have heard just what Timothy was talking about, and to whom he was talking.

"Trust me, I *can* dampen my aura, moron," Justin whispered as he rubbed his throat, angrily leering at the exit the Solarian had used to leave the starport. It *still* throbbed with pain whenever he took too deep of a breath, and Justin was *really* looking forward to returning the favor when it presented itself. However, right now, he had other concerns than revenge.

Once he was certain that Timothy was a good distance away, Justin rushed to the security modules. He stopped in front of one of them, certain that it was the one that Timothy had used. Normally, his superiors would have frowned on what he planned to do, but they had specified very clearly that it was of the utmost importance for Justin to bring the hacker to justice. He had quickly realized that Timothy had likely been put on the case considerably earlier, and so Justin needed to know whatever the Solarian knew.

Justin frowned. Had his father conceded to allowing Justin to pursue the case when he had first asked, Justin might not have been in this mess. As it was, it had taken a full ten-cycle before his father finally agreed… and that had put Justin at a considerable disadvantage.

Thus, the Kiros Knight was resorting to theft, of a sort. He slipped his hand into a sensory glove, and touched the keypad of the storage module. He waited for the processors in the glove to work out a compatible interface with the lock mechanism, and tapped in the appropriate commands on the wrist of the glove. Finally, once Justin had broken through the coded data, he just let the glove guide his fingers along the keypad, tapping out the correct combination. The door suddenly cracked ajar with a soft click, and Justin smiled in satisfaction, quickly opening the door like an anxious child ripping open a present... only to find nothing in the module.

Justin blinked three times, and realized the obvious truth. He had picked the wrong storage module. Glancing to his right and left, he knew that it was *one* of the modules nearby.

Looking back to the waiting area, it didn't appear that anyone was paying any attention to him, nor had any security officers been through recently. "Thank the Creator God for inept security," Justin mused as he shuffled one module to his left, repeating the process he performed on the first one. This one opened as well, and fortunately for Justin, *this* module contained the luggage pack he was looking for.

Justin examined the locking mechanism for a brief while, and then went over the combination he had spied off just moments before. Sliding the combination bars into their proper order, he heard the pleasant sound of the locks releasing, and pushed the top of the pack open. Now confronted with neatly folded and arranged articles of clothing and hygiene, he began carefully weaving through it in search of the PCU that Timothy had placed inside.

"Tsk... tsk... what a square. I wonder if he even folds his socks..."

...beep...

The sudden sound quickly drew Justin's attention. Most luggage packs that he had encountered didn't beep, regardless of the reason. He paused his search, looking for the source of the sound.

...beep...

Now he was concerned. Based on the little experience Justin had, Timothy was a clever and vicious sort when provoked, and Justin didn't doubt for one second that searching the Solarian's luggage pack would provoke him. Finally, he saw the small black detonator device underneath the front flap of the pack... its red light preparing to beep the third and final time.

Unfailingly, it did so, followed with a surprisingly large explosion.

Justin leaped back with all his strength as the luggage pack promptly burst into a plume of flame. Even then, he had to quickly teleport the remaining several Tacks to avoid being consumed by the fiery wake.

His teleport was somewhat haphazard, and Justin fell on his backside as the fiery plume died away, leaving only Timothy's unflappably resilient carbide armor remaining where once the entire pack had been. The walls around the security module were now painted in shades of charred black that gradually faded from the blast point.

The Kiros Knight panted heavily at his narrow escape, and then impulsively shouted, "That Solarian is a *lunatic*! He needs to be put away before he *kills* somebody!" In a softer voice, he added to himself, "Namely me…"

Justin then saw the approaching mass that was starport security. "Of all the times to decide to do your duty…" Justin mumbled before he jumped to his feet, and bolted at top speed out of the starport. By the time security also burst out the main exit, Justin had disappeared into the night.

*   *   *   *   *

Timothy followed the directions he had been given to the site of the network box in question. Glancing around to make sure that he wasn't disturbing anything, he jumped up the fire escape to the exposed terminal. It didn't take a long examination for him to determine that the box had indeed been hacked into. However, he would not be able to determine if Rumil was responsible without doing some hacking for himself.

In a sequence of events extremely similar to the one Rumil had just used a mere tenth-cycle before, Timothy had his PCU running the GalNet, trying to locate the user protocols that had passed through recently. He smirked as he connected his unit into the frayed wires of the beleaguered terminal box. He had sensed someone watching him back at the starport, and so had used a little sleight of hand to make said observer think he had put the unit into his luggage pack. *Anyone* who tried to then break into the pack would be in for a bit of a surprise.

Transmitting the request via his investigative status, he was then assaulted by all the users that had sent and received data through the box. Several hundred logins had been recorded, but Timothy expected as much. Even private GalNet usage had a considerable amount of logging, much less a business like the one this particular box was mounted onto. He scrolled the display down to the latest accesses, and his eyes finally stopped at the second to last one. All the other logins had a routing code, corresponding to the network console they had used inside the building. However, this one had no such number, suggesting the login came through *before* it split off into the various consoles in the building. Logically, he came to the conclusion that the hacker, whoever he or she was, used that login.

Timothy was ninety percent certain that the hacker in question was Rumil, but wasn't willing to bet it all just yet. There *were* a considerable number of notable hackers on just this planet, and so Timothy went deeper to gather more information, running the login through the public domain database. While the downside to public protocols was that anybody could get one with no personal information, at the same time the account's activity is open to be viewed by *anyone*, and Timothy didn't even need to use his investigative privilege.

What followed was a list of individual service protocols that extended almost as long as the login list for the network box. Hundreds of messaging protocols, chat protocols, site protocols, and others flew about the display. Timothy instinctively went to the fifth messaging protocol, but knew better than to be so naive. He would have to arrange to have eyes on *every* protocol, to ensure that he got exactly what he wanted.

He packaged up all the protocols that he was able to discern, just to make sure that none of them were being masked as something else, and had them sent to Investigative Services on Centris, capital of Solaria. He concluded with the message that surveillance of every protocol on that list was of the utmost urgency, and to return anything they may find with all due haste.

Satisfied that he had done all he could feasibly do, Timothy prepared to return to the starport, when he got another buzz on his comm display.

The same tired enforcement officer appeared on the screen, his face reflecting extreme disdain. "Knight Honore… I wish to inform you that your luggage pack exploded in South Starport Number 3."

"Any casualties?" Timothy asked with genuine concern. He had expected Justin Feroz – concluding that Justin was the only person who'd be interested in Timothy's luggage – to *at least* take the pack to a secluded location.

"Fortunately, no… but I am afraid to say that everything save your armor was completely incinerated."

"That's fine," Timothy answered, his voice reflecting his relief. "Clothes I can replace, lives I cannot. I'll return as soon as possible to collect my items. Thank you, Captain."

*   *   *   *   *

Timothy recovered his carbide armoring twenty ticks later, and put it on since he no longer had a luggage pack, but it was not until two tenth-cycles after dawn that he finally got word back from Centris. They came to report that they had indeed intercepted a transmission to one of the messaging protocols with instructions as to where a flight would be leaving off Talos.

Timothy regarded the instructions warily. North Side Starport #1, flight leaving for Fraus Starport in Iomet, Altair at 9.15 ET. It didn't seem like it would be this easy to hunt down Rumil again. He didn't need to consult his comm to have a pretty good idea just what time it was, but out of habit did so anyway, and the small device confirmed it was already 8.22 ET. Normally, that would have been plenty of time, but unfortunately, he had never seen *any* of the North Side Starports, and even if he had, it would likely be so hectic there that teleporting into the thick of it could be quite dangerous.

Thus, he hastened to the nearest rail station, which he was able to see from his position on the street. He waited at the sliding panel doors long enough for him to squeeze through, and rushed up to the ticket desk. A Demodian, her hair dyed a unique shade of neon green, scowled at Timothy's impertinence. "I'm sorry, sir, but I will have to ask you to get in line like everyone else."

Timothy flipped open his credit fold, making sure that his ID was clearly visible. "I am Solarian Knight Timothy Honore, working with the Talos Enforcement Office. I request *immediate* transit to North Side Starport number One."

The lady frowned, but couldn't adequately dispute Timothy's claim, the carbide armor painting as clear of a picture as possible that he was more than some fraud trying to get a quick seat. Rather than hold up the line any further, she conceded, "Very well, Sir. Board rail sixty-four on track seven, and we will arrange the rest."

"Thank you, miss. I appreciate your assistance," Timothy replied, bolting full speed towards the rail that he had been instructed to board. Once he literally jumped from the waiting pad into the door of the rail, he allowed himself to relax.

Seating on the rail appeared to be tightly packed at best. There were only five other people on the rail, but the seats looked as though they were made for humanoids less than a Tack and a half in height, which ruled out almost the entire Arcadian majority on this world. As it was, even Timothy's rather slight Erani frame would be crunched trying to fit in the minimal space between the blue padded-cloth bucket seats bolted to the rail floor.

Timothy addressed the group, and said, "I apologize for any inconvenience, but this rail will have to make a no-stop route to the North Side Starports. I am sure that you will be reimbursed for your trouble." Outside of five frustrated groans, there was surprisingly little objection to the statement.

Stepping along the grooved rubber flooring that was likely used to siphon off wet shoes and boots, he quickly slid into the front seat of the rail. Looking back to the front desk, he waved appreciatively as the rail door slid closed, and the automated systems kicked in. The rail initially jerked, and then smoothly slid along the fixed track with almost awe-inspiring speed, soon rising over the tops of all the buildings in the city save the tallest commerce towers. Had Timothy been a little less anxious as to his hopefully timely arrival, he might have allowed himself the luxury to examine the sight of Talos from this new vantage point.

Viewed from the high above, the city looked considerably less tainted than from street level. Someone on the rail would only see majestic buildings, both of antiquated brick and smooth polished hypersteel and fiberwall. The personal vehicles and people would appear merely as ants, so visitors would be unable to see the muggings, the prostitution, the crime and immorality. However, they would also miss the charity, the families, and the inner communities.

The bullet-shaped rail veered along the magnetic guide to the left, swerving past a towering skyscraper. Its mirrored windows reflected the rail as it passed, as well as the morning sun. Timothy was momentarily blinded by the gleam out of the corner of his eye.

Despite that, Timothy Honore never squinted, never even turned his head from its position straight ahead, as if his skull was fixed solid to his neck. His focus was dedicated to one goal, one purpose, and that one purpose alone. So intense was that focus he didn't even think to regard the powerful psionic aura following him from below…

*   *   *   *   *

Justin Feroz knew that there was no way that he'd be able to keep pace with the rail zipping over the city in the taxi vehicle that he had "commandeered." However, at least the Kiros Knight had a vague idea where his Solarian counterpart was heading, and could try to plan accordingly. Pushing the throttle of his hover to its full acceleration, he took off after his quarry.

Chapter Five

Rumil absolutely hated waiting in lines even under normal circumstances. Under *these* circumstances, her loathing and impatience was magnified a hundred fold. Coupled with her continuous nervous glances and ragged expression, she probably resembled a hyperactive addict going through withdrawal to the casual observer. And there were many such casual observers, as a matter of fact; a good twenty of them were ahead of her in line.

Had her eyes been able to do so, they likely would have just spun in complete circles, trying to keep track of all her surroundings at once. With every movement that her eyes caught, she was certain she would spot one of those Erani Knights.

Hundreds of people fought and struggled through the small space between the ticket counters and the departure gates. And if the people weren't enough, the assembly of employees, machines, and robotic units also trying to navigate to do their duties turned the already small starport into a veritable pit of chaos.

It didn't help her nerves much that there was a fairly large Erani presence in the starport. That wasn't terribly unusual; after all, this city itself housed a Solarian theological center and a military base. Regardless, any time one of the pointed-eared beings came into immediate view, Rumil's heart started to race, and she was absolutely convinced that they must be out to get her.

To her left, three Arcadians in business suits rushed past at top speed, as if trying to beat each other to the departure ramp for the shuttle, which drew her attention to the shuttle ramps outside the building.

For the amount of activity going on inside the building, there was an almost disturbing lack of activity going on outside it. The paved runway, slanted upward at a gradually increasing curve until it went out of view, had not seen a shuttle accelerate on it for the last twenty ticks. Rumil concluded that there was some backup on the taxiing lanes, which bode very ill for her attempts to get off-planet quickly: the longer she lingered on this world, the worse her chances to get out in one piece became.

From the escalator leading down to the lower level of the starport she suddenly saw the top of a brown carbide helmet. Fortunately, the head of the Arcadian maintenance crewman became visible just before Rumil went into cardiac arrest.

During all that, the line went forward one person.

Shutting her eyes in an attempt to gather her rampant thoughts, Rumil tried to calm down. If she kept this up, people *were* going to start getting suspicious. Just then, a hand fell softly on her shoulder…

Rumil didn't bother to get the name of the attendant that was handing out ducha to the customers waiting in line, nor did the blonde hacker care. All Rumil knew was that the black-haired Demodian girl who had touched her was *wrong*. Eventually relenting long enough to help the poor girl pick up all the spilled paper cups, Rumil also apologized to the startled attendant and the rest of the customers for screaming like she had been skewered on a spit.

It didn't take long for the people in the starport to return to their normal business, whatever that may have been. Taking several long, deep breaths, Rumil tried to slow her rampant internal workings. She had *started* to succeed, when four starport security officers worked swiftly through the crowd, making the straightest line they could to her.

For several demiticks, Rumil's mind flip-flopped between standing her ground and fleeing, but by the time she made up her mind to try to elude them, they were right in front of her. The two in front were large specimens, and had they possessed somewhat blue skins, Rumil figured they could have passed for Ubeks. They wore navy blue-brimmed caps matching their long-sleeved uniforms with double breast pockets, and neatly pressed black slacks. Small bronze badges were pinned to the right pockets, and at their waists were holstered large plasma pistols, apparently designed to maintain order by looking as aesthetically terrifying as possible.

Because of the hulking presence of the two security guards in front, she couldn't clearly see the pair behind them, except that they were red- and gray-haired. From what she could see, they wore the same uniform as their gigantic companions in the front.

"Are you all right, miss?" the first towering guard slightly to her right asked. "We heard a scream."

It was everything Rumil could do to keep from sighing in relief. "I'm quite well, thank you though. I'm just… a little stressed out, and one of your attendants surprised me."

"Are you sure?" the second giant Arcadian asked, "Is there anything we can do for you?"

"No… once again. I appreciate your concern however."

"Very well, then. Have a good day, miss." The two security

personnel turned to their smaller companions, then proceeded to weave back through the crowd to their posts. Meanwhile, Rumil turned back to find out that the line moved one more person forward.

Rumil groaned softly. If the two Knights didn't kill her, the anxiety would.

*   *   *   *   *

Timothy knew that Rumil was at the starport before he ever stepped inside. That tingle in the back of his mind was a dead-on indicator of the hacker's nearby presence. He refused to ponder the impossibility of the issue any further, however, until she was safely in custody.

Once he passed through the sliding doors, which might as well have been locked open because of the traffic, he discovered that he could see very little through the crowd inside. While he was tall for a Solarian, that didn't mean terribly much, and he was simply unable to get a clear view around him.

Thus, he had to rely on his extra sense, narrowing down Rumil's location by playing a hot and cold game with the tingle. The closer he got, the stronger the sensation was. Fortunately for him, when people saw his armor, they gave him as much room as they were able. Unfortunately for him, most of those same people probably figured he was absolutely gone in the head due to the way he constantly stopped and changed directions.

Taking great care not to trip on a Ruma that had suddenly appeared in front of him wielding a bare refreshment tray, Timothy finally found the spot where the power was strongest.

Only… the object of his search wasn't there.

Curiously, Timothy spun around slowly, trying to draw some clarity out of what his sense was telling him. This was where the presence was strongest, but it clearly wasn't her current position.

His eyes started scanning above and below him for any clue as to the reason for the psionic residue that he was feeling. That's when he spotted the escalator leading to the second floor through the massive crowd, and the left side of his lips twitched upward in a wry smirk.

Meanwhile, the party of ten in front of Rumil finally got all their business squared away and started to cut a nice long swath through the mass of "intelligent" life en route to their departure gate. Now she was the second person in line.

"Okay… better make sure my story is straight," Rumil muttered to herself, as she made certain that her eye contacts carrying forged retinal data, as well as the synthetic fingerprint and genetic material on her fingertips, hadn't fallen out or slipped.

The last customer in front of her, a green-scaled Ruma, stood on its tiptoes in order to reach up onto the counter. The receptionist, a tiger-striped Ferian – likely female, judging by its large stature – had slid a ticket through the small slot in the thick, clear blast shield separating the counter workers from the general public. The salesperson offered some subtle assistance by slipping her whole hand through the small partition, and the Ruma finally acquired its ticket and stepped away from the ticket desk.

"I apologize for the delay, miss," the Ferian salesperson said in a voice that Rumil almost mistook for an agitated growl… then again, she might not have. "We are experiencing some delays. If you wish to see which flights are delayed, the central display in the waiting area has a list updated every fifteen demiticks." With a brief thought, the Ferian then added acidly, "And please don't scream about it… people are tense enough as it is."

"Actually, I'm here to confirm passage for myself to Iomet, Altair," Rumil said sweetly. "It should have been arranged last night."

"How was travel purchased?" the Ferian asked, the large cat being's voice not gaining any cheer.

"My husband purchased it over GalNet at Faus Starport Network Sales," Rumil continued. "It should be under the name Rama Foran."

Nodding appreciatively after Rumil gave her all the information she needed, the Ferian turned to the console just to her left, and tapped in the required fields for confirmation. "Yes, you are all set to go; your travel was purchased and confirmed at 9.22 LT last night." Looking back at Rumil, she asked, "Do you need a ticket printed?"

"Yes, I do."

The Ferian then pointed to Rumil's right, towards an upright flat blue screen framed by light grey plastic, bolted to the desktop and tilted back slightly. "Please place your right fingertips on the screen for fingerprint identification."

Rumil did as ordered, and a yellow band of light zipped from the top of the screen to the bottom twice. The Ferian then ordered, "Now look at the screen, bringing your forehead about one Tackem from the screen."

Rumil once again followed the salesperson's instructions, and this time, the yellow light came in the form of two small beams that zapped right into the irises of her eyes. The beams weren't blinding, but did leave a nice retinal shadow when they disappeared.

"Very good, Miss Foran," the Ferian said, passing a small slip through the slot beneath the blast shield. "Have a safe flight." Rumil took the slip, her departure gate and scheduled time of departure printed on the top in red, and her destination and time on the bottom in blue.

"Oh, I don't know... I have a strange suspicion that 'Miss Foran' won't be making her shuttle..."

A pang shot down Rumil's spine, locking every muscle in her body into a tense, frozen position. She had only heard that cold, commanding voice once before, and once was all she needed. One thin hand, covered in carbide mesh, closed around her right bicep, and whirled her around.

Face to face with the Solarian Knight who had been hunting her like an animal since she arrived on Talos, Rumil decided that now was not the best time to resist. Maybe if she didn't put up much of a fight, the Solarian wouldn't hurt her... at least, not *too* badly.

"Will you just follow me, and not make a scene this time?" Timothy Honore asked softly, although his voice seemed to carry just as much power regardless of volume. "I really don't want to have to resort to extreme measures."

Rumil, at the moment, really didn't have the desire to test what Timothy deemed "extreme measures," and managed to nod slowly in a defeated daze. The Knight then pushed her in front of him, and whispered, "Go into that empty departure gate. We can talk there."

Without replying, Rumil began to walk, having to consciously tell herself to alternate her feet. She then looked down, and slightly behind her, noticing the carbide boots of the Solarian.

"Yes, Miss Bonamede, I am right behind you, so don't be getting any ideas," Timothy reminded softly. "You have tested my patience far too long as it is."

Timothy slipped in front of Rumil long enough to pull the elastic barricade out of the way, allowing them to both step into the long, glass-covered tunnel. The tunnel itself was bathed in royal blue carpeting, and extended almost a hundred Tacks until it ended with a pair of sliding clear doors, where a shuttle would normally be waiting for passengers to board.

"This is sufficient, stop right there," Timothy stated simply, and

Rumil quickly obeyed. Her best chance relied on Timothy letting his guard down at some point in the future. For now, it was in her best interests, not to mention her health, to cooperate.

Without prompting, she turned to the armored Knight, only to get pushed against the glass wall, his helmeted face getting threateningly close to hers. Timothy never rose his voice, but it still caused her to almost visibly cringe. "Okay, now that we can talk in peace and quiet, I want to know just who is running your little hacking operation."

"Pardon?" Rumil asked nervously. Out of a *million* possible questions that Timothy Honore could have asked, she would have willingly answered any of them save one, and that last one was it. "I don't know what you're referring to."

Timothy sighed. "You know… I don't need to be a psionic to see through that absolute lie for exactly what it is." The Solarian took one step back and commented, "I shouldn't be surprised though. I've encountered enough crime syndicates and pirate organizations to figure out how they work. I'll just tell you this; whoever is 'employing' you is eventually going to decide you need to removed, whether you help me or not. The way I see it, your *best* chance to live a full life span is by helping me and the proper authorities put them where they can't do more harm."

Sweet kid, Rumil thought. *Just naive enough to think that he can change the universe, and bring every last criminal to justice.*

"*I* can only do so much, *that* is true, Miss Bonamede," Timothy stated wryly, "But there are *many* like me."

"What's the point in interrogating me if you can just rip whatever you want to know right out of my head?" Rumil hissed. From what she knew of Erani, reading a person's mind without permission was in *extremely* bad taste. Then again, this particular Solarian seemed to have little problem with casting away taboos that he felt impeded his progress.

"I really don't want to do that," Timothy replied, "but I will if I eventually deem it necessary."

Suddenly, Timothy's attention was jerked to his left, back towards the main ticket room. From the mass of life forms scurrying about, a blue-armored Erani emerged, hitting Timothy with a flying tackle. Then, grabbing Timothy by the collar of his carbide armor, Justin threw the Solarian against the wall. Glass shattered, sending the young Knight falling from the suspended departure tunnel.

As the Solarian Knight disappeared from view, Justin Feroz quipped, "Seems like I've learned your 'first and last lesson' pretty well…" then turned to the young hacker he had suffered considerable pain and stress to locate. "Now, unlike your morally bankrupt friend down there, I have *no* problems getting the information I want from your pretty little head. So as long as you don't fight me, I won't have to *severely* hurt you."

Rumil frowned. "Again with the threats... again with promising pain... I swear all you Erani are exactly alike."

Justin appeared to snap back at the comment, when his attention suddenly whirled to where he had shown Timothy the exit, so to speak. Hovering just outside the suspended gate, defying the very nature of gravity with his psionic power, Timothy did not appear too happy. From inside the tinted visor, Rumil was almost certain she saw two white circles flicker for a bat of an eyelash, but it disappeared so quickly that Rumil managed to convince herself she was just seeing things.

Justin waited in an aggressive stance as Timothy stepped back inside the damaged tunnel. "I guess I shouldn't be surprised... you Solarians just don't know when to quit."

There was no reply from his Solarian counterpart, only a right hook that caught Justin on the side of his helmet, causing him to stagger. Rumil tiptoed back slightly as Timothy pressed his advantage, landing two fierce blows into Justin's carbide breastplate. It didn't take the Kiros Knight long to retaliate, and soon the pair were trading blows with vicious speed. Once again, the skirmish was almost awe-inspiring as the pair ducked, rolled, and attacked, each move inspiring a counter that was parried and countered in turn.

This time, however, Rumil didn't allow herself to be entranced by their combat. She slowly slid backward towards the group of customers and security that had bunched up near the entrance of the departure gate, as if not terribly sure what to make of the scene in front of them. Rumil then stepped backward again, and finally was convinced that neither Knight was paying any attention to her. With a devious grin, she flipped her hand in farewell towards the oblivious combatants, and squeezed through the mass of spectators into the waiting area.

Rumil noticed with satisfaction that her fist had crumpled around the ticket for her departure, but it was still readable. Almost skipping towards the departure gate that the ticket indicated, she handed it to the steward waiting at the booth leading towards the tunnel that connected to her shuttle. He ripped off the top half, handed the bottom portion to her, and stepped aside for her to proceed. "What is going on over there?" the steward asked as Rumil passed, pointing towards the scene she had just emerged from.

Rumil shrugged. "Just a pair of intoxicated louts who decided to settle an issue from what I gathered," then she proceeded into the covered tunnel. She had to quickly step around an elderly couple that wandered into her vision, then accelerated past them toward her destination. Handing the bottom portion of the ticket to verify her seat to the Arcadian stewardess waiting at the shuttle portway, Rumil turned left towards the front of the shuttle.

"Umm… miss?" the stewardess said sheepishly. "That's the Preferential section, your seat is in Standard."

"What?" Rumil snapped, looking back down at her ticket. With a sneer, she grumbled, "That little dunghill…" Displeased with the recent discovery, Rumil reluctantly turned right, and pushed aside the curtain that led to the Standard Seating section of the shuttle.

She frowned as she witnessed the cramped, beige-colored seats and walls already filled with passengers in varied levels of misery or discomfort. Looking down disdainfully at her ticket stub once more to confirm her seat assignment, Rumil huffed, and passed seven rows before finding her seat. Throwing her satchel into the compartment under her seat with barely veiled frustration, she slumped down into her seat with a scowl, waiting for the shuttle to begin its launch procedure.

Stealing a glance to the seat next to her, she beheld the grimiest excuse for an Arcadian boy she had ever seen. He couldn't have been any older than ten staryears or so, his face splotched with dirt, and his clothes looking like he had pulled them out of the dirty pile rather than from anything that had been washed within a ten-cycle. In one hand, he held a small plastic spoon, and in the other, a plastic cup that must have contained some form of treat at first, but had since melted into a congealed mess of blue, red, and yellow streaks and smudges. Trying to take another bite of the cup's unidentifiable contents, part of the half-melted treat slipped out of the spoon held by his unsteady hand, and splattered onto Rumil's leg.

The child looked down at the site of the accident, then up at Rumil, before he smiled broadly, and said with a giggle, "Sorry, lady."

Rumil didn't reply, just turned her head forward, and brooded internally. *Someone* was going to pay for the outrage, and they were going to pay dearly…

Meanwhile, the two Erani Knights were still engaged in their impromptu duel. They had since moved to swords, swiping and lunging with attacks that could deceive the untrained eye with their quickness. Security had managed to form a loose semi-circle around the tunnel, but didn't intervene directly, for much the same reason one didn't try to break up a fight between two Ferian; you'd likely lose limbs you'd much rather keep.

The sound of the shuttle taking off broke Timothy and Justin out of their combat hazes. The white shuttle shot up the inclined ramp before the boosters kicked into full power, and launched vertically off into the sky, quickly disappearing from view. It took them both nary a demitick to realize that Rumil was no longer in the tunnel, and had once again slipped away. From there, it took only a demitick longer to look around the departure tunnel, now ravaged by their errant attacks. Panels of the glass archway had either fallen or cracked, the support beams were bent, warped or slashed, and the carpet beneath them was scratched and gouged.

Finally, they turned their attention to the security detail that was finally approaching now that the skirmish appeared to be concluded. Justin and Timothy glanced at each other dejectedly, realizing they both had some explaining to do.

Chapter Six

One would expect that any establishment known for its service of the seedy and the suspicious would be a run-down, dark, foreboding dive somewhere deep within the bowels of a large city, run by a large, grizzled specimen that took no excuses nor IOU's.

However, as Timothy had learned quickly in his tenure, that was rarely the case, and this bar – which he had been reliably told was a hotbed of information for the criminally inclined – was yet another example to the contrary. Located in the suburbs of Iomet, this establishment could easily be classified as high-brow, with its bright, high ceilings painted a glimmering pearl and chandeliers of crystal and gold hanging every three Tacks. The entire barroom was bathed in a cascade of prismatic light, the colors shifting slightly as the chandeliers turned back and forth in some unseen air movement near the ceiling.

He himself sat perched atop a red wooden stool, elaborately carved, with a high-quality leather seat stretched over a down-filled cushion. Its pronged base had impressed itself into the antique carpet, which featured a pattern of cream and burgundy diamonds interwoven with wave-like frills interlocking the edges. It complimented the red and brown tints prevalent along the walls, tables, and counter tops.

"Not that I'm doubting your sources, mind you, but… are you sure this is a gathering place for the less than reputable?" his companion asked.

Timothy had almost forgotten that he had taken on a partner for the remainder of this hunt… and had almost forgotten that he was violating tens of social and moral taboos in doing so.

The pair had spent half a cycle in a Talos detention center while representatives for the Solarians and Kiros negotiated their release. Timothy had expected to be removed from the case after that skirmish, and was somewhat surprised to instead receive a commendation from the Knighthood for not allowing himself to be bullied by a Kiros.

Soon after being released, he ran right into none other than his adversary at the large exit leaving the detention center. Learning that his counterpart was also continuing to pursue the case, and ironically had *also* received a commendation for his actions, Timothy made a proposal that surely would result in a public execution if his father were to learn of it.

He had not expected the Kiros Knight to *agree*, displaying a level of rational thought that rarely surfaced amidst the nearly warlike interaction between the two sects. The deal was made, and the pair would pool their resources until Rumil Bonamede was in custody. Only at that time would they… settle… the issue of who would bring her to justice.

Finally, Timothy shrugged, and replied, "Perhaps even the legally bankrupt have dignified tastes."

Justin pursed his lips in a sort of half smile, half frown. "It just seems to me like I could bring my family here. It doesn't strike me as…" Justin's comment died away as he saw a large Ubek with lightly tinted blue skin duck underneath the door leading into the pub, dressed like a ceremonial warrior in a rather dingy skintight vest and trousers, wielding a ceremonial broadsword as big as Justin at his hip and a black plasma rifle slung across his broad, muscled back. A thick lock of white hair was pulled tightly back along his otherwise shaved head, and a line of yellow war paint stretched above and under each gray eye, joining at each ear and at the sides of his nose.

The thin Arcadian barkeeper, dressed most professionally in a red vest over white dress shirt and black uniform pants, suddenly paused, and hissed, barely audible to the two Knights three Tacks down the bar, "The… other entrance… is in the back."

Justin and Timothy looked at each other with devious smiles as the Ubek shrugged off the bartender's complaint. "I just want something quick to drink," the hulking humanoid specimen said with a deep, almost echoing voice, "then I have to leave again."

The Ubek stopped just behind Timothy, and although the Solarian Knight sensed this, he did not make any indication that he had noticed anything. "You're in my seat, little man," the Ubek commented with a derisive snort.

Timothy picked up the small glass of redberry giacano that he had been occasionally sipping, and looking at the almost blood red liquid with half-melted ice floating in it, commented, "Is that so? I didn't see a reserved seating sign anywhere."

Justin looked back at the Ubek, then at Timothy, and whispered, "You know… I'm sure you're a tough guy and all, but maybe you should just let our friend have this seat."

"I would listen to your little shrimp friend," the Ubek replied haughtily. "He seems to be interested in his future health."

Timothy ignored Justin, and replied dismissively, "Apparently you aren't interested in yours, or you'd walk away now while I'm still in a halfway decent mood."

Growling, the Ubek whipped Timothy's stool around, and the Solarian indifferently looked up at the large humanoid's face, then glanced downward where some of his drink had escaped the glass during the sudden movement, and splashed against Timothy's thigh.

Timothy pursed his lips in mild aggravation, and said in that same soft, flat voice, "Now you can pay for another drink. I was actually enjoying that."

"Gentlemen... there is no need to get angry..." the bartender began sheepishly.

"Sure, I'll pay for it," the Ubek smiled at Timothy. "I'll just take it out of your hide." The Ubek reared back with one meaty fist, and Justin's trained eye could see the muscles on his Solarian counterpart tense in anticipation, placing the drinking glass on the counter, as if unperturbed by the belligerent Ubek.

The Kiros Knight stepped in, pulling Timothy to the side off the barstool before the encounter could turn into something ugly. Meanwhile, Justin saw out of the corner of his eye a slight, four-fingered hand appear on the Ubek's forearm. The hand was connected to a brown-cloaked figure, his fine facial features partially shrouded by the cloak's hood. It seemed to calm the Ubek, who dropped his fist slowly, his arm finally falling almost limply at his side.

"Orion, follow me. *Now*," the cloaked Demodian said with a voice that rang with a clear, almost musical tone. Reluctantly, and casting several angry glares at Timothy in the process, the Ubek complied, eventually ducking back out the door.

"Are you crazy? Getting belligerent with an Ubek in a crowded place like this?" Justin sputtered. "I mean... I know you're a powerful psionic and all, you'd have to be, but picking a fight with one of those monsters isn't a good way to stay in the land of the living."

"I could have handled him," Timothy replied simply, his eyes narrowed in irritation.

Justin sighed. "I don't doubt it... but getting in a scrap here would really ruin our chances of getting in back where the *real* information is."

"It doesn't matter... they wouldn't have let us back there," Timothy answered knowingly.

"How do you figure?"

"I recognize the Demodian that was with him, and I am sure he remembers me."

"How could you tell?" Justin asked skeptically. "That cloak of his kept him pretty well hidden."

"The cloak perhaps, but there is only one Blood Hawk officer I know of that has his mark on that spot, and I know just about all of them at this point. If I don't miss my guess, he's their new leader."

*   *   *   *   *

Dewin Rio pulled Orion back around the bar towards the pirate's entrance. Fortunately, the Ubek was being cooperative this time, because it was unlikely that Dewin would have been able to force him anywhere.

"But… Mr. Rio… I just wanted a drink…" Orion protested.

"You can get one from the back while I warn them to watch out." Dewin snapped, the hood of his cloak falling back after a gust of wind had blown it off his head.

"It's dirty back there, and not fit for a warrior of my caliber."

"Yes, and apparently neither is a brain."

Finally Orion stopped, and the quick action nearly sent Dewin's feet out from under him. Whirling to face the Ubek, Dewin hissed, "What is wrong with you now?"

"Why are you going to warn the back about those two little twigs?" Orion asked curiously.

Dewin paused dumbly, and then he shook his head in disbelief. Not even an Ubek could be that stupid. "How long have you been traveling with us, Orion?"

Orion thought about this. "About ten staryears, Mr. Rio."

"And in those ten staryears, you have never encountered a Solarian Knight?" Dewin asked like he was quizzing a child.

"I've seen one before… but I never had the chance to fight him."

"Then you're simply ignorant. You're lucky I came when I did." Dewin sighed. "That 'little twig' could have seriously hurt you… if not killed you."

Orion obviously thought that idea was funny. "That… little man… hurt me?" The Ubek laughed loudly.

Dewin slapped him across the chest. While it didn't hurt the towering humanoid in even the slightest way, it managed to get his attention. "Yes. There's a lot of jolt in that frame, despite what you might think. A Solarian's strength lies beyond what you can see with those big eyes of yours."

"Yeah, most Solarians are psionic, just like the Kiros. That still doesn't explain why you seemed so scared of those two."

"I've met that Solarian before, and I very nearly didn't live to tell you about it. That particular Knight is named Timothy Honore, and he was the one that arrested our old leader three staryears ago."

"That's *him*?" Orion gaped. "That's the Solarian that had Mr. Gallan killed? Then why…? I must avenge my old leader!" Orion whirled around to return to the bar, promises of pain and suffering towards the little Solarian inside affecting his features.

Dewin quickly slipped in front of the towering Ubek, and held his hands out in an order for Orion to stop. "Have you listened to a word I just said? Getting revenge for Gallan is all well and good… but you don't accomplish that by walking back in there and getting yourself, and likely a good many others, killed."

Orion still wasn't sure just what about that Solarian Knight worried Mr. Rio. However, he understood that he wasn't the brains of the Blood Hawks either. If Mr. Rio was concerned about something, then there must be a good reason for it.

"All right, Mr. Rio… if you think that's for the best…" Orion finally said sheepishly.

Dewin sighed in relief, thankful that he had managed to get the Ubek to see reason. He could understand Orion's desire though, as one part of him wanted to charge into that bar and try and get his hands on that arrogant Knight himself. However, Dewin's first personal encounter with Timothy Honore had not gone favorably at all, and there was no reason to believe that a second would turn out any better.

With a resigned release of breath, Dewin ordered, "All right… now let's warn the fellows in back, and I'll grab your drink while we're in there."

*   *   *   *   *

About a tenth-cycle later, a young blonde woman trudged

nervously through the crowded streets of Iomet as evening began to wane above the city. She really did not like being here; she felt too exposed… too known. Granted, she had no real reason to feel that way, since it had almost been three staryears since she had last set foot in any public venue in this city, but she couldn't help but feel the occasional pair of eyes wander too long on her, as if they were remembering the "Beauty of Baramak."

Even now, the thought of the title made her lips curl in distaste. Despite actually being on the good end of the legal system back then, her current line of work felt considerably less dirty. Granted, she had not had much choice back then – the Tech Academy of Iomet had been expensive, and the only way she had been able to get enough credits to afford the outlandish tuition was through her dancing. Fortunately for her, she had learned enough to catch the eye of her new employer prior to the incident that terminated her dancing career…

*   *   *   *   *

Rumil watched Sasha disappear into one of the private rooms with a Demodian that looked like he had just come from a war zone. The blonde woman scoffed at her fellow dancer's extracurricular activities, wondering if she herself would ever lose enough dignity to do the same.

She heard the owner of the Sultry Siren call out her dancing name, and she took that as her cue to step out onto the catwalk. The group beneath her in the seats looked just like every audience that ever came to the club; lecherous, rich, and somewhat distasteful. However, there was a light tingling in the back of her head, like a small insect was buzzing around in the back of her neck, which she had never felt before. Forcing herself to ignore it, she began her dance.

Gritting her teeth as she smiled seductively, she began her routine. Just twenty-two more ten-cycles and she'd graduate, and then she wouldn't have to subject herself to this sort of debauchery any longer. She remembered her routine by heart, so it wasn't hard for her to just go through the motions. That's all the men expected anyway… they didn't care about the feelings of the woman on the stage. They just saw a piece of meat to be ogled and, if they were lucky, manhandled backstage.

Extending her right leg out to the crowd, she remembered that men, for some reason, found that using their teeth was somehow more pleasing and erotic than using their hands, so she quickly shook her head at the man who was starting to take off her ludicrously high-heeled shoe and bit suggestively. She wasn't even looking at him, nor did she look at the pervert who had removed the other. Her eyes were focused on the wall behind all the bodies, as one of the older dancers had suggested she do to cope with the leers and predatory stares.

Now able to walk comfortably, Rumil sighed inwardly as she strode towards the pole on the center of the catwalk. Spinning a few times for effect, she returned to the front. Another piece of advice from the more experienced dancers had been to interact with the audience. If they feel liked, they will like you in return, which translated to more tips to fill her creditfold.

The tingling sensation in the back of her head intensified. Instinctively, her eyes turned towards the source of the sensation. Sitting near the back, a clean-shaven man with a bowl cut of rich black hair and sapphire eyes was staring intently at her with a questioning glare that would probably have been creepy under any normal circumstances.

He looked so much different than the rest of the audience, but not by his dress. There were others dressed sharply like him, but his eyes didn't reflect the same lecherous thoughts that the other patrons were projecting. His was a look of a man trying to see something beyond physical appearance, his brow furrowed in deep concentration as if he was trying to see right through her. She raised her eyebrows, and smiled almost thankfully towards the unknown visitor. He definitely wasn't one of the regulars, she would have noticed someone like him had he been a frequent attendee.

Her thoughts were interrupted as one of the patrons in the front yelled at her, although she was so enthralled by the visitor in the back that she didn't clearly hear what he had said. She did notice two large Demodians next to him jump onto the stage, and quickly grab her by the arms. One of them ripped her slip off her body roughly, but since it hadn't covered anything to begin with, it didn't exactly embarrass her further.

Rumil yelped in surprise as she was pushed to her knees in front of the red-haired Demodian that had yelled at her. She knew better than to struggle, it would only get her assailants angrier and likely lead to her getting hurt.

"Did you forget that you were here to entertain *us*?" the ringleader of the trio demanded. "I think you owe us an apology."

"I'm… sorry…" Rumil whispered, hoping to appease them.

Unfortunately, the red-haired Demodian either didn't hear her or didn't care. He turned to the audience, and hollered, "Maybe this little slut should kiss my feet? Better yet… she should *lick* my boots clean.

Any of you out there favor that idea?"

The cheer that greeted the suggestion made Rumil physically ill. She glanced down at his boots, covered with dirt and grime, and had to stop herself from gagging. She began to wonder if anyone saw how disgusting this was… then when she decided most of them probably did, began to wonder if anyone cared.

Her head was forced down to Tackels above one boot, and clenching her eyes shut, she flicked her tongue out lightly over the footwear, fighting back another gag as she tasted the gunk encrusted against it. Unable to fight back the tears of humiliation quite in time, two small droplets fell to the floor beneath her.

She reluctantly took three more licks before she heard the sound of another body landing on the catwalk. "Don't rush me… you'll get your turn," she heard the boot's owner command to the new presence.

"I'm not here for my *turn*; I'm here to tell you to stop… right *now*," the person stated simply with a voice a little lighter and smoother than the deep grating bellows she had become accustomed to hearing during her working hours.

The boot pulled away from her, and she exhaled in relief. She tried to look up, but was unable to get much more than the bottom of their shirts into her vision.

"Could you care to repeat that, little man?" the leader of the trio demanded.

"Let me put it into words your drunken, narcotic-addled brain can comprehend. Cease and desist, before I rip that foot of yours *off*," the newcomer replied threateningly.

There was the sound of a fist slapping into a hand, then the Demodian howled in pain. As the red-haired humanoid fell to one knee, Rumil was pulled to her feet, allowing her to finally see the whole scene before her.

The man near the back had somehow slipped onto the stage, his hand clenched around his adversary's fist in a manner that must have been extremely painful. Rumil could barely control herself from smirking viciously at her assailant's discomfort. Moments later, the Demodian squealed for mercy, and Rumil was released.

Not even twenty demiticks had passed before the bar exploded in violence. Rumil had frozen in place, not sure what to do as fists and objects flew around beneath her. A barstool suddenly tumbled by, but before she could yelp in surprise about that, she yelped in surprise as a firm, strong arm wrapped about her waist, and another arm slipped underneath her thighs, pulling her up off the stage.

Rumil was too dazed to even scream as she felt the person holding her jump into the air, and landed behind the bar on one knee. The man who had rescued her from the Demodians glared at her, his almost-glowing sapphire eyes transfixed on hers. "Stay behind here, and *don't* move until I tell you it's clear," he ordered, but he turned away before he could see Rumil nodding violently in agreement.

He jumped onto the bar counter, and suddenly the sounds of plasma fire effectively stopped the melee. Rumil heard the Solarian – as she had just learned – calmly explain the situation. Her boss began to complain, but the man on the counter quickly silenced him, the pistol in his hand certain to convince everybody present that continued discussion was not going to be beneficial.

Finally, the Solarian declared it was safe to move, and she smiled at him in thanks when he helped her over the bar. Without all the people providing body heat to the establishment, the temperature inside had dropped considerably, and Rumil shivered involuntarily.

Suddenly, she felt the fabric of her rescuer's jacket fall over her shoulders, and she tried to give her thanks, but no sound came out of her throat. Flushing slightly at her vocal chord's betrayal, she settled for another sheepish smile.

The Solarian seemed to be looking for someone or something for a moment, and with a dejected sigh, apparently decided whoever or whatever he was trying to locate was not to be found. He nodded politely to her and the bartender, and as he prepared to leave, said to Rumil with a sympathetic smile, "I would strongly suggest, madam, that you find a new line of work… *quickly.*"

*　　*　　*　　*　　*

Rumil exhaled as her mind drifted back to the present. In a roundabout way, she had done exactly as the Solarian Knight had requested. About four ten-cycles afterwards, she had been fired unceremoniously by the club owner, and later received a secure communication from her current employer roughly a cycle after that.

Granted, even though she felt her new career was a step up from the previous one, she had to admit it was not the best of lives to lead. Hopefully, she wouldn't have to resort to hacking much longer. This job promised enough credits to easily set her up nicely. She could finish her education, get a legitimate career, and live peacefully… provided that she would be allowed to do so.

She looked up towards the Iomet skyline, and realized just what had prompted her nervousness and nostalgia. It quickly all fell into place why everything had seemed so frighteningly familiar to her. In her wandering around the city, she stumbled across the place where her current life had begun… the Sultry Siren.

Three men walked past her to enter the establishment, leering at her perversely as they disappeared into the increasingly crowded club. Their looks sent pangs of ill memories once again flooding through Rumil's mind, and suddenly in repulsion, she decided to get as far away from the Sultry Siren as she could.

Breaking out into a run, she burst out into the street, not looking back… and not looking at the headlamp of a hover vehicle bearing down on her.

Chapter Seven

"So… does the Blood Hawks presence complicate matters here?" Justin asked the driver.

"I got the impression that they weren't staying on Altair very long," Timothy replied. "I don't foresee any trouble from them."

Justin pondered that statement, as well as the summary Timothy gave of his previous encounter with the Blood Hawks. "But what if they decide that now's the time to exact their vengeance upon you for getting their leader executed?"

Timothy never turned his eyes off the road, but he clearly became just a little upset at Justin's unintended accusation. "First of all, I didn't get Gallan executed. That was the Solarian Adjucates' decision. Second of all, I know the new leader of that pirate organization. Gallan put Rio in the line of fire so that Gallan could protect his own hide. I doubt that Dewin would be particularly inclined to restore the old leader's honor."

Justin nodded. "I see… well perhaps you're right, but I'd feel a little more comfortable if you watched to make sure that no Ubeks will be pouncing on us trying to get to you."

Timothy emitted a sound that was something between a grunt and a chuckle, but made no further reply.

The pair continued down the road in silence for about a tick, when Justin finally spoke again. "I haven't heard from any of my contacts, or uncovered new information pertaining to Bonamede. Do you know of any other villainous haunts that we can crash?"

Timothy sighed, and answered, "They'll all be on the lookout for us now. We just have to keep our ears to the ground, and hope that someone sees her either hacking on this planet, or catches her leave it."

Justin snorted. "Wonderful… we're more likely to run over her in this hover before some layman finds that slippery little lady— *watch out*!"

A figure dashed out in the road, and Timothy had to apply full braking and turn the repulsor panels hard to the right in order to swerve around the young woman who had frozen in fear on the road. From there, Timothy had to swerve just as quickly to the left to avoid another vehicle moving the opposite direction. Finally, he braked to a stop, the vehicle hovering half a Tack in the air, and Justin allowed himself to breathe again. "All right… next time I'm driving."

"Hey, watch where you're going, rauche slime!" the pedestrian yelled poisonously.

Timothy and Justin would have recognized the voice by itself, but the psionic tingle that they both felt in her presence was all the confirmation they needed.

For a moment, Justin was unmoving, marveling at the irony, and he finally muttered, "Okay… that settles it, the Creator *indeed does* have a sense of humor…"

Rumil watched as two armored figures jumped out of the hover, and began to approach her rapidly. Combined with the increasing tingle in the back of her head that seemed to signify the approach of her two recent tormentors, she knew that this meant trouble. "Eep," she managed to squeak before breaking into a full sprint the other way.

She knew that she had no chance at all of escaping the two psionics in a flat-out race. However, if she could manage to lose them in the pedestrian crowd… her attention drew to a large gathering around a street side presentation of some sort. It appeared to be some sort of magic act, but the best Rumil could do was occasionally glance towards the performer as she squeezed into the middle of the group.

Rumil let her heartbeat slow. She would sit in this mob for a few minutes, and either wait until the crowd watching the show dispersed to slip away, or possibly slide into another large group of people if one happened by.

Unfortunately, because of her somewhat limited height, and her position in the crowd, she couldn't see either of her two pursuers. Then her mind started analyzing what she had just seen. Both Knights were in the same vehicle, and both had started to chase after her without so much as even trading an insult. "Wonderful… they're working together… Of all the times that a Solarian and Kiros could find a common ground…" Rumil muttered. It was apparent she could no longer count on using one against the other in order to spirit further escapes.

Once again scanning the crowd in hopes of catching a glimpse of the two Knights, she wondered just how hard it would be to find two people decked out like they were, about to enter a battle rather than a shopping center. She knew they had to be somewhere; that buzzing sensation in her head was still there, humming like a wasp.

A hand settled on her forearm gently, and a voice said, "Excuse me… can you come with me?" Rumil turned to face the person touching her. He was rather tanned, clad in a blue full-body stocking, and sported a wild mane of brown hair that didn't quite cover his slightly pointed ears.

She correctly assumed that this was Justin Feroz.

"You've been a very naughty girl, you know that?" Justin chided threateningly. "Now… why don't you just come with me so that we can have a little talk?"

Justin slipped his other arm around her shoulders to turn her in the direction he wanted to go, and started to gently pull Rumil through the crowd. His grip was just strong enough to resist her half-hearted struggling, both of them knowing that if Justin really wanted to, he could easily force Rumil to do what he wanted. However, he seemed to want to avoid making a particularly large scene… evidenced by the Kiros's lack of armor, which could have potentially stirred up the mostly Arcadian crowd. Upon this realization, Rumil's mouth turned upward in a mischievous grin.

"Let go of me you *pervert*!" Rumil screamed. "Stop groping me! Help!"

Justin turned to her questioningly, and asked, "What in the depths of Bannor are you…" His words died in his throat as he saw a good percentage of the mob turn in their direction, their eyes glaring dangerously at him. "Oh… well, this is no good…"

With that, Justin was buried in an avalanche of organic matter, and lost his grip on Rumil. Smirking victoriously, Rumil darted away from the mob, slipping through pedestrians traveling in various directions, until she found a dark alley connecting parallel roadways. Looking around quickly to see if she could spot the other Knight, she finally caught sight of him loitering underneath a light post, his relaxed posture suggesting bemusement at the carnage surrounding Justin. Now confident that Timothy wasn't actively searching for her, she dashed down the alley, and once she felt she was a safe distance away, called for a hover service to return to her hotel.

During Rumil's escape, Justin was having a hard go of things after being pushed to the ground by the mob. He really didn't want to hurt beings that were clearly duped into thinking a false scenario, but after having to kick away a Ruma that was trying to sever his ankles off for the third time, hurting was starting to become an appealing option.

Meanwhile, a boot connected with his abdomen roughly, forcing the wind out of his chest, promising to leave a nicely sized bruise. "Oh yeah… his boots just *have* to have hypersteel reinforcement…" he managed to gasp breathlessly. Another well-placed kick from a pointed shoe struck Justin in the back of his head as he curled up defensively, and finally managed to pull his creditfold out of his breast pocket. Raising it upward, he let one flap fall free, revealing his identification. "I'm a Kiros Knight! I'm not a molester!"

There were a few more half-hearted blows before the mob ceased, pondering the small bronze badge signifying Justin's rank and status. Puzzled looks occasionally fluttered through the various sentient beings as if they were deciding this recent development was reason to stop the assault... or to *continue* it.

Justin took the moment's pause to jump to his feet and make his escape to the other side of the street, where the light Timothy was standing beneath had just turned on in anticipation of the coming night. The Solarian was as close to outright laughter as Justin had seen during their brief cooperation.

Glaring, Justin commented, "You know... you could have helped me out..."

Barely managing to maintain just a humored chuckle, Timothy began handing Justin pieces of the Kiros's body armor. "I figured you could take care of yourself. By the time I realized that little girl was too much for you to handle, you had already managed to break free."

"Hey, those pointed shoes can hurt!" Justin protested as he clasped the panels of his form-fitting breastplate on, and moved to the leggings. "Besides, that little girl had about thirty friends. Did you see Rumil?"

Timothy shook his head. "There was too much commotion. I think she might have hitched a ride with someone, because her aura faded away very suddenly."

Justin finished attaching the various pieces of his armor, and Timothy took that as a cue that he was ready to return to the hover. Quickly falling into step behind the Solarian, Justin replied, "Well... I don't think we've totally lost her."

Timothy turned, his face now invisible through his tinted visor, but Justin could tell anyway that he had caught his counterpart's interest. Smirking to himself, Justin flipped a catch on the side of his left gauntlet and opened the panel that comprised much of its extra bulk, withdrawing his standard-issue mono-manual PCU from its housing where it interfaced with his armor's systems.

"I managed to slip a small tracker underneath our little hacker's collar as I was engulfed in that violent mass. I doubt she ever noticed me slip it on."

Timothy shrugged. "Perhaps, but I tried that trick before, and it got me about as far as a sandscrub going up a dune."

"Pardon?" Justin blinked. He had heard of sandscrubs, but the analogy was lost on him.

"In other words, it went nowhere."

"Ah."

The pair returned to their vehicle, Timothy once again sliding behind the operator's seat. "You need to keep your eyes on the tracking signal," he explained.

Justin's eyes narrowed suspiciously, and he said, "You don't think this will work, do you?"

Again, Timothy shrugged. "Maybe in her haste, she never saw it. Then again, I never imagined she'd find the tracker I placed in the restraints when she escaped from me the first time."

"Positive thinking is the first step to success," Justin replied cheerily, trying to convince his companion.

"It's also often the first step to a grievous disappointment," Timothy muttered wryly as he set to the controls, the repulsor panels shifting to allow for forward acceleration again. Justin fixed his eyes on his PCU's display, having downloaded a global street map of Iomet onto the screen, centered on his unit's own positioning signal.

"Next right, you should take it," Justin commented, trying not to sound too demanding. The traffic was beginning to increase as vehicles were either trying to get into the city as the nightlife began to take over, or trying to get out of the city for that very same reason.

Timothy finally was able to squeeze into the proper turning lane, and made the requested turn. "Next crossroad, go left," Justin dictated, and Timothy had to quickly swerve, cutting off the vehicle behind him, in order to get in the proper lane for the turn.

Suddenly, Timothy had to apply the brakes, nearly jolting the PCU out of Justin's hand. "What in Bannor…" The Kiros Knight asked angrily before seeing the large traffic jam that had plugged closed every lane of the street. Justin looked back down at his display blankly as their target pulled farther away.

"We might actually have better luck going about without the hover," Timothy commented.

"By the time that we walk past this blockage, the traffic will probably have cleared up," Justin replied testily.

"I never said anything about walking," Timothy replied. While Justin couldn't see the Solarian's face, he would have been willing to wager that a slight conspiratorial smile was creeping onto Timothy's features.

"Teleporting?" Justin replied incredulously. "Are you serious? It's a madhouse in this city! Added to the fact that you need a clear image of where you are going in order to ensure you don't pop up in the middle of wall or something!"

Timothy snatched the unit from Justin's hand, and said, "I recall a street corner about thirty Tacks from the transmitter's position. There is a rooftop that I once used while spying out Gallan. No one ever goes up there."

Justin paused, and replied, "Are you sure about this? I'm never terribly trusting of an image I don't know intimately as it is. Considering the fact that you had no problem trying to blow me up just a few cycles ago…"

Timothy interrupted the Kiros Knight, replying casually. "You don't have to follow me. You can take over the driving, and wait for the traffic to clear. I, however, am going to pull off to the parking lane, and I am leaving." Timothy did exactly that, drawing the hover vehicle out of the congestion, and onto the side of the magnetic roadway. Without further word to his Kiros counterpart, Timothy planted his right hand on the side of the vehicle, and vaulted himself to the ground below.

Justin sighed, and muttered, "Creator, help me…" before deactivating the operating console, and jumping out as well. "Hold on! *Wait up*! I'm coming!"

Timothy stopped, allowing the Kiros Knight to catch up and swipe back his PCU. "I figured you wouldn't like the idea of being left behind. Let's get into a relatively clear area, and then I'll give you the proper image."

The pair scanned the crowded sidewalk, their smaller statures not very conducive to seeing the entire area. Justin jumped in place twice in hopes of getting a better perspective, until Timothy grabbed the Kiros by the shoulder. "Will you *stop that*?" the Solarian asked, as if embarrassed, "You look like you'd been hitting the stims."

Tim turned his head away from the roadway, and then without releasing his grip on Justin, began to walk down the sidewalk. The crowd parted for them, likely stunned at the sight of a Kiros and Solarian Knight walking peaceably in a close proximity.

Timothy noted this with satisfaction, and then declared rather loudly, "Could we get some room here please?" The crowd slowly backed away as if in a daze, and Timothy nodded in approval.

"You want to teleport *here*?" Justin asked in shock. "In front of all these people?"

Timothy replied with a hint of amusement, "Why not? Are you afraid they'll copy us?"

"Well… no…"

"Then clear your mind, so that I can give you the necessary image," Timothy ordered. Justin closed his eyes, and instantly his inner sight was filled with a vision of a lonely office-building roof, its gray concrete railing, and loose gravel along the surface.

"Now," Timothy's voice commanded, and Justin reached out with his spiritual power, folding the fabric of space and time to his own will. To Justin, there was no sensation or feeling to the sudden travel, but to his impromptu audience, there was a strange waving effect to the air around the two Knights, then a flash of bright white light that engulfed the pair, leaving nothing in their place.

As suddenly as they had disappeared, Justin felt the sidewalk beneath him flash away, only to be replaced with air for a fraction of a second. He couldn't even open his eyes before he dropped onto the gravel below. Shocked by initial plunge, his balance didn't kick in quickly enough, and the Kiros fell firmly on his backside in the gravel.

Justin whirled his head around, and discovered his Solarian counterpart standing to Justin's right a little more than a Tack away. "You're funny, you know that?" Justin accused angrily, standing up and brushing off the smaller pieces of gravel that had wedged into his armoring.

"I forgot you were shorter than me," Timothy replied in a mildly apologetic tone, his eyes scanning the horizon blankly. "Where is the transmitter now?"

Remembering that there was a reason they had teleported here, Justin took out his display again. Moving out to the railing, he declared, "It's forty Tacks away now, almost due east… it's coming back this way…"

Timothy sighed dejectedly. "Now why would Rumil be coming *back* to the place she just *left*?" With another deep exhale, Timothy added, "Oh well… might as well check it out at least."

Justin looked around the roof, and then asked, "This may be a stupid question… but where is the stairway or lift down?"

"There isn't one."

"Then how are we supposed to get down *there*, from *here*?" Justin asked, pointing to the sidewalk and roadway below.

Timothy looked at Kiros Knight like Justin had suddenly grown a second head. "You can't levitate?"

"Well... yes... but... it's bad form to use such psionic power in non-emergency, public situations."

Timothy shrugged, and replied, "Very well... I guess you'll have to call a rescue team or something." The Solarian stepped out to the edge, and prepared to jump off the railing.

"Hold on!" Justin shouted in resignation, jumping up onto the railing next to Timothy, and commenting, "I'm just wondering if the Solarians have rules of psionic etiquette."

Timothy nodded. "Oh, we do... I just find most of them rather pointless."

Justin rolled his eyes, and muttered, "Of course..." before jumping off the railing, and floating slowly to the sidewalk below.

Surprised at the sight of two Erani dropping slowly on them from above, the pedestrians on the sidewalk quickly parted for the pair to land. Nodding appreciatively to the crowd, Timothy then asked, "Is it still coming this way?"

Justin quickly looked down at his display, and replied, "Yes... fifteen Tacks away. I think it's stuck at the intersection up ahead..."

"Which vehicle do you think it is?" Timothy replied, although at this point, Timothy had decided that their quarry had eluded them yet again. The strange psionic aura that accompanied Rumil was not around.

Justin seemed to reach the same conclusion. "It's in that transport service hover. She's found the transmitter... we'd know by now if she were nearby. Is there any point in wasting our time?"

"Not unless you want to recover the transmitter."

Justin shook his head. "It wouldn't be worth the time or effort. So, now what do we do?"

Timothy thought about this for a moment, and asked, "Does that tracking program record the transmitter's entire path?"

Justin paused. "Yeah... why do you ask?"

"Because I'm curious just at what point the hover in question turns back," Timothy explained.

"Do you think that's where she was dropped off?"

Timothy shrugged. "Maybe… maybe not. I'd guess the latter, since Rumil's proven she's anything but careless, but it's as good of a place as any to start."

The pair waited as the display plotted out the entire course the transmitter had taken up to that point. As it was doing so, Justin observed, "You know… I was thinking… about that psionic tingle we feel in Rumil's presence?"

"So you felt it too. Doesn't it strike you as a little odd?" Timothy queried.

"Perhaps she has some Erani blood in her somewhere in her family line," Justin responded with a shrug.

Timothy scoffed at the suggestion. "Enough pure blood to have that sort of aura? I don't think so."

Justin waived off the path the discussion was taking. "That's really not what I was trying to get at. I was just thinking that… if we can sense it in *her*… then maybe she can sense it in *us*."

Timothy slapped the forehead of his helmet. "It's very possible, the only time I had managed to sneak up on her was when I was trying to hide myself outside that old tavern on Talos. I had been shielding my aura in hopes that you wouldn't locate me… every other time, she had seemed to know I was coming."

"Perhaps we should move shielded from now on?"

Timothy nodded. "It might be prudent."

During this time, Rumil had finally managed to find her way back into her hotel room. That had been another escape far too close for her comfort. "That's it…" she muttered to herself. "Big-credit job or not… I'm calling it quits on this one."

Lurching in exhaustion to the work desk in her rather exquisite hotel room, she fell into the padded form-fitting chair, the soft gel-like cushions molding around her back. Sighing comfortably, she allowed herself merely a demitick of rest before she turned her attention to the room's console in front of her.

The system activated, and Rumil turned to the communication

codes that were quickly becoming her lifeline. Her fingers drummed nervously on the desk, hoping that her contact would answer her summons.

He did, but the exchange was predictably unpleasant.

>>What do you want this time?

>>**Those Knights are still following me, and now they're working together. The hassle is increasingly not becoming worth the payoff.**

>>The deal is the deal. If you don't like it, then too bad.

>>**At least get me away from them… really get me away from them this time. I can't do my work if I have to keep looking over my shoulder.**

>>Forget it. I put myself in an exposed position once already. You're on your own.

>>**You need me.**

>>Not that much.

Rumil's contact left, leaving her with a blinking cursor and no one to direct it toward. Slamming her open hand against the desk sharply in frustration, she clenched her teeth in an attempt to bite off her angered scream.

"Just great," she hissed to no one in particular. "I've got to get moving then while I've still lost them. Can't count on those two being off my trail for long."

A knock on the door to her room drew her attention. She had no reason to be expecting any visitors.

"Room service," a cheerful male voice announced.

Rumil's eyebrows furrowed, and she strode to the door quickly. Whipping open the door, she began to state with as much venom as she could muster, "You have the wrong room. I didn't order any…"

Her voice drifted from anger to a breathless babble within two demiticks. Justin Feroz and Timothy Honore, fully clad in battle armor, stood outside the door.

Justin stepped forward, and said with a frightening calm, "I think it's time we had a little meeting, don't you think?"

Chapter Eight

Rumil was somewhat grumpy at the moment, to say the least. Her hands were bound behind her back by crystalline restraints that she felt were completely unnecessary, and the grating against her scarred wrists caused significant pain if she so much as breathed too heavily. Added to the impending interrogation, her mood was sour at best. "So, the two zealots put their two brain cells together, huh?" Rumil sneered. "You know… only one of you can bring me in. You can't cut me in half, after all."

With a silence and quickness that could only be described as disturbing, Justin's hypersteel sword was removed from its sheath at his hip, and took one downward swipe. The blonde hacker cringed in spite of herself as the blade stopped suddenly mere Tackets above her head. "Don't tempt us," Justin threatened.

"That's enough, Feroz," Timothy softly intervened, nudging the Kiros away from the bed Rumil had been pushed down onto. "Don't forget, we have a few questions to ask her first." As an aside to Rumil, Timothy whispered, "For your sake, I would suggest being a little more cooperative than you were when I tried to question you the first time."

Rumil sighed, and replied, "I might as well… my contact dumped me. I have no reason to remain loyal."

Timothy knelt down in front of Rumil while Justin leaned back against the wall to her left, his arms crossed and left foot planted against the wall behind him. Despite his inherent menace in his full armor and weaponry, Timothy's voice was somewhat disarming. "Why don't you tell us who employed you to start with?"

The blonde hacker sighed. "You do realize that in telling you, I will have signed my death certificate."

Timothy replied coolly, "Well, if I may be totally honest, the Solarians aren't terribly happy with you, and knowing our justice methods, you'll probably be facing death anyway without your cooperation. I have no doubt the Kiros have an equal sentiment."

Rumil didn't miss Justin's subtle nod, and there was also no question as to the accuracy of Timothy's claim. She had been hacking into some very high-security, high-sensitivity servers, and knowing what the Solarians did to mere pirate leaders… her punishment could be quite messy.

Timothy slowly became impatient, and his voice began to reflect such. "I will not be nice much longer. Who employed you?" the Solarian hissed.

Rumil turned her head, and finally spat out, "Gregor Krennan."

Justin obviously didn't recognize the name. "Who?"

Timothy stood up, never taking his eyes off Rumil as he answered the Kiros Knight's question. "Krennan is an Arcadian media mogul. He owns about 50% of the legal GalNet transmission protocols, as well as owning several print publications, mostly of the somewhat dubious kind…"

Justin then commented, "That's right! He's the owner of the Galactic Eye! That's a pretty funny tabloid."

Timothy was about to comment on Justin's choice of reading material, but reminded himself that there was an interrogation that needed to be handled first and foremost. "What did Krennan order you to find?"

Rumil inhaled. "He wants information on the Baramak Slaughter."

Just mentioning that event sent a cold shiver down Justin's spine. At the time, Justin hadn't been old enough to understand, but as he aged and learned during his rearing for Knighthood, he had come to realize just how close the Kiros and Solarians had come to a full-blown galactic war. He wagered only a small handful of people knew exactly what had prompted a fusion bomb barrage on the Arcadian colony, turning half the planet into blackened rubble and killing almost four billion sentient beings.

"Why would he want that sort of information?" Justin asked curiously. "The Arcadians and the Galactic Alliance have all considered it a dead issue. Next question: why should we trust an admitted hacker's accusation against a very powerful businessman?"

"Maybe the fact that it's declared a dead issue is *why* he wants the information," Timothy replied to Justin's first question, and then asked after a demitick's pause, "You don't get many field assignments, do you?"

Justin bristled at the question, sensing the almost derogatory way that Timothy presented it. "Well… no, I don't get that many. I'm sure you know that my father is the head of the Kiros Knighthood, and thus only sends me out on missions such as these."

Timothy nodded, and stated with a voice hinting in pity, "I figured, since if you *were* out in the field frequently, you would know that Gregor Krennan is more than just a legit businessman. While he owns almost half of the legal GalNet transmissions, it's wagered he also owns most of the *illegal* GalNet transmissions. I know for a fact that the Solarians and the Kiros have been trying to pin him down for several violations of galactic law and treaties, like managing pirating operations, corporate fraud, and yes, even masterminding computer hacking."

Pausing only to take a breath, Timothy added, "Even the Galactic Alliance itself has run a few investigations into his practices, even if they were a bit half-hearted. Rumil is actually the third hacker Solarian Intelligence Command has caught over the last five ten-cycles. However, she's the first to actually label Krennan as her employer."

Justin nodded. "Well then… I suppose we need to… settle… who gets to bring in this young lady."

Timothy shook his head. "Maybe not just yet. With Rumil's little admission, we might have just gotten a hint of a bigger prey to hunt down. If you will excuse me…" Timothy left the room.

A tenth-cycle later, Timothy returned, closing his communications unit, and placing it back into one of the multitude of small packs on his belt. "Well, I have been cleared to continue with this. I suspect that they would allow you to proceed further as well, Feroz."

Justin regarded the offer. He was becoming increasingly less willing to fight it out with his Solarian counterpart unless it was absolutely necessary to do so. Secondly, if what Timothy spoke of was true, then Krennan would be a nice mark to try and apprehend. Maybe it would be just what he needed to convince his father that he could handle the duties the rest of the Knights were often given.

"So… what is our plan?" Rumil asked.

"*Our* plan?" Timothy asked.

Rumil nodded. "Of course! I pretty much just betrayed my employer. In Krennan's world, you get out one of two ways, either he dies, or you die. Since he's still around, I think you can guess the most likely method of terminating one's contract."

"So now you're on my side?" Timothy commented, apparently amused.

"As much as I can't believe I'm saying this, you two are probably my best chance of dying by natural causes," Rumil admitted. "Besides, if I help bring in Krennan… maybe my transgressions will be somewhat forgiven."

"I figured that you weren't going to help out of your own good conscience," Timothy replied, not surprised in the least.

Justin cut in, "You know… I have an idea that might work. If Krennan really wants information from the Baramak Slaughter… why don't we lure him out with what he wants?"

Timothy nixed the idea with a shake of his head. "I know where you're going with this, and it will *never* happen. Trust me, I know."

"How do you *know* that?" Justin demanded crossly.

"The Solarians refuse to release *any* information pertaining to *any* military movements and actions for the entire Staryear 3406. A team of Knights once tried the very plan you suggested about a staryear ago, and my superiors even refused to allow the team to *fabricate* a story pertaining to the Baramak Slaughter."

Justin scoffed. Timothy's know-it-all attitude was starting to get annoying. "Well, unlike you Solarians, my kind doesn't make a habit of hiding the truth and telling lies. Just wait, I'll get what we need."

Justin nearly slammed the door to the room shut as he left to get the necessary permissions for his plans. Timothy shook his head in disbelief, and said softly, "That is one green Knight."

"You sound convinced that he'll be rebuffed," Rumil stated.

Timothy regarded the hacker for about ten demiticks, then finally explained, "I had an adopted brother who died during the Baramak Slaughter. It took them ten staryears to even admit he had been killed during the attack. To this day, they refuse to explain how it happened, and I'm supposedly one of Solaria's most prominent Knights."

Then the Solarian's voice gained a hint of playfulness. "How about you? I can imagine that the 'Beauty of Baramak' would be interested to know the dirty truth behind her namesake's greatest secret."

Rumil blanched and managed to sputter, "How do you know about that?"

"I happen to know for a fact that you have met a Solarian Knight before," Timothy replied cryptically.

Rumil snorted, the deep exhale causing her wrists to ache again. "Maybe I have, but he was a hell of a lot nicer than you."

Timothy came about as close to an all-out laugh as he had in staryears. "You sound so certain of that." With that said, Timothy reached behind his ears to where the clasps of his helmet were located. The seals popped, and the entire helmet almost seemed to split, hinging on the crown of Timothy's head.

Rumil recognized the ragged black hair, light complexion, and penetrating sapphire eyes instantly. Her mouth betrayed her as Timothy regarded her with a cocky smirk, and he commented, "When I told you to find another line of work… this wasn't what I had in mind."

Rumil shook out of her surprised stupor in order to shoot back, "Well, it's your fault, you know."

Timothy's eyebrows raised. "*My* fault?"

"I was twenty-two ten-cycles from graduating from Iomet Tech Academy when you decided to play hero," Rumil explained, trying really hard to be angry. "Once I was fired, I couldn't make my tuition payments. The only place that I was able to get enough credits to live on was from Krennan."

Timothy looked around the lavish hotel room, and commented wryly, "Yes, I can tell you're barely managing to squeak by."

Rumil exhaled disparagingly, once again wincing in pain. "Well, I'm rather well-to-do now, ever since I established myself as one of Krennan's best."

"If you're one of the finest hackers Krennan employs, I find it hard to believe he'd cast you aside so easily."

Rumil shrugged passively. "He can always find someone else… this is a big galaxy, you know. He never places too much value in those working under him, either legally *or* illegally. Besides, Justin made a good point, albeit unintentionally. What society is going to believe me over one of the most influential people in the galaxy?"

"I would, but probably only because I have a better idea than most as to the sort of person your employer is." Timothy's eyes narrowed suddenly, and then he commented almost off-handedly, "Is something wrong with your wrists?"

Rumil again went rigid, but her mind quickly tossed out an explanation. "Oh… I just think in his zeal, our little Kiros friend latched these restraints on just a smidgen too tight."

Timothy nodded his head in the direction of her hands, and said, "I'll fix that then, give me your hands."

"No… it's quite all right."

Timothy smirked in amusement. "Now I *know* you're hiding something. You are the first fugitive I've ever met that has refused to be released from their restraints. Turn around."

Rumil shook her head, and replied nervously, "It's nothing really…"

The Solarian grew very stern and commanded, "I said, *turn around*, and let me fix your restraints."

Rumil sighed in defeat. The last thing she needed was to irritate Timothy more than she already had. After all, this man was hopefully her ticket out of a death sentence. She slowly turned on the bed to allow the Solarian Knight access to the alloyed bonds. When she felt the grating semi-metallic material fall away from her wrists, she sighed in spite of herself.

Timothy grabbed each of her forearms, and pulled them in front of her, turning her palms up in the process. The round scar on each of her wrists almost seemed to glow an angry red, with a small depression at the center of each welt. "I don't remember *those* the first time we met," Timothy stated bluntly. "Those must be painful."

"It's called makeup," Rumil retorted testily, "and I'm used to the pain now for the most part. I've had those little marks for as long as I can remember."

"How did you get them?"

Despite her initial determination not to irritate Timothy, Rumil snapped, "While I may be agreeing to help you, I don't ever recall agreeing to disclose my life story."

Timothy nodded. "I apologize. It was not right for me to pry." He attached Rumil's restraints again, this time in front of her, and higher on her forearms. He didn't appear to be insulted.

Rumil licked her lower lip, and broke the silence again. "Can... I ask you... an unrelated question?"

"Why did I help you three staryears ago in the Sultry Siren?" Timothy asked preemptively with a knowing smirk.

"You know, I thought it was taboo to read another's thoughts without provocation," Rumil said with an indignant snort.

Timothy's smirk broadened, and he replied, "Taboos hold no real use for me, but I didn't have to read your mind in that case. It was pretty obvious what you wanted to ask."

Rumil didn't reply, so the Solarian went with his assumption. "I actually asked that question of myself several times since the incident. I alerted my quarry long before I wanted to, and nearly got myself killed because of it, and all for some dancer that I figured I would never meet again." Timothy then drew his face about a half Tack from Rumil's, his eyes gazing into hers as if trying to find something in their depths. "And to this day, I still am not terribly sure. But if I had to hazard a guess, it's because of the sensations I get from you, the same that you no doubt feel when in proximity to me."

Timothy tapped the back of his neck with his finger. "You feel a tingle, a vibration of sorts in the back of your head when I get close. It's a psionic fingerprint if you will, each aura is different depending on the person, and each has a slightly different tingle. It probably all feels the same to you… but that tingle is how I knew you were here. Yours is very different."

"Are you suggesting I'm psionic?" Rumil gaped in disbelief. She gathered herself enough to chuckle. "I'm sorry to ruin it for you, but I'm an Arcadian, I can't be a psionic. That is strictly a talent that only your kind possess."

"I'm fully aware that you are Arcadian, and nonetheless, you definitely have some sort of psionic potential," Timothy reasserted. "Have you ever moved things with your mind or fashioned things that aren't really there?"

"If I could do that, I would have done it for all those stupid dances I had to do," Rumil scoffed. "I've never levitated anything or anyone, I've never evoked fireballs or lightning or the like, nor have I fashioned any illusions ever in my life."

Timothy seemed to think about this, putting his right hand on his chin, leaning against the desk that she had been working at ticks before, and he muttered solemnly, "Regardless, there is something about you that I cannot explain…"

Any further talk was interrupted as Justin stomped back into the hotel room, slamming the door behind him. Timothy's stoic features turned upward in a grin again and he said, "I told you they wouldn't give you what you wanted."

Seeing that Timothy had removed his helmet, Justin followed common courtesy and did the same, revealing his frowning features and muttering through clenched teeth, "Okay… you were right? Is that what you wanted to hear?" The Kiros Knight rubbed his temple then said with considerably less tension. "However, I was also cleared to continue the investigation, provided I can keep our informant in custody."

"Did you tell your superiors about our arrangement?" Timothy queried.

Justin looked shocked at the suggestion. "By Bannor, no! That would not have gone over well at all" Once again calming himself, Justin queried, "So… what's our next move? How are we going to draw Krennan out without the information he no doubt wants?"

Timothy took a deep breath before saying, "If our sects will not give us what we want... then perhaps we will have to *take* it." Gauging his companion's reaction, he went further. "Perhaps we should allow Rumil to continue her mission as if she was never caught... with the two of us hanging back to see what happens."

Justin was first with an objection. "If Krennan is as bad as you claim he is, don't you think he'd be watching Rumil in case of any subterfuge?"

Timothy smirked knowingly. "The information that Krennan no doubt wants is not going to be on record on any unsecured worlds. Rumil would have to go right into Kiros and Solarian secured space... Krennan won't dare send his eyes there."

Rumil shrugged. "Hey... you two are the ones in charge. I'll do whatever you tell me to do, if you make it worth my while."

Justin resigned himself at last. "I'd argue that this could get us discharged and shunned, but I get the feeling that the consequences won't sway our Solarian friend in the least. Besides, it's not like I have any better ideas..."

Timothy interrupted, "Then it's settled." He turned to Rumil, and removed her restraints once again before ordering, "Start packing immediately, and once you are done, leave for Iomet Central Starport. I'll have your future instructions waiting for you at the receptionist's desk."

As the two Knights turned to leave, Timothy added, "We'll be watching you, Miss Bonamede, so I would suggest against doing anything terribly rash."

Chapter Nine

"We should be arriving on Jun any time now," Justin stated matter-of-factly to the pair to his left. "You promise to keep a low profile?"

Timothy nodded. "I may be brave, but I'm not *that* brave. Are you sure you'll be able to keep an eye on our little friend all on your lonesome?"

"Of course," Justin retorted, then in an aside, he whispered, "Besides, I don't think she particularly wants to run. You probably should have remained on Altair, and just waited for us."

"Not likely," Timothy snapped back.

"Wait a minute," Rumil interceded, pointing her finger at Timothy from her seat between the Knights. "You're not joining us?"

"Walking around in broad daylight on a Kiros core colony?" Timothy chuckled. "I'll be busy just trying not to draw too much attention. Once we reach our reserved room, I'm probably not going to leave."

"Oh…" Rumil replied, almost surprised at the disappointment in her tone.

"Why so glum?" Justin said, his voice bordering on teasing. "I figured you'd almost be salivating at the opportunity of only having one of us watching you."

Rumil shook her head in disbelief. "Where would I run to? Even if I weren't almost in the heart of Kiros influence, I'd have no safe hideaways anymore."

Justin acknowledged her explanation, but with the air of a person who was convinced he was not told the whole truth. Seven ticks later they were jolted by Jun's atmosphere as the shuttle made its descent.

Technology had advanced to the point where two opposite ends of the galaxy could be traversed in about half a cycle. It could create a network of information that allowed even the most insignificant person to gather knowledge from anywhere in the galaxy. And yet, it still did not have an answer for the jarring force that accompanied atmospheric entry.

Once the tremors ceased, Rumil commented, "I hate that with a passion."

"As do I," Justin agreed, "but they are right… the newer shuttles do handle it considerably better. I was on an old Restir 400 class when I left Kiros for Talos. I was afraid that my body was going to shake apart."

Rumil seemed to ignore him. "You okay over there, Timmy?"

"I'm fine," Timothy replied blandly, as he released himself from his harness, "and I'd appreciate it if you didn't call me 'Timmy.' You sound like my mother when you do that."

Justin couldn't help but feel like a third wheel on an investigation that he was supposed to be jointly commanding. Rumil had not talked to him much at all during the entire flight, reserving the vast majority of her conversation for the Solarian on her other side, and Timothy simply didn't appear to have had much to say to either of them.

They slowly began to disembark from their assigned seats on the shuttle, and followed the procession out through the passenger doors, down the metal ramp to ground level, and taking a straight line to the starport entry, where several Kiros security officers were checking all incoming passengers.

"Planetary Security is going to be an adventure," Rumil muttered to herself.

"Leave that to me," Justin declared proudly, "I have special clearance. Just follow me, keep your heads down, and I'll take care of the rest."

It was that part that bothered Timothy somewhat. Justin seemed to be shielding himself from any mental probing that would shed light on the Kiros's plans. For all Timothy knew, Justin was planning on exposing him the minute they reached the checkpoint.

Only two things kept Timothy on stride with his fellow travelers. First, Justin had trusted him on Iomet. To Justin, teleporting on an unknown planet guided only by the image given by a member of his ages-old enemy was a great risk. Extending that trust seemed only fair.

Second, he was not going to allow Rumil out of his sight before it was absolutely necessary. He hadn't been totally honest to the hacker on Iomet when he explained why he had helped her three staryears ago. True, her psionic aura was an enigma that he would like to have answered, but something more had caused him to act on her behalf; a protective urge he had not often felt before. Discovering the source of that impulse was a close second priority during this investigation, almost beating out the desire to finally pin down Gregor Krennan.

"Those two are with me… they're about to be briefed on a

mission they are assisting me on," Justin explained, jerking a thumb towards the pair behind him, drawing Timothy's attention. Justin had stowed his helmet with his luggage, but was wearing the rest of his armor, complete with rank indicators on the right shoulder. Like Timothy, he preferred to leave them off his uniform, but while on Jun, he hoped that keeping his rank and name clearly visible would be the simplest means of removing any obstacles.

Despite that and his previous assertions, the Kiros security detail didn't seem terribly convinced. "There's something… odd about him," the commanding officer stated, as if questioning his judgment himself. "I'd swear he looks like a Solarian…"

Justin laughed at this, and even Timothy was somewhat impressed by how genuine it sounded. "A Solarian? With me? On Jun?" Justin glanced back at Timothy, his eyes reflecting his nervousness, before he finally turned to the detail once again. His voice softened slightly, carrying a hypnotic lilt, and the Kiros Knight droned, "Your worries are over nothing… besides, if you can't trust the Feroz family, who can you trust?"

For a moment, the eyes of his questioners seemed to glaze over as the psionic suggestion fell over them. Shaking themselves out of their daze, the officer in charge of the detail finally stated, blinking furiously, "You are free to go. I hope you have a pleasant stay on Jun."

The three quickly proceeded through the detail, and once they were clear, Timothy smirked and commented, "I never knew that psionic suggestion was acceptable among the Kiros."

Justin groaned. "If those security personnel ever find out what I did… I'm lucky none of them sensed it, or that someone sensitive enough didn't pass by." The Kiros Knight rubbed his temple as the doors leading out of the starport slid away. "If my father ever discovered that I had deceived my fellow Kiros for the sake of a Solarian…"

Rumil had sat silent ever since they had left the shuttle, but she finally allowed herself to speak. "Is it really that dicey between you people?"

Timothy sighed, visibly disgusted. "The grudges run deep and long between my people and the Kiros. Most Solarians actually bear very little ill will to the Kiros, but there is a fanatical following that continually stirs negative sentiment, and the people simply toe the line. I'd wager most of my kind don't even fully understand the reasons this feud started, they merely carry the hatred borne of generations ignorantly."

"You seem to bear your share of dislike for me," Justin scoffed.

"My *dislike* for you is completely on a *personal* level." Timothy glared, his eyes boring dangerously at the Kiros man.

Rumil stepped between the pair before the discussion could escalate. "You know, normally I wouldn't mind seeing my two holders kill each other, but when my neck is equally on the line, I'd appreciate it if you could at least try to get along."

Justin and Timothy turned to her, and Justin grumbled, "She's right, you know. I made this truce with you until this investigation is completed. I intend to honor it."

Timothy shrugged passively, like he had not thought the previous exchange to be that serious. "If you can manage it, then so can I."

Rumil turned her head slowly from side to side, and noticed the increasing number of pedestrians that were focusing on the trio. "If you two wanted to keep a low profile, then you both are failing miserably."

They were able to reach their destination without further incident. "The proprietor no doubt thought it was somewhat odd to see someone of your standing taking such a lowly room," Rumil commented to Justin as he swiped the key card through the magnetic lock of the motel room they had rented.

The two-room suite was smaller than the hotel room Rumil had rented on Altair, and she had been the only person in it. Needless to say, it was also in considerably worse condition. The walls, which she assumed were originally white, were now a dirty gray and flecked in places to reveal the unfinished fiberboard underneath. There wasn't even a separate kitchen or dining area; they were adjoined with the two bedrooms of two beds each, all four of which looked antiquated and in some semblance of disrepair.

"Actually, not really," Justin replied. "Kiros Knights frequently acquire the cheapest rooms they can find. Makes it easy to explain on the expense report. Don't know how the Solarians do it though."

Timothy once again replied idly, "I wouldn't know. I've never filled out an expense report. I just pay out of my pocket if I need something. Saves me unnecessary hassle."

"I've never found the accounting section of my Knighthood to be particularly boorish," Justin pondered thoughtfully. "Are yours really such misers?"

"To me they are," Timothy grunted as he finally set down his luggage cases. "While you two are out wandering, I'll probably wire the storage payment for my armor on Altair. The last thing I need is to have it impounded, and have to explain why I left planet without it."

"Fair enough," Justin said with a nod. "Well, I see no reason to wait around. If you are ready, dear lady, we can proceed into the capital proper, and begin our job."

"Fine with me," Rumil agreed. "I can barely breathe in here, much less stay for any extended period of time. If we can get this over with quickly, I won't be forced to spend a night." With a sudden concern for Timothy's approval, the hacker asked, "Is that all right with you?"

Timothy sighed before replying blandly, "Whatever you feel is best." The Solarian had been so indifferent lately that Justin was beginning to wonder if the few short flashes of emotion that slipped out of Timothy had been genuine.

"Okay," Rumil replied, as if trying to assure Timothy. "We shouldn't be gone any more than a few tenth-cycles, depending on how hard the system here is to crack." With that, she allowed Justin to escort her outside the motel, and towards the hover vehicle they had rented to take them back into Jun's capital.

Finally out of Timothy's earshot, Justin asked, "All right... what is that all about?"

Rumil turned her head to him and asked, "What is *what* all about?"

Justin shook his head. "Don't play dumb, it doesn't suit you. You know exactly what I am talking about; you and Timothy. You looked ready to kill him, and me for that matter, on Altair, then I leave the room and come back, and boom! You're swooning all over him."

Rumil blinked twice, as if not believing what she had just heard, "I am not *swooning* over anyone, much less some sanctimonious and arrogant Solarian."

"'You okay over there, Timmy?'" Justin said in a mocking falsetto. "'We shouldn't be gone any more than a few tenth-cycles.' 'Is that all right with you?' 'Wait a minute. You aren't joining us?' You looked like you had been kicked in the gut when you learned he wouldn't be following you around on Jun."

"Maybe I don't exactly trust you fully," Rumil snapped venomously.

"Yet you trust him?"

The hacker inhaled deeply before stating indignantly, "If you must know... I have met Timothy before, on Altair, as a matter of fact. He helped me out of a very… unfavorable situation. So, I suppose, yes, I do trust him. At least more than you."

Justin nodded. That definitely explained some of it… but the Kiros Knight didn't feel it really answered the question fully. "I see. What was this 'unfavorable situation' he rescued you from?"

Rumil scowled before she hissed, "That is none of your business, to be perfectly honest."

Justin mentally reared back. He supposed he could try and read her memories to find out, but cultural taboos aside, he had a feeling that Rumil would not be the only one to resent that idea. While Timothy didn't visibly express it, Justin could sense the subtle shifts in Timothy's psionic aura where the hacker was involved. It baffled him at first, but the recent discovery had cleared the picture somewhat.

"I suppose you are right," Justin finally agreed. "I won't bother you about it again." He then focused his full attention on the roadway again, maintaining a steady speed into the city.

Los, the capital city of Jun, did not resemble Iomet in any conceivable way. Where the largest city on Altair just seemed to be thrown together haphazardly, buildings constructed wherever they could fit, Los was arranged in such an orderly fashion that Rumil couldn't help but stare in awe. Every building was made with reflective panels and hypersteel, the exteriors painted in either a pearl white or metallic gray, reflecting the sunlight after being cleaned by the robotic units that slid and climbed along the outside walls and windows.

The feel of Los was different as well… there were no homeless on the street, and the stray piece of litter was an alarming rarity. The pedestrians, a majority of which were Kiros, even seemed to be dressed uniformly and professionally, walking in even strides that kept the movement on the walkways smooth. Further off the walkways were conveyor belts that moved even greater numbers of people through the city.

Before Rumil could even realize it, they were in the middle of the capital. As if sensing her question, Justin replied proudly, "In most Kiros-dominated cities, there are urban programs that allow only certain people to drive on certain days. It significantly cuts down on traffic, don't you think?"

Rumil nodded almost dumbly. Justin smiled and replied, "I take it you've never been to Kiros-controlled space."

The hacker shook her head slightly, and managed to mutter, "I never had a reason to."

"Well, we're going to have to get out here," Justin commented. "Another traffic law in most Kiros cities is that you must park as soon as possible once you are within a TackMet of your destination."

"Are you serious?" Rumil began. "How in the world is that enforced?"

"Mostly through good faith, I'll admit… but there are peacekeepers that keep an eye on this sort of thing. The fines can be pretty hefty, especially for someone of my standing. We're expected to set a good example, after all."

"Right…" Rumil began, dubious at the notion. "I wonder if you're the only one who—"

She was interrupted by one pedestrian suddenly taking notice of her; a young Kiros male with tightly slicked black hair, and the deceptively fragile features that were a trademark of the race. He wore a neatly pressed and starched navy blue business suit and matching pants, with a white sash across his chest and left shoulder bordered with a band of thick blue, bearing several broad gold pins. He carried a brown briefcase in his right hand, a finely polished wooden cane in his left, and his black dress shoes were shined so thoroughly that Rumil was almost blinded from the sun's reflection when she looked at them directly.

Rumil's eyes narrowed suspiciously as he began to approach her, his smooth stride suggesting that the cane clicking against the clean pavement beneath him served no real purpose. Once he was close enough, he welcomed her with a cheery voice. "Ah, greetings young lady. I can tell that you aren't from around here… it's always wonderful to get visitors to this city."

"Where I come from, it's not considered proper to engage complete strangers in idle conversation," Rumil stated tartly.

"Well, then I think you came from the wrong place," the Kiros man replied with a wink and a broad, almost phony smile. At that moment, the man caught sight of Justin in his body armor, and said with slight hesitation, "Oh… I was not aware you had an escort." Turning to Justin, the man asked, "Is this young woman in some sort of trouble?"

Justin leaned his elbows on the driver's side door, and rested his chin on his hands. "Nothing that should concern you greatly," the Knight replied with an amused expression on his face. "Do continue."

Bowing slightly in recognition of Justin's status, the finely dressed Kiros man turned his attention back to Rumil. "Perhaps it is best if I introduce myself. I am known as Mikael Antor, and I am a graduating student of the Los Missionary Academy."

"Missionary Academy?" Rumil asked. She figured she knew what they taught… she just hadn't been aware that there were actually schools for it.

"I'm am just about ready to go out into the rest of the galaxy to spread the light of the Kiros faith. In two weeks, I shall be deemed worthy of spreading the word and get my first assignment. Have you heard the words of truth, young lady?"

Rumil smiled with saccharine sweetness, and replied, "I've skimmed them. I especially liked the book by the fifth prophet… but I forgot his name…"

Justin's jaw initially dropped, but when he saw the horrified expression on the young student's face, had to stop himself from laughing out loud.

The missionary student's voice lowered, and he said, "For your future reference, it might not be wise to mention the false prophet while in the ears of the Kiros. His lies led to our greatest hero destroying himself along with the first Gate of Bannor."

Rumil gasped, and Justin marveled at her acting job, just phony enough for the casual observer to see it for what it was… yet just genuine enough for the self-absorbed to buy it. "Oh! I am so sorry, I meant no offense," she stammered in apology.

Mikael's mood brightened, and he said, "Think nothing of it. It can be very difficult to discern the lies of the Solarian prophet with the words of the true receivers of the Creator's vision. The deception is quite subtle, but it inevitably leads you to evil."

"I'll make note of that in the future," Rumil replied, the smile returning to her face. "I never knew it was so dangerous."

The student's face fell grim, and he stated solemnly, "Oh… it is… and the Solarians continue to try to deceive us to this day. Bryan Honore was a lieutenant of Zaal, the Treasoner, or the Defiler, you've probably heard of the fallen archangel called both. He and his family sought to corrupt the old Erani people, and it is what led us to the tragic War of Purification."

"The what?" Rumil asked. "I knew of the War of the Prophet… did the War of Purification come later?"

Mikael once again stiffened, and Justin couldn't help but allow a chuckle to escape. The student didn't appear to notice, whirling his head around towards the passing crowd nervously before explaining. "The War of the Prophet is what the Solarians call it, another of their numerous lies.

They sought to usurp the rightful King of the Erani, and eventually were forced out into what is now their desert home."

"Oh… I never knew that Solarians were so devious!" Rumil remarked, meanwhile internally grinning as she felt this meeting coming to its conclusion. "Well, then I wish you best of luck dispelling these lies and mistruths!"

Bowing with a flush on his cheeks, the student remarked, "Well… now that you mention it…" He reached into his briefcase, and removed a small red pouch in a fabric that looked like velvet. Inside, Rumil could see several gleaming silver credit chips, and several folded bills.

"Oh… why thank you so much!" Rumil squealed happily, reaching into the pouch, and pulling out a handful of coins and bills, dropping them into the satchel at her side. "Perhaps you are right, and maybe I do come from the wrong place! I've never had anyone just hand me credits before!"

The poor student wasn't sure how to respond to this. This clearly had not been his plan whatsoever. "I… I… but… ma'am… you… you're…" the young Kiros man stammered.

Justin interrupted him, pointing down the walkway and saying gently, "Why don't you just go on your way, Missionary? Might be the best choice right now…"

In a daze, Mikael agreed, "Yes… perhaps I should…" With that, he somewhat staggered past, his cane dragging with a grating sound against the walkway.

Justin shook his head, and chided his blond companion. "That was absolutely terrible."

"Hey, maybe he'll learn not to try and play his little con games now," Rumil said without remorse. "Besides, I didn't see you trying to stop me."

Sighing, Justin relented. "Well… I'll admit that some of those missionaries scare me a little. I understand dedicating yourself with zeal… but there comes a point that even I find disturbing." Then he added as they stepped onto the pedestrians' conveyor, "I wasn't aware you were so familiar with the faith."

Rumil smirked ruefully. "I've been hacking into Kiros and Solarian servers for half a staryear now. I swear I can't sneak into any of them without finding something about some mythological gate to the Erani hells."

Justin frowned. "There's nothing mythological about the Gates.

It's because of such a portal to Bannor that we have the Solarians and the Kiros at all. Are you familiar with that story?"

"Vaguely," Rumil answered. "I know that there was a war over the 'prophecy' of Bryan Honore, but not much details about it."

Justin nodded. "Would you like to hear it?"

Rumil shrugged and said passively, "Why not? It'll kill the time."

The Kiros Knight amended, "Now, bear in mind that if you asked our Solarian friend, you'll probably get a significantly different story, but I'll tell you how I know it."

"I'm sure," Rumil retorted.

Taking a deep breath, Justin began, "About nine hundred staryears or so ago, I'm sure you know that the Solarians and the Kiros actually all lived on Kiros, now known as the old Erani. The two most prominent families of Knights were the Honore and the Feroz."

"I take it Timothy and yourself are direct descendants of those lines?" Rumil asked, trying to sound somewhat interested.

"As direct as it gets over eight hundred some odd staryears," Justin acknowledged. "Anyway, the two families were actually very close, and among the families, Bryan Honore and Julius Feroz were the best of friends. Brian one day claimed to have a vision, and due to that vision, created the legendary Star Smasher, a weapon that he claimed could destroy the Gates."

Justin took another deep breath, then continued. "However, this is where the fissures began. The weapon had this very disturbing tendency to drive whoever wielded it to suicide. Thus, when Bryan claimed to have another vision, pertaining to the exact location of the first Gate, he was met with great resistance. Julius took a large risk by assembling a strike force, and departing with Bryan to what is now Solaria."

Gathering his words for his conclusion, Justin finally said, "Well… Bryan was right. There was a Gate on Solaria, but the strike force fell right into an ambush of hellish minions who were streaming out of the Gate. Julius realized he had been betrayed, and stole the Star Smasher from Bryan, using it to destroy the gate, but killing himself before he could kill Bryan."

"If Julius died… how do you know this is the true story?" Rumil asked.

"Members of the strike force that went with the two saw both Bryan and Julius fighting in front of the chamber that held the Gate. The survivors reported back that Bryan had tried to impede Julius's progress."

Rumil nodded flippantly, not really paying attention, her eyes wandering around the surrounding area. As they approached the base, another sight caught her attention. It was a large wire-mesh fence that enclosed what looked to be a shoddy campground. Ragged canvas tents occasionally dotted the dirty enclosure, and grimy and malnourished Kiros staggered around the distances or towards a dingy white trailer.

"What is that?" Rumil asked, pointing in the direction of the fence.

Justin replied quickly, "That's the homeless camp. Anyone who doesn't have a place of residence is likely there."

Rumil frowned, stepping off the conveyor, looking on at the deprived scene. "Well, that would explain why I didn't see any homeless people on the walkways."

"It's best for everyone. The less than privileged get somewhere they can go, and they don't clog up the streets," Justin commented. "I know it sounds pretty bad."

"They're like prisoners," Rumil grated, getting increasing angry at the scene before her. "And their only crime is that they can't afford rent."

"They *aren't* prisoners," Justin corrected. "They can leave whenever they want."

Rumil motioned wildly at the fencing. "And just *how* do they leave?"

"By checking in and out with the security details at the front gate."

"They have to *check in*?" she asked incredulously.

"Of course… we have to keep track of them in case they don't come back."

"Hmm… I can't imagine why they wouldn't want to come back to *this*," Rumil pondered sarcastically.

Justin was about to reply, but Rumil turned away from him, ignoring his retort. She had seen something that almost brought her to tears. About three Tacks past the fence, a young Kiros girl, maybe twelve staryears in age, her face streaked with dirt, stuck her head out the opening of a large box she had obviously procured for herself. Rumil approached the fence, getting as close as she could to the electrified wires as she dared. The girl looked back at Rumil warily, picking up her box, and slowly creeping away.

"No!" Rumil yelped then added soothingly, "No... I'm not going to hurt you... don't run..." The hacker reached into her satchel, and pulled out the handful of credit chips that she had taken from the missionary student less than ten ticks before, and tossed it through the fence with enough force to clear the electric field. "Here, I think you could use this more than me."

The girl's eyes bulged, and she quickly lunged out of her box, her head whipping about frantically to see if anybody else had noticed the treasure that had been tossed through the fence. Gathering up every last chip, the girl disappeared into the depths of the camp, out of Rumil's vision.

"What are you doing!" a gruff voice suddenly yelled. "Get away from there!"

Rumil's head jerked in the direction of the voice, and she jumped back from the fence as two Kiros peacekeepers were running towards her. The security officers stopped dead in their tracks at Justin stepped in their path.

"Don't worry, officers... I'm just taking her on a tour of the city, and she happened to notice this place. We were just leaving," Justin explained.

Obviously recognizing Justin's name and rank, and the status that went with both, the peacekeepers instantly turned docile. "Oh... yes, sir... please... take as long as you like," one of them stuttered in apology before turning around, and moving away almost as quickly as they had approached.

Justin grabbed Rumil by the shoulder, and half-dragged her back to the conveyor before demanding angrily, "What is wrong with you all of a sudden?"

Rumil didn't back down, gesturing with broad sweeping motions towards the camp. "What's wrong with me is that you don't see anything wrong with this."

*   *   *   *   *

Two tenth-cycles later, Timothy turned his head away from his PCU as Rumil and Justin entered the motel room. He instantly detected a hint of distress hanging over Rumil as she stumbled to the second room. "Did you find what you were looking for?" Timothy asked, even though he already had a pretty good idea as to the answer.

"No…" Rumil replied depressingly from around the doorway, increasing Timothy's concern.

Timothy turned on Justin and accused, "What did you do to her?"

Justin whipped up his hands as if warding off Timothy's anger. "I didn't do anything!" he denied, then sheepishly added, "She… happened to see Los's homeless camp. It apparently upset her."

Timothy frowned slightly and replied, "That's not surprising."

Rumil stuck her head around the open doorway, and queried with a hint of buried anguish in her voice, "Timothy, do the Solarians do that too?"

With a sigh, Timothy replied, "I'm afraid so. However, where I plan to take us next, you won't have to worry about seeing one."

"Why is that?"

Timothy turned back to his computing unit, as if confirming his statement. "Amat is relatively sparsely populated to begin with, and a majority of it is military installations. There is a civilian population, but it's too small to warrant creating a camp."

"Well, that's good… I guess," Rumil muttered. "I'm going to pack up what little I unpacked now."

Timothy nodded to her then remarked, "We're going to have to return to Altair, since no shuttles travel from Jun to Amat."

Justin guffawed, and stated, "Gee… what a surprise. That's good anyway, since I don't intend to do to you what you did to me. I'll just stay on Altair and spare all of us the worry of getting caught."

Timothy regarded this as if Justin had just told him the weather. "If you wish."

Then, the Kiros Knight's eyes twinkled, and he teased, "Besides, I think you two need a little alone time. Rumil said some very nice things about you…"

"*What?*" Rumil's voice hollered from the other room. "Justin Feroz, once I am finished packing, you are going to wish that *you* were behind an electric fence!"

Chapter Ten

Once the shuttle had successfully escaped the gravitational pull of Jun, and the tremors of takeoff had subsided, Justin finally felt it was time to ask Timothy to elaborate more on his plan. While the Kiros Knight wasn't going to be there, that didn't mean he wanted to be left in the dark.

"So… why are you going to Amat again?" Justin asked nonchalantly, as if he was trying to drum up innocent conversation as the shuttle entered foldspace, and the passengers were permitted to remove their harnesses.

Timothy barely glanced at Justin, and with a sigh stated, "Because I get the feeling that what Krennan wants to find won't be located on any public, low-security server. Your lack of success on Jun confirmed that for me."

"You plan on having Rumil hack into the storage drives of the Solarian Military?" Justin asked with a stunned hiss. "I can't imagine that they'll let you anywhere near that complex with a total stranger."

"You're right, they wouldn't. They probably wouldn't let me enter the complex without asking a lot of questions I don't want to answer yet, either," Timothy agreed, "which is why we'll have to sneak in. At least… I'll have to sneak in."

Timothy exhaled in disgust, then Justin heard the Solarian's voice in his head via telepathic communication.

I didn't really want to discuss my plan right now… but I suppose it is only fair that you are in the know, Timothy transmitted. *It will require me breaking into the storage drive complex on the Solarian military's main base, and fixing a remote transmitter inside the mainframe. From there, Rumil will be able to hack into the servers in question.*

Are you insane? Justin retorted. *Forget getting discharged… that could be construed as high treason! I'd shudder to think the consequences for that, especially since you Solarians are notorious for excessive punishment.*

Timothy's mental voice contained the same passive tone that his normal voice normally carried when Justin disapproved. *It's what will need to be done. I think you'd realize that given enough time… and frankly, I'm likely much more experienced in infiltration than you are.*

Does Rumil know of your plan of action? Justin asked.

Timothy admitted, *Not yet... but I think she'll agree. She strikes me as the sort of woman who can't resist a good challenge.*

Justin smirked, not realizing he was also doing so physically. *Oh, I agree that she'd do it... but not for the reason you're thinking of...*

Before Timothy could retort, Rumil's voice jolted them out of their psionic discussion. "I do not appreciate being left out of the conversation," Rumil huffed indignantly.

Justin blinked, and replied innocently, "I don't know what you mean..."

"Oh, give it up. I'm well aware that you psionics can communicate with just your minds." Then, the hacker added sheepishly, "Besides, the instant you two went silent, the buzzing in my head got worse than it already was." Somewhat pathetically, she added, "Is there some way to get it to stop?"

Timothy chuckled, in another rare display of any emotional reaction. "You get used to it after a while. Most psionics by your age are so exposed to the sensations that they barely feel it. Just give it time."

At that moment, the shuttle lurched roughly, like it had collided with something. Rumil was thrown forward out of her seat as Timothy reacted quickly to catch her, but the inertia sent him crashing into the seats in front of him instead. However, outside of a few bumps and muffled shrieks, there didn't appear to be any life-threatening indications anywhere in the passenger cabin.

Timothy was the first to piece together what had happened. "We've dropped out of foldspace..."

Leaning over the hunched pair to look out the window, Justin pointed out the panel while adding, "And I think I know why, too."

Rumil and Timothy crowded Justin out of the small window, and they saw the large, somewhat haggard-looking vessel less than thirty TackMets from their position. In blood red paint upon the patchwork hull, a symbol of a serpent and a bird of prey entwined within a circle keyed Timothy instantly.

"The Blood Hawks," he stated simply, as if not terribly surprised. "No doubt they used a hyperspace spear to knock us out of the fold tunnel. But that makes no sense... I can't imagine such an advanced shuttle model as this not having countermeasures for that."

"Should we..." Justin suggested, but Timothy would have nothing of it.

"Not with so many passengers," the Solarian declined. "We'd probably wind up doing more harm than good."

At that moment, Justin felt something poking him in the back, and it didn't feel like anything pleasant. Turning around, he confirmed the presence of four Demodians wielding pistols that were trained on the three. Glancing quickly around the passenger area, he witnessed the passengers being herded to the back of the cabin by two others. Without their business suits, the tattoos on their left shoulders were clearly visible.

The Arcadian pilot of the shuttle then emerged into the passenger area. He had taken off his uniform jacket, and then peeled off a patch of synthetic skin, revealing the Blood Hawks' mark on his left shoulder, just as the assailants wore. "I think they just answered your question, Timothy," Justin commented wryly while outside the shuttle, the large modified Blood Hawks battle cruiser approached with a slow and ominous speed.

Half a tenth-cycle later, the passengers on board the shuttle had been herded into the cargo bay of the cruiser, with several armed pirates serving as guards while the shuttle was searched for anything of value. It was during this time that Dewin Rio approached the Solarian Knight responsible for Dewin's new station.

"Timothy Honore... I really can't say it's a pleasure to meet you again," Dewin commented harshly, "but I suppose it's as good of a time as any to reacquaint ourselves. There are an awfully large number of pirates who would love to get their revenge on the one who killed their leader, including myself."

Timothy smirked and retorted, "Firstly, I wasn't the one that killed Regis Gallan. That was the work of the Solarian Adjucates. Secondly, I figured you would have thanked me. After all, you'd never be where you are now without my actions."

Dewin didn't rise to the bait. "Well, pardon me if I don't consider having to fight a two staryear-long civil war to restore order to this organization to be completely worth what I got out of it. Besides, I have a good appetite for tradition, and the Blood Hawks had been in the control of the Gallan family for over four hundred staryears. Now that line is ended due to you. Perhaps it's my Demodian values kicking in."

Timothy continued to smirk, as if he was calling Dewin on some unspoken bluff. "Some people are never satisfied," the Solarian said smoothly.

Dewin decided he had listened to Timothy for long enough. Besides, the pirate leader didn't want to do anything to anger the Solarian

Knight unless it was absolutely necessary. While the physical scars of their first encounter had healed quite nicely, the memories of that incident had not. Instead, the Blood Hawk leader turned his attention to Justin. "Justin Feroz, if I am correct. Your current companion must have drawn a few heads. I'll admit that I'd never thought I would see a Solarian and a Kiros walking side by side down the same street without drawing weapons."

"Desperate times call for desperate measures," Justin replied simply. "We have a common goal. Makes no sense to kill each other until that goal is attained."

Dewin's eyebrows raised, but before he could comment, he heard the heavy footsteps of an Ubek entering the cargo room. Groaning audibly, Dewin felt Orion move to his right side, directly in front of Timothy.

"From what I hear, you're the little twig that was talking tough in the Rose Room," Orion growled. The meeting in the bar was obviously still burning in the pale blue Ubek's mind. "I think now is as good of a time as any to pay you for the drink I spilled..."

"I doubt your boss would approve of that," Timothy stated simply.

Rumil, who was behind Timothy, put her hand on his left shoulder, and whispered, "It might not be a good idea to antagonize an Ubek. They're not known for being nice when angry."

Orion regarded the blond woman, "Well, what do we have here?" The large humanoid's grin turned almost lecherous. "I suppose you'd be a pretty little thing, if you had a little more meat on your bones and were about a Tack taller. I'd probably break you in half with one hand."

Orion reached out, as if trying to prove his point, when Timothy's arm snapped forward, grabbing Orion's arm. While the Solarian's hand only made it halfway around the gigantic Ubek's wrist, it apparently possessed enough force to stop Orion's progress, judging by the look of surprise on the giant man's face.

"You'd lose every finger that touched her," Timothy snapped, apparently starting to lose the cool that he initially possessed.

Orion ripped his arm away, and as Dewin protested, ordering him to stop, the Ubek swept with his other arm, backhanding Timothy across the left side of his face. The Solarian skidded across the floor of the cargo room, sliding five Tacks until he stopped up against the cargo bay wall. Rumil began to move to where Timothy had landed, but paused when two of the guards pulled their rifles in her direction. Justin dropped a restraining hand on her shoulder, trying to calm her.

Orion initially laughed with a bellow that echoed across the wide walls and high ceiling, but it only lasted for less than two demiticks, cut off promptly when Timothy flipped up to his feet, looking mildly cross. Striding purposefully back to his original position, he wiped a small trickle of blood from his lips in the process, and then glared up at the massive humanoid. Without turning away, Timothy asked, "Mr. Rio, is there a place that your friend and I can settle our differences?"

Before Dewin could answer, Orion had cut in with a bellow, "Why not right here in this cargo bay? It's plenty large enough, if we can get all these bodies to make some room."

"Very well," Timothy replied.

Dewin shook his head, he did not like where this was going, but he certainly didn't want to show any lack of faith in one of his most trusted lieutenants with so many of his pirates present. At least… not unless he had to.

"All right… you heard them, let's make some space," Dewin ordered. "Ramses, Tarvo, Felvanus, move our shuttle guests to the aft wall, and keep an eye on them, especially the Kiros Knight. If he even looks like he's going to try something, shoot him."

"Wait!" Justin shouted, and addressed Timothy. "Listen, my armor is around here somewhere. Most of it probably isn't your size, but I'm sure the arm and leg plates would fit."

Timothy shook his head and declined confidently, "That won't be necessary, Justin. Just make sure Rumil doesn't get into any trouble. This shouldn't take me long."

While Orion laughed at Timothy's boast, Dewin was trying to get the Ubek to see some semblance of reason. "Orion, be careful. I've already warned you that this Solarian is *not* to be trifled with," Dewin lectured. "Whatever you do, *don't get him angry.*"

Orion laughed even louder, and replied, "He'll be dead before he has a chance to get upset."

Timothy's pointed ears twitched slightly and his eyebrows rose in query. "Did I hear that right? You intend to kill me?"

"For what you did to my former leader, Regis Gallan, I will return in favor," Orion rumbled.

Timothy regarded this thoughtfully, idly rolling up the sleeves of his long shirt. "Well, if my life is on the line for this duel of sorts, then I think it's only fair that you have to put something at risk as well."

Before Dewin could cut in, Orion silenced him by placing one giant hand in front of the Blood Hawk leader's face as he agreed, "Sounds fine. What do you have in mind?"

Timothy glanced over at the shuttle on the port side wall, and to the passengers on the aft. "If I win, you let the shuttle, its occupants, and everything you took from both go free."

Once again, Orion cut off his leader before Dewin could cut in. "*Done!*"

Dewin did not like how he had completely lost control of this entire mess. If they lived through this conflict, he promised to make Orion learn never to interfere with Dewin's plans ever again. As it was, they were poised to lose a good haul, and there was no way he was going to countermand Orion at this point, as his support among the pirates was feeble already, to say the least. The last thing he needed was to develop a reputation for not allowing his people some freedom.

"Fine," Dewin hissed to Orion. "Just don't get yourself killed. I want that pleasure myself." He then walked away with as much dignity as he could muster towards the pirates who were admiring many of the trinkets and expensive items they had procured from the shuttle and its passengers. "You might as well put that all back where you found it now," Dewin suggested dejectedly.

The pirates were somewhat taken aback by their leader's order. "But... Mr. Rio... *why?*" one of them, his Demodian sensor officer, asked.

Dewin examined his ornamental timepiece that he normally kept in his breast pocket, and he bemusedly stated, "Because unless Orion's opponent decides to play around for a while, we're going to have to give it back in about five ticks."

"Do you honestly think that little Solarian is gonna win?"

Dewin sighed, somewhat frustrated. "There's a reason that only four people from Regis's personal crew returned from Canasa three staryears ago." Looking back to where the fight was about to begin, he added sadly, "I am afraid that Orion has no idea what he's gotten himself into."

Meanwhile, the one-on-one fight began with a burst of energy. Orion charged at his considerably smaller opponent, who braced himself as if getting ready to meet the hulking Ubek in a head-on collision. As the large humanoid closed to within striking distance, he brought one large, meaty fist down towards Timothy's head.

The clubbing blow was fractions of a demitick from striking, when Timothy almost seemed to flow out of its way like he was made of liquid. Spinning clockwise, Timothy planted his right foot onto the massive appendage and vaulted off it like a springboard, planting his left foot squarely in the center of Orion's broad, muscular chest.

Orion staggered backward from the blow, his shock stemming from two sources: that his opponent had evaded him, and – more importantly – the force that the slight Solarian had been able to pack into the kick. Rubbing his chest absentmindedly, Orion plotted his next move.

Timothy cocked one eyebrow smugly. Even though he knew that his attack had done little or no harm to the massive blue-skinned humanoid, it did bode well for the remainder of this contest. "I sure hope you're faster than that," Timothy taunted, "because if you're not, you might as well give up now."

Orion snarled and lunged forward again, swinging wildly as if in a berserker rage. The Solarian Knight dodged each blow, his ease of movement suggesting barely any effort. Timothy knew that Ubeks in general relied heavily on their brute strength, with little order or skill. While it was true that misapplied strength still did a good amount of damage, a disciplined warrior could easily fell an adversary even as large as an Ubek.

While the rest of the pirates cheered at the flurry of attacks, Dewin was quite solemn. He knew all to well that this fight was not nearly what it seemed, and that contrary to how it appeared, Timothy was completely in control.

Thus Timothy bided his time, waiting for the flailing fists and legs to slow. He knew that no one could maintain such a frenzied assault for a protracted period, and true to form, Orion began to tire less than two ticks later. Seeing the opening he was looking for, Timothy slipped in and dropped to his right knee, using his right hand to brace his weight. Kicking out with his left foot, he struck the Ubek squarely on the inner side of his left knee, then his right one. Orion buckled, and Timothy took the opportunity to jump to his feet, thrusting out with his right foot, connecting with a direct hit on the point of Orion's chin.

Rumil winced at the violent crack that followed. Orion toppled over himself, rolling head over heels twice before flopping roughly onto his stomach. Dewin dropped his face into his left hand, trying not to remember events long past.

The Ubek growled, but instead it came out as a sort of gurgle. Pulling himself up to his hands and knees, he used his right hand to examine his jaw, feeling the warm flow of blood and the shattered bone at the cleft of his chin. Orion's face contorted in rage, and he screamed several incoherent curses and threats before lunging at Timothy with a flying tackle.

Timothy smirked and jumped atop Orion's head, then propelled himself hard off of it, pushing Orion toward the floor before he was ready. As Timothy flipped through the air, he decided now was the time to really have some fun…

Unable to brace himself in time, Orion landed face-first onto the deck with a hollow thud. New pain flared through his broken jaw, and he lifted his head to see his opponent, hands on his hips and chuckling silently. Leaping to his feet, Orion charged with the heat of battle drowning out the warnings of his fellow pirates, who were pointing in the other direction. Orion swung, and he watched in satisfaction as the Solarian didn't move out of the way this time. The Ubek grinned, broken jaw and all, as his fist met his opponent, then frowned in confusion as it passed through entirely.

Again thrown off-balance after his attack, Orion fell forward, collapsing in a heap, his jaw arranging another painful meeting with the floor. Pounding his fist against the deck with enough force to dent the panels, Orion jumped back to his feet, sweat and blood dripping from his face.

Timothy was completely on the other side of the hold, once again chuckling inaudibly at his opponent. Orion charged again, but intended not to be fooled this time. Preparing to swing, this time the Ubek stopped short, whirling around to attack his real opponent who was coming down from above with a kick intended to take Orion unaware.

However, the fool turned out to be Orion again. The illusionary Solarian passed through Orion's fist, and the Ubek's jaw dropped. Turning back around slowly, Orion was able to witness Timothy display his flexibility, striking with his right foot across the side of Orion's face. The blue-skinned giant crumpled again, rolling three Tacks before stopping on his back, heaving for breath.

Timothy slowly approached his opponent, and commented with a victorious grin, "It's the moment of dawning comprehension that I absolutely revel in."

For once, Timothy appeared to be taken off-guard as Orion revealed he wasn't finished yet. With a viper's quickness, Orion jumped upright again, and was able to grab Timothy by both shoulders. Lifting the Solarian, Orion began to squeeze, as if hoping he could make

Timothy's head pop off.

Ten demiticks passed, then Timothy, who had previously looked to be in considerable pain, stopped grimacing, and smiled maliciously. Orion's triumphant expression melted into concern. Timothy bent his elbows so that his flat palms were pointed at Orion's chest, then bright blue fingers of electricity leaped from the Solarians hands, striking randomly into Orion's torso.

Each prong of electric power felt like an arrow of fire, ripping through the Ubek's gigantic frame. Orion bellowed in agony, his deep-throated wail almost shaking the walls. Unable to maintain his hold, Orion released his opponent, who nonetheless maintained the onslaught. Dropping to his knees, and then all fours, Orion's body began to spasm painfully from each finger of energy.

"It's over. Yield now," Timothy demanded.

Orion gurgled what sounded like refusal, still trying to regain his feet. After one tick, Dewin called out, "Knight Honore, cease and desist. I concede defeat on behalf of my officer."

With that declaration, Timothy ceased his attack, and Orion fell flat on his face, groaning weakly in anguish. Dewin shook his head as he regarded the Ubek, but silently acknowledged that Orion had given a good fight. "You have two tenth-cycles to prepare your shuttle for departure," Dewin stated to the shuttle's passengers and crew. "Gather your belongings and go." As the group did so, somewhat in a daze, Dewin turned again towards Rumil, "Miss… Bonamede, may I speak with you privately?"

Somewhat surprised to hear the Blood Hawk leader say her name, Rumil nodded, and said, "Sure… if you want." She slowly approached Dewin, and he motioned for her to leave the cargo hold.

As they did, Timothy warned, "If she is not back in two tenth-cycles, or you have harmed her in any way…"

Dewin dismissed the Solarian's threat with a wave of his hand. "I'm well aware what you are capable of, Knight. Let me assure you that I have no wish to test your limits again." Finally, Dewin turned to the prone Orion, still lying on the deck. "And could someone take Mr. Salazar to the medical ward? It looks like he could use some… attention."

Once outside the hold, Dewin asked with a wry smile, "I am curious how one of Gregor Krennan's finest computer hackers found her way into the care of two Erani Knights."

"I'm amazed you know me," Rumil answered honestly, "much

less who I work for."

Dewin laughed, and answered, "Your name popped up during a secured access bulletin from Krennan's camp. Supposedly, when you disappeared from his circle of influence, he grew concerned that you were planning to betray him."

"So… if I was found, I was to be killed?"

The Blood Hawk leader shook his head. "Actually no… I think our good media man has a soft spot in his heart for you. He just wanted you found. Besides, even if Krennan wanted you killed, I certainly would not have it done."

Rumil's face contorted in suspicion. "Why would that be? Pirates aren't known for giving mercy."

Dewin pursed his lips, and explained, "First of all, the Blood Hawks aren't one of Krennan's little pirating projects. As far as I am concerned, he is my competitor, and you don't do your competitor's favors. Secondly, the last thing I need is to irritate that little Solarian friend of yours again. Once was enough for me."

Rumil stated the obvious. "So you two *have* met before."

Dewin laughed bitterly. "You could say that. All but two of my fellow officers and Orion were killed defending Gallan when Honore cornered us on the planet Canasa. The crew was either severely injured or fled, and Regis Gallan himself was arrested… then summarily executed six cycles later. I'd rather not say any more about it."

"And I won't ask you to," Rumil said. Pointing back to the cargo hold, she added, "Unless you have anything else to tell me, I'd like to return to my companions."

"You never answered my original question," Dewin reminded with a smile. "Just why are you in the company of those two?"

Rumil grinned back, and replied, "They seem to think that if we can acquire certain information about certain events that took place in the Staryear 3406, we can lure Krennan into implicating himself."

"So you *are* betraying him. That's generally not good for your health."

Rumil put her hands on her hips, and glared. "Why? Are you planning on telling him of my delicate plans?"

Dewin raised his hands and shook his head. "As far as I am concerned, I never saw you. Besides, I wouldn't particularly mind seeing Krennan's little corporation collapse myself. Just if you get yourself in trouble over this... don't call me."

"I don't intend to," she replied simply, and without waiting for Dewin to dismiss her, returned to the cargo hold.

Chapter Eleven

The small and obviously antiquated shuttle departing Altair for Amat finally stopped shaking violently. Rumil had been almost certain the rusted seams of the shuttle were about to give way just before it finally escaped the densest portions of Altair's atmosphere.

"Now I know what Justin was talking about," Rumil complained as she rubbed her jaw. "I think I bit my tongue three times."

Timothy didn't reply to the statement except to reach into the backpack that he had just pulled from the carry-on compartment under his seat. He came out with a small red tube with a flip-top cap. "Squeeze some of this into your mouth, and swirl it around before swallowing. It should prevent your bites from getting infected and making sores."

Nodding thankfully, she did as Timothy suggested, then handed the tube back to the Solarian who promptly took his own advice. Before she could ask, Timothy confessed innocently, "I purchased this before the flight from Jun, anticipating this exact scenario in mind. I just hope the gash I made on the inside of my cheek isn't too deep for it to work."

"Bit yourself just now?"

Timothy shook his head. "No... from that freak of nature Rio called an Ubek when he cuffed me across the cargo hold. That *hurt*."

Rumil couldn't help but laugh. Timothy had come across as so unflappable and almost impervious to harm. That small admission seemed so out of his character that it was very amusing.

As her humor passed, the hacker's curiosity got the better of her. "Speaking of Blood Hawks, I... Dewin explained to me that the cruiser was not your first meeting. He seemed... reluctant to talk about it."

"And you would like me to fill in the holes of the story," Timothy finished. "I fail to see how that is any of your business."

Rumil shuffled her feet together nervously, and replied, "Well... I suppose it isn't. I just figured it would kill the time, and I'm more wondering how you got mixed up with such a powerful pirate group."

Timothy turned his head to his companion, as if weighing his options. "I suppose it wouldn't hurt anything to talk about it. Besides, it does involve you somewhat."

Rumil blinked repeatedly, somewhat confused. "How... does it involve me?"

Timothy grinned conspiratorially. "You'll see." So as not to disturb any of the other passengers, he began softly, "Not even three ten-cycles after graduating from the Centris Knight Academy, I was given my first assignment; to locate and apprehend Regis Gallan."

"I can't imagine that's a normal rookie assignment," Rumil commented.

Timothy nodded. "Not normally, but I was the one that asked for it."

Rumil almost couldn't believe that. "*Why?*"

"I knew I could handle it without the backup assistance the other Knights felt they would need," Timothy replied. "The Knighthood doesn't like allocating a large number of Knights in one place, understand. There aren't many of us, and we have a lot of responsibilities in a very large galaxy."

"Ah."

"Anyway, I won't bore you with the details of Solarian politics, but I was eventually approved to proceed with my plan. After initial planet-hopping, gathering information on the Blood Hawks, and coercing select people for the group's plans, it led me to Altair. Iomet, to be precise."

Rumil knew where this was going. "You were following Gallan, and he went into the Sultry Siren."

"I had learned that he frequented the place whenever he was on Altair, and that he preferred a dancer by the name of Sasha. My plan had been to arrest him with his pants down... so to speak." He added with a wry smirk, "Then, the next dancer distracted me."

"Because of me... Gallan escaped during all the commotion, I take it." Rumil sounded remorseful.

"He did... but it was merely a temporary setback."

Rumil smiled. "Of course. I mean, you obviously caught him anyway."

Timothy's smirk faded, and he continued, "Anyway, after he learned that a Solarian Knight was after him, he retreated to the planet he considered his stronghold, a neutral world not officially in the borders of the Galactic Alliance... a Galactic Rim planet called Canasa."

"You followed him there."

"Who's telling this story, you or me? But yes, I followed..."

Timothy's voice dropped off regretfully. "...and things got ugly."

Rumil's attention was fully directed to Timothy now. "What do you mean... 'ugly?'"

"I pursued Gallan and his crew to an abandoned factory on Canasa. They apparently didn't realize that I had not brought any support from the local enforcement or anywhere. Down the roadway the factory was on, a planetary company was leading tourists down the historical industrial section I was in. Thinking that the group was reinforcements, the pirates opened fire, killing everyone. One hundred seventy-four to be exact."

One hundred seventy-four didn't seem like a terribly big number on a galactic scale, but Rumil remembered that the Sultry Siren seated barely over two hundred, and that had always seemed like a lot of people to her.

Before she could make any comment, Timothy had continued, "From there, it all went crazy. I infiltrated the factory, and started methodically eliminating anyone in my way. Apparently, about half the crew decided not to continue, and fled, most of them not to return... the rest were either severely injured or killed." Taking another solemn breath, he said softly, "Gallan tried to escape out one of the other exits, and sent his remaining officers to stall me so he could get away. Rio was one of the four who met me in the reception area leading to the foreman's office. Only Rio of those officers survived, and he just barely."

Timothy's gaze became distant, as if he wasn't even speaking to her anymore, but telling the story to some unseen presence. "They didn't hold me off for as long as Gallan had apparently hoped. I caught up to him before he had even reached the south hallway, and I quickly overpowered him. There was this part of me, almost uncontrollable, that just wanted to kill him and be done with it. Fortunately, reason won out. Gallan was incapacitated and no longer a threat. What the Solarian Adjudicates wanted to do with him was none of my concern."

Despite his normally calm exterior, it was apparent that his first mission as a Knight still had a profound effect on him as he finished, "When the body count was finally confirmed, three hundred and eleven sentient beings were dead, one hundred and seven by my own hand. When I had heard the number, I had initially been beside myself; I hadn't thought I had killed that many. I had lost count somewhere around twenty."

The weight of the story fell on Rumil. It made perfect sense to her why Dewin didn't want to talk about this. "All that death... because you came to the aid of some pathetic dancer who didn't even think beyond her own graduation."

Timothy placed a hand on her shoulder. "I do not regret coming to your aid, if that is what you are worried about."

"Would you do it again?" Rumil asked warily, knowing the answer already.

Timothy surprised her once more. "Yes, even knowing what I do now, I would have done it again."

"But even after…"

"There was a method to the madness… those deaths were not at all in vain. Because of the incident on Canasa, the entire Blood Hawk organization was rendered inert for two whole staryears, and I can assure you that happening saved over one hundred seventy-four lives. It is likely Gallan would have lived to see more pirate raids had those tourists not died… the stories published of the event made a far stronger argument for capital punishment than any single death could. And as much as I might not like Dewin Rio, he is not Regis Gallan by any means. He won't panic and act out of fear, nor will he excuse wanton unnecessary killing."

"But, it's doubtful I would have been killed… sure, those pirates might have roughed me up a little bit… maybe even…" Rumil was trying to sound like the hardened criminal she was supposed to be, but she was failing miserably at it.

Timothy now took her shoulders in both his hands, and pulled her to face him, his eyes gleaming as if some strange light was trying to peek out from inside him. "Do not *ever* blame yourself, and do not insult the memory of those who died by wishing you had been harmed in their place. Instead, honor their memory by living your life the best that you can."

That advice offered little comfort. "I haven't even been doing that too well, have I?"

The burning intensity disappeared from Timothy's features, replaced by a mellow grin. "There is always time to start new. You'll find your way… I'm sure of that."

The rest of the trip was silent, as it was apparent neither of them really felt much in the mood for conversation. They both sat in a quiet reflection, trying to find some sense in what appeared to be a senseless event in spite of Timothy's recycled words of wisdom.

Timothy had warned her that if there was a polar opposite to Solaria, Amat would be that place. In short, the planet as a whole was wet and cold. Actually, it was *very* wet, and *very* cold. The rain falling on them at the moment was only a rather light mist, but it was still more than enough to be bothersome.

Rumil shivered through her large insulated coat, covered with a yellow hooded tarp that passed for a rainbreaker. "I don't get it… how can the temperature be below two CelMel, but the rain isn't frozen solid?"

"In this particular portion of Amat, the mountain ranges flanking this valley have a very high salt content. Due to the atmospheric winds that lie abnormally low on this planet, it blows that salt into the clouds, lowering the rain's freezing point," Timothy explained. "Now, the sooner we get into Frokslind, the sooner we'll be out of this mess."

"Couldn't we have just taken a hover?" Rumil asked, fighting off a shiver.

"No chance at all… the military would instantly see a hover coming in, and it would draw their attention. However, walking in on foot dressed up like some of the native population wouldn't. It's only two more TackMets to the town anyway."

A rather large splotch of rain slipped underneath the hood of Rumil's rainbreaker, splashing salty water onto her nose. "Is it because of the… unusual weather that the Solarians built the complex here?" she asked curiously.

"Yes, but not for the reason you're thinking of, most likely. The atmospheric salts make it very hard to get a clear sensor image from space."

Rumil huffed, and replied, "That actually *was* the reason I was thinking of, thank you very much. I am a computer systems specialist, after all. As if a rough rain would deter any military force with enough desire for this bog."

As soon as she had finished, she stepped down with her right foot, but instead of finding marshy ground, her leg continued to sink, knocking her off balance, landing with a splash into a shallow pool that had been camouflaged by a thin layer of mossy grass.

She jumped up, feeling the frigid water seeping through her rainbreaker, soaking into her coat and underlying clothing. While she stumbled out of the chilled quagmire, Timothy succeeded in fishing her luggage pack out of the pool.

"Hurry up and get changed," Timothy replied, thrusting the brown, ragged-looking pack into her arms. "Fortunately, these things are waterproof. Give me your coat, and I'll try to dry it out."

"What?" Rumil gasped, feeling the creeping cold already sinking into her skin. "You want me to change right *here*?"

"Only if you don't want to freeze to death," Timothy replied seriously. "Give me your coat now, and don't take too long."

"But—" Rumil protested.

"I won't look. I'll be too busy drying out your coat," Timothy interrupted. "Now stop stalling and get changed."

The Solarian Knight waited until Rumil slowly slid off her rainbreaker and peeled her soaked coat off the dampened clothes. Handing it to Timothy, she shivered as she took the pack, and Timothy wasted no time to turn around and give her as much privacy as was possible.

Rumil eyed the Solarian warily as she fished through the luggage pack she had been given. Fortunately it held up to its guarantee, as all of her clothing was still dry, which hopefully meant her PCU was as well.

Stripping down to her underwear, deciding not to remove them no matter how wet they were, the biting cold served as a not at all subtle reminder of why she had been so heavily bundled up to begin with. Pulling on the second set of clothing as quickly as she could without taking her eyes off of the back of the Solarian who was hunched over her coat, she declared, "All right, I'm finished." She was rather impressed that he had held true to his word, and had not taken even the slightest peek toward her.

Timothy didn't immediately reply to that statement, as if his concentration was drawn elsewhere. Finally, he slowly replied, "It will be just a little longer for your coat. I don't dare expend any more energy to drying it out. I know for a fact that there are several Knights in the main compound that would discover us."

"Well, hurry up… I'm freezing…" Rumil answered, jumping up and down repeatedly, her teeth chattering as she did so.

It took a little more than a tick for Timothy to finish. "It might still be a little damp on the outside, but we'll pick up our pace to compensate. It shouldn't take us more than half a tenth-cycle."

"What about my wet clothes? We can't put them in your pack, since it has my computing unit in there, and it would defeat the purpose to put them in mine," Rumil asked, pulling off her rainbreaker temporarily to put her coat back on.

With a frown, Timothy gathered up the wet bundle… then tossed them into the moss-covered pool. Before Rumil could protest, Timothy replied, "I'll buy you a new outfit. We just don't have time to deal with this right now. Come on."

Rumil grumbled to herself about the strange nature of her companion. One minute, he was acting like her personal protector, the next it was like she was nothing more than a common prisoner. Reluctantly following after Timothy's increased pace, she continued to mull over the issue until they finally reached the poor excuse for a city the residents of Amat called Frokslind.

Once they had safely taken a room at one of the two inns in the small town, Timothy revealed his plan to Rumil. She instantly had the same sort of objections as Justin had.

"First of all, you are assuming I'll be caught. Secondly, I have my own ulterior motives for finding out information on the Baramak Slaughter, remember?" Timothy replied lightly as he began to dress for his trek. "Besides, I get the feeling all would be forgiven if it manages to bring Krennan to justice at long last."

"But wearing your armor…"

"Actually might divert attention. A Solarian Knight would have reason to be near the installation… a native wouldn't. Besides, wearing that bulky garb would make moving with any semblance of stealth quite difficult."

Checking the PCU mounted inside his gauntlet panel, he confirmed that his armor's environmental controls were set for Amat's climate. "Once you get the remote transmission, just dump all the data from 3406 AW into the drive. We can sort it out after I return."

Not waiting for a reply, Timothy left out the front door. She looked out the window as he departed for as long as she could, then with a resigned sigh, took her seat at the work desk, preparing her computing unit for a large-scale transfer of data.

A tenth-cycle later, Timothy had arrived at the walls of the military complex that housed the high-security servers he felt contained the information Krennan wanted. Taking great care to ensure that he had not been spotted, and that his psionic aura was heavily cloaked to prevent detection, Timothy climbed the five Tacks to the ventilation shaft that would serve as his entry to the complex, then hung with one hand on the lip of the vent while scanning for any sensors or triggers that would alert the regiment inside. Finding two infrared sensors, he quickly disabled them and proceeded inside the vent, making slow progress as he continually searched for any more traps.

There wasn't much surveillance inside the shaft, obviously, but he did have to block out one heat-sensitive camera before Timothy finally found himself in front of a vent at the top of the large domed ceiling that housed the servers. Carefully focusing his psionic power to loosen the screws holding the vent in place, he pushed the grated metal forward from the opening, then slid headfirst out the hole, flipping in the air, and using another small surge of power to slow his descent and make a discreet landing.

His eyes darted around his surroundings, once again on the alert for any signs of detection or personnel. Still seeing none, he proceeded with the mission at hand. Checking his PCU again to confirm where he needed to place the remote transmitter, Timothy went to work with a small screwdriver from one of his belt packs, and began removing bolts. When the metal mainframe panel began to come loose, Timothy supported it with his free hand to make sure it didn't fall to the ground and make any undue noise. Once it was completely separated from the mainframe case, the Knight eased it to the floor, and prepared the wires he needed to splice, both on the transmitter and the mainframe.

Looking around the mainframe to check once more if anyone was approaching or entering the room, Timothy quickly finished the job, making sure he had tied the correct wires together before using the adhesive dots on the base of the transmitter, attaching it to the inside of the mainframe, then quietly replacing the panel.

Satisfied with his work, Timothy stood, then froze as another Solarian Knight with dull red hair stood on the other side of the case, his lips turned downward in a disapproving frown.

"At first I didn't believe it, but when security reported that something had slipped into the ventilation system without being clearly detected, and not radiating any psychic aura, I somehow knew that it could only have been you, Timothy," the red-haired Knight stated glumly.

"What are you doing out in this Creator-forsaken iceball, Emmitt?" Timothy asked as he removed his helmet, somewhat taken aback. He had trained with Emmitt Fransisca, and had graduated the same year, even with Timothy being four years younger. He was about as close a friend as Timothy made, despite the fact that the Fransisca family was never considered to be particularly high in standing among the

Knighthood.

"I could ask you the same question," Emmitt replied. "I am curious why you were attaching a remote network transmitter to one of the most sensitive mainframe servers in the Solarian Sphere of Influence."

"It's part of an investigation... that's all I can say."

Emmitt looked disappointed. "You can't give me any more tidbits? Perhaps I could help."

Timothy couldn't help but smile ruefully. "I'll let you know when I figure them out *myself.*"

"Does it have to do with the hacker you had been assigned to apprehend?"

Timothy's face expression didn't change, and he replied cryptically, "Yes... and no. That investigation has gotten complicated, which is what brings me here."

Emmitt sighed before returning the smile. "Why is it every investigation involving you gets complicated?"

"Because I don't say 'good enough' when there's more truth to be uncovered," Timothy replied, suddenly emotionless.

Emmitt rubbed his forehead as if figuring that would be Timothy's answer. "Let me guess... you found something during your search and seizure mission, and have convinced the Solarian Knighthood to open a broader investigation. However, the boundaries *still* aren't broad enough for you, and so you're taking matters into your own hands."

Timothy couldn't help but give a short laugh. "You know me too well."

Emmitt once again sighed, and stated, "You're fortunate I know you like I do. Otherwise, I'd have to consider you a security risk, and have you arrested. However, since you haven't managed to make a mess you can't clean up yet... I guess I can convince myself you were never here."

"Thanks, Emmitt. I'll owe you one."

Emmitt dismissed the pleasantry. "After all the flak you took on my behalf while we were still trainees, I probably still owe you a couple thousand favors."

"That was nothing. My 'father' *expected* me to be a troublemaker, so I wasn't disappointing anyone."

Emmitt had to laugh at that comment. "His opinion hasn't changed much, has it? I couldn't count the number of times he used the phrase 'loose cannon' while describing you last. I wonder where he got that idea?"

Timothy bristled. "Well, as much as I'd love to hear the story as to why you are stationed here, I don't think it's advisable for me to be sitting here unannounced for terribly much longer."

"You can go out like everyone else. I'll just inform them I had asked you to test the security system in this complex since you were in the area. I doubt anyone in the Knighthood will ask too many questions." He then grinned slyly, and added, "They'll be too busy defending their... epic failure."

Timothy nodded in appreciation, but before he could leave, Emmitt had another question to ask. "The Line of the Prophets celebration is coming up soon. Will you be there this time?"

Timothy shrugged. "I'll try. Depends on how long this investigation goes."

Emmitt clicked his tongue at his fellow Knight. "Tsk, tsk, Knight Honore. You've been suspiciously absent from the celebration for the last two staryears. Don't you realize the shame you place on your family name when you do not attend?" Despite Emmitt's teasing grin, Timothy did not find it at all amusing.

"I cannot cause my family any more shame than they inflict upon themselves without realizing it," he replied testily before excusing himself from Emmitt's presence.

*   *   *   *   *

"What took you so long?" Rumil asked once Timothy finally entered their room, about half a tenth-cycle longer than she expected he'd be.

"I had to dodge a little unwanted attention... but I managed. They won't find us," Timothy answered flatly. "Did you get everything we needed?"

Rumil huffed, and replied, "Not only did I successfully hack in and dump the data, I also managed to sort most of it out. I couldn't discern anything relating to the Baramak Slaughter."

Timothy just about cursed. "They have that information

somewhere, and not anywhere on Solaria. Believe me, I've looked."

Rumil held up her right hand to silence the Solarian Knight, before smiling smugly, and answered, "However… I think we might have something promising."

Timothy's eyes narrowed questioningly. "How so?"

"There is what adds up to be a top secret report, about two hundred pages long, with submission dates that do line up suspiciously with the dreaded Slaughter. However, the document itself is heavily encrypted and coded several times over, to the point where even the codes have their own encryption, which has their own codes. It's a mess that would require something a lot larger than this little PCU to crack."

Timothy rubbed his chin thoughfully. "That might be enough. I suppose it would depend on how badly Krennan wants this information."

Rumil smiled again, "Oh, he wants it pretty badly. After all, he sent me to find it." Then she grew serious. "Now, unless we have some other reason on the killing fields of Arcadia to be here, I would like to get off this frozen rock."

Much to her surprise, Timothy agreed. She concluded that something happened while Timothy was away that he did not like, she could see it despite his attempts to remain his normal stoic self. "Care to tell me what's bothering you?" she asked, trying to sound merely concerned.

"There's nothing bothering me," Timothy scoffed, then turned around to pack what little he had brought with him.

"You're a terrible liar… you know that?" Rumil asked, but when her companion didn't answer, she decided not to press the issue. She had learned that everyone has their own personal issues that they don't like to discuss. She had a good deal of those herself.

Chapter Twelve

"Okay… so maybe you were right," Justin amended as Timothy reported on what just might be the success of their plan. "I guess it was silly to suspect that our superiors would keep what they consider highly sensitive information in a place they couldn't be sure was completely secure."

Timothy shook his head. "Let's just wait and make sure that we have enough to lure Krennan out of hiding. He's been in the underworld for some time now, and I doubt he got there by being open and trusting."

As the two Knights continued contemplating their next move, Rumil was working at the desk on the other side of the room to ensure that there would even *be* a next move. As it stood, it was not going very well. "It might take a while to chase my contact down," Rumil commented, not really certain if Timothy and Justin were even listening. "This calls for the heavy artillery." Opening her satchel, she pulled out the headset and visor that was part of her virtual interface.

"Does that really help much?" Justin asked as the hacker slipped the headgear over her head.

"It allows me to interact with computerized systems on a more intimate level. Normally, it takes me about three demiticks to key in the average-sized command, while with a virtual interface it takes less than one," Rumil commented, as if it should have been common knowledge.

"Maybe I should get me one of those," Justin mused.

Timothy scoffed, "I'd love to see you explain having that on an expense report."

"Much less to a board of inquiry why I decided to purchase a piece of equipment illegal to the private sector," Justin added grimly. "But that doesn't mean I can't hope, right? You know, it's people like yon," he said with a gesture towards Rumil, "that make it impossible for normal people to have one."

Timothy made a sound somewhat between a chuckle and a grunt, and replied, "Is that right?"

"Well, yeah, it's because hackers figured out they could use the things to infiltrate and overwhelm codes and algorithms in fractions of the time it used to." Justin replied. "The Alliance pretty much *had* to outlaw them."

"Well, before you completely lay the blame on the hackers, make sure you give computing manufacturing and service companies their due share. They offered a good chunk of help to hackers in order to give the Alliance the excuse to make them illegal," Timothy lectured.

"What? Why?"

Timothy rolled his eyes. "Computing companies were set to lose a good chunk of money if the layman gained the ability to do their own fixes to PCUs that the virtual interface would provide. It was in their best interests to make sure the virtual interface didn't become a homestead staple."

"But—"

"Do you see hackers having a problem getting a hold of these units?" Timothy asked. "The Alliance didn't care at all about keeping the VI out of hacker hands. They wanted to make sure Sir and Madam Average couldn't clean or repair their own software systems."

"All right, quiet down. I'll need my full concentration," Rumil ordered as she inserted the interface connection into the corresponding port on her unit. "And here I go…"

Immediately, Rumil was plunged into total darkness, followed two demiticks later by the telltale yellow gridlines that marked the boundaries of her virtual surroundings. She had entertained the idea of programming solid textures to her program off and on over the staryears, but every time she was about to concede to it, function won out over form. Hackers needed to be able to operate at top speed and efficiency, thus bare-bones scenery was a necessity to ensure optimal performance.

The grid lines formed into a long hallway that extended beyond her line of sight, marked by dark gray doorways that signified entry protocols to the various rooms on this particular channel of the GalNet. She suspected that her former contact had been waiting to detect her entry to a room, and then switched to a different room before she could fully enter. Hopefully, she'd be able to catch him now.

Quickly opening the first door in the hall, she found seven wireframe visitors, suggesting they had no programmed avatars for virtual use, none of which turned to greet her in any way. Obviously, they were engrossed in a very private exchange. Not seeing her old contact anywhere in the room, she decided to leave the chatters to whatever they were doing, closing the door behind her.

The second door revealed another couple without virtual avatars, apparently an older couple judging from the text that was appearing just above their heads. However, Rumil knew better. If you were conversing on this channel, discussion was never what it appeared to be. Rumil left the room before either of the two could demand to know who she was or what she was doing listening in to their discussion.

Further doors were either similarly filled with unidentified people, or completely empty, until she came to the fifth door on the right and located her quarry. As she pulled open the door to enter, her contact whirled around and froze in place. He had been using a virtual interface of his own, explaining how he had been able to elude her up until now.

The avatar her contact was currently using was his most frequent one; a fat middle-aged Arcadian with long black hair, his unnatural red eyes drawing attention away from his double chin. She doubted his avatar accurately represented his real appearance, since he had been known to use several different ones. Fashioning a different GalNet appearance was another thing she had toyed with, but found it hard to look at herself with a different face. Besides, saving multiple avatar images required a lot of storage space that she could use for more important things.

"Gee… a girl would think you're trying to avoid me," Rumil sneered.

Her contact whirled away, not even looking her in the eye, and he replied snootily, "Our business is concluded, Bonamede. Why do you insist on getting me apprehended?"

Rumil snorted in dismissal of his statement. "Oh, get over yourself. Like anyone would be interested in the hacking equivalent of middle management? I just need you to deliver a little message to our employer."

"You want me to deliver a message from you, an abandoned hacker, all the way to the top? After you disappeared off the face of the galaxy for over a ten-cycle? No way, I have no idea where you've been."

Rumil grinned knowingly, and turning to her virtual satchel, pulled out the file that might just change the contact's mind, appearing as a thick ream of text-covered pages. "Are you sure? I found this on a Solarian server. It's dated 3406 AW, and sure seems to be pretty heavily encrypted. I wonder what happened that staryear that would require it to be coded so thoroughly…"

Sure enough, her contact whirled to face her, his interest definitely piqued. "You have confirmed the dates?"

Rumil replied smugly, "Indeed I have… from what I've been able to decode, the name 'Baramak' is used quite frequently."

The contact appeared quite apprehensive, weighing the potential risk to gather something that he obviously wanted very badly. Finally, he said nervously, "All right… just give me the file, and I'll pass it along. I'll contact you when Krennan decides what to do with it."

He reached out slowly for the file, but Rumil pulled her hand back, waving her hand at him. "I don't think so. I don't trust you anymore. You just tell your employer that his 'abandoned hacker' has happened across something that might be about the Baramak Slaughter, and then *he* can contact *me* directly if he's interested."

The contact's avatar didn't seem terribly pleased with this stipulation, but finally relented. "Very well… I'll pass along the message, but I think you're wasting your time."

The avatar disappeared, leaving Rumil alone in the room. She reached up to her head, pulling off her interface headset, returning her view to the real world.

"You know… it's kinda funny watching someone use one of those virtual interface units," Justin said with an amused grin, his left hand covering his mouth as if trying to stop from laughing. "I mean, watching you reach out for empty air like that was just absolutely hilarious."

Timothy shook his head. "Someone would almost think you're a rookie."

"I'm not a first timer," Justin answered indignantly, then sheepishly admitting, "Not really, anyway…"

Timothy then turned his head to Rumil, getting to business at hand, "So… did you find your friend?"

Rumil sighed, her voice laced with uncertainty, "I did, and he said he'd deliver my message to Krennan. Now the question is, will he actually do it."

"And will Gregor bite," Justin added.

They were answered a tenth-cycle later. Rumil received a message from an unknown source protocol that bore a very short list of directions. It directed her to a communications channel she had never seen before, and to plug in using her virtual interface.

"A channel is pretty top secret if *I've* never heard of it," Rumil commented. After a moment's thought, Rumil turned to Timothy and said, "You seem pretty good with computing units. I might need your help."

Timothy's eyes narrowed, and he asked warily, "For what?"

"Krennan didn't get to the top of the bottom by playing fair. He might… try something, and if I look like I'm in any sort of duress, I'll need you to send a jamming command into my terminal. I… might not be able to do it myself."

Timothy sat down quickly onto one of the plush beds of the room, and nodded to Rumil once his unit had fully activated. Taking a nervous breath, Rumil replaced her headset and jumped into the virtual scape of GalNet.

An avatar was already there, his height about two Tacks, lean frame and eyelids slightly red from the repeated surgeries he underwent to try and correct his vision. He had a slight dusting of facial hair around and below his chin, and a shallow face that reflected a man who had lived two lives for a very long time. His left leg was also slightly longer than his right, causing the man to have to use a small forearm-clipped crutch in order to keep his balance. All in all, the avatar was a very accurate representation of media top dog Gregor Krennan.

Of course, that meant very little.

"How do I know you're Krennan?" Rumil queried suspiciously.

The avatar opposite her laughed, and answered, "I suppose you don't. But then, I'm not going to ask for what you have right now, either. This meeting is merely to set up the *real* meeting."

"The real meeting, is it?"

"In person," the Krennan Avatar elaborated, "However, I do have a few concerns. One of them being your present company."

"My present company?"

Krennan shook his head, "Now, don't be coy. You know what I'm talking about. The two Erani Knights that have been with you, at least since your run-in with that upstart pirate Dewin Rio and his band of rag-tag pirates."

Rumil chuckled ruefully, "Of course… you have an ear, perhaps even an eye, on that entire Blood Hawk fleet. That is so like you."

"It pays to be in the know in my line of business," Krennan answered with a shrug. "And you have tried to deflect attention away from answering my query. That is so like *you*."

Rumil had to think quickly… then decided to tell the truth. "One of them is a Solarian who is helping me with my mission. He has a bit of an issue with his Knighthood, and probably wants to know the truth about the Baramak Slaughter even more than you do."

"Considering how often his name popped up on my radar, I suspect you're right." Krennan said slyly. "What about the Kiros Knight with you? What is his angle in all this?"

This was where Rumil had to fabricate the truth slightly. "The Solarian and I have merely been using him to gain access to some of the sensitive Kiros servers. Now that we have what we're looking for, we'll give him the dump. Hopefully he'll get the hint, and we won't have to..." she unconsciously gulped on the next words, "...kill him."

"Yes... I know how you do dislike death and blood," Krennan commented thoughtfully. "And by the way, I do know the names of those Knights you've been associating with. Timothy Honore would have considerable desire for intimate knowledge pertaining to that dark day. He is a bit of a rebel, and it wouldn't surprise me to know he's finally had enough of his fellow Solarians. But I figure you knew that already."

"Of course," Rumil lied. Truth told, she didn't know that much about Timothy at all, outside of the fact that he liked to bend the rules when it suited him, and that he had his heart in the right place... for the most part.

"That said, I suppose your explanation pans out. But why continue your mission after my contact so rudely decided you weren't worth the trouble anymore?"

"Because I could really use the credits this job could garner me," Rumil answered. "I might have panicked for a little while, but once I started to add up all the goods that payday could buy..."

"You felt you could end your employment on your terms," Krennan finished, then chided when he saw her surprised expression. "Oh, don't be so shocked. You had the air of a lady who was getting tired of her job, and I could tell your desire to call it quits. You know that's very unusual. I don't often release employees of this business... too many loose ends."

"Well, I have a little bit of leverage in that regard now," Rumil replied.

Krennan thought about that then flatly said, "Perhaps you do. But we shall negotiate the terms of this deal in person. It's much neater that way, and much more secure. I assume you know where my office building is in Pinnacle?"

"I do."

"Good. I shall arrange for a meeting for 7.35 ET two cycles from now. I hope that isn't too early for you. Do try to look nice so as to avoid any undue attention." He looked like he was finished, and then added as if in an afterthought, "And bring Knight Honore with you. I think I might have an additional offer to him. Now, I must bid you farewell, I do have other business to arrange."

The avatar left, and Rumil felt it safe to leave herself. Once back in reality, she whirled around to her two companions. "He knows about both of you."

Timothy nodded. "That doesn't come as a surprise. What did you tell him?"

Rumil knew that one of the Knights was not going to like this, and she had a pretty good idea which one. "I told him that you and I were in league with each other to get information on the Baramak Slaughter, and were going to leave Justin out of the loop before we left Altair."

Justin laughed. "Not bad." Then, given a moment to think, added nervously, "She *was* lying… right?"

"Considering that if Rumil and I *were* in allegiance against you, we would have gotten rid of you after Jun, I'd say that's a pretty fair assumption," Timothy said.

Now the part that Rumil knew Justin wasn't going to like. "Krennan has arranged for me to meet him in two cycles in his headquarters on Arcadia, in Pinnacle. He expects… Timothy to be with me… *only* Timothy."

Justin's eyes narrowed. "So you expect me to wait while Timothy makes the arrest, hoping that once he's got you both in custody he won't back out of our agreement? I didn't like the idea of leaving you two alone when you went to Amat. There is no way I'll let this continue without me *this* time."

Rumil began to argue her point again when Timothy cut in. "And you won't have to. You'll be with us on our trip to Arcadia."

"How?" Rumil and Justin asked simultaneously before Rumil continued, "Krennan is going to be watching our shuttle, if he isn't watching us already."

Timothy smirked. "He isn't watching right now… I had this room cleared of detection devices by local peacekeepers before we settled in. As for the shuttle issue…" He held up a small white box, opening it to reveal synthetic identification material. "With a little psionic trickery, and these little fakes, there will be no trouble at all."

Then the Solarian glanced at Justin before amending, "Provided our Kiros friend can maintain a self-illusion for almost a cycle."

Justin appeared almost insulted by the comment. "Of course I can… I'm not some weak-blooded Solarian."

"Then there shouldn't be a problem."

*   *   *   *   *

"Aren't you nervous?" Rumil asked when she and Timothy had reached their destination, the Arcadian capital of Pinnacle. "Not even I have met Gregor Krennan in person. He could have anything planned."

"Perhaps he does," Timothy agreed. "Which is why I wanted Justin along as insurance."

Rumil lifted out of her seat to scan her fellow passengers. "Which one is Justin?"

"He's not on this shuttle," Timothy replied quietly. "But he did just arrive on Arcadia."

"How do you know?"

"I can sense two distinct psionic auras in the city. One of them is yours, one of them is Justin's."

"You'd think if I was a psionic like you claimed, I'd be able to do that," Rumil sulked.

"I never said you were," Timothy replied casually. "I merely said you have a distinct aura. It is possible that your potential has yet to manifest itself. If you were an Erani, it should have happened long ago." Then he shrugged. "However, you aren't Erani; who knows what the rules are in your case."

As the pair stood to exit the shuttle, Rumil whispered to the Solarian Knight, "We have less than a tenth-cycle before our meeting. How will we know who Justin is?"

"We *won't*, and that's actually part of the point. I'll know if he makes it to the Multimedia Towers, but until then, we're just going to have to trust that he did his job."

"What if someone sees through his illusion?"

Timothy smirked, and words resounded inside Rumil's head, *On this planet? Not likely. Arcadians are about as talented in the extra-sensory arts as I am playing tali.*

"I thought Solarians were naturally adept at that game."

Timothy shook his head, and answered verbally, "Not myself. I'm terrible at it."

"I don't see why. You have all the physical tools."

"Never bothered to learn how to play. It never interested me."

"You're *not interested* in tali?" Rumil gasped in mock surprise. "What do you do in your spare time?"

Timothy retorted, "You assume I *have* spare time."

Once they had departed the starport, Rumil noted that they only had forty ticks to get to their destination, a pair of large stone circular buildings that towered above all but two on the city's skyline. At the top of the eastern skyscraper were red letters that gleamed in the increasing sunlight as it crept towards Pinnacle bearing the "Multimedia Towers" namesake.

"We're going to have to hurry. It shouldn't take that long to get there, but I do want to arrive early. As I understand, Krennan likes his appointments punctual."

"Of course. He would want his illegitimate guests on time so that he could push them out in time for his legit ones," Timothy commented ruefully. "Well, perhaps we can find a hover service to take us to our destination."

Two such passenger hovers passed by, totally ignoring Timothy's attempts to get their attention. Rumil gently nudged Timothy to the side, and said, "You're not doing it right. The drivers need… incentive." As the next hover approached, Rumil leaned over, the collar of her blouse drifting downward, one hand on her knee, and the other waving slowly as if in greeting.

Timothy frowned, and quipped, "Subtle."

"Subtlety is not rewarded on Arcadia," Rumil said through her bright, suggestive smile. "It just gets you passed over. See what I mean?"

She pointed to the hover, painted a bright orange with "Pinnacle City Services" in red on the side, and pulling to a stop right in front of them. Rumil once again smiled sweetly to the operator as Timothy opened the rear side passenger's door.

As the pair sat down inside, the operator wrapped his arm around the seat to look back at them, and said slyly, "Had I known that Arcadian women were so outgoing, I would have visited this place sooner."

Rumil froze. That voice, the tingle in the back of her head… but it couldn't be… "Justin?"

He shook his long green hair around his now Arcadian features, complete with a nose ring and tattoo of a heart above his right eyebrow. One eye was green, the other gold. "Like my new look?"

"You look like a freak," Rumil gasped, still not able to fully believe this was the illusionary visage that the proper Kiros Knight had decided to adopt.

"I just looked at some of the people who were preparing to board my shuttle here, and fashioned my appearance based on them." Justin then sighed, and stated, "I take it that it's no good."

"You could stop traffic," Rumil admitted. "How did you get hold of this hover?"

"Well, I actually got here about three tenth-cycles ago, and… borrowed this hover from a generous man who agreed to let me use it in exchange for not getting his internal organs smeared across the walkway."

Timothy grinned with an aloof amusement. "Getting violent with innocent bystanders? You're learning."

Justin turned his eyes back to the road, and answered, "Hey, even I am known to bend the rules slightly… if it is deemed needed. Besides, this gives me a perfect opportunity to be right in the position I need to be without drawing too much undue attention."

"Yes… just how do you plan on getting into Multimedia Towers?" Rumil asked. "This is one of the most tightly secure buildings in the galaxy. I'd wager there are even a few psionic detection systems in there."

"Oh, I don't doubt it. But by the time that security reports to the situation, we'll be long gone," Timothy replied confidently.

"There's no chance that I'm going to be privy to this plan, is there?"

"The fewer people who know just what is going to happen, the better," Justin retorted with a smile. "By the way… I got the image we'd need from our co-conspirator. He'll also be waiting for us on schedule, so everything is a go."

"Wait a minute!" Rumil interjected. "There's another person in on this? Who, and will someone *please* tell me what is going on?"

"Just something Justin arranged for us while we were exploring Amat," Timothy said with a smug expression. "And we can't tell you because we really don't want to ruin the surprise."

Rumil growled in frustration as the hover continued its path into the heart of Pinnacle, finally stopping in front of the main entrance to the east building of Multimedia Towers.

"Fifteen ticks to spare," Rumil muttered, glowering. She obviously didn't like being left out of the loop. "Let's get this over with." Timothy leaned through the front passenger side window, and appeared to pay Justin, but the hacker could tell from the sudden throbbing in her head that the pair was exchanging more than credits.

The mental conversation concluded, Rumil escorted Timothy up the fifteen steps leading to the main doors of the east building. Inside the lobby, Rumil pointed to the line of receptionists that stood almost like sentries in front of the lifts and stairways leading to the higher floors of the tower.

Taking her place in line with the receptionist furthest to the right, Timothy asked, "This is the longest line. Why are we—"

"This is Krennan's 'personal' secretary, the one that knows *all* his business," Rumil interrupted. "She'll be the only one who knows that Krennan is even *here* this early… much less that he has a meeting with us."

Timothy nodded in understanding. "I see…"

Fortunately, the line moved quickly. Timothy guessed it was because the occupants in this line probably weren't the type that liked being out in the open for very long.

Within six ticks, Rumil and Timothy were at the front of the line. "Hello, I have a 7.35 appointment with Gregor, Miss."

The secretary was a light brown-skinned Ruma, its skull ridge pierced with a series of twelve copper-colored rings spaced evenly along the edge. Its reptilian eyes narrowed, and it replied irritatingly, "I'm male, *Miss* Bonamede. Just put your hand here… and look in here…."

"Thank you," Rumil replied, as she placed her hand on the palm reader, at the same time looking into the retinal sensor. "I apologize for mistaking—"

"Yeah, yeah, we all look alike," the Ruma snapped as Rumil's identity was confirmed, waving them away with a flick of its scaled wrist. "Krennan is waiting for you in office number 13-16. Next!"

Rumil sneered at the Ruma's back as they proceeded. "He obviously wasn't hired for his customer service. Then again, his position rarely is."

"Leave any and all weapons here," commanded an Ubek, dressed in a brown security uniform. His skin was tinted darker than the one

Rumil and Timothy had met before on the Blood Hawk cruiser, likely a Halfblood, if Rumil didn't miss her guess. Timothy removed his sword and pistol without much hesitation, handing the two articles to the guard. "It is rather pointless to ask a Solarian Knight for his weapons, isn't it?" the Halfblood Ubek commented, surprisingly genial.

"Whatever makes you feel safer," Timothy replied nonchalantly as a second guard, this one Arcadian, ran several paddles around the Solarian, checking for any concealed weaponry or suspicious technology on his person. Satisfied, he did the same to Rumil, paying special attention to her satchel.

Finally, the Arcadian guard declared, "They're both clear."

The Ubek stated as if trying to be friendly, "Have a nice day." However, an Ubek voice rarely does "friendly" well, so it sounded like a medium-pitched growl that Rumil wasn't sure how to accept.

"We'll try..." she finally managed warily. Timothy gave her a gentle nudge on the shoulder, effectively breaking her out of her state. With an irritated glare, Rumil stepped into the lift, her companion not even half a Tack behind.

When the door opened to their floor, a small security detail was waiting for them. The lead, a being she assumed was Arcadian, wearing full combat gear complete with helmet and oxygen mask, pointed down the hall. "Mr. Krennan is waiting for you. Just follow me."

"You look like you're prepared for a war, not a meeting," Rumil remarked dryly to their escort as the remaining guards formed a circle around her and Timothy, and followed in close formation down the hall.

"Well, we've never had a Solarian Knight visit us," the leader of the detail replied. "Knowing the less than friendly regard that sect holds our employer in, caution was considered the better part of valor."

"It's quite understandable," Timothy stated humorously. "I wouldn't trust me either."

Timothy frowned slightly when the procession stopped before the proper door. The room clearly was aligned towards the center of the building, and that would make things a little more troublesome, but not too difficult to overcome.

Three of the detail stopped at the door, while the remaining two opened it and followed Rumil and Timothy into the darkened office. The moment they entered, the lights slowly brightened, revealing the figure of Gregor Krennan.

The media emperor stood in the center of the circular office, right above a small black spot on the red rug, radiating white spokes in resemblance of a wheel. There were no chairs or desks, and the black walls and ceiling made it seem like the small globe lights were floating in mid-air.

"I apologize for the lack of accommodations, but you can never be terribly careful when meeting people for the first time," Krennan stated, motioning for Rumil and Timothy to come closer. The guards had taken position on each side of the wooden door, rifles trained constantly on the pair.

"Can we get to business?" Timothy asked, almost coldly. "I really don't want to be here terribly long."

Krennan smiled without humor. "No nonsense, are you? I like that in a person. Very well, the reason I asked you here Knight Honore is to extend a special offer that I think you might find... intriguing."

The Solarian's eyes narrowed. "That would depend."

"I'll admit that I've wanted an eye inside the religious sects of Solaria and Kiros. They've been somewhat of a thorn in my side, and very dedicated to their cause. Finding someone willing to accept a few extra credits for a little reconnaissance work has been very difficult indeed."

Krennan glanced at Rumil briefly before addressing Timothy again. "I know that you aren't on the best of terms with your Knighthood, and I'd wager you distrust their motives as much as I do. With your aid, I think I can help keep them in check. I could make it worth your while."

Timothy did not hesitate in his reply. "I'd need to give that some thought before I committed to anything. I sincerely hope you didn't expect an immediate response."

Krennan laughed. "No, of course not. The best deals are always the most thought out. I shall leave you with instructions to contact me once you have made up your mind." Focusing his attention back on Rumil, he stated, "With that issue brought to light, I think it is time for us to discuss the primary reason for your visit."

Stepping away from the pair, Krennan began to pace the far wall, rubbing his chin thoughtfully. "As I understand it, you want full payment for the task, as well as a severance of employment. Am I correct, Miss Bonamede?"

"Considering how I nearly got myself vaporized in a skirmish with two highly gifted Erani, you should be lucky I'm only asking for double pay," Rumil almost sneered.

Krennan exhaled deeply, and said, "Normally, I'm not nearly so giving when negotiating. Though, admittedly, I'm very rarely on such equal footing with someone I'm negotiating with. You want out of your employment quite badly, likely about as badly as I want that file you are holding."

"That would be a fair assessment," Rumil agreed.

Retrieving a PCU from inside his suit coat, Krennan examined the terms of the initial deal with Rumil. "As I understand, the original fee was seventy-five million credits, correct?"

The number took Timothy by surprise. He knew that black market deals were usually pricey, but seventy-five million credits was well above what he had expected for a hacking job, confirming just how badly Krennan wanted this information. Meanwhile, Timothy felt Justin's signal. Slightly moving his eyes to his right in the direction of the signal, Timothy prepared to put their plan into motion.

"That's what I recall," Rumil answered tersely.

Finally, Krennan stopped pacing. "I'll give you one hundred and twenty million credits, along with an agreement for severance."

Rumil retorted, "Make it one hundred and fifty, and you have a deal."

Krennan bartered back. "One hundred and thirty."

Rumil thought about it, and finally said, "One hundred and thirty-five. I want half up front, as well as the severance agreement, in writing, before I hand over the disk containing the file."

"Done. The rest of the payment will be made after the document is authenticated."

Rumil sighed in relief once Krennan had agreed. She had been a little worried as to the shrewd dealings that the mogul had been known for, but his desire for information on the Baramak Slaughter obviously impaired his ability.

Then Timothy absolutely stunned her speechless. He lifted one hand three Tackems from the side of her head, and she could feel the occasional crackle of psionic energy tickle her hair. "Actually, Mr. Krennan, I don't think you need to pay her anything. The way I see it, she gives you the data, and hopes that she can walk out of here with her head still attached." He grinned maliciously as he continued, "She had come to me before our meeting, hoping that I would help her with an idea she had to arrange for you to implicate yourself. She'd get you to spill the beans, then I would arrest you."

Rumil shook out of her stupor, whirling around to face the Solarian, screaming in disbelief, "*My* idea?"

"Yes. I'm not that stupid, Bonamede. Did you honestly think I would take your side against someone as powerful as Krennan? Not even I am confident to mess with him without consequence."

The energy on his fingertips began to congeal into a blue-white ball, and Rumil was frozen in fear, her mind racing with thoughts of Timothy's betrayal. He had set her up to take a fall in order to get close to Krennan.

Suddenly, she heard Timothy's voice in her head, a loud command that almost made her wince. *Get down... NOW!*

Deciding obedience was her best option, Rumil complied, dropping to a crouched fetal position as the loud rush of energy zipped over her head, plowing through the dark wall like it was made of paper, disintegrating everything in its path. When the roar died away, a massive hole about four Tacks in diameter had burned through two more walls, and out into the open sky.

By the time Rumil had stood back up, Timothy had whirled around, and launched two invisible balls of energy from his fists that rippled through the air, striking the two guards with such force that they were knocked through the back wall and out into the hallway.

Krennan made a break for the door, but suddenly found himself caught in a grip of iron. Justin had appeared out of nowhere, having dropped his illusion. Timothy launched five more balls of energy while backing away, as the three remaining guards stepped over their fallen comrades and into the office.

Rumil shrieked as Timothy grabbed her by the shoulder, and with a flash of light, the world seemed to drop away, only to be replaced by a hard paved surface just underneath her feet. She dropped roughly onto Timothy's lap, who had seemingly collapsed in a similar fashion.

Justin stood over them, grinning, and stated, "Sorry... I wasn't terribly sure how tall you were."

Timothy would have replied, but Dewin Rio's voice interrupted them, "Hurry up and get in here before Arcadia's defenses realize what's happened."

Rumil darted up the ramp into the Blood Hawk cruiser from the roof of the corporate tower they had escaped to, while Timothy and Justin dragged Krennan aboard right after her. Several pirates waited inside to take Krennan off their hands and to the brig, as Rumil and the Knights followed.

"Where did Justin come from?" Rumil asked quizzically.

"I teleported through the hole our Solarian friend made," Justin replied triumphantly. "You see, psionics can't warp ourselves through solid matter, so Timothy had to make me a door."

"So that entire accusation…"

"Was a ruse so I could gather the necessary energy to make a sudden emergency exit," Timothy finished.

Once in the brig, Krennan was tossed inside a holding cell, and a forcefield was raised. Krennan laughed spitefully. "This is quite amusing. Do you honestly think the Alliance is going to believe the words of two Knights and a computer hacker over mine?"

Timothy grinned, and stated, "Of course not. Your own words will be more than enough." Reaching into his pants pocket, Timothy pulled out a small trinket about the size and shape of his thumb. Pressing the top end, resembling the tip of his finger, the brig suddenly filled with the words of the entire meeting.

Krennan's eyes looked ready to jump out of his head. "How did you get that through security?" he demanded.

"Knight Feroz here had slipped it into my pocket while Rumil was gaping at the Ubek you stationed at the lift. After we were declared clean, Justin waited for one of the doors to open, and delivered it to me."

"And so… while we were on Amat… Justin was arranging the rest of the plan with Rio here," Rumil gaped, finally piecing the entire plan together. "And since Rio was no friend of Krennan's, he apparently agreed to help."

"Exactly," Justin gloated. "The entire plan was simple enough to work without a hitch, but complex enough to not be easily discovered. Quite brilliant, I think."

"Speaking of which… I could say this entire investigation is completed," Timothy stated solemnly. "Perhaps we should settle our final issue now?"

Justin gulped nervously, knowing what the Solarian was referring to. "If you want… but I think I have a better idea."

Timothy's eyebrow rose, and he replied flatly, "Do you?"

Justin took the question as an indication that Timothy was not dead-set on fighting it out. "I mean, we can each take vital parts of this investigation back with us, and arrange for our leaders to jointly bring the case before the Galactic Alliance Legal Council."

Timothy's eyes narrowed, but he said thoughtfully, "The Knighthood would not like the idea… but King Frederick would probably do it. Krennan has irritated him considerably over the staryears, and he is rather level-headed as monarchs tend to go. I suppose it is a more humane option than one of us pounding the other into oblivion."

"So you'll help me?" Justin asked eagerly.

With a wry smirk, Timothy nodded. "I wasn't terribly keen on fighting you anyway. It might be clouding my judgment." The two Knights grasped each other's right forearms to seal the agreement.

"That's fine with me," Justin replied, smiling like a child given a large gift. "You can take Rumil and the evidence with you to Solaria, and I'll take Krennan with me."

Timothy frowned, and asked, "Why do you get to take Krennan?"

Justin stepped back, and shrugged passively, "Well, if *you* want to take him, I suppose I can bring Rumil with me to Kiros…"

Timothy grated as if annoyed, "No… that's quite fine. You can have Krennan. Perhaps it's for the best if you do."

"I do concur," Justin said, and then asked Dewin, "We're on our way to Altair, correct?"

"Indeed we are," Dewin nodded. "We'll be there in about five tenth-cycles."

Justin nodded, and concluded, "That should give Timothy and me plenty of time to arrange for travel back to our respective homes. Shall we?"

Timothy agreed with another nod, and the pair left the brig followed by Dewin and the pirates, save for those guarding the prisoner. Eventually, Rumil was alone with Krennan and the guards. With a hiss, the hacker said, "I'll consider this my severance agreement."

Then she left quite purposefully, the door sliding to a close behind her, to be followed a demi-tick later by a resounding thud, as if she had been hoping to slam it shut, and thus decided to punch it instead.

Chapter Thirteen

Rumil felt Solaria before she saw it, as a blast of dry, hot wind flooded the entire cabin of the personal shuttle, which Timothy had somehow acquired from his Knighthood for this journey. Stepping away from the pilot's console, he handed Rumil a small paper mask to place over her nose and mouth, and pulled her to her feet. She was reluctant to step out into what appeared to be a very inhospitable atmosphere, and reaching the shuttle ramp, she discovered that the planet was inhospitable in more ways than one.

Through the almost solid wall of sand blowing around in a gale force wind, eight military personnel waited at the bottom of the sand-swept runway. They were clad in brown battle armor similar to what Timothy wore now, with black plasma rifles held at the ready. Timothy appeared behind her, and queried sternly, "What is the meaning of this, Knight Datson?"

The Solarian at the back of the detail stepped forward, his custom-molded armor and lack of weaponry suggesting his membership in the Solarian Knighthood. Nonetheless, the Knight in question was visibly intimidated by the man he was forced to address. "High Commander Honore's orders were for me to take Bonamede into custody."

She heard Timothy growl softly in mild irritation, which was probably equivalent to full-blown fury for any normal person. "How about we argue once we're underground, Robert? I am in no mood to fight over this while we're in the middle of a sandstorm."

"Understood, sir," the Knight said with the customary Erani salute, right fist placed above the heart. He motioned for his detail to bring their rifles to standby, and ordered them into one of the two large vehicles that resembled a dune buggy on enhancing drugs. Thick roll bars formed a cage atop six wheels, each a Tack and a half in diameter.

Robert jumped into the driver's station of the second buggy, and waited for Timothy and Rumil to buckle in before starting to drive into the blowing sand. "You're fortunate you arrived when you did… we'd have had to relocate you to another landing strip… probably Gorgan."

"Good thing we didn't," Timothy replied. "The last thing anyone needs is my father brooding for a ten-cycle with no one worthy of dumping it on."

"I take it that this isn't the worst of the storm?" Rumil yelled over the rumble of the engine and the wailing wind.

"The worst won't hit for another tenth-cycle," Timothy answered.

Rumil could barely open her eyes due to the blasting sand, and silently wondered how it could actually get worse. Not that she figured there was terribly much to see. The surface of Solaria bore the scars of an unknown war that left the planet desolate, ravaged beyond even what modern terraforming could repair. Oceans boiled into vapor, the continental plates had ripped and split, approximately a quarter of the upper thermosphere had been ejected into space – all in one catastrophic event, forcing the original inhabitants underground. The civilization had been ancient during the earliest recorded history, its fate an enigma even to the Solarians, who had called this planet home for almost eight hundred staryears.

There was still some arable land, but water occupied barely two percent of the planet's surface area, and that was devoted almost entirely to agricultural use – not nearly enough to support its population. However, its abundant natural resources, initially fossil fuels, gave the Solarians more than enough trading power to maintain a good lifestyle. In recent times, the people of Solaria relied on mining amazingly pure veins of metals that were then smelted into amorphous alloys. These alloys were dearly valued by the Galactic Alliance, and the Solarians' skill in forging them was unparalleled. To own a Solarian piece of equipment was to own a very durable and efficient tool, to own a Solarian weapon was to own the finest piece of destruction money could buy.

No one could positively say why Solarian equipment was so superior. One theory was because the ore veins found on Solaria were significantly more pure than elsewhere in the galaxy. Another was that the Solarians adapted and stole ideas and technology from the abandoned civilization that came before. Perhaps it was both. Only the Solarians could say for certain, and they weren't exactly forthcoming with that information.

A bump from the undercarriage jolted Rumil from her thoughts and back on the maelstrom around her. From ahead, a large cliff face appeared on the dusty horizon, a looming door of solid metal extending at least fifty Tacks up from the lower floor, reaching almost to the top of the cliff. As if sensing the convoy's approach, the doors began to open inward, allowing the two vehicles to pull inside at full speed.

While Rumil cleared the sand that had clung to her eyelashes and clothes, the buggy began a gradual decline down into the depths of the desert planet. Only small red light bulbs on the sides and median of the roadway gave any indication as to where they were going, as there was no other lighting in the entire tunnel.

The buggy took a hard right turn, and then they exploded into a cavern brightened by artificial lighting that hung from the cavern roof about a TackMet above the floor. The horizon looked exactly like a normal city… only underground. She could see a mixture of modern skyscrapers and older stonework buildings near the heart of the city, and an assortment of smaller housing units littered about the proximity. Every so often, Rumil noted a worn stone ruin of civilizations past as they drove on.

Somewhere in the tunnel, Timothy had taken off his helmet, and tucked it under his arm. "Welcome to Centris," he commented, apparently amused by Rumil's slight amazement. "I suppose it is quite a sight to see in person for the first time, but the charm will rapidly die… trust me."

Robert pointed to his right, where a paved square was attached to a magnetic roadway for hover use. "We'll transfer into hovers there, and then proceed to Central Command. I get the feeling your father will want to talk to you."

"Once we get to the hover lot, I'll proceed to the complex on my own with my guest. I'd like you to deliver notice to the King's advisors," Timothy ordered. "Tell them to arrange for Frederick to meet me at my residence in two tenth-cycles, and tell him to be prepared for one outrageous report."

Robert was obviously disconcerted by the way that Timothy so casually referred to their monarch. "I'll do that sir… if they listen to me."

"Just inform them that if they don't deliver the message, I will, *in person*, the next cycle, and I doubt the King would approve of me having to do that."

Robert slipped a nervous chuckle. "And I think they know you'd do that too. Very well, sir, I'll see to it as you request. I just hope your father doesn't take it out of my hide."

"If he does, let me know," Timothy asserted. "Thank you, Robert."

The buggy pulled to a stop, and Timothy wasted no time leading Rumil to one of the black hovers bearing a shield with clenched fists side by side, and two swords crossed behind the shield, the standard of the Solarian people. Activating the hover, it lifted off the ground, and Timothy quickly accelerated towards Centris.

Just before they were about to enter the city, Rumil suddenly felt a sharp sting in her head, like someone had shot an arrow directly into the base of her skull. Dropping her head against the forward console, teeth clenched, she reflexively slapped her right hand onto the spot the pain radiated from.

Timothy stopped the hover, and leaned over in concern. "Are you all right?"

"If feels like somebody set off a pressure mine inside my head. What is happening to me?" Rumil grated.

Timothy had sensed a sharp spike in Rumil's psionic aura, and he had barely had time to strengthen the dampening field he had set around her when they had arrived on Solaria. Looking around, he figured the trigger likely came from one source.

Timothy pointed over Rumil outside the passenger's side of the hover, and the hacker followed with her hazy vision to a ruin about one hundred Tacks off the roadway. It looked like a stone box, but appeared to be in slightly better condition than most of the other relics they had passed. She noted how nothing seemed to be anywhere near it, even Centris itself seemed to be giving the ruin a wide birth, gouging a crescent shape into the otherwise circular city.

"What is that supposed to be?" Rumil asked, slowly getting accustomed to the sensation.

"That is the site where the first Gate of Bannor once lay," Timothy remarked, his voice reflecting some confusion. "To this day, remnants of its dark power linger, but we should be well out of its radius…"

"So the Gates really weren't something you Erani made up?" Rumil asked. She hadn't wanted to believe the religious doctrine, but the power she was just exposed to made it hard for her to dismiss quite so readily.

"Not in the least," Timothy affirmed. "This gate had partially opened, and minor minions of the lower plane had begun to rush out. Before the first Solarians had sealed the site in that block of stone, no one could go anywhere in this entire cavern without being affected by the evil, foreboding sensations radiating from what once was the Gate."

Rumil's eyes focused on the stone block, as if entranced. The inside of her head began to crackle, and then her vision went completely black. In the void, she slowly began to make out a shape approaching her. As it got closer, it gradually gained definition, taking on the form of a hand… but Rumil realized it wasn't any hand like she had seen. The palm was blood red, the fingers covered in scales of the same color, and deep black fingernails sharpened to points like daggers. Rumil wanted to get away from the approaching appendage, but seemed unable to move.

Behind it, she saw two eyes, glowing bright red, with large orange circles in the center, and two rows of sword-like teeth. An unnatural roar filled her ears as the hand suddenly lunged forward, grabbing her by the shoulder.

Screaming in terror, it took a while for Rumil to realize the black void had fallen away as quickly as it had appeared, and that Timothy had grabbed her on the shoulder, turning her to face him. His eyes were filled with concern as he asked, "You totally went blank on me. What's wrong?"

Rumil blinked rapidly, not sure how to answer that question. Rubbing her temple with her left hand, she finally said breathlessly, "I don't know...... I just... I want to get away from here. *Now.*"

"As you wish," Timothy replied as he accelerated the hover away from the ruin as fast as he could manage. He had expected some sort of reaction from Rumil as they had approached the old Gate site, but he had been taken completely off-guard by the second surge in Rumil's psionic aura, just as she had drifted off into a blank stare. He could only hope that he had dampened it enough to prevent anyone from detecting it. Something told him that Rumil's psionic potential would not go over well with many Solarians, especially the man frequently called his father.

It was a four TackMet drive to the official city limits of Centris. The traffic increased steadily, but not nearly as heavy as would be normal for a city of its size. "Ironically, despite the ire between the two sects, both the Solarians and Kiros adopt many of the same policies. In many ways, we're more alike than different," Timothy answered, as if sensing Rumil's question before she asked it.

The Central Command for the Solarian Military and Knighthood was on the other side of the metropolis, and so Rumil got a good look at the city itself. It struck her as very similar to Los in its orderly layout and lack of any... undesirable folk. "We're not going to have to drive near the 'homeless camp' here, are we?"

"No, we won't," Timothy assured her. "The camp in Centris is actually located outside the official city limits. It actually is pretty well maintained, and is probably one of the best such camps in the galaxy."

"That's like saying your feces are the cleanest in the decomposition tank," Rumil glowered. The idea of herding people like slaughterhouse animals simply did not set well with her.

Timothy took a deep breath, and admitted, "You're probably right... but like most things, there are some positives, as well as negatives. It's just a matter of people deciding if the benefits outweigh the detriments or not."

"I take it you don't share your society's opinion?"

"My fellow Solarians and I differ on many issues," Timothy huffed. "I'd rather not go into it." Then he pointed over Rumil's left shoulder, and declared, "That is Central Command."

There was a large contingent of soldiers waiting for them, and one displeased Knight with rich silver hair and angry brown eyes. His armor, sans helmet, was of a different style than Rumil had seen before; not sculpted to the actual shape of its wearer, but rather meant to make him look larger and more imposing than he naturally would, particularly with the wider, rounded shoulder plating. Timothy did not appear the least bit perturbed by his fearsome appearance however, jumping out of the hover and getting right into the face of the older man.

"Where is the detail I sent?" the gray-haired Knight demanded angrily.

"They're delivering a message to King Frederick, 'father.' I am sorry to tell you that I have orders that supercede even yours. I am meeting with the King in two tenth-cycles, and until then, I cannot report on anything that has occurred. Once that meeting is over, then, *and only then*, will I submit my report to *you*."

Without waiting for the older man to reply, Timothy whirled about sharply, then added threateningly. "Until declared otherwise by our monarch, Rumil Bonamede is a guest in my house. Anyone who so much as lays a hand on her without her permission answers to *me*." Turning his head back to the older Knight, he hissed, "And I mean *anyone*."

Niles Honore glared at the brat bearing his family name, as the young man climbed back into the hover and started to accelerate away. Ever since giving permission for Timothy to investigate and apprehend Gregor Krennan, he had been left in the dark until a cycle ago, when Timothy informed Central Command that he was returning to Solaria with Bonamede. He did not like being kept uninformed, especially when that bastard called a 'king' was involved. Nonetheless, Frederick was confirmed as the King of Solaria, and Niles's code of conduct required him to honor his king's wishes.

He didn't have to like it, though…

Meanwhile, Rumil asked nervously, "Is life at the Honore household like this all the time? Am I going to have to duck for cover when your father comes home?"

"No. We don't interact outside of Central Command," Timothy

replied. "He never visits me, and I never visit him."

"I can't imagine you don't run into each other once or twice on the Honore Estate, regardless of its size," Rumil commented, referring to the large clusters of mansions reserved for families of the Solarian and Kiros Knightoods. The more prominent the family – that is, the more Knights they produce, the purer their blood is, and so on – the larger the estate they are granted. The Honore Estate, due to the family's position as the premier family in the Knighthood, was likely as large as some cities.

"I haven't lived there since I was fifteen staryears," Timothy answered dryly. "I never felt terribly welcome there."

"You'd think the family would be thankful that there was a powerful psionic to maintain the family's status in the Solarian hierarchy."

Timothy smirked wryly. "It's probably the reason my father hasn't killed me yet." The hover stopped, and Timothy pointed up to a ten-story complex that was made out of a gray brick. "This is where I live. Seventh floor, actually. It's not terribly large… but it suits me."

Rumil would not have expected a member of one of the most prominent families of Solaria to live in such an area. It wasn't a slum, by any means, but it definitely didn't fit the mold that was expected of a Solarian Knight.

As they entered the apartment building's plainly decorated lobby, complete with tacky red and cream-striped furniture on top of a green carpet and pearl-colored walls, Rumil asked, "I can't imagine your family likes you living in such an… undignified place…"

"Most of them don't care," Timothy dismissed with a shrug, nodding politely towards the female clerk working the counter. Stopping suddenly, Timothy remarked, "Madam Cavarno, I would like to report that someone is robbing from your safe."

The middle-aged Solarian woman blinked twice then asked nervously, "What do you mean?"

"Well, when I was last here… I noticed my rent payment had been slipped under my door. I resubmitted it before I left, but I fear that it might have been returned again," Timothy replied innocently. "I sincerely hope you catch the thief… I do believe this happens almost every five ten-cycles."

As Timothy led Rumil through the lobby, he remarked wryly, "It's often a battle to get the landlords to accept my rent during every pay cycle. I had a rather long argument with her husband about how they do not need to pay me any undue favors."

"You are probably the first person I've met who demands to *pay* for a service," she said with a shake of her head.

"I don't like being treated as someone special. I am no different than anyone else here."

"Really? High-ranking Solarian Knights are all over this complex?"

Timothy glared at her, not appreciating the humor. "It is what I choose to do with the talent I possess, nothing more. It shouldn't be a free pass through my life." The implied finality of his statement told her that this line of conversation was concluded, and just in time for the lift doors to open.

"My apartment is at the end of the hall," Timothy said, pointing down to a door at the farthest end of the hall to his right. As they approached the apartment, the door on the opposite side of the hall opened, and a pale, blonde-haired Solarian stuck his head out, sky blue eyes dancing mischievously as he scanned the pair in the hall.

"Nice to see you back, Tim. This entire place seemed a little less secure while you were out," the Solarian chuckled, then his eyes focused on Rumil. "My... isn't this a specimen? Full score for style, but come on, surely there's a Solarian girl that could suit your tastes. Your father would go on a rampage if he knew you were fraternizing with an Arcadian."

Timothy clenched his fists tightly and released, finally slapping his left hand on the wall just to the left of the blonde man's door. "While I may put up with your antics for the majority of the time, Perkins, right now I am in no mood to deal with you, understand?"

Perkins jumped backward into the entry of his apartment, arms extended as if warding off Timothy's wrath. "Hey, just having a little fun, Tim. I personally don't care who you're—"

Timothy's glare intensified, and he grated with all the control he could manage, "I am not doing *anything* with *anyone*, for your information, and even if I was it is of absolutely no concern of yours."

Perkins was quickly realizing that a strategic retreat was in order. "Okay... well, I'll just leave you alone to whatever your business is." He swiftly shut his apartment door, holding the door as it closed so as not to slam it.

Rumil frowned disapprovingly, "He was only picking on you, Timothy. You didn't have to scare him to death."

Timothy relaxed, exhaling deeply. "Probably, but squashing that rumor as quickly as possible is in both of our best interests. The last thing either of us need is to have the wrong people thinking we're... involved."

"Why's that?" Rumil asked. "So what if a few people think we're having some mature fun in our free time?"

"It's... complicated. I'm surprised you don't already know."

"There's a lot I don't know about you people. You're a rather secretive lot for the most part," Rumil replied with a shrug. "It'd take me ten lifetimes to figure out all the rules you have."

Timothy's apartment was very plain, but she had actually come to expect that from the Solarian Knight. The main entry and living area was devoid of any character whatsoever; no artwork on the white walls, nor lavish furniture on the paneled wooden floor. Only a padded suede couch and one black metal chair standing in front of a holographic projector decorated the otherwise empty room.

Rumil stuck her head around the entryway corner, and peered into the dining and cooking area. There was a black multi-purpose cooker in the far left corner, a black refrigeration unit in the far right, and a clear plastic table with white trim and legs, with three white chairs around it in the center of the floor.

While she couldn't see the bedroom, restroom, or his office area, she had very little reason to believe it was no different from the rest of the apartment: plain, lifeless, and disturbingly spotless.

"One would think you have no life," Rumil remarked wryly as Timothy led her into the living area.

"About the only thing I use this place for is to sleep," Timothy replied. "Seems silly to waste credits on personalizing something so... irrelevant."

A high-pitched bell floated through the living area, and Timothy regarded the door warily. "Frederick isn't due here for another tenth-cycle and a half..." He stood up, and told Rumil, "Stay here. I'll be right back."

The Solarian stood up, and slowly approached his front door as the bell tones once again sounded in the apartment. From her position on Timothy's couch, she couldn't see who the visitor was, but soon later realized she didn't need to.

The Knight said only one word in greeting to his guest. "Mother."

At that, Rumil stood up, sticking her head around the corner of the living area, peering into the entryway. A Solarian woman with light brown hair, pulled back behind her ears, stepped around Timothy. Her features were smooth, appearing much younger than they apparently were, and her jewel-like green eyes twinkled with a vitality that did not do justice to her likely age. Rumil would never have guessed the lady in the entryway to have had *any* children, much less one in his adulthood.

"Timmy, one would think I taught you no manners while I raised you," the woman chided. "Whatever happened to proper greetings?"

"Why waste flippant courtesy on people who obviously don't require it?" Timothy retorted, gesturing to his mother to emphasize the fact that she had walked in without being invited.

The woman sighed, and shook her head comically. "And still no respect for your own mother, of all things. Living on your own has obviously destroyed all decency that I painstakingly instilled into your mind."

With this, Timothy smiled wryly, and said, "You have many strengths, but I wouldn't call decency one of them."

Finally, Timothy's mother abandoned her transparent façade, and embraced her only birth child. "I had heard that you had returned, and got here as soon as I could."

Timothy broke away, and his eyes narrowed playfully. "If your husband ever knew that you were folding about the city unsupervised…"

"It'll always be our little secret. Besides, how will I maintain my own inherent ability without a little practice?" the woman answered, then turned away from her son, looking over to where Rumil was peeking around the corner. With a pleasant smile, the Solarian woman quickly closed the distance, following as Rumil stepped back in surprise around the corner.

She took Rumil's hand gently, and broadening her grin said vibrantly, "And you must be the woman that was causing such a fuss with my husband. I am Celine Honore, Timothy's mother."

"Rumil…" the hacker answered nervously. She could feel significant psionic energy emanating from Celine, but it was quite different from the overwhelming presence of Timothy. "Rumil Bonamede. It's… a pleasure."

Celine appraised Rumil slowly, then declared, "You are indeed a vision, young lady. Pity that you aren't a Solarian, dear."

"Mother, do not…" Timothy warned.

"Oh, why don't you start writing your report, Knight Honore?"

Celine snapped, "I would really like to talk to this young lady, woman to woman."

Timothy frowned, but complied reluctantly, muttering as he retreated into his bedroom, "The things I let her get away with…"

"Do not mind my son," Celine said with a flip of her hand. "He just has no idea how to properly treat a lady. I sincerely hope he didn't get too rough with you."

"Nothing I couldn't handle," Rumil replied uncertainly.

Sensing Rumil's discomfort, Celine said conspiratorially, "Yes, I know what you are… despite my son's best efforts to shield your own potential. How much do you know about it?"

"About what?" Rumil answered. "My supposed psionic ability? I've never done anything like floating in midair, or starting a pyrotechnics show with nothing but my mind."

Celine smiled knowingly. "My dear, there are more ways to use psionics than cheap magic tricks." She moved towards the dining area, and motioned for Rumil to follow. "But enough about that. I need to make some huet. Come, have a seat."

Rumil sat in one of the white metal chairs as Celine pulled out a small kettle-like container, poured in some water out of the sink spigot, then placed it on the heating coils of the cooker top. As the water heated, Celine pulled a pinch of small thread-like roots out of a bag in one of the cupboards, and began crushing them into a fine powder using a rod and shallow bowl.

"Do you normally just do things without asking for permission?" Rumil queried. "That doesn't strike me as proper etiquette for a Solarian woman, especially from such a prominent family as the Honore clan."

Celine laughed. "Young lady, if you think all Solarian women say 'yes, sir' and 'what do you need of me,' then the rest of the civilized galaxy truly is as blind as I suspect."

With the water now boiling, she poured it evenly into two long and thin ceramic mugs, then shook equal amounts of powder into them. Grabbing two long-handled plastic spoons from the far left drawer under the countertop, Celine dropped one into each mug, and handed it to her.

"You might have to stir pretty quickly to keep the root powder from dropping to the bottom of the cup," Celine explained. "I have no idea how long Timmy has had that in the cupboard."

"You are aware he doesn't like being called 'Timmy?'" Rumil

questioned.

"I know," Celine replied with a mischievous grin.

"Can I ask you a personal question about Timothy?"

Celine paused. "This is about his father…"

Rumil growled, "Why do I bother even asking questions? Everyone just seems to take it out of my head anyway."

Timothy's mother started laughing. "Rumil, I figured it had to do with my husband because that is the only thing Timothy won't talk about himself. I think… in a minor way, Timothy blames me for the problems he and his father have."

"Why would he do that?"

Celine's features flattened grimly. "Well… it actually all starts right from his birth. It's not widely known, but my husband, Niles… is sterile. It's actually the reason we adopted Craig."

"The one who died on Baramak," Rumil remarked.

"Yes," Celine sadly stated. "Anyway, eventually I did get pregnant, and Timothy was born."

"Which Niles quickly figured wasn't his son," Rumil deduced.

"Correct. Niles sought to cut Timothy out of everything by labeling him an illegitimate child, claiming that I had conceived with another man," Celine explained.

"Did you?"

Celine straightened as if insulted, and she declared, "I have never been with any man but my husband. It was later proven when Timothy's genes were tested." Then the woman sighed. "But despite that, Niles remains unconvinced, and I don't think Timothy totally believes it either. Niles is certain Timothy is not his son, and thus, treats Timothy in private just like a bastard."

Rumil said, "He's pretty well-grounded despite all that," then added as she examined the lack of décor again, "If a bit bland."

Celine smirked, and retorted, "It was a difficult period. Timothy was always trying to gain his father's approval, never realizing that he really didn't have much chance. Finally, when he was about fifteen, just after his graduation, Timothy gave up, and left the mansion entirely. I've tried to be as much of a parent as I could be… but it *is* tough growing up without a father figure."

"I find it interesting that if there was so much dislike between

Timothy and his father that he would voluntarily join the Knighthood that his father commands," Rumil mused.

From the entrance to the dining area, Timothy replied, "Because while my father may decry my birthright in private, he can't do so publicly. One day, I'll command the Knighthood in his place, and I will do it right. It's worth a few staryears of grief."

"I think that is the first time that you have ever stated a life's goal, Timmy," Celine said, holding back a chuckle. "Normally when I would ask you what your purpose was, you'd never answer. Perhaps this young lady is having quite a positive influence on you." Celine winked at Rumil conspiratorially.

The Solarian woman then drained the rest of her drink, and stood. "Do be a dear, and wash this out for me, Timmy. I must be on my way. I don't want to be missing when your father returns from Central Command. Besides, I can sense Frederick is coming, and I don't want to get in the way of whatever scheme you two have been planning."

Celine gently took Rumil's hand again, and said sweetly, "It was a pleasure meeting you dear. It truly is a shame you aren't Solarian. By the Creator, we'd probably be even willing to accept a Kiros girl if it kept Timmy out of trouble."

"Mother, that's enough," Timothy nearly growled.

Celine grinned at him, and said, "Good day to you, Timmy. I shall show myself out." Which was promptly what the Solarian woman did, not waiting for any further farewells. Only opening the door wide enough for her to exit, Celine closed the door behind them.

"Your mother is not what I expected," Rumil commented.

"She definitely is a piece of work," Timothy agreed. "I personally feel that her life has been rather wasted."

Rumil placed her mug down, and propped her head on her hands. "Why do you say that?"

Timothy looked up at the door that his mother had just left from, and said, "Had she been born male, she'd likely be one of the most powerful Knights in the galaxy. But instead, she is trapped in this archaic system from before the Erani could even leave Kiros."

Rumil finally decided to ask Timothy something that had been bothering her since they had arrived at Timothy's apartment. "Okay... explain now. What is the deal with everyone picking on me about not being a Solarian and the deal with not wanting people to think we're involved?"

"Because if anyone could convince the right people that you and I were enjoying each other's company a little too much… it could mean the end of my career, if not your life," Timothy replied with a scowl.

"Are you serious?" Rumil sputtered. "Is the Solarian world still so uptight? You'd think a little premarital sex wouldn't be such a big deal in this modern time—"

Timothy interrupted her before she could rant any further. "To answer that question, yes, there are some people who still think that it's a very serious issue, but that's actually not the reason why it's such a grave offense."

"What is it then?"

Timothy took a deep breath, and replied, "The families of the Solarian Knighthood are very strict as to who I can associate myself sexually with. In order to maintain a predetermined purity of blood in my family, any potential wife or mate of mine is subjected to genetic testing."

Just as Rumil thought the Solarian lifestyle couldn't get any more bizarre, Timothy goes and proves her wrong. "Why would they do that?"

"Because the families of the Knighthood wish to maintain the purity of the ancient Se-Lan blood, in order to produce the best chance of talented psionics, and to maintain their status in the noble hierarchy," Timothy answered as if he was ready to spit in disgust. "This is especially true in the Honore family, who as a whole believes we are descended from the line of the Archangel Mican. Thus, over ninety percent of the Solarian population is already out of the question, much less some Arcadian woman."

Grabbing a bottled drink out of his refrigeration unit, he concluded, "Therefore, if I was tainting my 'pure blood' with an outsider… I could be stripped of my rank and even prosecuted. My 'father' would absolutely love that."

Rumil obviously was disgusted with the practice. "The way that you Solarians are so methodically restrictive should be outlawed."

Oh indeed, Miss Bonamede, a firm, tenor male voice resounded in her head. *And hopefully in a few staryears, I will finally have the support to banish these archaic customs once and for all.*

Timothy turned to the door, and opened it for his new visitor. "Frederick, you could just activate the door signal like everyone else."

"But where is the fun in that?" Frederick replied as the two exchanged a friendly arm clasp. The monarch was rather short, the top of his head barely making it to Timothy's nose, the jet black hair on the top of his head accenting his very pale complexion and gray eyes.

His face was somewhat lopsided and rough, not typically what would be considered "regal features," and coupled with his unkempt medium-length facial hair, it suggested to Rumil that he was more suited for a factory than a throne.

Timothy motioned for Frederick to enter, and the monarch stated, "You had caught me while I was investigating conditions in our forges. Now, my cover has been blown, so whatever you wish to report had better be worthwhile."

"Your cover?" Rumil asked, emerging into the living area.

Frederick smiled at her, and replied, "I will occasionally allow myself to be hired as if I am merely some normal Solarian man in order to judge how the common folk are being treated."

"Much to the dismay of many," Timothy remarked wryly.

Frederick waved his hand dismissively at Timothy. "Yes, yes… It's a little dangerous, especially considering the number of people who would simply love to see me in some 'tragic accident,' but in order to be an effective king, I do believe that I need the perspective of the people I am ruling over, do you not agree?"

"I'd rather you didn't have a preselected ruler at all," Rumil frowned.

Frederick sighed regretfully, "Well, there are some traditions that I doubt even I will have the power to change, and that is one of them. The Solarian Faith is the determinant in how this sphere of influence is operated, and they have been rather… reluctant to embrace change."

Timothy cut in before the pair could discuss the merits and flaws of monarchical government further. "I would like to give my report now, 'Your Highness.'"

Frederick whirled about, and his voice got serious. "Of course. I was informed that I probably would not believe what you have come up with. I must admit I am curious why you had brought Bonamede to Solaria… yet Krennan is suspiciously absent."

"Krennan is in custody with Kiros Knight Justin Feroz," Timothy stated simply, getting right to the point. "The two of us are waiting for you and the Kiros monarch to negotiate a joint prosecuting case."

Frederick blinked. "Cooperating with a Kiros? That might not be good for your career. Especially considering how close we are to success."

Timothy shrugged. "The more allies we have, the better, especially when they are 'the enemy.' The case against Krennan would appear considerably stronger if two hated races are willing to put aside their differences to bring him to justice."

Frederick weighed that point, and finally agreed. "Yes... perhaps that would be. The Kiros ruler is not always a terribly rational man, but I think I could convince him that cooperating would be in our best interests. Did you happen to secure a copy of the top secret information that Rumil had appropriated?"

Timothy nodded, and Rumil asked in disbelief, "You don't know what happened on Baramak either?"

Frederick sulked slightly, and replied, "The Knighthood has deemed that I do not need to be privy to the events of the Baramak Slaughter. It is also quite doubtful that anyone has been able to piece together exactly what happened. Too many people in power would like to forget it ever happened at all. I've been assembling what little I can, and Timothy has helped when he has been able."

"How does that make you any different than Krennan?" Rumil asked.

Frederick laughed. "I suppose on the surface... it doesn't. I do believe my motives are slightly different however. I want to know what happened so that I can try and ensure it never happens again. Krennan no doubt wants the information so that he can have the biggest galactic story in almost eight hundred staryears." Directing his attention back to Timothy, he asked, "So... is this all you wished to tell me? If so, then I probably should be on my way... as much as I tried to avoid it, there is some extensive paperwork that requires my hand."

Timothy nodded. The two Solarians clasped arms again, and Frederick said, "Be safe, my friend. I notice that you are also shielding our friend's aura from detection. I would suggest you continue to do so. There are elements in this society that probably would seek to actually harm her if they were to discover it."

"I shall do so," Timothy replied. "May you stay well, Frederick."

"I assume I shall see you next cycle?"

Timothy sighed dejectedly, and replied, "I'm rather obligated to be there."

When the Solarian monarch left Timothy's apartment, Rumil observed, "I take it you two are rather good friends?"

Timothy nodded slightly. "We've known each other since we were toddlers, and we've both had to fight legitimacy issues to get where we are. It's formed a close working bond of sorts."

"Am I privy to knowing what that working bond is?"

Timothy smirked knowingly, and answered, "I think you already know. You are a bright girl after all."

"So, what's going on next cycle that you have to attend?"

"The first day of Bryan Honore's ten-cycle in the Line of the Prophets festival. The entire book is read, then there is a feast and a ball. It's rather boring, tedious… and tradition."

"Ah… I'm sorry you have to be put through that."

Timothy smirked evilly, "I'd be more worried about yourself, since you will be attending as well. Frederick put it well; there are elements in this society that can be very dangerous, and they don't like outsiders. It would be best for your continued health to stay where I can see you."

Chapter Fourteen

Rumil was somewhat surprised to be awakened the following morning – or what passed for morning in the underground city – by Celine. The Solarian woman was looking down upon Rumil expectantly, holding two large plastic bags that appeared to contain some form of clothing.

"I was going to wake you up, dear, but you looked so peaceful that I just couldn't gather up the courage to do so," Celine remarked happily.

Rubbing her eyes of the enigmatic yellow crust that formed in them, a phenomenon that modern science had yet to explain to her satisfaction, Rumil asked sleepily, "Where is Timothy?"

"My son is in his office preparing for his recitation. He didn't get much practice, and he needs to make sure that he doesn't make any glaring mistakes. Here, I think I was able to find some dresses in this Annor-forsaken cave that are tall enough for you."

"Preparing for his recitation?" Rumil queried. "Why does he need to do that?"

"Didn't you know? The readers recite the passage they've been assigned by memory. But don't worry about Timothy, he shall be fine. He always is. You, on the other hand, need to get ready, and we don't have much time before the ceremony starts."

Rumil sat up in the bed, and tiredly pushed the two thin blankets off her. She finally seemed to notice the garment bags that Celine was holding. "What is in there?"

Celine pursed her lips, then repeated, "Dresses, dear. Fortunately, I was able to remember quite adequately how tall you were, and that Givni, the best tailor in Solaria, had fashioned some 'un-Solarian' sizes over the last couple of ten-cycles. However, I'm not sure which one would look better on you… or if they're even close enough to your body shape and size. So, you really need to get out of bed in case the tailor needs to do considerable work."

Finally succumbing to Celine's insistence, Rumil grabbed the garment bag in Celine's left hand, and mumbled, "What time is it?"

"It is 5.38 ET," Celine replied. "I know that it is early, but the ceremony begins at 8.00 ET, and I know how long it takes me to get ready for a public event. I have discovered that some things are universal among women of all races."

"Not for me," Rumil snorted.

"Well, I can tell. I doubt you've spent much time on tidying yourself up, but this is a special occasion, and we can't do Timothy a disservice arriving looking anything less than our best. Now hurry up and try on those dresses… the stylist is waiting for us in the living area."

Rumil was about to ask what a professional stylist was doing in Timothy's apartment, but finally decided that it was pointless to keep arguing. Examining the blue garment bags in her hand ruefully, the hacker sighed, and slipped into the bathroom to try it on for size.

As it happened, each bag contained three dresses of different colors and styles. Thus, it took almost half a tenth-cycle just to choose one. From there, Celine hurried Rumil and herself to the stylists waiting in the living area.

Two Solarians, a woman and a man, had set up two of Timothy's dining chairs in the center of the living area next to a collapsible stand, where several pairs of hair clippers and a small salon's worth of shampoos, conditioners, and gels were waiting for their clients. The man, with black hair and glittering silver streaks that shimmered when his head turned, drummed his right index finger on his chin, and said, "I shall take the Arcadian girl, Lucianna. I suppose I shall have to trust you with Madam Honore."

"Yes, Ihrman," answered Lucianna, the bright-eyed, red-haired woman. "If you would, madam?" she then asked Celine, motioning towards the chair in front of her.

Ihrman waited for about a tick, then snapped toward Rumil, "Well, hurry up, girl. Judging from what I see in front of me, it is going to take some time to make you into someone fit for the celebration, so we cannot dally. Take your seat, please."

Almost in a daze, Rumil complied. She wasn't even fully awake yet, and was already getting badgered by complete strangers. Ihrman ran his slender fingers through Rumil's hair, and sighed wistfully. "Such beautiful hair, yet it has been neglected for so long."

Rumil retorted, "Well, in my current line of work, function takes precedence over fashion. A simple gathered tail is all I've needed." Then she added with false sweetness, "I certainly hope it hasn't been damaged beyond repair."

Ihrman didn't appear to notice the sarcasm. "No worries, I know just what will suit you, and it shouldn't take terribly long to do, either.

Lucianna, may I have the grade-5 strength cleansing shampoo?"

It took a tenth-cycle for Ihrman to sculpt Rumil's hair into something that he deemed satisfactory, and even then, he wasn't terribly happy about it. "I really do not like being rushed… my work feels so incomplete that way," he bemoaned. "However, there are other things that I need to do besides your hair, and they must be attended to as well."

Rumil wasn't about to admit it out loud, but she was actually beginning to enjoy being pampered. It had been a long time since she had allowed herself the privilege of a professional treatment, being somewhat wary of them since her days as a dancer. However, the atmosphere of this treatment felt so different that she had very little trouble distancing this makeover from her old life.

The stylist had taken to giving her feet a massage and pedicure, using a sweet-smelling lotion that had the appearance of pink mud, then applying a wooden file to her cuticles. He then gave similar attention to her hands, and once that was done, reached for the makeup kit on the stand, only to stop thoughtfully.

Finally, Ihrman dabbed a splotch on her forehead over a small scar that she had received a few staryears back in an unfortunate accident with a broken piece of flying glass. He stopped thoughtfully again, and applied a lip gloss, a light dusting of eyelid color, and a slight hint of rose color to her cheeks. "Well… I certainly had expected to take longer on your makeup, but I fear that any more would detract from your natural radiance," he stated in honest wonder. "I suppose that's good; it'll give me time to make the final adjustments to your hair that I wanted to do…"

Then Ihrman caught a look at Rumil's wrists. "Oh dear… now *that* will take some work. Lucianna, do me a favor and hand me the dense covering cream, preferably the 'sand cream' color…"

When Timothy finally emerged from his office room, Celine, now fully dressed for the celebration, quickly imposed herself in his path and started to push him back, away from the living area. "Your guest is changing in there, and it would be extremely impolite to walk in on her. You know that."

Rather than argue, knowing it to be a fruitless endeavor, Timothy shook his head, and obeyed, but apparently not quickly enough for Celine's tastes, as she continued to push at his back as they retreated.

Fifteen ticks later, the blonde woman emerged from the guest bathroom, drawing an amazed gasp from Celine. Rumil spun around slowly, nervously showing off her ice blue backless dress, two thin straps on the front tied around her neck. The skirt was long, hiding her feet, and creating a small train behind her. White satin gloves gave a little color to the skin tone on her bare arms, and her normally long and straight hair had been given some lighter highlights, and curled up into an intricate bun along the back of her head, where two deep brown pins held it in place.

"Oh, my dear, you are absolutely exquisite," Celine marveled, waving down the hallway and giving Timothy permission to return.

Timothy did not sound quite as impressed, but his compliment still appeared sincere. "You look very good."

Celine turned to her son, and smiled, "Did you just compliment someone, Timmy?" Her eyes twinkling as she turned back to Rumil, the woman added, "Are you sure you aren't Solarian, Rumil dear? All we need to do is convince the right people…"

Timothy dropped his head into his left hand, and muttered with worn exasperation, "You're not going to let this go, are you, mother?"

"You are a vibrant young man who has been suspiciously void of a nice and charming woman to give you proper balance," Celine chided playfully. "Your father and I were married one staryear younger than you are, and we were on the late side in that regard."

As the two Solarians bantered about Timothy's lack of a love life, Rumil took the opportunity to examine her escorts to the celebration. Celine's brown hair had been trimmed into a layered mane that slid like one long wave down her shoulders and stopping at the small of her back. Dressed in a modest white dress that covered almost every inch of her skin save her neckline and wrists, Celine looked the perfect part of a Solarian noblewoman, pretty, prim, and proper.

Timothy was wearing what Rumil assumed to be a Knight's dress uniform, which superficially resembled his field uniform except that the armor panels were thinner and didn't seem to cover quite as much surface area. There was also a brown sash on his left shoulder, but she was barely able to tell its color due to the multitude of golden, silver, and bronze pins attached to it. Instead of his helmet, there was a thick gold circlet around his forehead, only visible across his temple as he had hidden the rest under his hair. She also noticed that on the right shoulder plate, there was a series of six gold bars, and four gleaming golden stars above them, the rank indicators that he never wore on his field armor.

Finally, Timothy took a deep breath, and stated, "As much as I would love to continue this discussion, it is customary for the families of the Knighthood to arrive early for the recitation. Thus, it would probably be prudent to leave now."

Celine nodded, "Yes… I should return to the manor myself. Poor Ihrman and Lucianna, I drag them here, and now I'm going to use them as my excuse for not being present during breakfast."

"Just be careful teleporting back," Timothy reminded. "My father is not senseless. If he detects your entrance…"

"Niles is already at the temple hall. He spent the night there with Priest Hightower, probably discussing Horace's 'liberal thinking' as of late," Celine said with a snort. "Sometimes my dear husband cannot see the most obvious of things." The Solarian woman shook her head slightly as if clearing her mind of the thought. "Anyway, I must bid you all farewell, and I shall see you at the temple hall. Peace be with you." Once again, Celine left the apartment without waiting for any parting pleasantries.

"Shall we be going?" Timothy asked, motioning towards the exit.

Rumil stood patiently, then her eyebrows raised questioningly as Timothy made no move. Finally the Knight sighed, and added, "It is custom for the lady to leave first. Normally, I would not care, but on days such as these, it is better to simply follow the tradition rather than cause a stir."

"Oh!" Rumil yelped in surprise, then quickly apologized as she stepped forward, initially stumbling on the ice blue high heels. Timothy righted her quickly, and Rumil hoped that he hadn't seen the flush through the makeup on her cheeks. "It's been a while since I've worn shoes like these," Rumil muttered sheepishly. Fortunately, it didn't take her long to regain the skill, soon moving with the same grace that she normally possessed.

Perkins was waiting in the hall as they left the apartment. "I saw your mother leave, Timothy. I keep telling you, she does not look like…" His jaw dropped when he got his first clear look at Rumil.

Rumil's eyebrows lifted in amusement, and she asked innocently, "Is something wrong, Perkins?"

"I think I've just seen a host of the heavens," Perkins gaped, his eyes drifting downward slightly, focusing on the bust line of Rumil's dress. The gown obviously did an impressive job of enhancing that quality of her physique.

Once again, Rumil replied with false decorum, "I don't know where. After all, it just us three in the hall." She looked around as if trying to find a phantom or some other stranger, conveniently displaying the rest of her dress and figure to the flabbergasted Solarian man.

When she faced him again, he was almost drooling. "I know who is in the hall…" Perkins gaped. "I just… you… look beautiful, miss."

Rumil smiled at the compliment, inwardly somewhat revolted by Perkins's reaction. She had seen that type of expression far too many times in her life, proving to her that Solarians weren't nearly as upright and pure of heart as some believed.

Timothy placed his hand on Rumil's left shoulder, and pulled her back against him almost possessively. "Perkins, we are on a tight schedule. I'm sure you will have plenty of time to gape when we return."

Rumil batted her eyelashes, and replied, "You aren't attending the ceremony, Perkins?"

Perkins shook his head, serving as both a negative response as well as clearing his thoughts. "No, I'll be attending the celebration, just not the same one as our Knight friend. I'm not permitted into the 'distinguished' noble gathering."

"Oh… well that hardly seems fair," Rumil mused, her innocent tone starting to disappear.

"We can discuss this later," Timothy interjected, "but as I said, we are on a tight schedule. We must leave now." With that, Timothy led Rumil down the hall to the lift, softly chiding. "You didn't need to encourage him."

"I was just having a little fun," Rumil replied. "Besides, after your bland reaction, I needed to make sure that Celine wasn't just being nice."

"Would you have rather have had me wax poetically about how your beauty compares to the solar winds as they play across the starry night?" Timothy asked. "I had assumed you were above such empty compliments."

Rumil pursed her lips as the lift stopped at the lobby floor and they proceeded out to Timothy's hover, trying to decide just what Timothy had been saying. Did he really think that she looked that nice, or had he simply thrown it out for the sake of argument? It wasn't always easily to tell what Timothy was thinking just from the words he said and the tone he used.

"Would you *please* get in?" Timothy asked from inside the hover.

For the second time in the last five ticks, Rumil felt herself color, and hurried into the vehicle, lifting her skirt in order to step into the passenger seat. The hover began to hum, and lifted off the roadway. Timothy geared it forward, and they were finally on their way.

"The 'nobles' have their own ceremony that the 'common' folk aren't permitted into?" Rumil asked disparagingly. "Talk about archaic. You know, I'd like to invite your society to the Staryear 3421."

Timothy glowered, then answered, "Yes, we know how the Arcadian tradition values fair and equal treatment. The next time a low-level worker is turned away from a high-brow eatery, I'd advise you to keep your own words in mind."

"Are you suggesting that the medieval caste system you Solarians practice is no different from the rest of the galaxy?" Rumil scoffed.

"It's all a difference of how the power is distributed. Rather than power by blood, it is power by credits," Timothy replied. "Money buys influence, which buys special treatment." Then the Knight frowned, and added, "But you're right… things on Solaria need to change. Hopefully, the chance to do so will come soon."

Neither of them spoke the rest of the short trip from Timothy's apartment to the Solarian Temple to the north side of Centris, where the majority of the Knighthood manors resided.

There was only one road leading into the upper-class section of Centris, and it was heavily guarded by a small regiment of Solarian soldiers manning a checkpoint, complete with roadblock and sentry house. They quickly identified Timothy, and thus his hover barely had to stop before the gates were lifted.

Within half a TackMet, the main road began to branch off several times, leading to the various family estates, although only a few small mansions were clearly visible from the main road. Directly ahead was their goal, the three brown brick spires visible over the next rise signifying the Solarian Temple of the Knighthood.

Once over the rise, Rumil was able to see that the spires were actually a small part of the massive sprawl of the temple, its seven different wings connected by a long circular hall along the outer edge, so that the entire structure resembled a large spoked wheel. Several stone sculptures of giant Solarians, fully armored with their hands holding long swords in front of them, stood sentry surrounded the temple, their making so elaborate that it almost seemed like they would come to life against any perceived threat.

They had to walk past the hulking statues after parking in the lots across the roadway from the temple, and they looked just as detailed up close as they did from afar.

"Each of these represents the patriarchs of seven of the families of the Knighthood," Timothy explained as she had stopped to admire the intricate handiwork.

"I thought there were eight families considered of Knighthood status," Rumil added.

"There is. The temple itself is for the Honore family," Timothy replied. "It's where the shrines to the family 'patriarch' Bryan Honore resides."

Rumil had caught the subtle sarcastic tone that Timothy had used when referring to Bryan. "Something tells me there's more to this story."

Timothy smirked, and said, "You see, Bryan never had any children before he was killed. His only relatives were his two sisters, who were given a little exception to tradition, and were allowed to keep their family names. Thus, Bryan Honore really isn't the patriarch of the family, but it's awfully convenient to believe it so. It helps secure my family's position as one of the eight simply on tradition."

"So the family that was questioning your legitimacy is somewhat of a fraud itself." Rumil smirked. "Talking with you makes me wonder if there are any redeeming traits of Solarian society."

"It had its place… but it is quickly becoming obsolete. Our rigidity is what is slowly causing our downfall. Without a change, the Solarians, the Kiros, and all we stand for will fade away into history, and eventually be forgotten."

"This is a bad thing?"

Timothy almost glared, and replied, "While our society may be flawed, the pillars of the faith we hold are honorable, and dedicated to improving the way we live. The battles we fought, and the trials and errors we made should never just be dismissed like a deluded myth, eventually to be discarded as flights of fancy." Timothy turned to the temple. "Let's keep going. I'm probably going to get some grief for not being perfectly on time as it is."

The pair entered the circular hall from the wing facing the main roadway, passing through a huge set of double doors, etched with a grand representation of who Rumil assumed was Bryan Honore. Only a couple of older men were in the entry, evidently retired members of the Knighthood, and they exchanged pleasantries with Timothy before the young Knight motioned for Rumil to proceed further inside.

The wing they had entered was either new, or recently renovated. A springy red carpet led down the length of the straight wing, and on each side, walls of fiberboard occasionally framed contemporary sliding doors. "These are study halls in which priests will often go to analyze and restore older texts," Timothy explained as one such religious leader suddenly burst out in front of them with a large tower of books blocking his vision. The man was dressed in a long, flowing, formal robe, the top half hanging about his waist, suggesting that he had been trying to sneak in some study before attending the recitations.

Finally, they approached another older wooden door with carvings of various scenes, most of them apparently battles judging from the bared weapons and conflict etched into the surface. Timothy paused dramatically before he pushed the door open, and motioned with his free arm for Rumil to continue on.

This portion of the wing was similar to the first, in that it really was nothing more than one long hall. However, it looked considerably older than the previous, the floor was stone rather than wooden paneling, and the walls were made of brick as opposed to the more modern fiberwall.

Hanging from the brick were a series of canvas paintings and the occasional sculpture. The figures depicted in the artwork looked somewhat similar to Solarians, but carried significant differences. The features were even more delicate in appearance, their frames thinner than normally carried on the slight Erani race.

"This is the Hall of History," Timothy declared softly. "These works depict scenes and characters from the most devastating war in history, the Archangel War."

Rumil had heard of the mythological war between the higher and lower planes of existence. The Galactic Staryear Standard was based on the acronym AW, or After War, in which 0 AW marked the supposed end to the brutal conflict.

It was an age shrouded by the passing of time. Every race of the Alliance had some story about catastrophic events that ravaged their homeworlds at that time in history, and the Ferian even claimed that theirs was the site of a battle between the planes. On some planets, there were indeed scars of mysterious and ancient warfare, obviously fought with weaponry that modern technology still couldn't match.

However, the truth of that war still was up for debate. Rumil remarked, "Some would argue that it wasn't really a war between heavenly and hellish powers, but simply a conflict between now forgotten and highly advanced civilizations, their awesome power causing the unenlightened predecessors of modern times to think they were some sort of gods."

Timothy smirked, and answered Rumil's thoughts. "Erani history would suggest a little of both. The angelic host of Annor had mortal progeny on the material plane called the Se-Lan, who were forced from their ancestral home of Mydor after the final battle of the Archangel War. Eventually, they made their way to Kiros, where they intermingled with the native population, giving rise to what was the Erani, now split into the Solarian and Kiros factions."

Timothy then continued, "Meanwhile, the demonic hordes from the lower planes gave rise to the Democs, half-demon kind which mysteriously disappeared after the Archangel War. No one is terribly sure just what happened to them."

Rumil would countermand the suggestion, but knew that several independent researchers had discovered remains of strange humanoid beings from the time of the supposed Archangel War that didn't appear to coincide either genetically or physically with any existing race. Many mused that they were specimens of what the ancient peoples would label the Democs.

From there, she looked at the artwork; glorious and somewhat Romantic images of battles from the Archangel War. Rumil scoffed at those, thinking that if the wars of the past were anything like the wars of modern history that there would be very little glorious about them.

The sculptures did grab her attention, however. They were full-body sculptures from marbleized rock, most of them of cloaked beings with blank faces. Timothy noted her attention, and stated, "Those are representations of the Archangels. Their faces are blank because conventional belief states that no one who looked into the eyes of those heavenly beings lived to tell the tale. Their essences were so pure and powerful that no mortal could hope to survive their direct gaze."

The first robed Archangel carried what appeared to be some sort of stringed instrument that resembled a lyre, but with squared edges rather than rounded. "That is Gabrin, the messenger of the Archangels. He is often the one that is claimed to have delivered the visions of the future to the Erani prophets," Timothy said then turned Rumil around.

The one across from Gabrin held a book under both arms and had a crown with five prongs on his head. "That is Mato, the lord among the heavenly host, leader of the Archangels. He was the one who plotted the strategy and was the wisest of the angelic kind."

The final two sculptures were three Tacks beyond the first two. The statue on the right held a swallow, a weapon with a blade extending from both ends of the hilt, as well as a large towering shield that was almost as tall as the statue's body.

Timothy gestured to it, and said, "That is Mican, the general of the hosts of Annor. He was the one who led the armies onto the field of battle, and is considered to be the most powerful of the Archangels. Solarians believe that the essence of Mican still exists on the material plane, to be born in a mortal body in preparation for the opening of the Second Gate."

The final sculpture looked nothing like the first three. The figure was slouched over, as if slinking stealthily. It carried a menacing curved dagger in its hand, and where the other faces were completely blank, a pair of scowling, narrowed eyes could be seen, radiating pure malice.

Timothy exhaled, and said with a hint of disgust, "That is Zaal. He is also known as the Defiler and the Treasoner, among other things. Zaal at one time held the position that Mato now resides, but in a time before recorded history, decided to betray the God of Creation, and tried to seize Annor for his own. He roused the chaotic demon kind to be his army, and that was what led to the Archangel War. The one-on-one battles he had with Mican are considered to have been the most devastating ever known. Planets were said to have collapsed and disintegrated under the power of their clashes. Some believe that Solaria became what it is now because the two engaged in combat here in a time before record."

Suddenly, another Solarian emerged into the hall, a red-haired man dressed in a manner similar to Timothy, but with about half the number of pins on his sash. "Oh... you did arrive," the Knight commented, looking at Timothy. "We must hurry, your father wants all the presenters in the main temple immediately."

Timothy nodded, "Rumil, this is Emmitt Fransisca. Emmitt, Rumil Bonamede. He was the one who gave us some... assistance... while on Amat."

Emmitt whirled around quickly then motioned for Timothy to keep quiet. He whispered, "Could you *please* not incriminate me in the middle of the Noble Temple? Besides, all I did was conveniently look the other way." Finally, Emmitt addressed Rumil with a genial smile. "So... this is the hacker that brought down the mighty Gregor Krennan. If I did not know Timothy as well as I do, I would have suspected now that his decisions would have been influenced by more than just his mission."

Timothy frowned disapprovingly at Emmitt, and grated, "Did you not say that my father wanted the presenters immediately? Then let's not waste any more time."

Without further ado, the three approached the large arched double doors, carved with the image of a Solarian man, his arms extended as if welcoming visitors. With each Knight pushing on one door, they motioned for Rumil to walk across the threshold first.

As she stepped inside the temple proper, she felt like she had suddenly been thrown two thousand staryears into the past. The mosaic floor work was done completely in black, gray, brown, and red stones, not seeming to carry any set pattern. There were four columns and thirty rows of finished wooden pews, with padded cushions covered by what appeared to be red velvet. Twenty Tacks above, a series of flying buttresses merely added to the gigantic feel of the temple. She could see the holes in the ceiling that indicated the placement of the three towering steeples that she had spotted on their way to the temple.

In the rear portion of the temple, there was a dais surrounded by a four steps covered in red carpet. Behind the dais there was a large looming statue of a figure like the one on the door outside the temple, and in the center was a Tack-high altar once likely meant for sacrificial purposes, but fortunately it looked like it hadn't been used for some time.

High Commander Niles Honore didn't make any comment towards Timothy's arrival – not out of any courtesy, but because it appeared he was engaged in a very one-sided conversation with a brown-haired Solarian man in white robes with brown and gold trim, signifying his status within the Solarian priesthood. The priest himself seemed quite uninterested in what Niles had to say, but the elder Knight didn't seem to realize this

Timothy strode purposefully towards the raised dais that Niles and the priest were on, and said flatly, "Horace has many things to do, father. Perhaps you could leave him in peace to do them?"

Niles whirled about at the sound of the voice, and snapped back, "It's about time you got here. And it is High Priest Hightower, Timothy. I suggest you show proper decency to his status."

"He shows proper decency in his actions, rather than his words, High Commander," Horace retorted softly. "But he is correct. As much as I would love to debate the merits of maintaining the status quo, I do have many things to prepare for the celebration."

Niles's face turned into a disgusted scowl just as Rumil and Emmitt approached the dais as well. The elder Knight pointed at the blonde woman, and accused, "What is she doing here?"

At that point, Rumil noticed how intimidating the High Commander could be up close. Despite being a handful of Tackems shorter than her, he cut an imposing figure made all the more disconcerting by the heavy, archaic dress uniform he wore, consisting of broad, nearly angular shoulder pads covered with a full two-piece russet brown suit. A red sash was barely visible through a blanket of metallic medals and pips, and a heavy woven cape of the same dark red color hung fixed to his shoulders, likely the proper style from when he had been initiated into the Knighthood.

Timothy retorted calmly, "She is my guest. It is not proper form to invite my guests with me to distinguished events such as this? First you berate me for not displaying proper decency, now you berate me for displaying such decency. Would you please make up your mind?"

Niles cheeks turned violently at the unsubtle jab. Shaking a finger violently at Timothy, the elder Knight said, "You think you are so smart, don't you? Keep in mind that you are not in command of the Knighthood, and you do not arbitrarily decide what is proper and what is not."

"Not yet, anyway," Horace added slyly, a smug grin starting to play on his features.

With a barely contained growl, Niles stomped away, bellowing, "You and Knight Fransisca have five ticks to meet me in the priest's study. While you may ruin our livelihood in the coming staryears, I intend to make sure one tradition stays pure until then." The elder Knight then disappeared into the study behind the dais, slamming the wooden door violently as he did so.

"I apologize for our High Commander's rudeness, madam," Horace said graciously to Rumil with a bow. "His manner as of the last six staryears is that of a man under siege. He has seen two young, and somewhat unconventional, thinkers take the positions of High Priest and King, and can clearly see his son following that path as the successor to his position. That sort of stress rarely brings out the best in people."

"It doesn't bother me any, High Priest," Rumil said politely, trying to be as genial as possible. The last thing she needed was to make more enemies. "I'm used to dealing with that sort of behavior."

With a nod to Rumil, Horace quickly turned his attention to Timothy. "Frederick has informed me of your ambitious plan. Cooperating with the Kiros in a common cause… quite ingenious. I can sense the seeds for a new future free of this old and meaningless conflict taking root."

Emmitt looked somewhat nervous, and glared at Timothy accusingly. "Cooperating with the Kiros? I didn't hear anything about this."

"Does the idea bother you, Knight Fransisca?" Horace asked.

Emmitt sighed, and said, "I suppose I should say it doesn't

surprise me. I would like to warn you that many in this society would find the idea of assisting the Kiros in any way, even in a common goal like prosecuting Gregor Krennan, to be quite unfavorable."

"I am sure they would, but I do believe that it is time that our peoples proceed beyond the petty squabbles that have tainted our true mission. Both the Kiros and the Solarians seek to end any threat from the Gates of Bannor. Our division merely weakens our resolve and our efforts."

Emmitt clearly was not comfortable discussing these things in such a public arena. "I think I shall report to the High Commander. With your pardon, High Priest." The Knight bowed slightly, and retreated to the study.

"Poor Emmitt. He agrees with what I say, but in the back of his mind, he still feels like he is being somewhat treacherous to think so," Horace explained, and Rumil initially didn't realize he was talking to her until he continued, "I am sorry that you appear to have been dragged into what might be a somewhat ugly time in our history, Miss Bonamede. This final transition of power from the old generation to the new might not be particularly smooth."

"I am just glad that you Solarians are slowly deciding to join the rest of the Galaxy," Rumil answered.

Horace laughed, as if amused by the statement in a way. Once he had composed himself again, he said to Timothy, "Perhaps you should join your father in the study, Timothy. Fear not, I shall keep Miss Bonamede company until you return."

*   *   *   *   *

Timothy did not return before the ceremony started, but Rumil had run into Celine in the reception area of the temple... or more appropriately, Celine had hunted Rumil down. Thus, the young hacker found herself sitting next to Celine while the procession of presenters lined along the back of the dais, with Horace standing in front of the altar.

The High Priest raised his hands to the sky, and said, "Welcome humble followers of the Creator God, and in those who follow the words of the first Solarian Prophet."

The assembly then replied, "May his words give us strength."

Horace lowered his hands, and said, "The story of the first

Solarian Prophet is a tale of joy, a tale of tragedy, and a tale of warning. On this day, we honor the man who received the vision of the Creator God, and the sacrifice he was willing to take for the sake of the betterment of all."

Horace then turned slightly to the row of Knights who were to present the text. "Knight Emmitt Fransisca will begin with the recitation of the Book of Bryan Honore. If you may, Knight Fransisca."

Emmitt bowed respectfully, and took Horace's position after the High Priest had stepped aside. Taking a deep breath, the Knight said with as firm a voice as he could manage:

I had my first vision when I was merely sixteen staryears old. At the time, I had no idea what it meant... was it just a dream? Even then, I knew it could not be a dream... it felt like something more.

The hand of a warrior, but none yet born, and a weapon for that hand, one that no other hand could wield. It made no sense... until I let myself believe. Believe in the visions I had received, and believe in my ability to complete them.

I had my success... the weapon was made... the Star Smasher had been forged. From the toughest Durium and finest craftsmanship my dearest friend Julius could manage, it was made according to the vision I had in my head, the vision that had become my sole purpose.

Emmitt eventually came to stop, and the next in line took his place, and so on, through the story of the battle on Solaria, and the sealing of the first gate. Through their voices, Bryan Honore bemoaned the death of his friend, Julius Feroz, and his inability to stop his friend from his final act.

Rumil started to daydream, but it struck her as a very odd thing to daydream about. It was as if she was seeing some sort of battle from the eyes of one of its participants. She was on a ledge in front of a pair of old, rotting wooden doors that apparently led to a central chamber. With her was an Erani man in ancient combat armor and long black hair. Suddenly, the long-haired man grabbed an intricate swallow from her hip, and shoved her to the ground roughly, charging into the chamber. There was a rumble, then a loud explosion that jolted Rumil to full alertness.

Rumil slowly turned her head to look around the assembly, wondering if anyone had seen her nod off. Celine put her hand on Rumil's arm, silently imploring Rumil to settle down. Meanwhile, Rumil's eyes met Timothy's, who was looking back with her with mild concern.

> *But I waste my time. This is not a book of the past... the past can be known in any history book. This is a book of the future...*

Thus, eight different speakers went through the entire book, and Rumil continually was assuaged with frequent daydreams... images of what she was beginning to realize were images from Bryan Honore's life, seen from his eyes as if she were in the prophet's place.

While it initially confused her, Rumil decided that the Knights were utilizing their telepathic talents to give a picture to the words they were reciting. That is, until Timothy took his place as the final speaker.

Timothy's voice was soft, but it carried a power that carried throughout the entire temple. He didn't seem at all pleased to be doing what he was doing, but then again, Timothy never really showed much enthusiasm for anything. Even as the book reached its climax, his voice never wavered:

> *I have seen the Second Gate. The ancient war that decimated the Se-Lan's ancestral home has returned for another battle. From the Gate, a lieutenant of Zaal, an Arch-Demon, shall rise with his hordes to do battle. Ichor stains his clawed hands, blood flows like spittle from his mouth. No mortal being could hope to stand before this creature's wrath.*
>
> *When all seems lost, on the moment that hope begins to falter, the time of our greatest triumph is at hand. We are not abandoned by the heavens, we are not left to our own devices. Even though the heavens are sealed from us, they watch... and are prepared.*
>
> *The general of the Annor host, knowing such a time would arise, gave himself to the mortal coil, to be reborn for this event, to do battle with the Arch-Demon. This is what I have seen... this is what I know to be true.*

Timothy's voice stopped… but the images burned into Rumil's mind didn't. She did indeed see the Arch-Demon towering over the battlefield, its skin the color of blood, black slime dripping from its talons, its mouth more resembling racks of knives then a set of teeth.

It glared in her direction, as if it could see she was there. It reached out with one stained hand, drawing closer to her. She barely withheld a scream of terror as she recognized the beast as similar to the one that she had seen in her head outside the Gate Memorial on Solaria… the same sort of monster that had haunted her nightmares as long as she could remember.

But before the creature reached her, there was a sudden flash of bright light that completely enveloped her entire vision in its blinding radiance. A strange being, covered in brilliantly gleaming armor and metallic, serrated wings emerged from the light, then imposed itself between herself and the demon.

The image then shifted to a large assembly of what appeared to be the entire nobility of Solaria and Kiros, standing at attention before the shimmering metallic being and the Gate. The being hovered above them, hand outstretched, before bringing them together with a resounding slap… then the planet itself seemed to tremble. Fissures split the ground, hot magma bursting into the sky, scalding any beneath it. There was the sound of agonized screams in her ears, and the smell of burning flesh in her nostrils. Fortunately, any suffering was short-lived, for there was another blast that seemed to tear the very planet apart in one catastrophic explosion… then there was nothing…

"Rumil!" Celine shouted in panic, shaking the blonde woman back to the real world. "Dear, what is wrong?"

Rumil was trembling in terror, cold sweat pouring down her face, her breathing labored as if she had just run twenty TackMets. Eventually, Rumil began to whimper fearfully, "There's more… there's more… to the story…"

The crowd had fortunately dispersed and returned to the reception area, so very few witnessed the almost catatonic state that had overwhelmed Rumil. It wasn't until Timothy picked Rumil up and shook her that she appeared to snap out whatever was terrifying her.

She buried her head in Timothy's chest, barely restraining the tears that threatened to liberally pour out of her eyes. "I… saw things… like it was… more to the story…"

Timothy's voice was surprisingly soothing, betraying his normally stoic character. "It's all right now…"

"It was terrible… what did I see?" Rumil sobbed.

"I don't know," Timothy answered compassionately. *But I might have a guess…*

Rumil suddenly lifted her head, blinking in confusion. It had been one of Timothy's thoughts, but the tone it had carried suggested that it was not one he had intended to share. "You have a guess… about what I saw?"

Timothy stiffened nervously, his face once again going flat, as if closely guarding his thoughts and emotions. "No… it's nothing, Rumil. Don't worry about it just now. Once you calm down, we can talk about it more fully."

Rumil nodded blankly, thankful that he didn't want to press the issue. She wasn't sure if she wanted to bring it up again, now or ever.

Meanwhile, Niles Honore was watching from the doorway, his face growing increasingly grim with each word that escaped Rumil's lips. This situation would have to be dealt with… quickly.

Chapter Fifteen

"Are you sure you're up to this?" Timothy asked Rumil as they stood outside the entrance to the ballroom of the Honore family estate.

"I need to do something… *anything*… to get my mind off what happened earlier," Rumil replied. "The more I think about it, the less I want to know."

"Well… I hate to disappoint you, but there isn't going to be much happening in there. The ball is nothing more than a slew of nobles moving in a set pattern of steps. It's rather boring."

Rumil sighed. "You have to attend this anyway. What would your contemporaries think if you were absent because of me?"

Timothy grabbed Rumil's shoulders, and said with a surprising sincerity, "Right now, I am not concerned with how certain people will view my absence. I've skipped this ball plenty of times in the past, so I doubt it would surprise anyone."

Rumil pursed her lips then replied slowly, "I don't want to be left in my thoughts right now. I need a diversion, and right now this ball is the best chance for me to find one."

Timothy knew this might be a potential nightmare, especially if she had another one of the psionic spikes that had become quite frequent since arriving on Solaria. The last one had been so sudden and intense that it had taken a combined effort on the part of Celine, Horace, Frederick, and himself to shield the surge from the rest of the assembly.

However, it appeared that Rumil was quite set on attending, and so with a defeated sigh, he said, "As you wish…" Timothy then pushed open the doors leading the ballroom, and extended his arm for Rumil to enter.

The ballroom was expansive to say the least. She had seen athletic arenas smaller than the room that the Honore family held events in. Like the Temple of the Nobility, the ballroom had an extremely high ceiling that made it seem even larger than it already was. About thirty intricate lighting units similar to silver-colored chandeliers hung from the towering roof, bathing the entire room in a soft white glow.

The dancing floor was a polished mural of painted images of Solarian history, spiraling outward from the center of the floor, the latest events lying at the edge just before the small step that led to the rest of the ballroom.

At the moment, there was no one on the ballroom floor itself, the inhabitants either at the refreshments table, or seated around several other white tables positioned in a circle around the dancing floor. Along the north wall was a raised stage, where a group of Solarian men were preparing some form of musical entertainment. Solarian music appeared to be heavy in percussion instruments, as she could see no fewer than seven different drums on the stage in a large arc around the rest of the instruments.

Celine was waiting just inside the door like a good and proper hostess. "Oh, Rumil dear, I'm surprised you actually came. Are you sure you're up to this?"

Rumil nodded with a slight, weary smile. "It's for the best. Besides, what else did I have to do with Timothy watching me every single tick?"

Celine chortled, "He's just trying to watch out for you. Over-protectiveness does tend to be a Solarian trait." She then added in a conspiratorial whisper, "Besides, in your case… you can never be too careful."

Timothy's mother then looked back, to where her husband Niles was starting to take long, purposeful strides towards them, his trademark bitter scowl once again on his features.

"So now she's coming to exclusive celebration balls?" Niles snorted, pointing an accusing finger in Rumil's direction. "Since when was it tradition to invite Arcadian criminals to events of nobility? I want this… *harlot* to leave my house immediately—"

Niles demand suddenly shifted to a yelp of surprise when Timothy moved in between Rumil and Niles, seizing the older Knight by the wrist. Timothy's voice was almost an animalistic growl when he threatened, "If you demean my guest in my presence once more, I fear that I might forget your rank and position."

The idle conversation of the ballroom died into an awed silence. It had not been a secret in the least that Timothy and his father rarely saw eye to eye, and that Niles's treatment of the younger Knight bordered on abuse, but this was the first time that any of them could recall Timothy visibly and publicly reacting in kind.

Horace and Frederick quickly closed the distance while three other subordinate Knights tried to pry Timothy's grip off of Niles's wrist. Rumil doubted they'd have much luck unless Timothy released voluntarily. She had seen her Solarian escort stop an Ubek's progress cold in a similar fashion, and figured that the considerably slighter Solarian frame would not fare much better.

Fortunately, Frederick decided to utilize his own status to end the confrontation. "Knights, I would expect this sort of behavior from Initiates, not from two of my highest-ranking officers. You will cease and desist right now!"

The monarch said to Timothy, "I know that your personal feelings towards High Commander Honore are less than friendly, but he *is* your commander until further notice. I expect you act accordingly."

To Niles, he had this to say, "For a man who preaches decency, you have shown absolutely none to your son's guest. This is completely inexcusable, and I would hope that it changes… *quickly.*"

"Yes, Your Excellence," the two Knights said in unison, still glaring at each other almost murderously. Finally, Niles ended the stalemate, stomping away indignantly, apparently to chide the entertainment on the stage for taking so long to prepare. His berating apparently worked, because the music soon began, a light waltz-like tune with a low hum from the drums underlying the soft tunes of wind instruments.

Frederick then made a request to Celine, "Madam Honore, could you escort Miss Bonamede to the refreshment table? Your son, Horace, and I have business to discuss that isn't fit for public ears."

Celine bowed respectfully, and chirped, "Of course, Your Excellence. Rumil, dear, right this way."

Rumil complied, somewhat reluctantly. Something about Frederick's tone did not sound good. "I don't like this…"

"Frederick is informing Timothy that King Lionel of Kiros rejected the offer to present a joint case before the Galactic Judicial Council. Gregor Krennan was thus released last cycle," Celine explained.

"How do you know that?" Rumil asked.

The Solarian woman smiled, "I have my share of ears as well." Then she turned serious, and added, "I think it's pretty obvious what this means. Frederick will try to keep it quiet, but eventually, it'll be found out that your value here is nil. I'm sure that those three are trying to plan a way to get you out of Solaria before Niles learns this, and decides that it is time to cut his losses, and make an example of you."

Rumil glowered, and replied, "I mean no disrespect, but I am developing a significant dislike for your husband."

"That's understandable. These last few staryears have been

difficult on him. He feels that it is the Solarian tradition that makes us what we are, and to see Frederick, Horace, and Timmy apparently disregard it so… he feels like he is defending Solaria from ourselves." Celine's voice then became almost pleading. "Niles really is a decent man, if a bit old-fashioned. He's only doing what he thinks is best… even though he might only be making it worse." The Solarian woman sighed. "He doesn't see that we *need* to change. It's time for Solaria to advance beyond the castes that we have applied for ourselves, as sacrilegious as that may sound, but adhering to policies and traditions that are hundreds of staryears old, leaving us behind while the rest of the galaxy moves forward, just doesn't make any sense."

"Whatever did you see in him in the first place?" Rumil queried.

"Well, to be brutally honest, I didn't have much of a choice," Celine answered with a roll of her eyes. "When my father was approached with the opportunity to be linked with the most influential family of the Knighthood, he took it without question, and thus I was bequeathed to our High Commander. I was barely four staryears at the time, so I didn't even fully understand what had happened until much later."

"You were only four staryears?" Rumil gaped.

"That was the way it was done at that time. One of the first things Niles helped to eradicate. It's rather ironic, really. When Niles was Timothy's age, he too fought tradition and the norm. He hated the idea of arranged marriages, among other things that he deemed 'meaningless' and 'antiquated.' Had it not been for my husband, it's likely that Centris's homeless camp would be no better than the filthy hovels that most Erani cities have."

Rumil's interest was even more piqued. "I just can't picture that bitter old man to ever have been a rebel."

Celine laughed. "He was. But as he got older, he began to grow attached to the ways he had fought to forge. He can't imagine the next generation dismissing what he had fought to achieve so easily, and thus became the very thing he railed against as a younger man… a slave to tradition. In some of the more peaceable moments, I find it remarkable how similar the father and son are… and how anyone could think anything but that they are related."

Rumil then smirked, that troublesome gleam in her eye. She spotted the Knighthood's High Commander sulking in the corner, apparently sharing his woes and concerns with two older men wearing similarly antiquated dress armor, likely retired Knights once under Niles

Honore's command. She then asked, "So, your husband is a slave to tradition, is he?"

"Oh indeed, bless his spirit," Celine mused.

"So, he probably really dislikes the idea of a woman taking initiative, am I right?" Meanwhile, her eyes took in every detail of the very deliberate and planned dance that various couples were just starting to engage in.

"That is a quick way to get under his skin, I suppose, but why are you asking… oh, Rumil dear… you aren't…"

Rumil grinned mischievously. "Are you going to help me, or not?"

Celine's eyes narrowed, but finally the Solarian noblewoman relented, "What do you need me to do?"

Rumil gave it some thought before replying, "Ask them if they know any music with a more energetic beat, perhaps something with some brass horns. If they do, have them wait for my signal to play it."

"Are you sure you want to antagonize my mate?" Celine asked again.

"From what I'm gathering, I don't have much more time here anyway. I might as well make the most of it."

Celine shook her head in disbelief. "You are indeed a spirited young woman. Are you *sure* there isn't *any* Solarian blood in you?"

Timothy was right; that *was* starting to get annoying. "Even if I did, Celine, I doubt anything would come of your son and me."

Celine sighed wistfully. "I'm a mother, dear. I have to try. I'll see what I can do for you, though." That said, the Solarian woman turned away, and proceeded towards the stage.

Rumil smiled, and took one more long appraising look at Niles Honore, who was still chatting with his two companions. She was definitely going to have some fun with this. Finally, she caught Niles's eye and smiled broadly, making purposeful strides towards the wall, fully aware of the elder Knight's glare.

Had Timothy been keeping his eye on Rumil, he would have noticed she was up to something, and probably would have nipped it before it had taken root. However, his full attention was on the planning phase between himself, Frederick, and Horace. The trio had taken up their meeting at one of the tables in the southeast corner, their backs turned towards the wall.

"I could give her sanctuary," Horace stated grimly, "but considering the crimes that Niles would no doubt bring against her, my influence would not hold for long."

Frederick shook his head in refusal. "That wouldn't be that great of a plan anyway. The longer she is here on Solaria, the more danger she is in. Our best chance is to slip her out after the ball."

Timothy nearly pounded the table in frustration. "If she leaves Solaria, she is as good as dead anyway. Once Krennan sniffs that she has left our sphere of influence, every hunter and assassin in her quadrant will be looking to bring her in dead or alive... preferably dead."

"I agree," Horace said. "It's also possible that we can use her duress as a defense for her actions. What Krennan is capable of is well known to anyone in the know, even in our little corner of the world."

"I know what the Adjudicates are like," Frederick insisted. "Once they realize that Krennan is out of the question, they will be looking for someone, *anyone*, to sink their claws into. Rumil is the rational target."

Timothy frowned, "I might be able to arrange that it never gets that far. I never gave that disk Rumil downloaded from Amat to Krennan. If my father knew I had it, I might be able to convince him not to press the issue."

Frederick had to keep himself from jumping out of his seat. "We haven't had much success deciphering the report, much less uncovered anything particularly damning."

Timothy smirked knowingly. "My father doesn't need to know that. Just give me the salient points, and I think I can concoct something that would deeply concern him. Besides, the fact that we have this information at all will probably give him great pause."

Horace rubbed his chin, and suggested, "Perhaps we can allow Rumil to decide what she wants to do. After all, it's her head on the block, so to speak. Surely the situation will not turn significantly dire by next cycle?"

Frederick sighed, relenting. "No, I suppose not." The monarch decided, "We can allow Rumil to hear her options. Perhaps she can even think of something we have not. She is a rather bright girl after all."

Horace sensed someone approaching, and turned towards the approaching figure. "Speaking of the hacker..."

Timothy and Frederick sat straight and found that Rumil was less than three Tacks from them, her hands behind her back. She looked like a personification of innocence... if only the three didn't know better.

"Timothy, I'm bored," Rumil softly stated.

The Knight shook his head knowingly. "I told you that you would be. Would you like to leave?"

"Actually…" Rumil began softly, then said a little louder than she probably intended, "I'd like to dance, and need a partner."

Timothy's eyes narrowed suspiciously, then he felt the piercing sensation of his father's scrutiny from behind Rumil. The young Knight frowned, and said softly, "You're intentionally trying to aggravate my father."

"Oh, and threatening him isn't intended to?" Rumil snapped back.

"This dance is very meticulous. Even the slightest mistake could be construed as an insult to our tradition," Timothy warned, as if trying to find a reason not to go with Rumil's plan.

The blonde woman scoffed. "I've been watching those dances. They're all pretty much the same dance with different variations of upper body placement. Child's play, really. I could engage in more complex moves while asleep."

"You're not planning to do anything improper, are you?"

Rumil looked insulted, and then motioned with her head to where the elder Knight was absolutely scowling. "Trust me; this dance will be true to your tradition." She then made a slight feminine bow with a swirl of her long gown skirt.

Horace smirked deviously. "This would definitely make a statement to your father."

"This is a ball, and people dance at balls," Frederick added. "Why should this young lady be denied what everyone else has the right to do?"

Timothy glared at them as if they had just committed treason, before accepting what appeared was rather inevitable. "Very well… I suppose if no one else has a problem with it, neither should I." Then toward Rumil, he added, "I should warn you, I am not much of a dancer."

Frederick objected. "He lies, Miss Bonamede. He has a natural grace and agility that lends well to the ballroom floor. He just never had much reason to display it."

Timothy exhaled in annoyance before taking Rumil's hand in his, and moving out to the dancing floor. "Are you sure you want to do this?" he asked one last time.

Rumil did not get a chance to answer as the music began –

nothing more than a replay of the first song the group had played. The pair bowed to each other before joining hands at arm's length in front of them, leading with a right step forward that brought them closer.

Rumil had not been boasting, Timothy realized, as she made each step and combination perfectly. He guessed he shouldn't have been quite so surprised; after all, the Arcadian woman was certainly experienced with elaborate routines and procedures, and probably did find this very meticulous dance to be rather simple.

When the music died, Timothy realized that many of the nobles off the dance floor were applauding the couple, evidently impressed by Rumil's flawless display. Even Niles was nodding somewhat appreciatively. From the corner of his vision, he saw Celine grin, which Timothy initially dismissed, until he turned back to his partner.

Then, Timothy saw Rumil's troublesome gleam, and realized that his father's approval was going to be extremely short lived. "You told me you weren't planning anything…"

Rumil smirked, "I said *that* dance would be in your proper tradition. This one however…" She then pointed towards the musical group, and as if from out of thin air, three members of the group had picked up brass instruments, and they began a much more energetic song, one that was considerably out of place with the rest of the music.

Rumil then stepped away from Timothy and turned her back to him, taking several long steps with an exaggerated motion of her hips. Then with her back still towards him, she lifted her hands in the air, and swayed from left to right in a wave-like movement, before suddenly snapping rigid, facing her partner again.

I can tell you're listening to my thoughts, wondering what in the depths of your hells I am doing. Rumil accused as she began to stride back towards him. *Good, because I want you to right now. Just keep in tune with me, and do what I tell you to. Got it?*

Before Timothy could reply in any way whatsoever, Rumil was less than a Tack from him. She threw her upper body backward, and with impressive flexibility, placed her left leg on Timothy's shoulder. It stayed there for less than five demiticks, when she slid the limb down his arm, spinning twice once it had touched the ground again, her back pressed firmly against Timothy's chest. Her right arm slid up like a serpent, brushing his cheek with a feather caress, when he felt Rumil's thoughts order him.

Put your left arm on my waist, and spin me to face you. Then place your other hand on the other side of my waist.

Timothy's reluctance was for the slightest of moments, then he complied without further question, his rational thought overwhelmed by that compulsion that he often felt in her presence. Once he had done his part, Rumil fell backward, Timothy quickly recovering to keep her from falling to the ground.

Rumil then grabbed his shoulders, and pulled herself upright, Timothy rearing back as well when her face stopped with their noses almost touching. He could feel her warm breath against his lips as she wrapped her left leg around him, sliding down the length of his body before suddenly popping back to her feet and sliding away, meanwhile thinking of her next command.

Now take my right hand with your left, hold it above our heads, then place your other hand on my far hip once we meet.

Once Timothy had taken his cue, Rumil spun several times to close the distance, the skirt of her gown billowing in an ice blue flurry. Once again, her back was to him, his arm draped around her waist while she energetically thrusts her hips from side to side.

Let go, then catch me as I fall back, spinning me three times before you pull me back up.

This pattern of orders and execution continued for about two more ticks, finally ending when the song cut off with a sharp, piercing note, coinciding with Rumil's last move which thrust her body almost completely against his, looking into his eyes with a triumphant grin.

There was an awkward silence immediately afterward, as none of the entire assembly could seem to totally believe what had just transpired. There was a dull thud from the seating area, and Timothy quickly identified it as one of the senior Initiates literally falling out of his chair.

Timothy allowed himself brief glances at the audience, trying to gauge their reactions. Most of them were still stunned to silence, blank, uncomprehending looks pasted onto their faces. He caught sight of Robert Datson in the second row of tables, nervously adjusting the collar of his dress armor as if trying to cool himself.

His gaze then inexorably turned to Frederick and Horace. The Solarian King seemed deep in thought, as if he were analyzing a diplomatic brief rather than an impromptu dance. Horace, on the other hand, had a glazed over look, his jaw dropped limply so that his mouth hung open.

Finally, Timothy spotted Niles, whose face and neck were growing steadily red with each passing demitick. His boiling anger was then dispersed by the sound of applause. It began with one spectator, was gradually picked up by others with some trepidation, then eventually expanded into full appreciation of the unorthodox dance.

Meanwhile, Celine stood next to the table in which Frederick and Horace were sitting, looking pleased with herself for her quick thinking that diffused the tension in the ballroom. She then asked, "Priest Hightower, is something wrong?"

Horace shook his head to clear his thoughts, rubbing his temple. "I'll admit that I started to have some thoughts that a man of my position probably should not be having."

Without looking at her, Frederick asked, "Let me guess, you had nothing at all to do with this."

"Now why would I trouble you by stirring my husband's ire?" Celine asked with false innocence.

"You're the one that has to live in the same mansion as him," Frederick wryly reminded.

Celine then dropped her face into her hand, pretending to sob, "Oh indeed. After all, I am just a weak and submissive Solarian woman. There is no telling what my husband will do to me. Whatever will I do?"

Frederick frowned, and replied, "If anyone believes that, then our society has more fools than I figured."

*　　　*　　　*　　　*　　　*

As the Late Ten began to wane, the ball was mercifully ended, although some could argue that it had been over tenth-cycles ago, after Rumil had turned the entire event on its head with her demonstration. From that point on, nothing else had come close to comparing.

Timothy opened his apartment door, and waited for Rumil as she stepped inside, her face still fixed in that victorious smile that he had seen just after their dance. "Now *that* was how you're supposed to have fun."

"I'm amazed my father maintained his composure, and didn't have you executed on the spot," Timothy mused wryly.

"Oh come on, from what I've gathered, by tomorrow I'll be dumped off on my own to wait for Krennan to hunt me down. Allow me this little bit of enjoyment." She tried to sound flippant, but deep down, she was quite terrified. The prospect of being on her own with Krennan free and doubtlessly looking for revenge was not a pleasant one.

Timothy seemed to sense this. "We're not certain just what we're going to do yet. It's very possible you won't be leaving Solaria."

"I doubt your father would allow me to stay here."

"That, frankly, isn't his decision," Timothy snapped. "If I wish for you to stay, there is precious little he can do about it, especially once he learns that I have a little piece of information that he has desperately tried to keep secret."

"Do you think that's wise?" Rumil asked. She didn't like the idea of Timothy possibly angering Niles's further just for her sake. "He already is acting like a cornered animal... telling him that you have information regarding the Baramak Slaughter might just push him over the edge."

Timothy shook his head. "He's grown too deeply in love with his power and position to do something that stupid. He may be old-fashioned, needlessly conservative, and downright blind at times, but he isn't foolish. He knows that I'll eventually learn everything anyway once he inevitably retires, so I doubt he's willing to risk doing something drastic over it. However, it might be enough to convince him to be peaceful."

Rumil rejected the request with a shake of her head. "I couldn't ask you to do that for me."

"Well, that's fine, because I'm not asking," Timothy reiterated. "You aren't leaving, not with Krennan running about unchecked."

"Excuse me?" Rumil snapped. "Perhaps you haven't noticed, but I'm not one of these helpless Solarian women who just blindly accept anything any man says. This is my life, and if I want to leave, then I can and will!"

If her rant had rattled Timothy, he wasn't showing it. "I guess the question is; do you want to leave?" he asked.

Rumil paused. "Not really... but I'm not going to put you in any more grief by keeping me here." She took a deep breath. "You and your friends have a chance to change this society for the better, and I'm not going to let you risk that just for me."

Timothy began to speak, but Rumil silenced him by putting a finger on his lips. "You told me as we were traveling to Amat that I needed to live my life the best I can. You also told me it was never too late to start. I guess... I would like to start now."

"Are you sure this is what you want to do?" Timothy asked with a resigned sigh.

Rumil inhaled in exasperation. "I really am tired of being asked that question today. I am positive. I may not like it, but it's what I want to do."

Timothy pulled his frame tight, as if about to say something he really was not too keen on saying. "Very well, I shall inform Frederick of your intentions immediately, and next cycle, probably in the early ET, we'll arrange to have you transported to wherever you wish. I suggest that you get some sleep then."

Rumil complied, admitting to herself that fatigue was starting to overwhelm her. "I think I'll do that." Before she disappeared into Timothy's bedroom, she added, "I guess... I should thank you... for everything."

*   *   *   *   *

Rumil had slept reasonably well, considering that she probably wouldn't have too many more nights to enjoy. Once she left Solarian space, her life might as well be over. She ruefully admitted that she might not even last that long. She slowly awoke to hear the sounds of arguing coming from the living area. Timothy was evidently quite irritated about something.

"It's pure coincidence that my father demands my report right now, isn't it?" Timothy snapped.

"Now, don't shoot the messenger," the other voice, which she recognized as belonging to Emmitt Fransisca, answered hastily. "I'm just here because Frederick told me to take Miss Bonamede to the starport in your stead."

"I'm not about to—" Timothy began.

"Listen, it's the perfect chance. While Niles is busy with you, it shouldn't be terribly difficult to get Rumil out of here."

Timothy seemed to accept this line of reasoning. "I suppose you're right. But be careful, Emmitt. My father can be tricky, and could have people waiting for her to leave. He doesn't have to be present to be a bother."

"I know... he's my commander too," Emmitt assured. "I suppose it's time to wake up your guest, so that we can all be on our way."

With that cue, Rumil opened the bedroom door quickly, and stepped out. "I'm already awake, and I packed up my belongings last night. I suppose I'm ready to go."

Timothy took one look at the blonde woman, and quipped, "Perhaps you have time to fix your hair before you leave. Your locks haven't exactly returned to their normal shape."

Rumil didn't doubt the appraisal. Ihrman, Celine's stylist, had placed so much holding gel in her hair that it had hardened tougher than the carbide helmet Timothy wore out in the field. She asked Emmitt, "Do I have time to freshen up, Knight Fransisca?"

Emmitt blinked warily, apparently taken aback by Rumil's mussed appearance. "Yes, I suppose we do. The last thing we need is for people to know what went on in here last night."

For the briefest moment, it seemed like Timothy's eyes flashed with an unexplained white light, before returning to normal, and clapping Emmitt so soundly on the shoulder that the Knight yelped in pain. "Absolutely *nothing* happened between Miss Bonamede and I, do you understand me? She was understandably tired, and thus didn't prepare herself for bed as she probably should have."

Emmitt was so intimidated by Timothy's sudden and uncharacteristic burst of aggression that he could barely squeak. "Of course, Timothy… I was wrong to think that you… well… I apologize."

Timothy released Emmitt with a low growl of irritation. "I suppose I shall get ready for my debriefing while Rumil cleans herself up. In case I have left before you emerge, Rumil… wherever you choose to go, I ask that you send me some sort of message once you have arrived."

"Why?" Rumil asked teasingly. "Do you want to check up on me?"

"It's doubtful I'll have the opportunity to do that," Timothy remarked sourly. "But wherever you decide to go, I can deliver a message to some Knights I trust to at least keep a passive eye out for Krennan's friends."

"All right. I'll try," Rumil agreed. Timothy obviously was going to do everything he could to keep her in the realm of the living, as little as it would probably be. It was annoying and sweet at the same time. There was another awkward silence as all of three of them merely stood in place, as if they were all waiting for someone else to add something. Finally, Rumil broke the silence, and pointed towards the restroom. "I'll… just get cleaned up then."

Once Rumil had slipped into the restroom, Emmitt said slyly, "Okay, just be honest with me."

Timothy cut off his colleague's line of questioning before it even started. "I'll say this once more in the hopes that this time you'll be able to remember it. *Nothing happened* between Miss Bonamede and me last night."

"Be serious," Emmitt retorted. "Had you come in on me, and I had a lady in my home all trussed up like that, what would you think?"

Timothy snarled, "First of all, I wouldn't have barged in on you. Second of all, I wouldn't have asked. But for the sake of argument, if I *had* done those two things, third, I would have let it drop after the first time. Whether you were telling the truth or not would concern me little."

Emmitt raised his hands, trying to ward off Timothy's anger. "Very well, I suppose you have a point there. You better get ready. The longer your father has to wait, the angrier he tends to get."

Ten ticks later, Rumil emerged from the restroom, looking considerably better than when she had entered. Her fancily-done hair had reverted to its normal style, and all the smudged makeup had been wiped away.

Emmitt stood up from the chair he had appropriated from the dining area, and said, "Timothy left already, so I suppose we should make our exit with all due haste as well."

Rumil was somewhat reluctant, but agreed. Due to the rather early hour, the apartment complex was devoid of human activity, which probably served their flight for the best. The fewer people knew of her departure, the better.

Emmitt had precious little to say as they climbed into his hover, and began their trip out of Centris toward one of the main gates leading to the surface of Solaria. "I really hope I don't get seen doing this…" Emmitt muttered. "I'd really like to still be commissioned when Timothy finally takes over the Knighthood."

Rumil rolled her eyes, and asked, "Has anyone told you that you worry too much, Knight Fransisca?"

"All the time," The Knight replied, "but when your family's position among the Knighthood is tenuous at best, you have to do everything with extreme caution. One misstep, and the next generation of my family would be completely out of luck. We'd probably have to leave Solaria, and take up a Knighthood station on another planet."

"Is that so bad?" Rumil asked.

"To be one of 'The Eight,' one of the 'True Knighthood,' is an honor among honors. My family could definitely claim a Knighthood designation from almost any other planet in Solarian influence… but it wouldn't be the same."

"I figured the families were set in stone," Rumil commented.

Emmitt laughed at that thought. "Oh, for families like the Honore clan, the chance that they'll be unseated *is* truly impossibility. My family, on the other hand, only has a history in the Solaria Knighthood for about a hundred and twenty staryears. Compared to the other seven, that's a blink of an eye." The Knight made a quick turn onto another roadway, and added, "We'll need a few more generations of strong talents before we can really feel at all comfortable about our status."

"I get the feeling once Timothy takes charge, his little triumvirate will make a lot of changes," Rumil said, hoping that would cheer him up.

"Possibly. At least I can hope so." Emmitt sighed. "Timothy, Frederick, and Horace seem so convinced that society will accept the changes they are pushing for. I hope they're right… but I can never be too sure about anything with my status."

Finally, the pair reached the main gate. "The roadway ends here, so we'll have to switch to a sand vehicle once we get outside," Emmitt explained as he stepped out of the hover and Rumil followed behind. The Knight nodded to the four military guards serving as a security detail.

The guards let Emmitt and Rumil through without any trouble, asking nary a question. Emmitt proceeded to the smaller service door that was actually a part of the large metal gate, pulling it open with a grunt.

Sand began blowing into the cavern, and Rumil realized that the sandstorm that had been raging as she had arrived clearly had not settled much at all. She got a sinking feeling that something wasn't right.

Her concerns were confirmed when the detail closed around her, grabbing her by the arms, and escorting her to the service door. Emmitt looked on forlornly as the guards prepared to push her outside.

"Frederick didn't send you at all, did he?" Rumil accused.

"Actually, he did… but High Commander Honore had very clear orders as well," Emmitt replied. "I may respect Timothy, and will be his most ardent supporter when he takes over the Knighthood, but until then, I must display that same loyalty to my current commander."

All conversation was concluded when the guards literally threw Rumil outside into the blowing sandstorm, closing the service door quickly with a resounding metal thud.

Chapter Sixteen

To say that Niles Honore was not taking Timothy's report well would be a gross and potentially dangerous understatement. The High Commander of the Solarian Knighthood was barely maintaining any semblance of control as he berated the man who claimed to be his son.

"Let me make sure I have this story right," Niles growled. "You attempted to arrange a *cooperative* venture with the *Kiros*?" The elder Knight paced back and forth behind his desk twice before slamming both open palms against the wooden surface. "In case you missed that portion of training, the Kiros are the *enemy*!"

Then Niles began to chuckle spitefully. "And then... *and then...* our exalted monarch and that brain-addled High Priest actually *helped* you plan this dim-witted and, dare I say, almost *treasonous* scheme!"

"The planning was mine," Timothy asserted. "Frederick and Horace merely agreed it was the best course of action."

"I don't care whose plan it was!" Niles bellowed, spittle flying from his mouth in varied arcs. "And to think I was actually contemplating stepping down in the near future, thinking that maybe you had gained some sense as you gained field experience! As it stands, I'm going to have to live forever to keep you from destroying our entire society."

"As it stands, our society will fade into nothingness," Timothy replied. "I will prevent that descent, and there's little you can do about it."

Niles grew solemn, and his voice sounded like the growl of an angry animal. "Are you suggesting you'd try to force me out? Please... say it, so that I can have you executed for mutiny."

"I won't give you the pleasure," Timothy retorted. "It's simple fact that no one lives forever. Time is on my side."

There was a beeping signal from the sliding door leading out of Niles's office, indicating that someone was requesting entrance. "I am in a meeting!" Niles screamed towards the doorway.

"I- I... am... deeply sorry... sir..." the low-ranking receptionist stammered from the other side. "But... High Priest Hightower... requests communication... with Knight Timothy Honore. He- he... says it's... urgent..."

"I don't care how urgent the communication is!" Niles replied. "My subordinate will contact him when I am finished with him!"

"Actually, I do believe we are finished," Timothy answered crossly, then said flatly to the receptionist, "Have it transferred to my remote comm, Subjucant. I thank you."

"You're… you're welcome… sir," the receptionist answered, and apparently stepped away from the door.

Timothy reached into one of the pouches at his belt and pulled out his PCU, flipping it open and holding it to his ear to keep Horace's end of the conversation private. "Horace, I was told it was urgent…" The younger Knight stood in silence for about ten demiticks then his face twisted into a venomous scowl. "Oh, he did…" Timothy stated, glaring directly at the High Commander. "Thank you, Horace."

Timothy reigned in his anger, gently returning his communications unit to its place, and then declared, "Did you not think that I have eyes and ears around Solaria too? I think we're done here, and I apparently have other business to attend to."

As Timothy turned to leave, Niles commanded, "I order you to not leave the command complex!"

"You *order* me?" Timothy answered angrily.

"As long as you are a Knight under my command, you will obey my orders. You are not to leave the complex," Niles reiterated.

In response to this, Timothy ripped the nameplate off his armor and removed his pistol, throwing both to the floor at Niles's feet. The rank badge in Timothy's billfold, and the indicators on his shoulder, soon followed. "Consider that my resignation, then," Timothy spat, and whirled around to leave once more.

* * * * *

Timothy could only marvel at how fast news traveled in Centris. He had barely returned to his apartment when his mother became the first of what would be many visitors.

"Your father sent me to try and talk some sense into you," Celine sighed. "Could you care to tell me just what is going on?"

Timothy grudgingly explained the situation while he gathered supplies for what would be a considerably perilous rescue. Added to the fact that the longer Rumil was outside in that sandstorm, the worse her chances were, lent itself to a very brief explanation. "My father decided to do Krennan's work, but didn't have the guts to do the dirty deed himself. Thus, he had Knight Fransisca toss Rumil out into the sandstorm."

Celine gasped, and then quickly grabbed the armload of canteens that Timothy had gathered. "Well then, I'll go fill these up while you prep the rest of your gear. Time is of the essence."

Timothy just finished the preparations on his armor for travel through the extreme conditions of a Solarian sandstorm when he received his second visitor. Celine reached the doorway first to reveal Emmitt, looking quite nervous.

"Oh... Madam Honore... I was hoping to meet your son— *uuurrk*!" Emmitt's voice was cut short when Timothy reached around his mother, and grabbed his fellow Knight by the neck, pulling him roughly inside the apartment.

Emmitt had just begun to regain his breath when it was forcefully pushed out of him again by Timothy slamming him roughly against the interior wall of the entryway. "I don't particularly care for your excuses or rationale, nor do I have time to hear them." Timothy ended the very short discussion with a swift punch directly to the side of Emmitt's head. The Knight's head recoiled flaccidly from the blow, and his body went completely limp.

Timothy let Emmitt slide lifelessly to the floor, and acquired his helmet from where he had tossed it upon Emmitt's visit. "Stay here with Knight Fransisca. When he wakes up, inform him that we are not finished with our discussion."

He reached the lobby of the building just as Frederick entered from the outside door. Before the monarch could say anything, Timothy held up his hand, "I am short on time, Frederick. If you have anything to say, you can meet me at the main gate."

Frederick protested, "Are you sure you've thought this through?" but by the time he had finished the sentence Timothy had already left the apartment complex, and had teleported away. The monarch quickly followed, and when the pair rematerialized before Centris's main gate, quickly began to question Timothy.

"What in the name of the great Creator of Annor are you thinking?" Frederick demanded. "Everything we worked so hard to accomplish, you've completely thrown away over some Arcadian woman!"

"You know as well as I do what Rumil could mean... to everything," Timothy answered simply.

"*Could* mean!" Frederick emphasized. "What if you're wrong?"

"What if I'm right?" Timothy replied as he looked over all his equipment one last time, finally satisfied that he had everything he could need.

The King turned to Horace, who evidently had seen Rumil's expulsion take place and had been waiting at the gate since. "Could you help me talk some sense into him?"

The High Priest smirked, and replied, "Are you certain Miss Bonamede is who you claim she is?"

"I cannot be sure, of course, but I have to find out," Timothy answered, still checking the seals between his armor plates to make sure they would not allow the blowing sand outside from becoming a major bother.

Horace shrugged then replied, "Then he must go, Frederick. I just pray you are right. It would indeed be tragic to lose all we have fought to build over this and then learned we gained nothing in return."

By that point, Timothy had stopped paying attention to the pair, and had advanced towards the main gate. The chief guard, a rather dangerous-looking figure, declared, "By the order of High Commander Niles Honore, once you leave here, we are not allowed to allow you inside again. Do you understand this, sir?"

"I am more than aware of the circumstances for my actions, Guardsman, now step aside," Timothy nearly growled. Each moment he wasted inside Centris was one less moment he could have spent searching. When the guard didn't move quite as quickly as he would have liked, Timothy finally pushed him aside with a force that sent the poor guard onto his bottom.

From there, he grabbed one of the massive double doors by its thick handle, and pulled. Normally, it took three Solarians to pull open the gates of Centris without mechanical aid, but Timothy alone nonetheless succeeded in yanking the thick, sealed doorway ajar with relative ease. Sand began to blow into the underground city, and the wind howled with the anger that could only come from nature's wrath. With a steeled resolve, Timothy stepped through the gate, closing it with the assistance of the guards behind him.

Outside, the storm was considerably more violent than Timothy had first assumed. Visibility was minimal at best, as if he was surrounded by a wall of flying sand. A gust of wind took the Knight by surprise, actually blowing him off his feet, and depositing him an undetermined amount of Tacks away from his previous location. Regaining his feet, he had to utilize his psionic energies to anchor him to the desert surface in order to prevent another wailing burst of wind from doing the same thing yet again. Gritting his teeth, he started to fight his way through the billowing dust and wind, deeper into the sandy maelstrom.

This was not good for Timothy's hopes. If he was having such difficulty in this sandstorm, how was he to expect a young woman who had no experience dealing with these conditions to survive? He quickly banished any negative thoughts from his head, reminding himself that Rumil was quite a resilient young lady. She must still be alive, somewhere in this desert. If, by chance, she had found some sort of shelter, or come across the remains of the long-departed surface civilization, or even perhaps found a Solarian military outpost that had been abandoned by the coming storm, she could be trying to wait it out. When he thought about it that way, her survival didn't seem nearly as impossible.

Just highly improbable.

He reached out with his psionic sense, hoping to locate the unique aura that the Arcadian hacker possessed. While he didn't sense anything right away, he allowed himself to cling to some hope that she could have traveled some distance, even in this sandstorm. She had a consideral head state to move around, and could be likely anywhere.

However, he had to discern just which way she had decided to go. For a moment, he entertained the idea of following her psionic footprint, but rationalized that she likely didn't have nearly enough power in order to leave a trail strong enough for Timothy to detect, much less follow with any accuracy. Nevertheless, with rapidly dwindling options, he decided to least make the attempt.

Timothy closed his eyes, gathering his focus and adjusting his senses to try and pick up on the tiny residual fragments of power that Rumil might have unwittingly left. Gaining such proper focus proved to be difficult as the storm seemed to intentionally double its efforts, the gale winds picking up even more velocity, almost covering up the crackle of electric energy gathering in the clouds. The heart of the storm appeared to be closing in.

With a determined grunt, Timothy pushed the ever-increasing sounds and sights of the maelstrom out of his mind. It would take every available fragment of his energy not devoted to keeping himself upright to even have the remotest chance of catching Rumil's trail.

Finally, he felt he was ready, and he opened his eyes, promptly closing them again at the scene before him. Rather than faint specks of psionic energy lingering in the air and ground, there was a large cloud of bright golden residual power floating almost directly in front of him, unmoved by the storm buffeting everything in the area, its remarkable density nearly blinding him. Now prepared for it, Timothy noticed that it formed a rather clear line to his northwest. It dwindled rapidly, but at least the Solarian Knight had a general idea as to where his target had gone.

About three TackMets from the initial residue, there was another large cloud of energy hovering in the air. Timothy suspected they were what remained of Rumil's occasionally spiking energy, likely from the visions that had been plaguing her since arriving on Solaria. This time, the energy seemed to point him due west, suggesting that Rumil was merely stumbling blindly, looking for any sort of shelter. That bode ill for her continued survival.

Then again, Timothy himself was largely stumbling blindly through the sandstorm. He didn't hold total confidence he could even find his way back to the Centris gate, had he not Rumil's little trail to follow. Pushing those thoughts aside, Timothy faithfully followed the westward direction of the residue trail, and finally got his first glimpse of hope. It was extremely faint, but he could recognize that life aura easily. She was nearby, hanging on through the storm.

Rumil? Are you there? Timothy called instinctively as he reached out with his psionic sense.

Her reply would have carried the tone of a breathless gasp as she felt him say his name. Timothy was surprised, since he was not trying to read her thoughts, suggesting that she was telepathically projecting to him. Was she even aware of what she was doing?

Priest Hightower informed me of my father's little plot, he answered. *I'm coming to you, so don't move.*

Rumil's indignant snort caused the Knight to chuckle. *It took me eternity and a day to find a spot that was somewhat out of the wind and sand. Let me assure you I'm not going anywhere.*

However, fulfilling his request would be easier said than done. The storm's intensity was steadily increasing, forcing Timothy to expend more of his energies into remaining upright and moving forward. The sand kicked up and swirled even faster, reducing his already minimal sight to mere Tackems in front of his nose.

It was due to this low visibility that he never even saw the steep drop-off of the dune he was climbing until it was too late. He tumbled down the decline in a fashion very contrary to his normal agility and grace, going limp as he fell to limit the chance of spraining or bruising anything along the way.

He finally landed with a metallic clunk and a grunt onto the bottom of the decline, then he heard a startled yelp from behind him. There was a small burrow in the dune face, likely carved out and abandoned by one of the small number of creatures that actually managed to survive on the Solarian surface. Inside it, Rumil was huddled against the deepest wall, the left sleeve of her blouse ripped and wrapped around her mouth and nose as a makeshift filter.

As he staggered inside, she said, "Nice of you to drop in like that. I think my heart pumped an extra staryear out of me."

"I'm always looking to make an entrance," Timothy smirked from behind his visor, then plucked one canteen off his belt. "You look like you need this."

The way Rumil snatched the canteen and poured almost the entire contents down her throat confirmed his suspicion. Once finished drinking, she wiped her lips, and stated, "I hope you realize you're not going to convince me to stay on Solaria."

"I know. I'm not too enamored with it myself," Timothy replied, and noting Rumil's quizzical expression added, "I had to resign my commission to hunt for you."

She scowled, and said, "You are truly an idiot, you know that? Did you hear a word we discussed yesterday?"

"I did," the Knight answered flatly. "You were wrong then, and you're wrong now." Kneeling down next to the ragged-looking blonde, he continued, "I've already told you that there's something about you that I can't accurately explain. You're going to do something special, something that no one else can do, and my duty, beyond all others, is to make sure you accomplish that."

"You sound so certain," Rumil replied warily. "What do you think you know about me that makes me so special in your opinion?"

Timothy rubbed the back of his helmet, and said, "I can't say specifically. I just know that something is compelling me to keep you safe, and I've given up fighting that urge."

Rumil couldn't help but feel that he wasn't telling her everything that was on his mind. However, rather than press the issue – and ruin the one little bit of good fortune she had received that day – she decided to change the topic. "So… what's the plan?"

Timothy looked outside the burrow, where the sandstorm was showing no signs of letting up. "We'll wait out the worst of this storm, then make our way back into Centris. Hopefully by dusk, the heart of this storm will have finally passed over us."

"Why do you want to go back in there?" Rumil asked disapprovingly.

"Because I still have unfinished business with certain parties, first of all, and secondly, that's the closest place we'll find a shuttle in which to make our escape. If you think my 'father' is going to just assume the storm has finished us off, you're mistaken. We'll need to get off Solaria, and as soon as possible."

Rumil agreed with that idea, but with a playful grin, she commented, "You know, just last night, you didn't want me to leave."

"The situation changed. Besides, perhaps you're safer off this sand rock," Timothy said with a defeated shrug.

"That may be true. I mean, it appears I'll have you tagging along now."

Timothy looked at her almost expectant expression, and tried to reassure her, "I'm better than anybody I could have sent to keep an eye on you."

"That may be, but you've only got two eyes, and now we'll have to be watching out for Krennan and your dear old father."

"We'll worry about that if we get out of here in one piece," Timothy said, finally taking a seat next to her. "I shouldn't say 'if.' We will get off Solaria, and I will keep you safe. I can't afford to fail."

Rumil threw her head back, and looked at the top of the burrow. "Why are you doing this? What do you want from me?"

"What do you mean?" Timothy asked. "What could I want from you?"

Rumil snorted, "No one helps me without expecting something in return. That's the way life is."

"Sounds like you grew up around the wrong people."

"That goes without saying," Rumil said wryly.

Timothy put his left hand on her right shoulder. "Tell me about it."

At first, Rumil didn't realize just what he was referring to. "About what?"

"The people you grew up around. The life story you didn't want to talk about on Altair."

"What makes you think I want to talk about it now?"

"Because I want show you how I'm different from all of them."

Rumil didn't sound terribly convinced. "And how do you plan to do that?"

His voice seemed tinted with a hint of playfulness. "Tell me, and then I'll show you."

Rumil frowned, then nervously admitted, "I don't remember much of my youth outside of the name I was given. The only real memory I have from before I was four or five staryears is one where I'm restrained to some table, with strange clear tubes pushed into my wrists and ankles. I just remember it hurting… a lot."

"Is that where these scars came from?" Timothy asked, gesturing to her wrists.

"Presumably," the hacker replied. "From there, it's all a haze. Something happened apparently, because I was free, living under cardboard boxes on Urundal, the capital city of Baramak, scrounging for food, picking out of trash, or getting sympathy from passers-by. I was eventually found and placed in an orphanage… they arbitrarily decided I was six staryears old, and tossed me into the system. I don't even really know how old I am."

Rumil planted her chin on her right hand before continuing, "The woman in charge of the orphanage used our terrible stories to receive countless donations from the public, talking about how terrible our conditions were, and how they desperately needed money every year. She'd parade us out onto holovision and the GalNet, and say how we barely had enough food to eat, let alone anything else that would make our lives worthwhile."

Another depressed sigh slipped out of her mouth before she said, "Well, I think you're a smart fellow, so you see where this is going. We'd rake in the credits for her, enough for her to afford these lavish hovers and mansions out in the countryside, where she didn't have to deal with us dirty little orphans. Then, the next year, she'd parade us out again with the same old sob story, and the public would just eat it up, never asking questions."

"This orphanage was operated by Krennan, I assume?" Timothy asked, but was already fairly certain of the answer.

"I didn't know it at the time, but he ran and donated a lot of money for the survivors of the Baramak Slaughter, and when my talents at computer science were noted, his connections influenced me to move to

Altair for further training. At the time, I thought he had come to my rescue... 'miner trash', as Baramak survivors were called, helping miner trash. I was obviously wrong." She sighed, then added, "I should have realized it sooner, although fat amount of good it would have done me."

"People like Krennan are everywhere, although fortunately not all of them wield his sort of influence," Timothy remarked. "Often a person will go through life meeting thousands of such people, all wonderful on the surface, yet rotten to the core, and never know it."

Timothy was then silent for a second, then he finally asked, "So, what about your parents?"

This caused Rumil to suddenly choke back what appeared to be a sob. "Maybe this is a bad thing to say, but I don't remember anything about them. I once had this rather heroic notion that they died in the Baramak Slaughter protecting me from harm… but I just have no memories at all of them."

Timothy smiled wryly, and quipped, "Sometimes I wish I had that luxury…"

"You shouldn't," Rumil retorted somewhat testily. "Your mother really cares about you, even if she's a little annoying at times. Granted, I can't think of any redeeming qualities of your father, but I'd trade a thousand bad memories of my dad for none at all anytime."

"You're probably right," Timothy said in apology. "I didn't mean to offend."

"Well, now you know the abridged version of my story. Now, you tell me how you're different than any of them," she challenged him with narrowed eyes, as if she was not about to be swayed by any answer of his.

Timothy wasted no time, gesturing out to the sandstorm, and said, "How many of them would have braved this to find you?"

Rumil's eyes narrowed even further, and asked, "Depends on how valuable they thought I was to them."

Timothy brushed his free hand under her chin, turning her head upward so she was looking directly at where his eyes were faintly visible through his visor. "Well, I'll admit, I think you are quite valuable, but not in the same way you are no doubt thinking. As I said earlier, I sense something in you, something special, something I want to be a part of."

"I can't imagine you playing second to anyone," Rumil said.

Timothy took a deep breath then asked, "Alright then, how about this? Of everyone who had taken advantage of you in the past, how many of them would have been willing to give up everything to make sure you were safe?"

At that moment, Rumil realized just what Timothy had done. He had been in line to become High Commander of the Solarian Knighthood, had been in position to alter the course of the Solarian people as a whole, and apparently had tossed that all away to find her. She wrapped her brain around any possible reason he'd do something like that, what she could possibly offer that would be greater than what he already had in his grasp, and came up with nothing.

"What if I don't believe you?" she finally said, trying to maintain a cynical stance.

"Do you honestly think my father would have let me go? He appears to want you dead, remember?" He paused, then added, "He hasn't exactly wished for my continued health either." His hand on her shoulder then slipped behind her back to gently hold her other arm. "In the end, I suppose this could all be some elaborate trick to get myself into your good graces, but you have to admit that it's highly unlikely. I've cast my allegiance with you, wherever that takes us. You'll have my support, no matter what fate decides to throw in our path."

Once again, Rumil swore she heard a slight hint of emotion in the Knight's voice. For a moment, she was able to banish the cynical thoughts from her head. He sounded so sincere… and she couldn't think of anytime that he had proven to have deceived her. Even when he was hunting her as a criminal, he had seemed to try to avoid hurting her.

Then of course, there was their first meeting in the Sultry Siren… and how he had actually fought an Ubek that had merely tried to touch her on Dewin's pirate vessel… and all the times he had stood up to his father on her behalf… In just a few short ten-cycles, he had done more for her than anyone else she had ever known. Maybe… just maybe… he *was* different.

She leaned in against her companion slightly, and said, "All right, let's assume I believe you. You're really behind me until the end? Well, I suppose you'll get your chance to prove it." Even as she said it, she had decided that if she couldn't trust Timothy after all he's done, there probably wasn't anybody trustworthy in the galaxy.

At the same time, Timothy was plotting their next move. Without a doubt they had to get into Centris, and the main gate was clearly out of the question. The only other way he knew inside the underground city was not going to be easy.

Somewhat to his surprise, he felt Rumil slowly snake her arms around his waist, allowing him to fully support the weight of her upper body. She suddenly sounded like the frightened little girl she no doubt was for so long when she asked, "You promise you aren't using me?"

"I promise," Timothy replied, at the same time, feeling like he was lying somehow. Granted, he wasn't going to exploit her for his own gain, but at the same time…

Rumil broke off his train of thought when she laid her head gently on the breastplate of his armor, and muttered, "That'll have to do for now, I suppose."

She said nothing further, and Timothy didn't particularly feel like breaking the comfortable silence they had just achieved.

Chapter Seventeen

Due to the wall of blowing sand, it was hard to tell just how long Timothy and Rumil had spent hiding in the abandoned burrow in which they had taken refuge. Once the winds began to die down to something just below a hurricane gale, Timothy checked his gear in preparation of their departure.

"What are you doing?" Rumil asked suspiciously.

Just tenth-cycles before, Timothy had displayed hints of sympathy and caring. Now, he was all business once again. "We have to move soon, as my father will likely mobilize to find us once the weather is deemed passable."

"Therefore, you figure we have to get going while it's unfit for any reasonably safe travel?"

"To put it bluntly, yes. I wouldn't worry too much. It looks and sounds like the heart of the storm has finally passed over. It will only get better as time goes on." He then stepped gingerly out of the burrow, as if trying to brace himself for any degree of wind. Seemingly satisfied, he stepped out fully into the gale, and after about ten ticks, stepped back inside. "Yes, I barely even need to use my power to anchor myself. I'd wager within two cycles, the storm will have completely moved by. Oh, by the by, this is for you…" From the pack he carried on his back, he managed to fish out a small, clear nose and mouth mask with a black circular disk on the front, and an elastic strap. "I suspect this will be a much more effective air filter than your shirt sleeve."

Rumil silently agreed, and felt the device almost instantly reshape itself to firmly fit around her face. "Hmm… not too shabby. You Solarians know how to fabricate tech."

Timothy shrugged. "Wish we could take credit, but as I understand, those filters came from an Arcadian manufacturer. We do trade quite frequently, and not just for food."

Rumil grinned sheepishly. *Now if only other parts of their society were not as expected…*

The beauty of generalizations is that they tend to carry a hint of truth, making them difficult to dispel, Timothy answered with his thoughts.

"You know… the fact you can read my mind without my approval does not help your trustworthiness," Rumil chided, displeased.

"I didn't read your mind at all. You projected that thought for anyone gifted to hear. You had no idea you were doing that, did you?"

Her companion's declaration gave Rumil pause. "Obviously not. Are you saying…"

"That you've been telepathically communicating? Yes. I haven't had to reach into your mind at all, even when I first found you earlier. It does appear that your psionic abilities are indeed awakening."

Is that so…? Rumil asked herself, trying to see if Timothy had picked up on it. "Well?" she finally asked when the Knight didn't reply to the mental question.

"Well… what?" Timothy asked, confused.

Rumil shrugged. "It appears you were wrong then. I just tried to ask you a telepathic question, and you didn't answer. Anyway, you were the one who said we had to get going, so let's go." She then stepped out of the burrow, nearly getting knocked over by the still rather powerful wind. Adjusting to the sudden change in environment, Rumil managed to right herself before falling over, looking back at Timothy expectantly.

Timothy meanwhile was lost in thought. At first he had thought that Rumil simply had transmitted her telepathic question incorrectly, not knowing the tricks involved, but as he pried deeper, he soon discovered that the aura that had been about her just moments before had dissipated, as it had when he finally apprehended her on Altair.

Most curious… he commented mentally before finally rejoining Rumil outside the burrow. "Stay behind me, and I'll try to block out most of the wind," he suggested in a tone perilously close to an order.

His eyes scanned eastward, where the Solarian sun was actually visible, albeit barely, through the waning sandstorm, starting to disappear over the desert horizon. However, looking around, he discovered that was about all that was recognizable. "Well, I have good news, and bad news."

Rumil rubbed her temple, and muttered ruefully, "Good news first, please. I need some."

"I can see the sun, and thus can put together directions, and I also know where we need to go."

"Okay… now the bad news…"

Timothy was silent for a second before sheepishly admitting, "I'm not terribly sure where we are."

"What?" Rumil asked in disbelief. "This is your home planet, remember?"

"Yes… but I don't just wander about on the surface. I know that we're somewhat north-northwest of the main Centris gateway, but beyond that… nothing."

Rumil sighed, "I knew it… this plan is going straight to the trash already. Hey, can you just make a rough guess?"

"I suppose I can. We can't be more than a few TackMets from the main gate… Perhaps while we're on our way, the storm will lessen up even further, and then I can try to pick out some landmarks."

"Sounds like we have our course of action then," Rumil stated. "Now lead on, since you are so intent on trying to block the wind for me."

Timothy shrugged, "If you feel you don't need my help…" He then stepped aside, putting Rumil just outside the minor psionic barrier he had placed. A sudden burst of wind actually picked up the hacker, and prepared to deposit her back on the ground in a less than gentle manner, but Timothy had deftly moved himself to catch her as she came back down.

Rumil didn't immediately feel the desire to be placed back on her feet, and it startled her somewhat. "You know… there are easier ways to make your point," She chided.

"But none more effective," Timothy retorted, before settling her back on her feet. Despite not being able to see his face, Rumil was almost absolutely certain he was barely containing his laughter. He looked back towards the setting sun as if to gather his bearings, then turned to the direction of their destination.

At this same time, Rumil had a burst of inspiration. "You know… you can teleport, correct?"

Timothy cut off that idea before it had time to develop. "If I teleport to our destination, it will be like throwing up a huge glowing beacon telling my father exactly where I am. It's possible to redirect the energy I would discharge, but considering this entire planet is filled with sensitives, there is absolutely no way I could teleport that sort of distance and not be detected. I'm rather loathe for such a thing to happen, as you may guess."

Rumil hadn't thought of that. "Oh. I see…"

"It was a good thought though. To bad reality had to get in the way, right?"

"Rather than teasing me about it, you can start moving," Rumil snapped crossly.

With a casual salute, the Knight said, "Yes, ma'am."

As they began their march to wherever it was that Timothy was leading them, a small clump of sand, roughly about a tackem wide, smacked her on the cheek. She didn't think much of it until it actually seemed to stick to her face. It felt a little warmer than sand was supposed to be, and she quickly decided something was not quite right about what had just struck her.

She rubbed it away with her hand, just to discover that it had now adhered itself quite firmly to her index finger. She shook her hand violently, and eventually it did fall off, squarely onto her boot. From there, she noticed several other such sandy looking clumps all over her boots and calves. With a shriek, Rumil tried to kick whatever they were away, but with little effect. The billowing sandstorm was bringing in a wave of the things, finding a home on Rumil's person, shielded from the winds.

Timothy whirled around, and at first, Rumil thought he was laughing at her. "What are these things?" she demanded angrily once she ascertained that was *exactly* what he was doing.

After another chuckle, he finally answered, "Sandscrubs. They're all over the Solarian surface, eating the microorganisms that live on the sand. They can't move on their own, and often rely on sandstorms such as this to get from one place to another."

"How come they aren't sticking to you?" Rumil said in a voice bordering on a whine, motioning to Timothy's relatively clean armor, save for a few sandscrubs that had managed to latch onto his body suit underneath.

"They don't adhere to carbide terribly well." He then appraised his companion's situation – almost her entire front side was covered in the small insects, making her look like she had fallen face first into a sand dune.

At that moment, one slapped right onto her lower lip, and stayed there despite her efforts to spit it off. "I hate them! Get them off! *Now!*"

"They're harmless. Let me assure you they won't mistake you for food."

"*I don't care*! I swear, if you do not get these things off me *this instant*, I will make you suffer agonies that you could never even begin to imagine!" In the meantime, she was flapping her limbs and brushing her shirt and trousers in a vain attempt to brush them away.

"We'll wait until this little colony has blown by us, then I'll coax them off you," Timothy reassured her. "At this moment, however, any attempts would be rather counterproductive."

Reluctanly, Rumil agreed to that line of logic. "How long will that take?"

Timothy shrugged. "There could be billions in this sandscrub colony. I can't imagine it would take any longer than a tenth-cycle."

It was everything Rumil could do to keep from crying on the spot. It wasn't that she was some little girl scared of bugs. She spent plenty of time living next to all sorts of grimy, disgusting little insects in various alleys during her early years… it's just that none of those had ever stuck to her like adhesive.

"I understand it's disconcerting, but hang in there," Timothy said, trying to be reassuring. "They won't hurt you, you'll be perfectly fine. Maybe you should try closing your eyes, and try to imagine they aren't even there."

Rumil did so, only to feel the familiar slap of what could only be another sandscrub attaching itself onto the upper lid of her right eye.

"Well… maybe that wasn't such a good idea after all…" Timothy mused, while Rumil harnessed all her reserve to keep from slapping him. After about twenty ticks, Timothy declared, "I think that's the lot of them for the most part. Come here, and I'll see what I can do."

Rumil shook her head. "Why don't *you* come *here*?" When Timothy hesitated, she decided he was having far too much fun with this. "I'm serious. Get over here and get these things off me!"

"All right, I'm coming," Timothy said, laughing outright at her predicament. "Now just stand still. This might shock you a little."

He pointed one finger at Rumil, and a small blue spark of electricity jumped between the point of his finger and the sandscrubs latched to Rumil. Wherever the tiny bolt went, the insects plopped off, falling to the sand below. She did indeed feel a slight jolt wherever the energy touched her bare skin, but nothing much worse than the shock one got from a static electricity charge. That was fine until the little bolt started wandering to more… sensitive areas.

"Watch it!" Rumil yelped as the finger of energy started to drift in between her thighs, and Timothy recoiled as if stung. "I think that'll be fine, Timothy."

Timothy reminded, "You said you wanted them all off, though," gesturing towards the insides of her legs, where a small group of sandscrubs was still attached to her trousers.

Rumil pursed her lips, and said, "All right… then keep going, just don't get any ideas."

Timothy's posture suggested he was completely oblivious to what she was referring to, and his next question supported his expression. "What *are* you talking about?"

It was too hard to for Rumil to tell if Timothy was simply being coy, or if he truly had no idea what was concerning her, thus she gave up trying. With a defeated groan, she said, "Fine, just hurry up and get it over with."

Timothy shook his head, and took little time removing the few remaining insects. Once free of the legless bugs, Rumil was in considerable hurry to reach their destination. "Let's find where you want to go before another one of those colonies decides to blow by," then after a moment's silence, added, "Just where are we going anyway?"

"A somewhat unconventional entrance into the underground capital," Timothy replied.

"And that means?"

"Did you notice the river that runs through Centris? It was on our way to the prophecy recital."

Rumil thought about that before replying, "I did."

"Presently, it runs totally below ground, but at some point long in the past, it flowed along the surface before falling into the caverns that make the city. We can use the cave that was formed by the river, then follow said river towards Centris."

"Is it really that simple?"

"Navigating the underground Centris Riverway is not easy. Depending on the water table and speed of the current, it can be quite perilous indeed. It's actually because of the dangers that my fellows don't put too heavy of security along it."

"Don't you think they'll know of that way in, and be expecting us?"

Timothy shrugged. "Possibly."

"That wasn't reassuring."

"It wasn't meant to be," Timothy retorted. "But it's our best option at the moment."

"Do we have to go back into Centris?" Rumil asked. "I'm sure there are other cities on this planet."

"Not ones that are within feasible distance. Besides, as I said earlier, I have some unfinished business down there."

Rumil didn't exactly like Timothy's decision, but at the same time acknowledged she didn't have much room to complain about it, nor did she have enough knowledge of Solaria to know if he was speaking the truth.

Their progress eventually moved down a slight slope. At first Rumil thought it was just another of the endless multitude of dunes scattered about the desert planet's surface. However, once she felt hardened, caked earth under her feet rather than sliding and yielding sand, she instantly noted this was just *a little* different. The ground was indeed hard and tightly packed together, like it had been subject to a great amount of weight. There were several small cracks and fissures that ran down the slope, parched and broken from lack of water.

"Is this…?" Rumil began.

"The ancient river bed," Timothy finished for her. He then turned slightly to the east, "Which means the cavern we are looking for should be somewhere in that direction. Are you up to it, or do you want to sit down for a bit?"

Rumil shook her head. "The sooner I am off this planet, the better," then with a slight apology, she added, "No offense."

Timothy scoffed, "Of course it was meant to be offensive. However, I do not blame you in the least… and in some ways, I suppose I share the sentiments."

The pair followed the bottom of the riverbed east. Because of the harder surface, Rumil could move at a more comfortable pace and not feel for every step she took, she slid two backward. Nonetheless, the trip was starting to grate on her nerves.

"How much farther do we have to go?" she asked, her voice again teetering precariously close to a whine.

Timothy appeared oblivious to her tone, since he shrugged and answered, "I'm not sure. It depends on how far off our intended course we have drifted. If I had to make a guess though, I can't imagine we're more than a few TackMets away."

"A few TackMets" didn't really answer anything. That could mean half a tenth-cycle, to almost half a cycle. Added to the fact that all this walking was starting to get rather boring, and her feet hurt. She had never been much of a walker in the first place thanks to the scars on her ankles, which were still quite painful to go plodding upon for any great distance, and the distance she had traveled today would have tested people of greater stamina than she.

Timothy stopped abruptly, and asked, "Do you need a rest? You look somewhat… beleaguered."

Rumil shook her head. "I can manage."

Timothy didn't seem to believe her. He knelt down, and ordered, "Well, climb on. I can take a faster pace this way."

Rumil scowled. "I said I can manage."

"You can't even take a step without grimacing, and you've been steadily slowing down this entire tenth-cycle." There was silence before he added, "Did you think I wouldn't notice? Now, climb on, and let's keep moving."

Deciding that it would be nice to get off her feet, Rumil abandoned her prideful statements, and complied. As if she weighed nothing at all, Timothy straightened without so much as a grunt, and began walking again at a surprisingly brisk pace. She initially found herself somewhat awed with yet another display of the Knight's deceptive strength, then decided not to treat it as anything out of the ordinary.

After trying to find some interest in the barren scenery, she found herself overwhelmed with another feeling even more nagging than fatigue… boredom. Then, as her mind began to drift, she got the sensation that she had done this before. She knew for certain she had never been to Solaria, but something about her current situation seemed so familiar, like a fuzzy memory that can't quite be recalled.

It was at that point, as Rumil's head started to drift thoughtfully against Timothy's shoulder, she noticed her companion was not without his own scars. The neck of his bodysuit had been tugged free from under the joint of his helmet by Rumil's weight on his back, revealing a flesh-colored gash along the right side of his neck, partially hidden under his helmet, and disappearing underneath his bodysuit, aimed towards his back.

She figured she shouldn't be terribly surprised that Timothy bore marks of battle. After all, he was a prominent Solarian Knight who had no doubt seen his share of skirmishes. She herself had witnessed him in combat on a few occasions. However, something about this mark struck her as different, telling her that he had not received that blemish through fighting. Rumil drug her index finger lazily along the scar, feeling Timothy cringe slightly as she did so. Somewhat pleased to know that she had discovered something that rattled her companion, albeit subtly, she asked slyly, "And where did you get this, dear sir?"

Timothy shook his head. "I'd rather not say."

Rumil slapped him softly on the back of his helmet, and growled, "Hey, you made me spill my deepest secrets. Don't you think it's only fair that you let me in on yours?"

Timothy sighed, but she more felt the heaving in his chest than heard the sound. "I got that little scar you saw there when I was five staryears old. My father whipped me for appearing before a noble gathering. He was still in his 'deny-I-even-exist' phase at the time, and didn't want his fellow Knights to see his 'bastard' son. One of his lashes went a little high and sharp, and cut into my neck."

Rumil gaped. "That sort of punishment was outlawed thirty years ago by the Galactic Alliance. It's considered child abuse."

"And perfectly acceptable by Solarian custom. The people tend to have selective vision in regard to it," Timothy replied. "Had I received prompt treatment, it could have been healed without scarring, but after getting lashed, I was promptly locked back in the basement, and it was three tenth-cycles before my brother returned, and let me out."

"Didn't your mother do anything?"

Timothy chortled, "She called my brother. It had taken him three tenth-cycles to arrive from where he had been posted. Outside of that, there wasn't much she could do. If you think current gender issues are bad, over ten staryears ago, they were remarkably worse."

"Well, at least your brother was a decent enough fellow, it seems."

"He was," Timothy agreed. "I guess he felt for me, since he wasn't a 'legitimate' heir himself, being adopted and all. He never took my father directly to task for anything that had happened, but it was for the same reasons I never did the same when I became a Knight."

"Is that some of your 'business' you still have in Centris?" Rumil asked warily.

"Only if our paths cross. As much as I would love to have him answer for the last twenty-one staryears, it would not be wise to actively search him out."

Rumil sighed gratefully, then asked, "Tell me more about your brother."

Timothy answered warily, "Why do you want to know?"

"Just curious. No reason other than that. You don't talk about him. As a matter of fact, you barely talk about yourself."

Timothy smiled at the observation, although the lady on his back couldn't see it. "My brother was an interesting character. He was in line to inherit my father's position, as well as control of the entire estate, until I was born."

"Really? I would have figured that there were other Honore children that would have been given the honor, rather than some adopted son."

"Well, the rules governing transition of the male line are rather vague. It doesn't necessarily just move down the line cleanly. As a matter of fact, it could have gotten somewhat messy, even with my father's blessing to Craig... that was my brother's name, by the way. I'm not sure if I told you that."

"I see. Then when your heritage was confirmed, your brother was suddenly supplanted." Rumil remarked, "That must have been an interesting relationship."

"The irony in it all is that the one person who you would think would be thankful for a male heir, to ensure that the Honore family didn't break down into chaos, never was, yet the one person who you would think would have hated me for it never did." Timothy sighed wistfully, "He was the one person, until his death, that I could count on."

Timothy had mentioned his adopted brother's death in passing once before, and given his more open demeanor at the present, Rumil figured he might discuss it. "Your brother's death really affected you."

"My father seemed to take a perverse glee in telling me I had no right to know about what happened on Baramak. The fact that I've never been able to find out how he died, and what he was doing, still haunts me. It's why I had endured my father's asinine antics for this long."

Rumil apologized, "I'm so sorry I ruined that."

"You have nothing to apologize for," Timothy retaliated. "Your safety is more important right now. And as I say that, we arrive at our destination."

Through the clearing sandstorm, Rumil could indeed see a gaping black cavern directly ahead. While the distance could have been deceiving, it didn't appear to be terribly tall – almost five times in width what it was in height. Nonetheless, there was more than enough room for seven people to have stepped inside without lack of space in either direction.

"I'm going to set you down now. I'm not terribly certain of the footing inside," Timothy said simply, then slowly crouched down so that

Rumil could return to her own two feet.

"I've been on your back long enough, actually," Rumil stated, her legs feeling considerably refreshed having been granted the short rest. She tried to glance inside the cave cautiously, and due to uncharacteristically dim light on the Solarian surface, was able to make out only vague details of stalagmites and such, along with a ragged floor. She could also hear the faint rumble of rushing water, obviously from the river running through below.

Timothy heard it too, and did not like what it meant. "The current is running fast, and likely high as well. This could get entertaining."

Rumil snorted, "You have a queer idea of entertainment."

"That goes without saying." He then took the lead again, stepping inside the cave carefully in order to maintain his footing against the uneven floor. Twenty Tacks inside, he declared, "Right about here the cavern starts to decline down to the river itself. You'll need to be very careful once you get to this point."

With that, Rumil followed. She figured that humid air from the river below mixed with the dry surface, and the combination led to a very cracked and unstable ground. Less than a Tack into the cave, Rumil encountered the very slippery surface covered in loose rocks, and nearly fell on her bottom. Almost miraculously, she maintained her balance, but was certain that her luck wouldn't last.

As fate would have it, the normally sure-footed Timothy was the one to lose his footing first, and he landed hard on the cave floor. His fall served to topple him over the slope of the cavern, and he began to swiftly slide downward, his surprised yelp echoing into the darkness.

Rumil gingerly made her way to the edge, and peered downward. "Timothy?" she called out, but when she didn't hear any answer, save the rushing of water below, she began to grow concerned. She had no idea how far the fall was, but was now worried as to Timothy's well-being.

Unfortunately, a flock of small flying nocturnal creatures made up her mind for her. Obviously awakened from the noise the pair of travelers had made, they flew with a fright towards the exit of the cave. Rumil, stunned as the flock rushed past, stepped over the edge of the slope herself. After three Tacks, the slope abruptly ended, and she plummeted through open air down towards the underground river.

Chapter Eighteen

Not even Rumil heard the splash she made as she hit the water over the sounds of the raging underground river leading to Centris. From there, she had to fight a horrific undertow as the waters continued to plunge deeper into the Solarian crust. The pull from the river, coupled with not taking a full breath would bode ill for even the most expert of swimmers, much less a computer hacker who had barely learned the skill at all.

Fortunately for her, either pure random chance or a higher power intervened on her behalf in the form of a slight eddy in the river created by a small earthen shelf. The outcropping lent her an escape from the frightening current and allowed her to surface for desperately-needed air. She reached for the shelf, hoping for some sort of handhold, but it was covered with algae and slime, and her hand slipped off ineffectually. She floated past, eventually to be swallowed up in the torrent yet again, and her lack of expertise in swimming did not allow her to hold her breath for terribly long. In less than half a tick, her lungs were once again screaming for oxygen.

Yet fate favored her once more. She could not clearly see what she had bumped into in the darkness, but when she felt herself collide with a hard surface, Rumil flailed out for something to grab and this time found purchase, the fingers of her left hand clenching around a lip of rock along the side of the river.

She quickly realized within a demitick that she had not grabbed onto anything made of rock. It was too smooth and too uniformly polished to have come from nature's design, and once she had pressed her body flush against her perch, she discovered it was a humanoid shape. As her eyes adjusted to the darkness, its details began to emerge from the blackess; the familiar shapes of a carbide breastplate and helmet.

"Timothy!" Rumil yelped, embracing the Solarian, only to feel them both shift precariously into the current yet again. It then struck her that Timothy had not reached out for her, nor had he said anything when she grabbed onto him. Closer investigation revealed that he was not hanging on to anything at all, but that his belt had caught along a small prong of a stalagmite sticking up out of the center of the river, a prong that appeared to be cracking under their combined weight and the powerful current.

She then realized that there was a deep crack on the right side of

Timothy's helmet just above the visor, and what that could possibly mean to the man inside the armor. Slowly pressing her ear to the mouthpiece of the Solarian's helmet, she was relieved to hear the faint sounds of breathing.

Not wanting to risk too much movement, but at the same time needing to know the extent of the injury, Rumil slowly unclasped his helmet, and gently tossed it away. There was a small trickle of blood from the same area as the crack in his helmet, but it fortunately did not appear to be terribly serious. Nonetheless, he was clearly unconscious. She had to wake him before their lifeline snapped.

She slapped him along the left cheek gently, all the while softly calling to him. It took almost a full tick, but she began to feel movement in her companion, then a pained groan. His left hand began to drift towards his head, but he shifted his hips to do so, and that caused the pair to slide further into the current. The sudden movement jerked Timothy to almost full alertness, although he was understandably a bit disoriented.

"We fell into the river," Rumil began, stating the obvious more to test Timothy's current state rather than to state the obvious. "Your belt luckily caught against this rock here, and I luckily bumped into you. Do you remember what happened?"

Timothy's brows furrowed, and he commented, "Not really... I remember falling, then blacking out. I think I might have hit my head on the way down."

"You must have hit hard, your helmet was pretty badly cracked. Had that not been Solarian carbide, I fear what would have happened."

"Guess my home is good for something, huh?" Timothy remarked wryly, valiantly trying to shake off his grogginess before getting to business at hand. "With the water levels so high, I'm rather certain that the entire waterway is flooded from here all the way to Centris."

"That's a problem, I take it?"

"How long can you hold your breath?" Timothy asked, somewhat rhetorically.

"Not terribly long," Rumil admitted.

"And I'm not exactly an expert swimmer myself." His voice trailed off thoughtfully, "I guess we don't have much choice."

"Of what?"

Timothy shook his head slightly. "I was hoping I could save this little trick for later, but it can't be helped. I just hope I can gather enough air for us to make it."

Rumil still didn't quite get what Timothy was getting at. "What are you planning on doing?"

Timothy smiled, and replied, "You'll see. I just ask that once I'm finished that you don't breathe unless you absolutely must."

Before Rumil could ask again what Timothy was talking about, she saw him close his eyes. Initially worried that he was fading out again, she then noticed a small shimmering field forming around their heads, barely visible save for the occasional crackle of energy along its surface, inflating like a balloon until it had completely encased about a Tack of area from her shoulders upward, eventually merging into one large bubble of crackling energy.

"Are you sure it's safe to be using your psionic ability after taking a blow to the head?" Rumil asked skeptically, figuring her companion was the source.

"No," Timothy answered honestly. "But if I don't, then it's going to be a very slow death by drowning for the both of us."

"Well, when you put it that way—" Rumil began, but Timothy pulled his belt free, and they were once again swept away by the river. As the Solarian had predicted, the head room inside the cave rapidly diminished as it plunged further into the depths of the Solarian undergrounds, and the movement of the river pulled the pair beneath the water level as it did the same.

It was a somewhat surreal experience to hear the roaring current all around her, yet not feel it against her face because of the air bubble surrounding her head, nor see it because of the pervasive darkness from the depths of the flooded cavern.

"How far is this cavern?" Rumil asked as she exhaled slowly, preparing to take another breath.

Timothy's reply was telepathic. *I'm not terribly sure, but it can't be anymore than fifteen TackMets or so. Don't speak, it takes up more air. Use your thoughts.*

Rumil smirked. *You just like reading my mind.*

Timothy's telepathic voice seemed laced with amusement. *You're doing it again.*

Doing what again?

Telepathic communication. It's quite curious, really. One minute, you're projecting a rather impressive psionic aura, the next, nothing.

Rumil thought about that for a moment. *Well… I don't know what to say. It's not like I'm doing it consciously. Maybe when my life is in danger or something, it kicks in with my adrenaline. Who knows?*

Timothy didn't sound totally convinced. *Perhaps…*

Not certain what else to add to that topic of conversation, Rumil went silent, trying to peer into the darkness for any sign that their trip was nearing an end. When there was no indicator that such was in the immediate future, the hacker gave up, trying to come up with anything that would take her mind off her current situation.

In this, she failed miserably. She found herself wondering how much longer the air in their little bubble would last, how long they would have to be underwater, which would be worse; suffocating or drowning. In other words, things one really shouldn't think about when trapped underwater with only a small balloon of air keeping him or her alive.

After an indeterminable amount of time, Rumil was overcome with a cough in the depths of her lungs, and after it finally had escaped from her mouth, she discovered she couldn't breathe out. Rumil immediately panicked, the fear of a woman about to face her own death. She couldn't think of anything to expel the horrid air from her lungs, and was certain that she was starting to discolor from the lack of oxygen. Her grip on Timothy tightened, and she tried to say something to him, but since she was having no luck breathing out, speaking was also out of the question. Finally, Timothy's voice entered her head, offering one piece of advice.

Inhale.

For less than a demitick, Rumil went almost totally limp as she mulled over Timothy's suggestion, then did as he requested. As she felt the soothing air fill her throat, she realized what had happened with great embarrassment. In her panic… she had forgotten to breathe.

After that gaffe, Rumil scratched off any sort of conversation, even of the telepathic type. She was starting to feel hot, and silently wondered what that meant. Figuring out that the heat was actually from the accumulation of heated exhaled breath trapped inside the air bubble took her mind off other things.

Suddenly, they took another dive, and fell with the river as it plummeted straight downward. The abruptness of the fall caused Rumil to scream, quickly cut off when Timothy slapped his hand over her mouth.

They hit level water yet again, and after some random tumbling from the wake of the waterfall, they were once again taken by the river's current. Instantly, Rumil noticed a significant difference. This time, the current wasn't nearly as swift as before, and she noticed Timothy kicking upwards towards the surface of the water. Rumil eventually joined him in his efforts, but upon afterthought began to wonder if she was interfering with the Knight's efforts rather than assisting.

Regardless, the pair broke the surface of the river, and Timothy released the psionic field he had been maintaining, as evidenced by the sudden rush of fresh, somewhat damp air that was common with the Solarian underground. Rumil soon realized that they were now in a small tunnel that had one bright semi-circle about a TackMet away.

"Once we reach that exit, we will be about five TackMets north of Centris proper," Timothy stated simply. "We're going to have to be really careful now. My father no doubt will have security on the lookout for us entering the city, and might have some people waiting along the river."

"So… then… what's the plan?" Rumil asked.

"Well, keeping out of my father's sight won't be terribly difficult," the Knight boasted. "I'm fairly certain I could at least shield a short teleport from detection if we need to, and besides, I have my share of assistance in this city."

"Then could you start backing up your boasts? I don't know how long I can tread water," Rumil said with mild annoyance.

"As you wish," Timothy replied lightly, then the pair slowly began to progress towards the end of the cave that emptied the river out into the cavern that held the underground capital, their slow kicks working in time with the considerably gentler current.

As they drew closer to the end of the brightening tunnel, Timothy suddenly warned, "Be ready to take a deep breath. We may have to quickly duck under the water, and hope we continue to avoid detection."

"What a wonderful idea…" Rumil quipped. "When having a hard time treading water, just let yourself go under…"

"Well, it turns out that won't be necessary. It appears Knight Datson got my message," Timothy then commented.

Rumil looked up to see what he was referring to. Just outside the cave, a single figure was standing vigil as if waiting for something… or someone. Rumil couldn't see the person clearly enough to identify it, but once the pair emerged out into the cavern proper, the figure slowly became clearer. Robert Datson didn't even notice the two swimmers' presence until they were almost right underneath him. Then, with a discreet wave, and glancing about half a TackMet downriver towards a small patrol mulling about, he slowly helped Timothy and Rumil out of the river.

A pair of towels suddenly tumbled onto the ground next to them, and Robert smirked, "I'm sure mother won't mind that I borrowed these." With another glance towards the patrol, he said with a devious grin, "I sent them further down, just in case you 'slipped my detection.' However, I can't imagine they won't eventually spot you with me, so I'd strongly suggest you move on as quickly as possible."

Timothy had eschewed the towel, since his battle armor and body suit weren't easily soaked to begin with, and not even Rumil spent long wiping herself down, figuring that she'd be on the move quickly.

"Thank you, Knight Datson," Timothy replied softly. "You've been of great help, especially since my position is no longer one you can benefit from."

Robert scoffed, "You'll be back. I'm certain of it. Besides, Priest Hightower was quite adamant that I assist you all that I can. One learns not to aggravate the High Priest."

"Well, we will need to meet with him shortly, so we shall thank him for his efforts. Be well." Timothy then grabbed Rumil by her left shoulder, and before the other Knight could give a farewell of his own, the pair had teleported away.

Once again, the movement through space and time was too quick for Rumil to fully process what had happened until they were standing just outside an all too familiar temple, where some of Rumil's most lucid visions to date had assailed her. Because of said visions, she had not been particularly keen on going inside, but Timothy managed to convince her.

"I'm not going to allow you to sit out here where you can be easily spotted," Timothy chided. "Unless, of course, you *want* my father to find you."

It hadn't taken much more than that for Rumil to get the idea. She followed the Knight into the temple with some trepidation, worried that if she looked at anything, she would be assailed with horrifying images. She kept her head down and looking at the back of Timothy's legs, refusing to even so much as glance at any of the statues or murals or paintings. Granted, it helped that they were rather nice legs... his bodysuit and carbide plating fitting his contours so well.

Settle down, girl! Rumil snapped at herself, even as she couldn't help but notice how very well-toned Timothy's calves were.

In my chosen profession, it's generally a good idea to stay in peak fitness, Timothy stated matter-of-factly.

Rumil wasn't certain if he had pried into her mind, or if she was indeed broadcasting telepathically, but she flushed nonetheless. For the second time, she had been thinking along more mature lines, yet Timothy seemed totally oblivious to it. She still couldn't figure out if Timothy was being coy or not. But before she allowed herself to delve too deeply into that line of thought, there was one thing she wanted to know.

"I'm curious; how does a psionic shield their thoughts from being heard by every other psionic in the area?" Rumil then bit her upper lip nervously, hoping he didn't ask why she wanted to know. She wasn't sure she'd be able to lie convincingly enough to fool herself.

Timothy shrugged. "Normally, unless someone wills it, thoughts aren't communicated telepathically. I've never seen a situation like yours, where your thoughts are broadcast as if by their own volition."

"Wonderful. Then how about keeping others from reading my thoughts?"

Once again, the Knight shrugged. "Different people envision such a mental shield in different ways. The trick is finding a method that works for you. I personally see my mental shield as a helmet around my brain. It may appear odd… but it works for me."

Rumil wasn't sure she could envision Timothy's helmet wrapped around his brain, and thus was doubtful she'd be able to do the same without laughing at the absurdity. Then, she remembered a somewhat amusing response some ancient Arcadians made out of fear of the mind-reading abilities of their Erani visitors when first contact had been made. The slightly ignorant group got into the practice of wrapping their heads in metal foil, thinking it would protect their thoughts from being read. Later revelation proved it to be totally ineffective, but at the time, the Erani had said nothing, likely finding the entire act to be mildly hilarious.

It was this image that she put into her mind, of her head wrapped from the temple to the back of her neck in a silvery foil, then decided to test her results. Pursing her lips, she went forward with full abandon. *I find Timothy to be quite attractive, especially when he's in such tight clothes.*

When the Knight didn't react in any way to the statement, she still felt the need to ask, "Did it work?"

Timothy's reply was a stoic, "Yes."

Her eyebrows crinkled slightly as she added, "Would you be honest with me even if it *didn't* work?"

Timothy stopped, turned his head, and smiled in a way that wasn't exactly reassuring before continuing down the hall. Rumil emitted a soft, breathless squeak as she felt the blood rushing to her face, then noticing that he was leaving her behind, had to scamper to catch up.

Nothing further was said, nor was anything significant thought, until they entered the center of worship. Horace was waiting for them at the entrance, and quickly grabbed Timothy's right arm.

"Could you give us a moment, Miss Bonamede?" Horace asked politely, and in such a sweet manner that Rumil didn't feel she could say 'no' without appearing quite mean-spirited. Horace then led Timothy several Tacks away, out of the hacker's hearing. Once they started talking, and occasionally glancing back in her direction, it made her wish she knew how to read minds herself…

Meanwhile, Horace began grilling Timothy on the past, present, and future.

"Well, I have arranged for Knight Fransisca to have a personnel shuttle ready at the south hangar for you," Horace said, then asked offhandedly, "Are you *certain* she is who you think she is? Because both Frederick and I sensed some doubt when you last answered that question."

"I'll admit I cannot be entirely positive," Timothy answered, as he made a passing glance towards Rumil, "but it looks quite likely. All the signs point in her direction. Surely you can understand why I had to do this."

Horace nodded. "I do. But, do you honestly believe you can protect her from both your father *and* Krennan on your own?"

"I won't have to do it on my own."

The High Priest shook his head. "While you may have considerable sympathy and sway from your fellow Knights, you cannot expect them to aid you unless…" Horace's face went ashen, then he asked nervously, "You aren't planning on starting a civil war, are you?"

Timothy almost laughed at the suggestion. "Of course not."

Horace exhale of relief was audible and animated. "Thank the Creator."

"I now have ties with the Feroz family, and should be able to find sanctuary there."

Horace's face dropped as if he had been told that Timothy hadn't accidentally killed his favorite pet, but rather had accidentally killed his mother. "You aren't serious! I mean, I'm all for new ties with the Kiros sect, but your father would waste no time construing that as high treason."

Timothy wasn't at all perturbed. "I'm already likely charged with dereliction and insubordination. Might as well go for the trifecta."

Horace finally managed to stop looking like Timothy had inexplicably kicked him the gut in order to say, "If you feel you must… but your plan even makes me wary. I sincerely hope you know what you are doing."

"So do I." The Knight then turned away, and rejoined his companion. "We shall need to be going now. Tell Frederick that I probably will not be able to contact him, and make sure that he doesn't allow my father to do anything foolish."

Horace bowed slightly. "Of course."

With Timothy's business completed, the pair left the way they came. Less than five demiticks after they had emerged back into the "outdoors," Timothy had once again grabbed Rumil and whisked the two of them away to another location.

They reappeared on the south end of the Centris cavern, more than six TackMets from the city itself. Several small personnel shuttles were lined up in tens of rows, about twelve shuttles each. One shuttle was on a lift that extended up to one of thirty metal hatchways on the roof of the cavern, where the shuttles were brought to the surface for takeoff.

Before Rumil could ask why, Timothy commented, "Well, looks like Emmitt did his job after all."

The voice of Niles Honore responded, "Yes, he did his job very well." From there, thirty armed military personnel accompanied by twelve Knights emerged from inside and from behind several of the shuttles. They assembled into a semicircle in front of the pair, partially surrounding them and blocking the path to the shuttle on the lift. The soldiers formed the front line, dropping into a kneeling position and training their rifles on Timothy, while the Knights stood behind them in relaxed and ready stances, calmly awaiting the order to strike.

Niles took his place at the center among the line of Knights. From there, it was easy for him to appear cocky, particularly with the numbers so heavily in his favor. Yet in spite of this, the Solarian High Commander was considerably worried. It was the reason be brought such heavy numbers in the first place, and even with them, he didn't much care for his odds should this become a real fight. Instead, he decided to try and play a slightly more diplomatic mode at first.

"Knight Fransisca promptly told me about what you asked him to do. You know I can't let you leave the planet with this criminal," Niles said, attempting to be soothing.

Timothy smirked coldly, knowing that he hadn't asked Emmitt to do anything, contrary to his father's belief. In fact, Horace was likely the one who had Emmitt set up the shuttle for departure. Timothy felt a small bit of glee for yet another reminder that his father's control was not nearly as absolute as the elder Knight would believe… or wanted Timothy to believe, for that matter.

Meanwhile, the High Commander continued, "I'm going to offer you a chance. Release the woman into my custody, and it'll be as if nothing had happened. We don't need to make a scene out of this."

Timothy was not about to do any such thing, and made that point perfectly clear. He crossed his arms, and retorted darkly, "I can't and won't allow that. If you want Rumil, it will be through my corpse."

Niles couldn't help but laugh somewhat bitterly. "I can't… I just can't believe *this*! You'd be willing to kill yourself over some worthless computer hacker?"

Timothy smirked again. "For a woman who is so worthless, you seem to be willing to spend an awful lot of effort and manpower to eliminate her."

"I simply wish to bring her to justice, nothing more. What the Adjudicates decide to do is none of my concern."

This time, Timothy laughed. "So, your idea of justice involves locking her out in the middle of a sandstorm, and leading a detail of Knights armed and ready to kill? Your actions up to this point have suggested that you'd much rather leave the Adjudicates out of this. I wonder why?"

The gleam in Timothy's eyes rattled Niles. His "son" *knew*… somehow he *knew*… but how? Had the boy gleaned that information from High Priest Hightower, Niles would have eventually known about it from the elder Knight's ears inside the priesthood.

Niles felt the gravity of the situation fall into place, and suspected the lengths that Timothy would go to protect this woman. He wasn't going to stand down… the only peaceful resolution would involve Niles and his Knights retreating.

I have an opening, my lord.

Niles's eyes flashed open in frantic horror, recognizing the voice behind that bold claim. Niles had summoned Knight Kenseth Dutis not for his combat awareness, but for his raw power, hoping that if the standoff came to conflict that Kenseth could at least go toe to toe with Timothy long enough for the rest of his men to take control of the situation.

That was before Niles had realized that Timothy would go as far as he needed to preserve Bonamede's life. And in that case... no mortal being or agency in the length and breadth of the galaxy would likely be enough.

"Damn it, Dutis! Stand down!" Niles ordered, but the brash young Knight had already committed. A thin needle of energy burst from his fingertips, intended to pass just over Timothy's shoulder and into Rumil's forehead.

That thought came to a crashing halt in much the same way as the psionic needle struck and splintered off the shield Timothy had constructed before fading into nothingness. Timothy stared down Kenseth with lips curling with malice and disdain. With little fanfare or warning, Timothy's eyes erupted in a brilliant, painful white light that heralded a spike in psionic power so intense that the Knight detail momentarily staggered back from the mind-scrambling surge.

There was nothing that could have been done for Kenseth, Niles knew. By the time any order would have reached Knight Dutis's ears, it would have been far too late. Timothy ended Kenseth's existence with one move, a thrust of his left hand that erupted in a blue-white screaming beam of raw psionic energy. The beam consumed and incinerated Knight Kenseth Dutis on the spot, the young man not even given time to scream before his entire being was reduced to vapor and plasma.

"Fall back! Regroup at Central Command!" Niles ordered, but that still wasn't enough time to save two more of his detail. Timothy lunged forward, disappearing and reappearing in visibly the same instant in front of his next victim. Timothy seized the Knight by his neck and infused his body with so much energy that he visibly swelled as he became a living bomb, then threw him with effortless force into the Knight nearest them, both exploding in a gruesome shower of shredded flesh and gore.

The shockwave from the blast knocked Niles off his feet, but his meeting with the ground was interrupted by a vice-like grip grabbing his forearm, wrenching Niles's shoulder from its socket with a painful tear and popping sound. The momentum of his fall contributed to the following throw that sent Niles's back slamming into the edge of the raised shuttle pad, snapping vertebrae and numbing the older Knight from the waist down. As Niles began to slump to the ground, Timothy's boot slammed into his neck, pinning Niles's head to the top lip of the pad, and leaving his legs dangling lifelessly just inches from the polished floor.

Niles forced himself to keep his eyes open in what he was sure was his final moments; Timothy deserved that respect, and Niles's honor dictated nothing less than to face his demise bravely. Just a subtle twist from Timothy's ankle would be enough to end it all, unless the enraged man had something more gruesome in mind.

"Timothy! Stop this!" Rumil voice shouted frantically, scrambling to the Knight before he killed any more of his kind. Timothy felt Rumil's presence as she lightly laid a hand on his left forearm, and the rage and overwhelming aura dispelled. His eyes slowly faded back to normal, and he reluctantly released Niles who at last crumpled lifelessly; alive, but in hardly any condition to stop their escape.

"Timothy? What just happened?" Rumil asked in concern. Wherever that mind-blowing eruption of power had come from, it seemed to have taken half of Timothy's natural vigor with it. He looked exhausted and pale – or at least paler than normal.

The Knight shook his head, unwilling to discuss it. "Don't worry about it. It's a long story that we don't have time for right now. Just get in the shuttle, and strap yourself in. We might be looking at a bumpy ride."

Rumil nodded, but didn't get terribly far ahead of Timothy, worried that he might collapse at any moment. Finally, she asked, "So… just where are we going?"

Timothy smirked warily, and replied, "As odd as it might sound… we're going as directly as we can straight to the very planet of Kiros itself."

Chapter Nineteen

One staryear ago, if anyone had told Justin Feroz that a prominent Solarian Knight would appear outside Kiros High Command in the capital city of Senter, asking for him specifically, Justin would have asked to see a sample of whatever narcotic that person was using.

Now, he probably would have marveled over said person's uncanny precognitive abilities. Because when one of the office staff contacted Justin's comm unit with a breathless voice, and informed the Kiros Knight that a prominent Solarian Knight by the name of Timothy Honore had just appeared outside High Command, and had asked for him specifically, Justin didn't even bother to question the news. He simply put down his stylus, pushed in his chair, and quickly left his manor for High Command.

Surprisingly, the staffer didn't lead Justin to the detention area, where Justin would have expected his fellows to put a Solarian who had the gall to appear in the heart of Kiros space. Instead, Justin was led to the primary conference room, where he discovered his father, High Commander Joseph Feroz at the head of the rectangular table, along with fifteen Knights of very high rank on both sides. At the far end was the far too recognizable face of Timothy Honore, and just to his left sat the somewhat bemused Rumil Bonamede.

Thankfully it doesn't appear that my comrades tried to separate those two, Justin thought wryly, *or that might have gotten messy.*

Joseph wasted no time getting to the point. "Justin, do you know this man… more than in passing?"

Justin cringed, trying to gauge how his answer would affect a multitude of things, most notably his career. Finally, he remembered his father's own words; that honesty never had the worst consequences. "Yes… I assisted him in the apprehension of Gregor Krennan. I had informed King Lionel of the plan to bring forth a joint case against Krennan, but kept it from your knowledge knowing the sensitive nature of the attempt."

Joseph frowned, but didn't do much more than that. "That's what I wanted to know." Looking back at Timothy, "Our Solarian guest here informed us that he is willing to… switch sides, but I wanted to see how trustworthy his story was."

Justin's mind flopped in mild shock. No wonder Timothy was

being treated well. He also had a hard time believing that his Solarian counterpart would just arbitrarily decide to embrace the Kiros faith. Timothy might have been unconventional, but was still strong in his beliefs… some of which were wholly contrary to Justin's sect.

Joseph then continued, "However, the Solarian Central Command issued an edict to the general galaxy that anyone matching the description of these two is to be reported immediately. The list of charges against Timothy is quite… extensive to say the least, and include several serious offenses that the Solarian military will not simply take lightly. If word were to come to the Solarians that Timothy was here on Kiros… this council can easily see full-blown conflict emerging."

Justin was still a little taken aback by the fact that Timothy was here, and that he had supposedly offered his services. Thus it took him a while to catch up with everyone else. Finally, he asked Joseph, "Father, may I speak with you… in private?"

Joseph grinned, "I was about to suggest the same. Meet me in my office." He stood, and nodded politely to the rest of the assembly. "I will return, gentlemen."

It wasn't a particularly long walk from the conference room to the office of Joseph Feroz, so Justin didn't have adequate time to sort out the mess that had conglomerated in his brain. Because of this, his father had to repeat his first question because it hadn't registered through the muck.

"Justin!" Joseph snapped, finally getting his son's attention. "Do you feel we can trust this Honore character?"

Justin nodded emphatically. "Implicitly. I'll admit, his offer to join us is somewhat out of character for him, but in my experience, when he says something, he does it."

"So, you don't think he is a Solarian spy?"

Justin didn't quite succeed in fighting back a laugh. "My impression of him is that he's not exactly the biggest fan of the way his sect does things. I can't imagine him submitting himself in such a way." He then added slyly, "You're thinking of taking him up on his offer, aren't you?"

"I'm weighing the option, of course," Joseph admitted. "The advantages of having someone of his stature, with his knowledge of Solarian methods and plans, would be the biggest boon to us since Tan's decision to give our sect Kiros eight hundred staryears ago."

"But…?" Justin queried.

"But the disadvantages could be just as profound. The Solarians won't just let us have someone of his stature. As I mentioned earlier, the Solarian military has demanded to the general galaxy that he be returned, basically dead or alive… preferably dead. The vehemence of these demands suggests that if they were to find out he is *here*, *on Kiros*, they would not hesitate to go to full-blown war."

"First of all, the Galactic Alliance would never allow it," Justin argued. "They've always been preaching the right to choose your own life, and it appears that his desire brought him here. The Solarians, if they were to bid for the Alliance's aid, would be rebuffed, and I doubt the Solarians would have the gall to challenge the entire Galactic Alliance for one man."

"What about his little friend? Isn't she the computer hacker you were sent out to find initially?"

Justin gulped. "Yes… she was going to be our prime witness against Krennan. She's a decent enough girl, I suppose. A lot of her problems stem from her situation. A situation Timothy appears to believe wasn't completely under her control. I got the impression that they had met before she had been apprehended."

"Which you cooperated with Mr. Honore in doing," Joseph remarked.

"Yes, sir…"

Joseph's face remained emotionless, "You do realize that your actions violate numerous amounts of our own regulations? It's not like you to shirk our rules of conduct."

Justin bristled, knowing how correct his father's analysis was. "Not usually… but in this case, I felt the advantages to be gained were worth bending the rules slightly. It's not my fault King Lionel couldn't see reason if it bit him on the nose."

Joseph chuckled at the comment. "Perhaps not, and your actions might have come to advantage of us anyway. I still don't like the idea of how Solaria will respond once the truth becomes known."

"Well, let me ask you, doesn't it interest you why the Solarians want him back at just about any cost?"

"Because of what he knows. He was the Commandant of the Solarian Knighthood, after all."

Justin shook his head. "Not just that, I'd wager. I mean, plans can be changed, codes can be altered, or bases can be rearranged."

"That is true. What else do you think is affecting their decision then?"

Justin took a deep breath, as he really didn't want to admit this. "I… was in a couple skirmishes with him before we decided to pool our resources. His combat and psionic abilities are *easily* equal to mine…" his voice then trailed off slightly, "… if not a little *better.* I suspect they don't like the prospect of that power in our hands."

This piqued Joseph's attention. A psionic along Justin's level was rare indeed. Justin was in some situations equal to several regiments of non-talented units, and to have *two* such people at Joseph's disposal was indeed an interesting thought.

"We'll see if your estimation of Timothy's ability is true enough. I am currently having his output analyzed, and once our scientists feel they have a decent approximation of his power, we'll compare the two."

Justin snorted. "Those estimations are never precise."

Joseph waved a finger in chiding. "No, they are not. However, along with what you have just told me, it can be somewhat confirmed. If our people estimate that his psionic power has a maximum around the eleven to thirteen Toule range, I'll be able to safely consider *your* estimation correct…" then with a grin added, "… and then obviously decide that the positives far outweigh the negatives."

Justin smiled. "You'd probably be better off just asking him to demonstrate his maximum capability. He'd probably do it."

Joseph shrugged. "Possibly… but I don't want to give him the impression I'm merely out for his power."

"Of course…" Justin mused, somewhat sourly. "Appearances are everything, aren't they?"

Joseph's face turned thoughtful. "You're somewhat fond of that Solarian, aren't you?"

Justin admitted sheepishly, "It's been hard to fit in with my fellow Knights, due to my last name, and my abilities. I sense considerable jealously and apprehension from most of my peers. I've never gotten those same feelings from Timothy, likely because he comes from a similar background, and has had to deal with the same issues. He's the closest I've had to a true friend in a while."

Joseph's expression softened. He had known that his son never felt like he was one of the group from as early as he could remember, knowing he was different than all of them, but never fully understanding just how different he was.

Justin had been a blessing to Joseph, and he had always tried to make his son as happy as possible. "Well, when you put it that way… I'll see what I can do."

"Thank you… father," Justin said sincerely.

Joseph waved away the thanks, and said, "Perhaps we should return to our guest, no?"

Before they could do that, Joseph's receptionist called in. "Sir, Kenseth is here to see you. He has the results you were asking for."

"By all means, send him in," Joseph said, his voice lilting in anticipation.

The middle-aged Kiros man, with dark skin and a half bald, grey-haired head, looked almost like he had seen a ghost when he slipped inside the door. His pudgy frame – as pudgy as an Erani frame gets, anyway – was trembling in something that looked like a mix of fear… and amazement.

Both Feroz men caught onto this quickly. "I take it you have something grand to tell us, Sir Kenseth?" Joseph asked.

Kenseth nodded violently. "Oh, yes, sir. I could hardly believe it myself… We ran the numbers through our equations several times because we thought it couldn't possibly be right."

"Out with it," Joseph ordered sternly.

Still, Kenseth continued to prattle on. "I mean… it bodes really ill for us if Knight Honore is at all indicative of Solarian Knights. Even if he is considered one of the finest of his sect, it's still disturbing."

Joseph had to grit his teeth to keep from yelling from the man, but still snapped with great annoyance, "Just tell us, and we shall decide how disturbing the news is. What did you calculate?"

Kenseth mumbled what appeared to be a number, but not loud enough for either Knight to discern.

Joseph was about ready to scream. "I will rip it out of your head if I have to, I swear, Kenseth. Now, one last chance."

Kenseth, as if finally realizing just how upset the Kiros High Commander was, yelped then nearly shouted, "Around twenty-two!"

Joseph wasn't certain he heard right, so he asked, "Did you just say… twenty-two Toules?"

Kenseth nodded. "Yes, sir. I know how it sounds, but we ran the numbers several times, and it always came up around that point."

Justin finally cut in. "That's not just unbelievable. That's impossible." He then addressed his father. "I've already told you I've fought him, I've seen his abilities. He couldn't possibly be much stronger than I am."

Joseph found himself playing the devil's advocate. "Could he have intentionally been holding back?"

Justin shook his head. "We were competitors for the same target at the time I mixed it up with him. With that sort of output, he could have turned me into a messy smear across a roadway. For what reason would he have held back?"

Joseph acknowledged that point. "But at the same time, the psionic calculations have never been that far off-target. Could he have improved?"

"You're telling me he almost doubled his power in a matter of about two ten-cycles? You know as well as I do that's just as impossible as the number Kenseth tossed at us."

Joseph rubbed his forehead. "Well, I do believe I'm going to have to take you up on your suggestion, my son. Kenseth, get to the analysis lab, and prepare for a psionic trial. Justin and I will try to convince our Solarian friend to submit himself to a slight measurement."

*   *   *   *   *

Unfortunately, Timothy did not seem particularly inclined towards Justin's idea.

"Why would I want to do that?" Timothy asked.

Justin crossed his arms. "We received some conflicting information regarding your psionic potential. We'd like to sort it out once and for all."

"Why does it matter? You know that I'm at least your equal," Timothy said with a shrug.

"We'd like to know precisely," Joseph retorted. "Consider it simple curiosity. What is your maximum energy output?"

Timothy shrugged. "I don't rightly know."

Justin blinked. "What do you mean, you don't know?"

"I've never had it tested, nor do I want to." The Solarian's tone suggested that it was rather non-negotiable. "The Solarian military was also intent on fixing a number to what I could do. I, on the other hand, have never seen the point."

"Knowing what you are capable of will help us determine what I can use you for," Joseph explained.

Timothy glared as if in challenge. "I'm capable of anything you assign to me."

Finally, Joseph played his final card. "Our discussions towards your conversion will proceed no further until you submit to a psionic trial."

Timothy's glare flattened further, causing Rumil to take two steps back. She remembered the last time he stared like that, and it hadn't turned out terribly pretty. Fortunately, this time, nothing unusual occurred. Timothy grit out an emotionless, "Very well. What do you need me to do?" which served to drain the tension from the room.

The group started to filter out, but once Rumil tried to leave the room, two soldiers imposed themselves in her way. "Miss, we can't allow you any further into the complex. They will return when the trial is completed."

Not surprisingly, Timothy found that totally unacceptable. "Miss Bonamede does not leave my sight under any circumstances."

Joseph protested, "She can't be in the room you are testing in anyway."

Justin deftly stepped in to stop the situation from escalating. "Father, I will be responsible for Rumil. She can be in the analysis room with us. She won't even touch any of the computers there, right?"

At that point, Rumil just felt it was a good idea to simply agree. As much as she hated the idea of being treated like a troublesome little girl, arguing the point in the middle of the Kiros military headquarters didn't seem to be particularly prudent.

While Joseph didn't seem entirely happy with the plan, he didn't have any strong objections to it, either. "I suppose we can make an exception in this case. Nothing you see can ever leave this facility, do you understand, Miss Bonamede?"

"Clearly," Rumil replied, trying to sound as sincere as possible. Granted, she certainly wouldn't have minded half of a tenth-cycle of free time at one of the terminals in the facility, but she wasn't so brave to do it with so many eyes keeping close tabs on her.

With a resigned sigh from Joseph, the procession continued

towards a lift at the end of the hall. Once everyone crammed themselves inside, it began to drop downwards towards the lower levels of the complex. Due to the lift's darkened windows, Rumil couldn't see outside, but could feel tiny pangs in the back of her head… possibly from psionic experiments being performed on the floors.

She then noticed that Joseph was looking at her with a confused expression on his face, like he had seen something disappear into the wall of the lift behind her. Finally, he blinked several times then started looking forward again.

A demitick later, she heard Timothy and Justin's voice in her head.

That was too close for comfort, Timothy commented.

So I take it we're out to keep Rumil's… little tingle… a secret? Justin replied.

How do you think most Kiros would react to know that an Arcadian woman was demonstrating psionic ability?

Good point.

Somewhat irked, Rumil finally interjected. *You know, I am right here.*

Justin's mental voice made a little gasp. *Did she just…?*

Timothy seemed inflected with a slight humor. *Indeed she did.*

When did she learn to do that?

She picked up a few tricks while on Solaria. Not even I am terribly sure how it happened, Timothy replied.

Just know now that you can't have these little private conversations anymore. Rumil couldn't help but sound a little cocky as she made the comment.

Justin was amused by the boast. *We'll see about that.*

The pair then went silent, but Rumil was quite certain that they were still communicating at a telepathic level, she could feel it in the back of her head, just shielded from her attempts to pry. She glowered at them, then the jolt as the lift stopped abruptly at the designated floor nearly knocked her over.

"Stay close, Rumil," Justin stated, as the group slowly began to filter out of the lift. "The last thing we need is for you to get 'lost' down here."

Timothy agreed, "Yes, you don't want to 'accidentally' get 'left behind,' understand?"

Rumil sighed, "I wouldn't try hacking around here for all the credits in this whole cursed galaxy."

Timothy and Justin replied simultaneously, "Good," then took step behind the rest of the procession, Rumil behind Timothy, and in front of Justin. Clearly, they didn't totally trust her not to stray. But to be fair, she wouldn't exactly trust herself either. No doubt the answers to her muddled history could be found somewhere in this facility, if she was given enough time to find them. However, she wasn't so stupid as to intentionally wander off looking for it, as the two Knights implied.

They suddenly took a left down an intersecting hall, Justin's hand falling on her shoulder as if to guide her. Scowling at him, she noticed they were passing by a multitude of rooms, their windows heavily tinted, just like the doors of the lift. Occasional flashes of light were dimly visible nonetheless, coinciding perfectly with the gentle tingle that implied the use of psionic power.

No doubt the Kiros are just as heavily into psionic experimentation as the Solarians are, Timothy remarked.

Rumil had to admit that confused her. *Why do your people still experiment? You'd think after all the centuries being blessed with the power, you'd have it pretty much figured out.*

One would think so, Timothy agreed wryly. *Truth is, there is a great deal about our psionic gifts that we simply don't understand, and we are just starting to get the sophistication and technology necessary to explore it.*

Rumil couldn't help but try and pry. *Such as?*

What causes an Erani to have psionic power, for one. The very origins of the skill are still a considerable mystery. All we know for certain is that it comes from the Se-Lan race, but we still have no idea as to what in that ancient heritage gives us our power.

Suddenly, Justin's voice slipped into the conversation. *We have had the typical Erani genome mapped for centuries, but found nothing. Recently, there has been a breakthrough in gene protein analysis that sounds promising. The Arcadians first developed the science, a guy by the name of... umm... ah! Sams Fidel! That's it!*

Rumil froze in place upon hearing the name. It was like Justin had reached out, and plucked a neuron in her brain like a harp string. Justin bumped into her, knocking her to the ground, but by then, her mind was already fading in on itself.

She vaguely heard Timothy hiss telepathically, *Bannor take us, it's happening again. Help me shield this coming surge, Justin.* Then she totally slipped into her vision…

She was on a table, strapped down, with her arms straight out at her sides, and her legs slightly spread. Outside of the metal grain of the table, she could barely see much else due to the odd darkness. Two long clear tubes were attached to her ankles, right where her future scars would form. Another such tube was embedded into her left wrist. Turning her head to the right, she saw a young, smooth Arcadian face, topped with a disheveled mess of black hair that completely covered his temple. His eyes reflected great regret as he held another tube in his hand, and turned her palm upward to reveal the angry mark on her wrist. He said something that Rumil couldn't hear then pushed the tube into her wrist.

Rumil screamed in pain, and it was at that moment that she realized that she was just a child, reliving a moment of her past. The man gently rubbed her forehead while she sobbed, his lips moving in what Rumil assumed were supposed to be words of comfort.

The man disappeared into the darkness, and everything was silent for several demiticks, when a glowing white substance started pouring down the tubes and into her body where the tubes had been injected. Flaring pain flashed through the contact points, and another agonized scream ripped out of the little girl's throat.

Much to Rumil's embarrassment, the vision disappeared instantly, and she discovered herself screaming like she was being murdered in the middle of the Kiros Military High Command. It had drawn a great deal of unwanted attention, as just about every person inside every room along the hall had stuck their head outside trying to find out the source and/or reason for such wailing.

*What was **that** all about?* Justin asked telepathically.

Timothy ignored him at first, because Joseph had asked a considerably more pressing question out loud.

"By Annor's host, what is wrong with her?" the High Commander of the Kiros Knighthood asked.

Timothy quickly answered, so quickly that Rumil was certain he had rehearsed it at some point. "Your son and I quickly learned that Miss Bonamede occasionally suffers from debilitating headaches. Solarian medical officers had tried to determine the cause, with little success."

Joseph turned to his son, and asked, "Is this true?"

Justin froze, two thoughts battling in his brain. On one hand, he didn't want to lie to his father, but at the same time, he didn't want to expose Timothy for a liar either. Eventually, he muttered dumbfounded, "Yeah… but I don't recall them to ever be quite this… violent." He figured that Timothy would eventually explain himself.

Joseph nodded. Something about all this was setting off warning signs in his head. His son was not one to intentionally deceive him, but at the same time, he couldn't help but think that Rumil's little episode was more than a simple headache. Joseph finally decided not to let it trouble him at the moment. He was a patient man, and was certain he would get to the bottom of the issue given enough time. The Kiros High Commander then turned back about abruptly, and resumed his previous pace towards his destination.

The area that the test was supposed to take place looked like a large warehouse, with one large central room with exposed piping running along the ceiling in between the hypersteel girders that supported the floor above. There was nothing in the central room outside of a pair of thin, black poles topped with black, translucent orbs that were about the same diameter, coming about waist-height to an Erani. The posts stood on a small raised portion of the floor, and Timothy was guided onto it, though he cooperated somewhat sluggishly.

Rumil followed Justin, Joseph, and the rest of the procession into the smaller room annexed to the south side. It had the same high ceiling, but considerably less surface area. The wall facing the central room was comprised of window paneling on the upper half – no doubt shatter-resistant – and a long series of monitors and computer terminals linked together in one long table on the bottom half. Fortunately, Justin's duty to keep an eye on her allowed her to be in the front rather than crunched in some corner by the large number of onlookers.

Joseph leaned into an intercom on the center console, and said, "Knight Honore, just place your hands onto the receptors, and focus all your energy into them. Keep doing so until I inform you to stop."

Timothy complied, yet sulking as he did so. Less than five demiticks later, the center of the orbs started to glow with a soft yellow color, gradually brightening until the entire balls were completely lit with the gentle light.

From there, the attention turned to a blonde Kiros technician to the far left, who was looking closely at some form of digital display, calling out numbers as the readings rose.

"He's at nine Toules… ten… eleven… leveling off at eleven point four… sitting solidly at eleven point six," the technician finally declared.

Justin bought that assessment about as much as he had bought into the original estimate of his friend's potential. "That's too low. It has to be."

"Not necessarily," Joseph corrected. "I doubt the two of you actually went off trying to blow each other to pieces with your maximum ability. It's quite possible he just put a little more into it. Although, I'll admit that our estimates have never been that far skewed."

Hearing Justin's disbelief merely supported Rumil's initial thoughts. She had been almost certain that the back of her brain was about to explode from the buzz she felt during his outburst just before they had escaped from Centris. The sensation she got now was like the buzzing of a flying insect, barely detectable over the background "noise" from the other Erani present.

She pushed her way to the intercom as the two members of the Feroz clan argued back and forth, her sudden movement surprising Justin to the point where he stepped back to let her pass without thinking. She leaned around a technician the next console over, nudging Joseph out of the way in the process.

"Will you quit fooling around, and show them everything you're capable of so that we can get this over with? I'm roasting in here!" she bellowed into the receiver, causing Timothy to jolt like he had just managed to avoid jumping.

The Solarian then glared daggers at the hacker, who returned the look as Joseph reclaimed his original position.

"Knight Honore, if you have more than what you've demonstrated so far, I suggest you show us," the Kiros High Commander commented.

Still scowling at Rumil, he showed no indication that he had acknowledged Joseph's request, until the orbs at his sides again began to glow even brighter, pulsing rapidly as if struggling to keep up with the man testing, while the technician at the console began to count upwards again.

When the technician hit fifteen, it drew some impressed nods. When he reached seventeen, the nods became an excited murmuring from the Knights in the back. Then, when the increasingly amazed technician counted to twenty, there was simply an awed silence.

"Twenty-one... twenty-two... leveling again at twenty-two point three... now sitting solidly at twenty-two point four Toules," the tech shook his head swiftly then peered at the display again as if thinking he might have misread it.

In the now completely silent room, Rumil leaned close to Justin's ear, and whispered, "That's good… right?"

Justin turned his eyes toward her, and peered down like she had suddenly grown a second head. "The highest I've ever tested at is a little over twelve."

"Oh," Rumil replied simply. "So that *is* good."

"Try more along the lines of incredibly infeasible… then throw in a practically impossible and stupendously unreal, and then you'd be somewhat close."

Meanwhile, Joseph stared dumbly at the Solarian then finally jerked to reality in order to say, "Knight Honore, you can stop now." Taking a few moments to gather the thoughts he had been putting together before the unexpected display, he continued, "Would you like to know the results?"

Timothy frowned, and replied with a tone bordering on sour, "Not particularly."

"Well, then… we'll just go through a standard physical, and pending a clean bill of health, I should make my decision as to your usefulness by the end of the day."

Justin smirked, and asked, "It'll take you that long?"

Joseph couldn't help but smile back, "I will wait until I receive the results of the physical for posterity's sake, but as it stands… the Solarians' loss is our gain. They can make all the threats they want, and go straight to the depths of Bannor. He's *ours* now."

Chapter Twenty

In reality, High Commander Feroz's official decision took less than two tenth-cycles, demiticks after the physical confirmed that Timothy had no nagging genetic conditions or illnesses. Shortly thereafter, Timothy had been shuttled off to the tailor and armorer to get all his gear squared away.

Timothy slowly fastened the claps of the carbide breastplate he had been given, having just been cooled from the molding bin. They had told him to see if it fit properly, which the Solarian found somewhat amusing, since they had actually created the mold from his own body for the purposes of making his armor pieces.

It wasn't Solarian carbide, and not just as a matter of quality. While it likely didn't hold a candle to the alloys molded by his native sect, no others would either, so that wasn't the issue. He simply wasn't prepared for its color.

The royal blue breastplate fit to his body like a glove, as did all the other pieces of his armor… but it didn't exactly fit his mind. It served as a strong dose of reality. There was no going back now.

Had he made the right choice? What if he was wrong about all of this? What then? Could he live with the mistake, of no longer being able to have any relations with his old people? True, the society he lived in on Solaria was archaic and riddled with mindless traditions… but he highly doubted that the Kiros way was any better.

His mind drifted to his mother. No doubt she was worried ill over her only birth son, and contacting her to let her know where he was… well, that was simply out of the question. If she knew what he was doing now… as progressive as she was, she was still a Solarian. No reasoning Timothy could ever give would make her understand.

The Knights who had supported him through all his father's abuse… who had told him to stay strong, who would have been willing to defy orders, even perhaps go up in arms, for him… what would they think? They certainly would never be able to understand. They would see the man for whom they had been willing to die suddenly wearing royal blue, nothing more than a traitor. They would feel cheated and used, and would no doubt look for any opportunity to rectify their misplaced trust.

Frederick… no doubt Horace had told him about Timothy's plans. While it appeared that the Solarian King had not informed Niles about

Timothy's whereabouts, by no means did it mean that he liked the idea. Even Horace had paled at the idea, and the High Priest had been one of the most forward-thinking men Timothy had ever known.

What about Craig? What would he have thought to see his adopted brother wearing the armor of a Kiros Knight? The man who laid his life on the line countless times, defending the honor of a family that he wasn't even a member of by blood? What would his choice have been?

As suddenly as the doubts had mounted, Timothy banished them as far back in his mind as he could. He had made the decision that was the best he could make with what he knew. That's all anyone could have asked of him. If no one other than himself understood, that was not his concern.

"Looks odd, doesn't it?" Rumil said from the entrance to the small dressing room. She was leaning with her right arm against the door frame, her head cocked slightly towards the shoulder. He had been so absorbed in his thoughts that he hadn't even sensed her presence.

"Slightly, but I suspect I'll get used to it," he remarked flatly.

She abruptly wrapped her arms around his waist, and pressed her cheek against the back of his neck, whispering, "You're not as good at hiding your thoughts as you might think. I think I'm finally figuring out how to read you."

"Is that so?"

She nodded, and he could feel the movement through the bodysuit covering his neck. "You've said before one doesn't need to be a psionic to know what a person is thinking. You had the look of someone who was afraid he had made the biggest mistake of his life."

"Don't concern yourself too much with that," Timothy dismissed. "It was my choice, and I don't regret it. Your safety remains my primary concern, no matter how many enemies I make in the process."

Suddenly, Justin's voice interrupted them. "I'm not… disturbing anything, am I?"

Rumil tensed, and released her hold, whirling around as Timothy slowly turned to face the Kiros. He stood in the doorway with his arms crossed, a knowing and conspiratorial grin tugging at the corners of his mouth.

"You *wish* you were interrupting something," Rumil retorted with a disdainful snort. "You have the demeanor of a gossipy old woman."

Justin's smile broadened. "If that was the case, then half of this compound would know of your little psionic episode."

Timothy glared. "Well, they probably do *now*." His eyes scanned the dressing room. Technology had made surveillance equipment so small it could be attached to a person, and they would never know it.

Justin remained cool. "Nobody's listening to us right now. Nonetheless, we can continue this discussion once we leave. You better have some pretty good answers for my questions, Knight Honore."

He turned around, then stopped briefly, and added over his shoulder. "For all it's worth… I think you look good in blue."

Once Justin had disappeared back into the halls, Timothy allowed himself the slightest of smiles.

* * * * *

"I don't imagine sending you out on any missions into the far reaches of the galaxy at the moment," Joseph stated in his final briefing to Timothy. "I would like the issue of your defection to cool down slightly before sending you off-planet."

Timothy laughed in his mind. If Joseph Feroz thought that the Solarians would ever let this go, he was definitely mistaken.

Then the High Commander added, "On the other hand, I'm not going to have you patrolling around the core planets. If you think the Solarians dislike the idea of having one of their number in the Kiros sect… imagine how some elements of Kiros society would feel."

Joseph released a heavy breath that bordered on a sigh, "I guess what I'm saying is that I don't have much for you to do initially… except any insider information you might have on the Solarians."

Timothy shrugged. "I'll tell you what I can, but bear in mind that the Solarian military is no doubt going through a full-scale changing of their every process, even if they don't know where I am exactly, just in case." Surely Timothy's father had instantly classified him as a security breach, and acted accordingly.

Joseph nodded, acknowledging that appraisal. "True… but I was more talking about the people running operations, who *won't* change. Everyone has their tendencies, and knowing those tendencies could make things considerably easier for us if it goes as far as conflict."

"I'll do what I can," Timothy replied.

"There's one more issue I'd like to bring up. It's about Miss Bonamede."

Timothy's eyes narrowed suspiciously. "What about her?"

"It's that, well… we Kiros have a very strict policy about who we can… you know… engage in strong relations with. I'm sure the Solarians do something similar."

"Meaning?" Timothy was getting increasingly impatient, as he could sense where this conversation was going.

"I know that your situation is a little… different… than the rest of us, but I've been thinking that your obvious psionic gifts could be of great use augmenting our genetic pool, so to speak."

Timothy rolled his eyes. "Let me explain something to you. There is *nothing* sexual about my relationship with Miss Bonamede. I made a promise to keep her safe from Krennan, and I'll admit, she's become a very close friend of mine, but there is nothing beyond that."

"Good… then I was wondering if you'd be—"

Timothy cut him off sharply. "However, if anything *does* stem from my relationships, that will be *my* concern, and no one else's. My father made the mistake of thinking he could control me. I suggest you be careful about doing the same."

Joseph liked to claim that no man had ever made truly afraid, but Timothy was testing the limits of that boast. The Kiros High Commander wondered if this was the same thing his Solarian counterpart had to deal with, and what made things so tenuous between the pair. Perhaps it's best that Timothy didn't know his own strength, so to speak. The knowledge that one is much stronger than anyone else could make for a dangerous change in a person, especially when the gap is as wide as it is in Timothy's case.

"Well, nonetheless, I won't keep you any longer. I suspect my dear son wishes for you to meet his family," Joseph finally finished, his words and tone suggesting that he had said all he wished, or dared to, at the moment. "You are dismissed."

Timothy saluted, then meandered out of the High Commander's office, where Justin was indeed waiting, looking quite excited about something. Rumil, who was just behind him, was fiddling with her hair somewhat absentmindedly, but nonetheless, looked more than pleased with herself.

"Guess what happened while you were talking with my dear father?" Justin almost chirped.

Timothy blinked, and replied, "I've never enjoyed guessing games."

Rumil finally nudged Justin aside, and said, "The Kiros Military has decided my expertise at hacking and computer sciences could be put to good use by bulking up their own security."

Timothy's expression turned amused. "I'm surprised they're letting you within a TackMet of their mainframes."

"Oh, I can't touch anything." Rumil snorted. "They're just using me as a consultant, I suppose. But hey, since it appears we're going to be stuck here for a while, I might as well be doing something with my time, right?"

"Anyway…" Justin interjected, drawing a withering glare from the blonde woman who he had just stepped in front of, "Julianne more likely than not has the evening meal ready, so it would probably be best if we made our way back to my home. We'll teleport to save time, then after we dine, I'll show you where the two of you will be staying."

"Who's Julianne?" Rumil asked.

"My wife," Justin remarked. Ignoring Rumil's disbelieving gape, he added to Timothy, "I guess you'll finally get to meet Jonathan after all. He's never met a Solarian before, so he'll probably be real interested in you. He's always been attracted to new things."

In a daze, Rumil asked, "Is Jonathan your… your…"

"My son. Yes. He turns three staryears in about two ten-cycles. Cute as a Ferian cub, too. Fortunately, he inherited his mother's looks."

Rumil found it extremely hard to believe that carefree, somewhat quirky, Justin Feroz, was a *father.* "Why didn't I know this before *now*?"

"Hey, it's not like you were exactly forthcoming with your past, Miss Bonamede," Justin replied. He then smiled mischievously. "Why? Are you upset to know that I am spoken for?"

It was slight, and it didn't stay very long, but Justin was certain he saw a flash of irritation on Timothy's face. *Are you jealous too?* He asked in a tight mental thought to the Solarian.

Timothy's telepathic reply came at the same time as Rumil's spoken one, exactly word for word. "Get over yourself."

Justin laughed heartily then said, "Well, at any rate, come along. I'll give you the image you need, Timothy, and I'll trust you to transport our other guest." He then led the pair through the multitude of hallways to the exterior of the complex. Pushing aside a pair of dark red hypersteel double doors, they emerged into a large courtyard, empty save for one large yellow sign on it that almost seemed to glow in the increasing darkness as night fell on the Kiros military complex.

"That's to give us a landmark that we can easily commit to memory for teleportation," Justin explained. "This entire courtyard is largely for high-ranking Knights to get in and out of the facility quickly."

"That seems like a pretty sloppy backdoor into a highly regarded facility," Rumil remarked.

"Why? Only high-ranking officers even know it's here, and we do have security watching this courtyard just in case. High standing has its perks."

At one time, I thought that Timothy and Justin were dropped from the same mold. Then I got to know them... Rumil thought wryly.

Justin hasn't had to ask himself the type of questions that challenge the very core of his own person and faith like I have, Timothy observed. *Psychology is often a lot like physics, in that regard. A mind at ease will remain at ease until an outside force acts upon it.*

Frowning at the fact she was broadcasting telepathically, Rumil asked, *I take it Justin heard that?*

Timothy looked over to the Feroz, who was still waxing about what they will have waiting for them at his home, and quipped, *It doesn't appear so. Most curious.*

Finally, Justin whirled about, and said, "Well, you all ready to go?" His features then flattened when he noticed that his two companions didn't respond right away. Even more disturbing was the fact that they likely had shared a telepathic communication that he had not been aware of in the least. Once again, Justin pushed the thoughts aside to be asked later, when he was in the relative safety of his own home. Transmitting the proper image of the back lot of his home to Timothy, he transported himself through foldspace towards his destination.

Somewhat to his surprise – and yet at the same time, not to his surprise – Timothy and Rumil were already at their destination by the time Justin appeared.

If either of the others noticed that Timothy's travel took less time, they certainly didn't comment on it, as Rumil was quickly taken aback by the size of the manor in front of her. It was a large monstrosity with seven balconies and four levels, the fiberwall paneling in a rich forest green with brown trim that almost perfectly matched the neatly trimmed greenery and occasional earth tones of the large hill the manor was built upon.

"Just… how many people live here again?" Rumil asked incredulously.

"Just myself, Julianne, and Jonathan… and during the day there are a few helpers around," Justin replied. "However, at this time of the day, our primary attendant Fiona is usually the only one around, and she returns to the servant manor when Justin is put to sleep."

"Just the three of you… in *that*?" Rumil gaped, her left hand gesturing towards the large homestead.

"At the moment," Justin said with a suggestive grin. "Julianne and I are hoping to have a few more little Kiros running about. Can't ever have too many potential Knights, after all."

Rumil snorted disdainfully. "Leave it to you to make such a delicate act as sex sound both remarkably crude and disturbingly political at the same time."

Justin might have had some form of reply, had they not heard the high-pitched shouts of a young boy from inside the house. "Daddy's home! Daddy's home!" the voice shouted gleefully, and the sounds of someone running down steps quite enthusiastically could be heard.

A woman's voice, logically belonging to Julianne, cut in chidingly. "Jonathan, what have I told you about running around in the house?" Julianne began with a huff. "Just because your father is reckless and uncontrollable does not mean I'm going to let you grow up and be the same. Go back upstairs, get dressed, and wait for your father to come inside rather than run him down in the garden."

"Yes, mom…" Jonathan replied, his voice dying away, probably because he was walking away from the sliding glass door that led outside.

Justin rubbed the back of his head, embarrassed, and asked, "That's the family… got to love them, right?"

Then the sliding door whipped open, revealing a slender Kiros woman with night black hair and threatening gray eyes, dressed in a simple royal purple dress that appeared to be soaked through. With a scowl and a tone that made Justin visibly recoil, Julianne huffed, "Justin Feroz, you are going to get your son to take a bath after you have explained to me just why in the depths of Bannor you disappeared earlier today without so much as a warning when you said you were going to try and fix our GalNet console—oh!" Her tirade was cut short with a startled gasp when she finally acknowledged Rumil and Timothy's existence. Julianne stumbled over her next words a couple of times before finally managing, "Oh dear… I was not expecting company. Oh curse you, Justin, look at me! I am a mess, and I don't have anything ready for guests. Well, please, come inside, come inside… I shall be with you once I tidy myself up."

Timothy smirked wryly as Julianne disappeared into the manor again, leaving the sliding door open. "If I were a betting man, I'd be accepting wagers on how long it takes your wife to boot me right back out."

For a brief moment, Rumil wasn't certain what Timothy meant, until she turned to look at him and realized that she could barely see any of the Solarian's features… especially the paler skin tone that marked him as clearly descended from the Kiros's rival sect.

"I'll try and explain it to her…" Justin began, as if he just realized the potential problem. "Besides, you're still wearing your armor, so that'll help your case. At any rate, don't worry about it, and just leave it to me."

*   *   *   *   *

Fortunately, Justin had no need to explain anything. After an initial start of surprise, Julianne recovered quickly, and seemed determined to play the part of the perfect hostess, regardless of whatever guests Justin dragged in. It helped Timothy's case immensely that he, with Rumil's help, volunteered to repair the faulty GalNet console that Julianne had been fussing over while Justin watched over his son's bath time. "Do you work with computing units, Miss Bonamede?" Julianne asked with awe as the hacker identified the faulty programming and hardware that had been causing the malfunction.

"Yeah… something like that," Rumil replied calmly, deciding that there was really no need to go into detail as to her career choices for the sake of continued good relations. "This may sound silly… but why does it seem like every Kiros name I come across start with the same letter?"

Julianne sighed wistfully, "That's just something members of the Feroz line tend to do. It is done in honor of our greatest patriarch, Julius Feroz. Have you heard the tale?"

Rumil nodded vigorously, hoping beyond hope to dissuade a retelling. "Oh yes. I have been made familiar with it."

"What about you, Mr. Honore?" The family name came awkwardly from Julianne's lips. The woman was still getting used to the idea of the first son of the premier Solarian Knighthood family on his back underneath her GalNet console, replacing damaged cards.

"I would wager I am more familiar with the nuances of your family and your faith than you are, Madam Feroz," Timothy replied flatly. "Just as I would probably be a little surprised to learn the sort of things your husband knows of my family."

At that point, a nagging suspicion snuck into Rumil's thought process. "Wait… did they make you change your name to Julianne when you married?" she asked worriedly, knowing that it was quite unlikely.

"No… why would they?" Julianne replied with a small degree of confusion.

"Then it's just coincidence that your name starts with the same letter as Justin's… right?" Once again, Rumil hopefully asked the question, although she was increasingly certain that she would be once again wrong.

"No… Justin and I are both members of the Feroz family. We shared the same great-grandfather."

Fortunately, Rumil turned back to hand Timothy another replacement card, because her lips coiled into a repulsed sneer, and the hair on her arms was standing on end. Timothy was grinning up at her playfully.

When you require certain levels of genetic purity, and the politics of nobility get involved, those sort of close ties can happen. Several Solarian couples are even closer than third cousins, but I know they try to keep the inbreeding as minimal as possible, the Solarian said.

Was that why you were so adamantly unattached? Rumil asked curiously.

Timothy's reply was carefully thought out. *That… was part of it. There were other issues that concerned me enough to keep me from pursuing a family.*

Rumil decided not to query further on said issues, not that it would have mattered anyway. The sounds of tiny feet rushing down the stairs to the right of the living area drew her attention.

The scruffy-haired blur dressed in nothing but a pair of padded underpants pulled to a sudden stop just before he collided with Rumil's knees, then looked up slowly at her.

Their eyes met, and transfixed instantly. "I take it this is Jonathan."

Julianne sighed in mild disgust. "Yes, that is the little monster himself, and he knows better than to run around the manor half naked, now doesn't he?"

Justin had not been boasting about his son. He was indeed a cute child, with his mother's smooth facial features, but when he popped his index finger into his mouth, his eyes twinkled with his father's mischievousness, looking precious in the way that most children do when they aren't your own. "Yes…" Jonathan finally mumbled around his finger, the slightest of naughty grins on his face.

Julianne was completely unperturbed. "Well, then don't you think you should do something about it?"

Jonathan smiled broadly, and then chirped, "No!" before dashing out of the living area giggling violently.

His mother scowled darkly, crossing her arms and tapping her foot rapidly. "He thinks because we have company, he can act as badly as he wants. Sometimes I swear I gave birth to a Bannor spawn." Then with a yell that caused Timothy's boots to visibly curl, she added, "Justin! Get your son to behave this instant!"

Demiticks later, there was a squeal from around the dividing wall, and Jonathan howled with glee, "Daddy! Let me go!" Justin emerged back in the living area with Jonathan slung over his right shoulder, the young child ineffectually kicking and punching, all the while laughing animatedly.

Justin set his son back down on the ground, and said softly, "Why don't you go upstairs and let Fiona dress you up real nice so that you can meet my friends I brought with me?"

Reluctantly, Jonathan nodded then disappeared around the wall once again, the sounds of the boy dashing up the stairwell, calling out Fiona's name.

Timothy then slid out from underneath the console, and pulled himself to a sitting position, his hands behind him to prop himself up. "That should take care of your reception problems. It's amazing it operated at all with as many damaged cards it had in there."

"Well… I leave those sort of things to certain people in this household, who of course shall remain unmentioned," Julianne said with a scathing glare towards Justin. "A certain person who promised to arrange for its repair before he left…"

Justin quickly waved his hands in front of him, trying to ward off his wife's ire. "I was called out to duty rather unexpectedly, love. You know that happens on occasion. Take it up with my dear old father." As if trying to derail that track of conversation as quickly as he could, Justin turned towards Timothy, and said, "Knight Honore and I have some things to discuss in private. If you could accompany me outside?"

Timothy nodded, and silently the two Knights walked back towards the sliding door that led to the manor's back rotunda. Rumil and Julianne watched passively as the Justin slid the door closed and the two began talking.

Within demiticks, the conversation grew quite animated... at least Justin was growing animated. He was gesturing wildly, the obviously soundproof door muffling his sounds. Meanwhile Timothy stood straight as a board, arms crossed, possibly interjecting briefly.

After a tick, Justin appeared somewhat mollified, and the dialogue between the pair became subdued, although Justin took occasional quick glances towards the manor's interior, locking eyes with Rumil each time.

"There are times where I feel they are intentionally keeping something from me," Rumil mused sourly. "I wonder where I get that idea."

"Men will be men," Julianne replied with a slight shrug of her shoulders. "I've reached the conclusion that if they want to worry themselves to an early death trying to keep me from doing so, they can go right ahead and do that."

At that moment, small feet once again proceeded down the steps, much slower this time. Jonathan appeared into the living area once more, in a matching set of blue trousers, blue button-up shirt, and with black dress shoes adorning his small feet. His black hair had been combed neatly, and Rumil was certain she smelled a slight bit of forest scent. Fiona apparently was quite thorough; the child who had just re-emerged barely resembled the urchin that had blatantly defied his mother earlier.

"Sorry, mother," the boy said mournfully, tapping the heel of his right shoe on the toe of his left.

"Apology accepted, Jonathan," Julianne answered. "We will address further punishment tomorrow. For the moment, you can introduce yourself properly to our guest."

Rumil knelt down to accommodate the toddler, and held out her left hand. "My name is Rumil, are you Jonathan?"

Jonathan nodded, as if suddenly shy. He looked warily at Rumil's hand, obviously uncomfortable with the gesture. Glancing at his mother questioningly, and not seeing any disapproval, Jonathan finally reached out, and grabbed Rumil's fingers. The tactile contact drew a smile from

Rumil, and then their eyes locked on at each other. Jonathan's pupils bulged into discs that almost swallowed the rest of the iris. It was Rumil's only warning that something was about to happen.

The image blasted into her mind so quickly that she never even saw it coming, and for a moment was confused as to what it actually was. It wasn't until the picture focused that she realized she was being assuaged by another mysterious vision.

She seemed to be floating above the scene, looking down on two figures locked in combat. She recognized the first as the gleaming white winged figure that she had seen once before, the other a young adult Erani man dressed in deep red carbide armor. Rumil instinctively understood that she was watching an older version of the young child in front of her.

The white figure had the upper hand, throwing Jonathan's older self like a rag doll into a drab hypersteel wall with such force that the metal dented. As Jonathan stumbled to his feet, the white figure's face burst into a blinding, white-hot light that filled her sight.

The vision ended as abruptly as it came, and Rumil jumped back when she heard Julianne scream Justin's name. Both Justin and Timothy burst back into the manor upon hearing Julianne's outburst, and for a moment Rumil didn't understand why.

Then she noticed that Jonathan had pulled away from her, and was trembling violently, looking like he was about to fall over. Rumil began to approach him in concern when Timothy grabbed her and pinned her against the wall, as if trying to shield her body with his.

That's when it seemed like Jonathan yelled in anguish, and blue lancets of energy ripped out in all directions, piercing the ceiling and walls, ripping through the floor, and smashing the GalNet display that she and Timothy had just fixed. About seven or eight such bolts struck Timothy in the back, but were harmlessly deflected by a psionic shield that Timothy had constructed as if expecting something like that would occur.

When the outburst ended after merely two demiticks, nobody moved, as if trying to decide what to do next. Finally, Jonathan spun about in a full circle, surveyed the damage then instantly put his comfort finger in his mouth just before he said guiltily, "Sorry…"

That served to break the mass paralysis in the room. Justin dove towards his son, snatching up the small boy and tossing him the air, catching him with arms outstretched. "Well done, young man!" the elder Feroz exclaimed proudly. He quickly turned to Julianne, and ordered,

"Get my father on the comm, he's going to want to hear this!"

Julianne dashed out of the living area, and into the dining hall, most likely where they kept a spare unit, as the one in the living area was completely wrecked. Meanwhile, Justin had pulled his son into a tight hug, muttering, "I am so proud of you. Just incredible. With any luck, you'll surpass your old man, and then some."

Finally, Rumil whispered what she felt was a very important question to Timothy. "What exactly just happened?"

Timothy looked at her strangely for a moment, then replied, "You mean, you don't sense anything different about Jonathan?"

"No." But just as the word escaped her mouth, she did feel something in the back of her head. It was almost shrouded by the tingle that she recognized as Justin's, but she did feel a small flicker of another psionic presence. It was very faint, and barely detectable, but it was there.

"You mean…"

Timothy raised his eyebrows. "Jonathan's psionic talent just manifested itself."

Rumil gaped at the damage caused by the child's outburst. "This happens *every* time a psionic comes to his power? No wonder there are so few of you."

Justin cut in after hearing Rumil's comment, "Actually, homes are prepared for this sort of thing usually, and aren't always so violent in their manifestation. Noble children with purer bloodlines generally do cause more damage than most, though. Julianne and I were getting ready to do the same in the next few ten-cycles, but it appears this little guy snuck up on us." Justin then frowned, as if truly realizing that his guests were still there. "Actually, I suspect that I'll hand Jonathan off to Fiona for a little bit, and take you two to your new residence now. You probably won't want to be around when the rest of the celebration inevitably comes."

*   *   *   *   *

It was barely five ticks later that Justin dropped Rumil and Timothy off at the small lakeshore cabin that was to be their temporary home until they had time to decide on a permanent place, leaving once he had pointed out where every room was.

"Justin sure wanted us out in a hurry," Rumil mused.

"Because he didn't want to answer questions about your part in the episode," Timothy said with a critical glare.

Rumil, taken aback by Timothy's accusation, she asked, "What are you blabbering on about now?"

"The average Erani child first manifests his potential around the age of six staryears," Timothy answered. "While it's true that Justin also came about at an early age, Jonathan's emergence is still rather young, far younger than he possibly should have."

Timothy approached rapidly, pinning Rumil up against the wall, his arms planted against the wall just above her shoulders. "You did something to trigger his power."

Rumil violently shook her head, once again trying to comprehend how a person can go from so gentle to so cold with barely any change in his voice at all. "If I did, I didn't do it intentionally. I saw another odd vision… then it happened."

Timothy seemed to accept that, as he backed away and took a considerably less threatening posture. Meanwhile, his mind was mulling over what had occurred, hoping that no one else managed to put together the puzzle.

Chapter Twenty-One

Joseph knew the communication protocols for his Solarian counterpart, and the reverse was also true. This was done to prevent the lack of communication that led to the Baramak Slaughter. The implied meaning was that the protocols would only be used in the most dire of circumstances. Thus, when a call came through the GalNet from Niles Honore, Joseph Feroz instantly knew there was some form of trouble. The Solarian High Commander wouldn't try to communicate just to chat.

It had been so long since the pair had met in person that it took Joseph some time to recognize the face on his console's holographic display as belonging to his counterpart. Fortunately, he remembered that Niles tended to be direct, as the Solarian High Commander got right to the point. "I assume you are aware as to the warrant issued against my… son," Niles remarked flatly.

Joseph noted the pause that the Solarian had put just before that last word. Joseph had been aware of the controversy of Timothy's birth, of course, but had been unaware that the issue still lingered so evidently. "I was made aware of it, yes," The Kiros High Commander finally replied, with a casual coolness.

"Well, since it appears he has dropped off every sector of my intelligence, I can only assume he's hiding in the one place I don't have eyes." Niles instantly became accusing. "You wouldn't happen to know anything about that, would you?"

"Even if I did… what would lead you to believe I'd tell you?" Joseph was internally reveling in the advantage he held over the Solarian High Commander.

Niles sighed ruefully, and admitted, "Okay… let's forget my treacherous little boy for a second. To be honest, he's not who I'm looking for."

"Then who?"

"Rumil Bonamede. She accompanied that traitor to wherever he disappeared to. She needs to be eliminated, immediately."

Joseph's eyebrows raised in query, and he asked tauntingly, "Now, why is that? Did she hack into your private diary?"

Niles didn't appear amused, and seemed somewhat irked that Joseph wasn't taking this with great seriousness. "Have you read the Fifth's Prophecy?"

Joseph scoffed, "Of course I have."

Niles paused. "The *whole* prophecy?"

Now it was Joseph's turn to take stock of his thoughts. "I have, indeed. Are you implying…?"

"I sensed… an aura about Miss Bonamede while she was on Solaria. It had been well hidden, but she was definitely a psionic, and appeared to have received some sort of vision. She knew that there was more than what was told." Niles didn't wait for Joseph to reply, as if he was eager to end the conversation. "I'm just suggesting that if you know anything about the whereabouts of my 'son,' that you might want to act… and rather quickly."

The holographic display died, leaving Joseph to his thoughts.

*   *   *   *   *

Justin's first visit to his two friends since the episode with Jonathan three days ago was not as well received as he had hoped. Rumil opened the door and saw the Kiros Knight clad in athletic gear, with elbow and knee pads, a smooth red helmet tucked under one arm, and a small circular ball under the other. "Oh… it's you," she remarked sourly, but stepped aside to allow him in anyway.

"Listen, I know I've been gone some time…" Justin began as he entered the cabin, his eyes roaming the entry hall. "Things have been rather hectic around the manor, as you might have guessed. We finally decided to hire the same man who trained me to oversee Jonathan's development."

"Why? It obviously didn't work for you."

"Okay… I'll comm you more often. I would have figured you'd *like* some alone time." Justin's tone lilted in that suggestive manner Rumil found irritating.

"Time clearly hasn't cured your delusions," she snapped. "Timothy barely has enough time in between training sessions to eat and sleep." Rumil flushed slightly then quickly added, "If I were honestly interested in anything else… which I'm not."

"Where is Timothy, by the way?"

Rumil gestured with an index finger towards the interior of the cabin. "Inside the 'simple' training room, in the middle of this 'simple' cabin."

Justin grinned playfully, "You're still on that privilege of wealth thing, aren't you? I didn't make the rules, I just play by them."

Rumil snorted, not bothering with words to reply. She turned on her heel, and took a brisk pace through the hall, stopping at a pair of large reinforced hypersteel doors. "You can go first. The last time I walked in there I was just about ignited."

Justin slowly pushed the thick metal door open with some small degree of caution, but fortunately, Timothy wasn't doing anything particularly high-risk. He was performing something similar to push-ups… only done from a handstand.

His warm-up suit was neatly folded near the door, leaving the Solarian clad in nothing but his athletic shorts as he performed his exercises. His back was to them, but he didn't seem at all perturbed by their entrance. His voice didn't even reflect any fatigue whatsoever, even though his body was slick with sweat, dripping occasionally on the floor below.

"What can I do for the two of you?" Timothy asked flatly.

Justin stepped further inside, and asked cheerily, "Just wondering if you were up to playing some tali with me and some of my friends."

Timothy grunted, but not from exertion. "I don't play."

Despite that answer, Justin didn't seem at all convinced. "Nonsense, every Erani boy plays tali."

"Not this one."

Justin pursed his lips. He had not been anticipating any reluctance on Timothy's part. He then decided to use the next weapon in his arsenal: guilt. "Come on, I haven't had the chance to be around for three days, and now you tell me I'm not worth your time?"

"I can't imagine you will be playing tali all day. I am quite certain you will have some extra time to spare later on."

Finally, Justin reduced himself to his final tactic… pleading. "Help me out here. One of the regulars got one on his arms broken on his last mission, and even under accelerated therapy, he's out of service for four more days. There's no telling when we'll be able to play again. I need you to do this for me."

Timothy stopped his exercise, yet remained standing on his hands, at last muttering ruefully, "Very well. Allow me to finish my cool-down then I'll clean up. Shouldn't take any more than twenty ticks."

Justin looked like he was about to clap his hands and skip happily. "Now that's what I wanted to hear! Very well, then, I'll let you finish up, then we can be on our way. Of course, you're welcome to join us, Rumil."

"Of course she's coming," Timothy replied in a very non-negotiable tone.

Rumil frowned disapprovingly at Timothy's demanding statement, but slowly shrugged it off, as if she were becoming accustomed to that behavior from the Solarian. Regardless, Justin got what he wanted, thus he didn't think much more beyond that.

When Timothy finally emerged from the training room, dressed neatly in athletic shorts that hung to mid-thigh and a loose, light blue sleeveless shirt, perfectly pleated along the hemlines, Justin shook his head. "Don't tell me you press and fold your athletic wear too…"

"It fits easier in the drawers that way," Timothy responded simply.

Rumil had to agree with Justin. There was a point where you crossed from tidy to disturbing.

"What about you?" Justin suddenly asked Rumil. "Don't tell me you're gonna play dressed like that."

"Excuse me?" Rumil gaped. She had cleaned up, and dressed casually in long pants and a white button-up collared shirt, expecting to sit in one of the spectator seats and watch Timothy severely hurt people… perhaps even unintentionally.

"Oh no… if you come along, then you're going to at least try," Justin teased, his left hand plucking at the shoulder of Rumil's shirt, which she swatted at angrily.

"It's not even my choice," Rumil growled, turning her ire in Timothy's direction.

Timothy smirked, and was unrepentant. "If I have to play, so do you. I suspect they just want to make themselves look better in comparison."

Justin waved off the idea. "Nah… I just want to see Rumil throw a tali ball. She looks like she could really put some force behind it."

"How about I throw my fist at your face instead?" she threatened, half cocking her arm in the process.

"Oh, come on… please?"

Timothy was still smirking, and finally, Rumil relented. "Fine.

Give me a few ticks to see if I have anything I can throw on…"

Justin stopped her. "I'm sure we can hunt down something in the stadium. We don't want to be too late after all."

*   *   *   *   *

The hover slowly lowered to the parkway surface. The Knights had chosen not to teleport since it was no great distance at all from the cabin to the nearest athletic grounds. Rumil looked up at the towering stadium, the refracted panels of its golden dome casting beautiful rainbow hues along the ground, and the large blue-tinted windows framed in silver beams gave a slightly shaded view of the two levels inside the building.

"Yeah, I know. But this is rather small in comparison," Justin remarked, anticipating Rumil's thoughts. "The actual city stadium is about twice this size. This is just for the use of the nobility manors." A hint of guilt crept into his voice, in apology to Rumil.

The former hacker sulked ever so slightly. "Let's just get this over with," she muttered, stepping out of the hover and proceeding at a brisk walk towards the rotating door that served as the entrance to the stadium, not waiting for her companions, who took a brisk jog to catch up.

Once they entered the stadium, Justin wasted no time in moving to the athletic lockers, making sure that his two companions were following. He turned down a wide hall with a slight decline that branched off from the circular causeway, and stopped at the first blue door on their left.

"Just tell the assistant inside your size, and they should set you up quite nicely," Justin said cheerily to Rumil as he pushed the door open. "Timothy and I will be on the playing floor proper."

Rumil gave him another dark glare before stomping inside. Unperturbed, Justin turned to his friend, and said, "Well, let's move on. I assume you're familiar with the rules?"

Timothy rubbed his forehead, before replying, "I might need a reminder… it has been quite a while."

Justin grinned. "So you *have* played before."

"When I was younger, the other Knight trainees played in little matches to test their skills. I played a few times, but decided it wasn't worth my time."

The three emerged in front of a wooden paneled floor, divided down the middle with a thick red line. A blue painted circle with a white drawing of a bird in flight rested directly in the center of the floor. About seven Tacks from each side of the center line, another pair of red lines crossed the floor, the tip of a blue semicircle meeting near the center of each of those. Near the ends of each floor was a cage, also semicircular, and a mesh net attached to the inside of the bars.

"Okay, the goal is to put this ball here," Justin began, gesturing to the orange tali ball in his right hand, "into the cages over there."

"That much I remember," Timothy answered wryly. "Shots can be kicked or thrown, and any shot beyond the blue circle is worth two points. Inside the circle is one point. First team to ten points wins."

"Humor is lost on you isn't it?" Justin shook his head. "Anyway, each team has two attackers, two defenders, one center, and one goalkeeper. From the end of the floor to the first red line is one zone… from there to the third red line is the neutral zone, and then from there to the other end is the last. Defenders can only move from the defensive end to the opposite end of the neutral zone. Attackers can move from the defensive zone line to the offensive zone. Centers can move anywhere. Got that?"

Timothy frowned. "For the most part. I think I can handle it."

"Okay… since we're all psionics here, do you remember the rules that apply to our power?" Justin asked. "Don't worry if you don't… they sometimes confuse me."

"There is a three-Tack sphere around every player that they can use their psionic ability in, and only on the ball. The only exception to the rule is in the case of a shot, in which the shooter can control the flight of the ball through the entire shot."

"For someone who hasn't played in a while, you sure seem to remember the rules pretty well," Justin remarked skeptically, his eyes narrowing in accusation.

Timothy shrugged in a passive manner. "I must have a better memory than I thought."

"Well, anyway, let me introduce you to the others. They've probably already sorted out teams for the most part. I trust you won't be insulted if they don't look on you with customary kindness at first."

Timothy suddenly turned grim as he retorted, "I'd expect nothing less."

When Rumil reemerged ten ticks later, still wearing the garb she arrived in the stadium in, Justin shook his head disapprovingly. "And what is going on here?"

Rumil smugly retorted, "They didn't have anything in my size."

Justin had to admit the strong possibility, as Rumil was built in ways that the more waif-like Erani women definitely were not. When one of his teammates voiced a desire to actually begin their game, he waved for Rumil to take a seat, and the two teams huddled together on opposite sides of the court.

Justin quickly assigned his teammates to their respective positions, finally asking Timothy, "Think you can handle playing an attacker?"

Timothy shrugged apathetically, "Sure."

With that, Justin's team broke out of their huddle and he took his place inside the blue circle as his team's center, his counterpart doing the same on the other. From above, a silvery receptacle hovered ten Tacks above the circle, and then the orange tali ball was fired directly downward at a surprising speed. It hit the center of the circle, bounced back upward, and that was when the two centers literally leaped into action.

Justin and his opponent collided at the hip. Being somewhat smaller than his adversary, Justin gained a slight amount of leverage, and was able to nudge the other center away just enough to reach up with his right hand, and slap the ball back towards one of his defenders behind him. Once Justin hit the ground again, he took a return pass from said defender, and surveyed the scene as the other team backed away into their defensive scheme.

Justin slowly stepped forward, ball propped between his side and his left hand. Out of the corner of his eye, he saw Timothy gesture slightly, as if requesting a pass. Noting Timothy's position just inside the offensive zone, Justin shook his head slightly, motioning for Timothy to move deeper into the zone.

I can score from here, Timothy stated confidently.

Justin shrugged, and snapped a quick pass off his wrist that Timothy caught smoothly, the ball barely making a sound as it smacked against his palm. The Solarian spun on his left foot to face the cage, and his arm pulled back to gauge the throw.

Justin watched in concern as Timothy's right foot rose up, and then lunged forward, pulling the rest of his body with it. Timothy's left arm then extended fully, swinging in a circle over his head, his hand releasing the ball perfectly at the apex of the motion, and the ball shot forward with a speed that Justin almost wasn't ready for, and because of that, the Kiros Knight nearly lost track of the ball's position.

The ball's flight was so smooth that it almost didn't appear to be guided at all by Timothy's psionic ability until it skipped off the floor less than a Tack in front of the first defender, bouncing between the right knee and elbow, and then continued unimpeded on its path despite the obvious psionic attempts of the second defender.

Due to the distance in which the shot was taken, the keeper moved into position with plenty of time to spare. The ball skipped again just in front of the crouched keeper, then ricocheted at almost a right angle parallel to the cage. The keeper followed the ball, trying to remain imposed between the ball and the cage, meanwhile trying to wrest control from the shooter, with predictably little success. The ball bounced the opposite way again, only much faster, and the keeper jumped sideways to try and intercept the path, and unwittingly crashed into the bar of the cage. As the keeper reeled from the impact, Timothy gently rolled the ball past the goal line into the cage.

The keeper scowled angrily at his defenders, rubbing his shoulder from where it smacked the cage. "You could have slowed that down!"

One defender managed to mumble, "I tried…"

Meanwhile, Justin teammates crowed happily as they took a 2-0 lead. The keeper prepared to put the ball in play, while the defender opposing Timothy's position slowly drifted over to the Solarian.

"Pretty nice shot there," the man said sourly.

"Glad you thought so," Timothy answered. He recalled that the Kiros attacker was named Glyn from when Justin had introduced the group before the game had started.

"Did you learn those tricks from your father?" Glyn said, hinting with a sneer.

"No."

"I guess I shouldn't be surprised," Glyn replied, prepared to move to his punch line. "I mean, the Solarian High Commander is generally worthless. I was simply hoping that maybe he had some use."

"Sorry to disappoint," Timothy said, largely unperturbed.

This took Glyn by surprise. In order to get into someone's head, you generally had to get them to react, not agree in an implicit manner. Pursing his lips, Glyn then tried again. "So… why are you here? Why play traitor? Is it that pretty little Arcadian there?"

That got Timothy's attention, Glyn noticed. It was subtle change in the Solarian's facial expression, but it definitely appeared to be a sore point. Glyn pressed further on that line, asking suggestively, "Did you think that perhaps the Kiros would allow you to play with your Arcadian?"

That did it... and did it far more effectively than he had planned. Glyn rushed past the flatfooted Timothy, and lunged forward to catch the pass that had been thrown as the he broke free in the neutral zone.

However, the ball no sooner hit Glyn's hand when something else much harder connected solidly with his exposed midsection. Glyn barely registered Timothy's angered expression as the Solarian escorted him rather roughly into, then over, the wall that separated the floor from the spectator seating.

Rumil yelped in shock, and managed to scramble away as Glyn tumbled past her, and finally came to an awkward stop upside down on the back of one bucket seat four rows up. By the time Glyn recovered his wits and body enough to gather some indignant anger, Justin had called a cease to play, and imposed himself between Glyn and Timothy as Glyn climbed back onto the playing floor.

"Hold yourselves!" Justin hollered as he held Glyn at bay with one arm, and put his other arm on Timothy's chest, not so much to hold back the stoic, unmoving Solarian as to give him a means to prop himself against Glyn's pushing. "This isn't the Commissioner's Trophy we're playing for here."

To Timothy, Justin said, "We're here to have fun, not necessarily kill each other." To Glyn, the Kiros Knight asked suspiciously, "Just what did you say to him?" On a psychic vein, Justin added, *If you were talking about Rumil, I suggest you not do it again. He's grown rather protective of the lady, and I'm not terribly sure just how far he'd go to defend her honor.*

Glyn nodded, as if suddenly aware that Timothy was not one to trifle with. Justin himself became aware of Timothy's power building, but so subtly that by the time he recognized it, Timothy had already teleported away.

The Solarian popped back into existence in front of Rumil, who once again squealed in surprise, but not because of anything Timothy had done. Timothy had reacted just in time to fashion a psionic shield that harmlessly deflected a rifling plasma burst from the luxury section on the other side of the stadium.

Several of the players gasped and shouted, all of them focusing their attention on where the shot appeared to have been fired from. As they gaped, however, Timothy went into action again, making another teleport into the luxury boxes. There was a masculine scream, the sounds of another shot, then a loud crash.

Justin turned towards Rumil, her chest heaving with deep breaths, and his eyebrows furrowed in confusion as he muttered to himself, "That shot was meant for her… but… why?" Deciding that Rumil might not be totally safe, Justin jumped over the dividing wall, and helped her to her feet. "Are you all right?" Justin asked as Rumil numbly brushed invisible debris from her shirt.

She nooded somewhat dumbly, and mumbled, "I felt… something was about to happen. Something like the visions I've been having… but not really. Just an overall feeling of dread, and when I told Timothy about it, that's when I saw some man in the luxury suites holding a rifle."

Justin took her by the arm and said, "Well, why don't we see what Timothy has found up there?" Without waiting for Rumil's reply, Justin had teleported themselves up into the suites as well.

Where once there were two separate glass-paneled boxes, there was now one. The fiberwall that separated the suites was in shambles, the guiding beams bent unnaturally. Along the far wall opposite Rumil and Justin's position, Timothy had cornered the assailant… "cornered" meaning slammed against the wall, being held off the ground by the angered Solarian while the would-be assassin screamed in a combination of terror and agony.

As Rumil and Justin approached, they could see the reason for the mixed wail. The air was so thick with residual psionic energy that it was buzzing loudly even in Rumil's head. From the light tone of the fiberwall interior of the luxury box, they could see the reflection of intense white light from Timothy's eyes.

Justin finally gathered the courage to try and pull Timothy away, with little success. It wasn't until Rumil managed to convince the Solarian that she was indeed still alive, and in fact, quite unhurt, that the tension eased in Timothy's body, the gleam in his eyes faded, and he allowed himself to back away.

Then, as if he had done nothing out of character, Timothy asked flatly, "I assume this is your other friend who simply couldn't play today?"

Justin confirmed the suspicion when he addressed the hurting assassin. "Yes, it is awfully strange. For a man with a broken arm, you sure seemed to hold a rifle pretty well." Then Justin snorted derisively. "I hope your hand *is* broken now. I demand you tell me who set you up to try and kill one of my friends."

The assassin was clutching his right hand painfully with his left, despite what appeared to be a series of nasty cuts along his face and a left leg that was bent at a very unhealthy angle. "I can't tell you…"

Justin then angrily swatted at the attacker's injured hand, and yelled back, "Is that so? I suspect maybe a little more time with my Solarian friend will change your mind…"

In the meanwhile, Rumil noted that when Justin had slapped the assassin's arm, the man's glove had been thrown a considerable distance away. She then looked back to the man, and noticed that his hand wasn't broken… it was gone, the assailant grabbing painfully at nothing more than a stump just below where the wrist would normally be. Glancing once more at the glove laying neglected across the suite, she saw gray ash scattered about the article.

Justin turned his attention back to his two companions, and said testily, "Well, considering there is only a handful of people who make orders I am not privy to… I think I have a fairly good idea as to who is responsible for this attempt on Rumil's life."

"I get the feeling you have a prime suspect," Timothy asked.

"I do… as much as I loathe saying so. That man is a specialist directly under my father's command. It seems more than likely that any orders would have come from my father himself."

*　　*　　*　　*　　*

Base security was a little surprised to see Justin Feroz appear at the nobility entrance, dressed in his armor somewhat hastily, with Timothy Honore and Rumil Bonamede in tow.

"Knight Feroz… you weren't expected on base today," the security chief said in confusion, looking down at the duty chart displayed on his PCU.

"Emergency circumstances require my presence, High Guardsman," Justin replied. "Has my father arrived?"

"I'm not certain, sir… I can contact his assistant to find out."

Justin shook his head, "That's quite all right, High Guardsman. Can I just see your PCU?"

The guard blinked, then with a confused nod, handed the

computing unit over to Justin. The Kiros knight tapped in several menu commands on the unit's touchpad, then said with a smirk, "Yes… he is definitely in… very good…"

Further planning was cut off as alarms from all over the base blared almost simultaneously. Fearing that the high alert was for the three arrivals, Timothy took a rigid battle stance, hands hovering at his weapons while raising his psionic aura steadily. Rumil dropped to the ground in anticipation of some more sniper shots, and even Justin found his hand drifting to his sword warily.

However, the guard didn't seem to be any more in the know than any of the three. "What in Bannor is going on here?"

His answer came when one of the lower enlisted personnel emerged into the courtyard. "Sir, the headquarters have been compromised!"

"Compromised?" the High Guardsman asked, his head swiveling in all directions due to the wailing cacophony. "By what army?"

"It was a large-scale job, sir," the enlisted man replied hurriedly, "Rumor's floating about that it was the Blood Hawks."

Justin's eyebrows raised. "The Blood Hawks? How could they have gotten within three systems of Kiros… much less in our main military facility?"

It seemed at that time the enlisted man finally recognized that there were other people in the courtyard. "Oh, Knight Feroz, sir! Of course, I can't say anything for certain… I've just heard rumors, and was told to report here to backup the guard detail in this section."

"Well, I suppose I shall locate my dear father, and get to the bottom of this mess," Justin growled. "Do pardon me…"

"Of course, sir!" both guards said at once, parting to both sides of the automatic door leading into the base.

Justin motioned for Timothy and Rumil to stay close as they entered into the deafening noise that echoed and rung throughout the halls of the complex, and were promptly nearly run down by a large security detail of about twenty soldiers as they stormed past. Another detail came through the hall five demiticks later, going in exactly the opposite direction.

"Well, I can see that the famed Kiros discipline is everything it's billed to be," Rumil quipped as Timothy helped her up from the floor after the second detail had knocked her over in their haste.

Justin pursed his lips in concentration, trying to get mental images of what was happening. "I'm only getting a sense of utter confusion. No one I scanned has any image whatsoever of any physical invasion… it doesn't make any sense at all. Everything is in utter disarray… I can't believe my father would allow such a complete breakdown of order."

"We have other concerns anyway," Timothy reminded. "And the current state of the base could actually lend itself to our advantage."

Justin seemed to balk at the statement at first, as if he had momentarily forgotten the reason the three of them were on base in the first place. "Yes, I suppose we do, don't we?" After a moment's silence, he added, "Let's get to it, then…"

The trio worked their way through the halls bathed in the red lights of the alarm system, and largely ignored by everyone in the facility. The elevator details that are supposed to check every potential passenger, regardless of rank, barely glanced at Justin's identification before letting him and his two companions through the checkpoint.

As the elevator descended to the lower floors, Justin simply shook his head, trying to make sense of all that had happened. "My father orders an assassination… the entire base is in chaos… I'm going to wake up from this nightmare anytime…"

Timothy's next words weren't exactly comforting. "I suspect things are going to get worse before this nightmare is over."

Justin then seemed to snap. "And *that's* another thing! You told me that my sect would possibly be after Rumil… how did you know that?"

Hearing this, Rumil got in on the yelling. "You said we were coming here because I would supposedly be safe here! What is it about me, that all you Erani want me dead?"

Justin then turned to the former hacker. "You mean you have no idea what that was about either?"

Rumil was fuming as well. "He's been keeping me in the dark since I was dumped out into the middle of a Solarian sandstorm! I've been hunted like an animal, ambushed by the Solarian Knighthood, nearly drowned in an underground river, been the target of a sniper attack, and I've gotten nothing out of that man other than there being something 'special' about me that he can't into terribly good detail about."

Finally, they both turned simultaneously towards the Solarian, their eyes glaring accusingly. They said nothing, but the unspoken question was rather clear.

Timothy sighed, and then said, "I'm not terribly certain on any of it myself, but I suspect several of our answers will be found in the High Commander's office." He then stepped through his two companions as the lift doors opened.

The office levels were just above the testing facilities that the trio had been to earlier, and were largely empty. It seemed most of the high-ranking officers were on the higher floors trying to restore some semblance of sensibility, and the few that were still in the office area understandably had their attention on other things. At the end of the mostly abandoned hall was a pair of large, carved, wooden double doors with brass-colored handles and a shimmering gold plaque that bore the name of Joseph Feroz. Without acknowledging his father's secretary at the adjacent desk, or bothering to request entry in any way, Justin pulled the doors outward and stood in the entry.

At first, Joseph was surprised, then angry at the intrusion, his psionic power abruptly building against an unseen foe, then dispelled with a sigh of relief when he recognized his son. "Justin, I am so glad you are here…"

"You won't be, I'd gamble," Justin answered cryptically, his expression considerably less than pleasant.

"On the contrary!" the Kiros High Commander exclaimed as he rushed to his son. "As you may have noticed, the complex is in complete chaos. There have been several reports of infiltration, but for some bizarre reason, we can't confirm any of them… oh, dear…"

Joseph had been interrupted by the sight of the two companions just behind Justin outside the office. The man fell back as his son literally guided him back into the office with a hand on his chest, until the High Commander's desk stopped his progression. "I see… I think I may know what this is about…" Joseph finally muttered guiltily.

"Well, then, I don't need to waste my time angrily demanding answers then," Justin scowled. "But, I want to know… did you order one of our Knights to assassinate Miss Bonamede?"

Joseph was bordering on frantic. "Justin… allow me to explain…"

"Yes… or… no…" Justin grit out slowly. "Do *not* make me force my way into your mind and find out for myself."

With an expression of utter defeat, the Kiros High Commander muttered, "Yes…"

Justin's next question was laced with near homicidal intent. "Why?"

Before Joseph could even begin to fashion an answer, another voice interceded. "I suspect I can shed light on some of that."

Four faces turned full about to see a cloaked figure in the doorway, his four-fingered left hand clutching a battered, hide-bound book at his side.

"Rio! how in the Defiler's name did you get in here?" Joseph demanded, his earlier anxiety replaced with righteous fury.

"Oh, come now… surely you do not think that I have no friends on Kiros?" Dewin retorted almost mockingly.

"So the Blood Hawks were responsible for this mess?" Timothy asked.

"Well, yes and no, to be quite honest," Dewin admitted. "Not a single one of my pirates has set foot on Kiros… save myself, obviously. But, I knew several people willing to make the right people believe we had. I was just waiting for the right opportunity. The attempted killing of our little hacker friend was just what I was looking for."

"Why would that be?" Rumil queried.

"Well, because frankly, I have a bit of an old debt to settle with our dear High Commander, and what better way than with the current conundrum Mr. Joseph Feroz finds himself in?"

"You wouldn't dare…" Joseph threatened.

"None of you are making much sense…" Rumil groused at the same time.

"I will in time, but do bear with me, because we have a considerable amount of material to cover," Dewin said silkily, his mouth turning upward in a predatory smirk. "You see… I wasn't always an interstellar pirate. As a matter of fact, at one time I led a very upright and proper life." With a pause for effect, Dewin continued smoothly, "I grew up on Tanis to converted parents, and much to their glee, I enlisted myself into the Kiros military. Due to an exceptionally keen eye, I was drafted into the flight academy, and became a very prominent fighter pilot. So lauded was my skill, that I was granted a most unusual role for one of my race; a patrol pilot above the home planet of the Kiros themselves."

"Now, as is expected for the heart of the Kiros sect, things were rather docile. However, there was one… bizarre incident… so totally unique, that members of the Kiros hierarchy felt it would best be prudent if it just wasn't discussed."

"Rio, I am warning you…" Joseph once again threatened, his

voice reflecting increasing nervousness.

"In all due respect, father, do be quiet," Justin snapped.

"Thank you, young Feroz," Dewin said, with a slight and sarcastic bow. "I remember that Kiros morning quite well. I was on my patrol shift, and I'll admit, my instincts were somewhat dulled from the sheer monotony of my current duty. I suppose in the end that is a fortunate thing, because otherwise I would have promptly blasted the unidentified escape craft that popped out of foldspace into debris. You see… there was a very innocent life in that craft, most probably ejected from a doomed vessel trapped in foldspace. It was a young Kiros infant… and after recovering the baby, I reported my findings to the proper authorities."

"Well, apparently, this child was quite special, because the High Commander himself decided to watch over the babe, and sought to eliminate anyone who knew about the infant's less than conventional history. Fortunately, I got lucky, and slipped out of Kiros with my life."

"You aren't serious…" Justin growled, and then turned towards his father. Much to Justin's surprise, Joseph Feroz looked beaten and drained, not even attempting to resist Justin's mental probe. It confirmed every word of Dewin's story, even the attempt on Rio's life to keep the truth silent.

Timothy grimaced, sensing Justin's mental state crack like a mirror struck by a large rock. The young Kiros staggered away from where he had cornered his father against the desk, backing into the far wall, then slumping down to a sitting position, eyes looking upward through the ceiling.

"Well, he took that better than I expected," Dewin remarked ruefully.

"So… my mother didn't die while giving birth to me," Justin finally said.

Not sure how to respond to that, Joseph shook his head. "She did pass on a day after you were recovered, along with the child she carried. It just seemed—"

"Like a good cover for your little charade?" Justin then screamed, leaping to his feet and lunging at Joseph, grabbing the elder man by the arm holes of his dress uniform breastplate.

"Now *that* was more what I was expecting," Dewin quipped.

Timothy then merely stole the pirate leader a glance, and muttered with soft viciousness, "I think you have said quite enough for now, Mr. Rio."

Dewin suddenly went completely rigid, the sanctimonious smirk on his face instantly flattening into an emotionless pursed line. The only thing that moved were Dewin's eyes, stealing ever so brief peeks at Justin and Joseph before fixing back on the Solarian, as if afraid of what would happen if Timothy caught him looking away.

Meanwhile, Justin had demanded of his father an answer to one simple question.

"Why?"

Joseph sighed, and his head lowered slightly, as if he had been trying to formulate an answer to that very question for some time. "It's a complex story. When I saw you… I should have just been rid of you, but I just couldn't take it upon myself to be responsible for the death of someone so young, so pure…"

"What in your Creator-forsaken brain are you blathering about?" Justin hissed, his face contorted into such an angry visage that he was barely recognizable.

"Perhaps I can offer some answers to that as well," Dewin cut in again, as smug as before, although with a subtle wary glance in Timothy's direction. Once he was satisfied he had the office's attention, he lifted the book he had been carrying over his head with his left hand.

Joseph's face drained completely of all color. "How… When…?"

"Well, as I said, I really wanted to pay you back for the courtesy of what you did to me, Mr. Feroz, and happened to stumble upon this little tome on my way here. What better way to twist the dagger than reveal the hideous little plot you and every single one of your predecessors for the last eight hundred some-odd staryears have been running with?"

"Excuse me?" Justin and Rumil asked at the same time.

"Does anyone here know what this book I am holding is?" Dewin asked slyly.

Dewin was somewhat surprised to hear Timothy answer, "It's the complete and unedited book of Bryan Honore, I'd wager."

Dewin's eyebrows lifted. "So, you're familiar with this?"

Ignoring the accusing glares from Rumil, Timothy continued to look straight ahead, saying, "I have a passing knowledge, yes."

Dewin nodded, then playfully patted the book with his free hand. "Well, anyway, I haven't had much of a chance to read this thing, but the story I've managed to glean in my days in the underbelly of society plays something like this…" Dewin stepped forward, then leaned against the desk, playfully flipping through the pages of the book. "The conspiracy theory goes that at the end of the Schism War, both sides agreed to… edit… portions of Bryan Honore's prophecy. Guess there were things in there that they didn't want anyone to know. But at the same time, they kept several copies so that they'd know what to look for when the time Bryan spoke of came to pass."

Dewin then pointed with the book to Justin, "Apparently, your appearance tipped Joseph off as something he had read in this book. His twisted little logic probably would have required him to kill you before you became a problem… and that's probably what he meant to say just now."

"Listen to me, Justin." Joseph began. "You weren't supposed to learn it this way."

"According to what I'm hearing, I wasn't supposed to learn it at all!" Justin nearly screamed. "I want some answers out of you, right now!"

"I had hoped that I could raise you the right way. You see, you're a special child. Your destiny was spoken of long before you were born… but there has to be a better way to fulfill your calling in this life."

Justin growled in frustration. That was obviously not what he meant by answers. "I wish I could simply trust you like I used to."

"Don't pester your father, young Feroz," Dewin cut in again, "especially when you can learn first hand what he's talking about."

Justin turned just in time to have Dewin thrust the book into his stomach. "Why are you giving me this?" he asked suspiciously.

Dewin shrugged. "I certainly don't care to keep it. As I said, my only concern here was getting back at this wonderful High Commander."

Finally, Rumil interjected herself into the conversation. "What about me then? What's the deal with wanting to kill me?"

Suddenly, Joseph became overcome with a subtle ire. "You… I can sense it now… now that my son and your Solarian defender aren't trying to hide it anymore. It's as obvious as I can think… you'll be the end of everything I have ever defended, what I have built and maintained all my life."

Rumil blinked. "Wha—?"

"It's the ramblings of a man trying to rationalize his actions," Timothy interrupted. "I wouldn't pay him one more demitick of your attention."

At that point, the sounds of approaching Knights and security drew everyone's attention. Dewin clicked his tongue, and remarked, "Well, it appears they've finally found me. I probably have overstayed my welcome."

Dewin looked back at the door, as if realizing for the first time that it was the only exit. "Would you think it would be possible if you helped me find an exit, Mr. Honore?"

Timothy frowned, but acknowledged the pirate leader. "We were just planning to leave anyway… unless Justin has some other business to attend to."

Justin scowled, and whirled away quickly from Joseph, who sank down to a squatting position, head bowed. "No, I think I'm done here," Justin hissed, taking a place right in front of Timothy.

"Then why don't you make sure Mr. Rio comes with us?" Timothy stated, placing his left hand on Rumil's shoulder as he did so. His other hand ignited with a yellow flame, bursting in one bright beam straight at the ceiling once he extended his arm.

"Subtlety is not exactly your strong point, is it?" Dewin asked wryly, cringing slightly when Justin roughly grabbed his forearm.

Timothy didn't reply, and a demitick later, had teleported away. Justin frowned, and remarked, "Gee, that was helpful… thanks for the heads up, Timothy."

"Could you just take me to my vessel then? My shuttle is only about a TackMet from here," Dewin requested.

Are you coming or not? Timothy's telepathic voice interjected. Justin instantly sensed Timothy's presence almost exactly a TackMet away, at the same spot that Justin had gleaned from Dewin's mind. No doubt Timothy had done the same, without the pirate's permission, figuring it to be the best course of action. Apparently, subtlety wasn't Timothy's weakness either. By the time security finally arrived at Joseph's office, Justin had also vanished with Dewin.

The pair reappeared on the Kiros surface, in a small clearing of an artificially maintained tropical forest among the outer courtyards of the military complex. Justin shook his head, trying to comprehend everything that had occurred in the last ten ticks. He decided to start with something simple. "Just how did you, the leader of the Blood Hawks piracy ring, manage to slip his way onto one of the most heavily guarded planets in the Galactic Alliance?"

Dewin sighed as he ushered his new guests aboard the small shuttle. "As I said, I have my connections on Kiros, old friends of mine, you could say. They managed to convince the right people to conveniently look the other way as I arrived."

"Okay... then why is this book in my hand anywhere on a Kiros Core Colony? I thought we rejected this sort of trash..."

Timothy bristled at the statement. "Perhaps Joseph did as well, but perhaps he saw something in yourself and Rumil that prompted him to act just in case. Nonetheless, he's not the first person to reach that conclusion."

"And just what conclusion would that be?" Rumil demanded as Dewin sealed the shuttle door, and took his seat at the controls, preparing for a rather quick take-off.

"Perhaps we'll have time to get into it once we're in a place not full of people looking for blood," Timothy stalled, fastening his seat harness.

Rumil was about to demand that Timothy explain himself when the shuttle jerked, throwing her roughly against her seat, prompting her to secure her person before the craft reached any great velocity.

Surprisingly, Dewin's pirate cruiser was actually in Kiros's orbit, floating along the far side of the planet's lone moon. "Just how many friends do you have on Kiros?" Justin asked as the craft docked with the large pirate vessel, and the four filtered out.

"Enough that owe me some significant favors," Dewin answered cryptically. "However, not enough that we can just sit around chatting." The pirate leader stepped quickly across the shuttle bay to the rear wall, which hosted a line of communication terminals. "Orion, get those engines running, I need full sub-light drive as soon as possible. Make sure the vector coordinates for the fold generator are ready."

"Yes, sir," the Ubek's voice replied. Then, there was a sudden gasp, "We've got company! Three Kiros heavy cruisers, approaching at quarter light speed!"

"They found us sooner than I would have liked," Dewin cursed. "Begin evasive maneuvers."

"But then we might have to recalculate our fold coordinates!" Orion protested.

"Unless you think this rickety old clunk can last two ticks against three cruisers, then we're going to have to."

"No you won't," Timothy said. "They aren't after you or your crew… at the moment, at least." The first sounds of weapons fire began to echo through the shuttle bay. Timothy regarded the blasts briefly, then continued, "You know as well as we do that Justin, Rumil, and I am the Kiros' targets."

"I won't deny that," Dewin agreed. "Then what do you propose?"

"Let us… rent out your shuttle," Timothy proposed. "It will be obvious to the Kiros that the three of us are on it, and that should give you proper time to make your escape."

Dewin shrugged. "I'm certainly not going to tell you not to take on such a suicide mission."

"Are you insane?" Justin demanded, "I don't know about you, but I frankly would like to see my family again!"

"And if you stay here, you stand just as little chance of survival, as well as take the entire crew of this ship with you," Timothy replied. "Is that the way the honor of Kiros Knights work?"

Justin glared darkly, as if he had been slapped. Another volley rocked the pirate craft, and Orion once again spoke over the communications system. "Mr. Rio! The deflector arrays are nearly overloaded!"

Timothy turned about, and began herding Rumil and Justin back into the shuttle. "The discussion is over."

Suddenly, Dewin jolted. "Feroz… one moment of your time."

The Kiros Knight paused, and slipped out of Timothy's grasp. Timothy allowed the brief transaction, escorting Rumil to her seat and beginning the power-up procedure.

Dewin retrieved a small, battered slip of paper that appeared to have come at one time from a patrolman's notebook, and slipped it into Justin's right hand. "About twenty-three staryears ago, I made note of the origin point of a small escape pod I happened across. Perhaps… you'll find some use in it."

"Justin, we must leave now," Timothy insisted.

It was obvious that Justin had other things he wanted to say, but he only had time for one last request. "If it's at all possible… could you have some of your friends… keep an eye on my wife and son… make sure they're handling everything all right? I don't think I can trust them totally to my father's care."

Dewin frowned slightly, "I don't blame you. I'll see what I can do,

I suppose."

Justin managed rushed thanks, before nearly diving into the shuttle as a third volley of shots rocked the pirate craft. The hatchway to the shuttle closed, and Timothy wasted no time maneuvering the small vessel out of the magnetic airlock, and into space, accelerating rapidly.

As Timothy had predicted, the firing ceased, and two of the cruisers broke off in full pursuit, the third lingering in lunar orbit as if waiting to see if the shuttle would try and return to Dewin's cruiser.

Leaning into the communications panel, Dewin said, "All right… if all of you still have the fold coordinates set… go to full speed on my mark. Create the fold the instant we are clear of this moon's gravity well."

Orion replied, "We're good for foldspace, Mr. Rio."

Dewin gave one last second to regard the three who had just left, now completely out of his sight. "I can't believe I'm wishing them well…" he mumbled before activating communications to the command center once more. "Move out!"

*   *   *   *   *

Rumil shrieked as another high-density accelerated round from one of the cruisers came perilously close to vaporizing the shuttle. Justin asked solemnly to Timothy, "How much longer do you think we can keep this going?"

"How long do you need?"

Justin ran his thumb across the faded numbers that Dewin had given him. "Long enough to calculate at least a semi-reasonable fold to anywhere other than here."

Timothy glanced at the sheet, then quickly returned his attention long enough to evade what would have been a most unpleasant conclusion to their flight. "Those coordinates aren't anything like what I've seen before."

"No kidding," Justin remarked when the coordinates were plotted. "These are way out… beyond the Galactic Rim even, outside all known space."

Rumil forgot the exploding weapons fire long enough to comment, "You mean to fold us completely outside the galaxy itself?"

"It's been done before," Timothy remarked, "although I don't recall anyone going out quite as far as those numbers are pointing. It'd definitely be out of anyone's eyes." Then to Justin, he asked, "Does the fold generator have enough power for that sort of trip?"

Justin nodded, "One-way, at least."

"You are going to assume that there's something on the other end that can recharge us once we get there?" Rumil challenged.

"Apparently, I came *from* there, Rumil," Justin answered.

"Which brings up another issue… Who's to say that whatever is out there is any friendlier than here? I mean, I can't imagine infants get sent out in escape pods as standard procedure."

Timothy cut in again, "While that *may* be true, I happen to *know* that there aren't many friendly havens in this galaxy any more. I figure we don't have many other options."

Finally, Justin declared, "Got it! Though, it might not be terribly accurate considering the way we've been bouncing around."

At that moment, the navigational alarms alerted them that making a foldspace jump under the current conditions would be ill-advised.

"Yeah, we know!" Justin growled at the computer, overriding the alert, and clearing the programmed course through. "All set here."

"And not a moment too soon," Timothy grunted as he rolled the shuttle away from what might have been a torpedo lock. "All right, here we go…"

He slapped his hand on the console in front of him, and the shuttle lights dimmed from the drain being caused by the fold generator. Within demiticks, a black circle crackling with swirling energy formed in front of them, snapping shut almost instantly as the shuttle disappeared inside.

www.ingramcontent.com/pod-product-compliance
Lightning Source LLC
Chambersburg PA
CBHW071131170626
46809CB00002B/567